**Praise for #1 *New York Times* bestselling author
Stephanie Laurens**

"All I need is her name on the cover
to make me pick up the book."
—*New York Times* bestselling author Linda Howard

"Laurens's writing shines."
—*Publishers Weekly*

"Superbly sensual...elegantly written...
splendidly entertaining."
—*Booklist*

**Praise for *USA TODAY* bestselling author
Nicola Cornick**

"Her books are fabulous."
—*New York Times* bestselling author Julia Quinn

"A rising star of the Regency arena."
—*Publishers Weekly*

"A wonderfully original,
sinfully amusing and sexy Regency historical
by the always entertaining Cornick."
—*Booklist* on *The Confessions of a Duchess*

A Lady of Expectations

and other stories

STEPHANIE LAURENS

NICOLA CORNICK
KASEY MICHAELS

HARLEQUIN®

entertain, enrich, inspire™

ISBN-13: 978-0-373-77723-5

A LADY OF EXPECTATIONS AND OTHER STORIES

Copyright © 2012 by Harlequin Books S.A.

The publisher acknowledges the copyright holders of the individual works as follows:

A LADY OF EXPECTATIONS
Copyright © 1995 by Stephanie Laurens

THE SECRETS OF A COURTESAN
Copyright © 2009 by Nicola Cornick

HOW TO WOO A SPINSTER
Copyright © 2009 by Kathryn Seidick

Recycling programs for this product may not exist in your area.

CONTENTS

A LADY OF EXPECTATIONS   7
Stephanie Laurens

THE SECRETS OF A COURTESAN   303
Nicola Cornick

HOW TO WOO A SPINSTER   383
Kasey Michaels

A LADY OF EXPECTATIONS

Stephanie Laurens

Readers can contact Stephanie
at slaurens@vicnet.net.au. For information on
all of Stephanie's books, including updates on
novels to come, visit Stephanie's website
at www.stephanielaurens.com.

CHAPTER ONE

"LADY ASFORDBY, OF ASFORDBY GRANGE, requests the pleasure of the company of Mr. Jack Lester, of Rawling's Cottage, and guests, at a ball."

Ensconced in an armchair by the fireplace, a glass of brandy in one long-fingered hand, the white card of Lady Asfordby's invitation in the other, Jack Lester made the pronouncement with ill-disguised gloom.

"She's the *grand dame* of these parts, ain't she?" Lord Percy Almsworthy was the second of the three gentlemen taking their ease in the parlour of Jack's hunting box. Outside, the wind howled about the eaves and tugged at the shutters. All three had ridden to hounds that day, taking the field with the Quorn. But while both Jack and his brother Harry, presently sprawled on the chaise, were clipping riders, up with the best of them, Percy had long ago taken Brummel's lead, indefatigable in turning out precise to a pin but rarely venturing beyond the first field. Which explained why he was now idly pacing the room, restless, while the brothers lounged, pleasantly exhausted, with the look about them of men not willing to stir. Pausing by the fireplace, Percy looked down on his host. "Lend a bit of colour to your stay, what? Besides," he added, turning to amble once more, "You never know—might see a golden head that takes your eye."

"In this backwater?" Jack snorted. "If I couldn't find any golden head worth the attention last Season—nor during the Little Season—I don't give much for my chances here."

"Oh, I don't know." Unconsciously elegant, Harry Lester lounged on the chaise, one broad shoulder propped against a cushion, his thick golden locks rakishly dishevelled. His sharply intelligent green eyes wickedly quizzed his elder brother. "You seem remarkably set on this start of yours. As finding a wife has become so important to you, I should think it behoves you to turn every stone. Who knows which one hides a gem?"

Blue eyes met green. Jack grunted and looked down. Absent-mindedly, he studied the gilt-edged card. Firelight glinted over the smooth waves of his dark hair and shadowed his lean cheeks. His brow furrowed.

He had to marry. He had inwardly acknowledged that fact more than twenty months ago, even before his sister, Lenore, had married the Duke of Eversleigh, leaving the burden of the family squarely on his shoulders.

"Perseverance—that's what you need." Percy nodded to no one in particular. "Can't let another Season go by without making your choice—waste your life away if you're too finicky."

"I hate to say it, old son," Harry said. "But Percy's right. You can't seriously go for years looking over the field, turning your nose up at all the offerings." Taking a sip of his brandy, he eyed his brother over the rim of his glass. His green eyes lit with an unholy gleam. "Not," he added, his voice soft, "unless you allow your good fortune to become known."

"Heaven forbid!" Eyes narrowing, Jack turned to Harry. "And just in case you have any ideas along that track, perhaps I should remind you that it's our good fortune—yours and mine and Gerald's, too?" Features relaxing, Jack sank back in his chair, a smile erasing the severe line of his lips. "Indeed, the chance of seeing *you* playing catch-me-who-can with all the enamoured damsels is sorely tempting, brother mine."

Harry grinned and raised his glass. "Fear not—that thought

has already occurred. If the *ton* stumbles onto our secret, it won't be through me. And I'll make a point of dropping a quiet word in our baby brother's ear, what's more. Neither you nor I need him queering our pitch."

"Too true." Jack shuddered artistically. "The prospect does not bear thinking of."

Percy was frowning. "I can't see it. Why not let it out that you're all as rich as bedammed? God knows, you Lesters have been regarded as nothing more than barely well-to-do for generations. Now that's changed, why not reap the rewards?" His guileless expression was matched by his next words. "The debs would be yours for the asking—you could take your pick."

Both Lester men bent looks of transparent sympathy upon their hapless friend.

Bewildered, Percy blinked and patiently waited to be set aright.

Unable to hold a candle to his long-time companions in the matter of manly attributes, he had long since become reconciled to his much slighter figure, his sloping shoulders and spindly shanks. More than reconciled—he had found his vocation as a Pink of the *Ton.* Dressing to disguise his shortcomings and polishing his address to overcome his innate shyness had led to yet another discovery; his newfound status spared him from the trial of chasing women. Both Jack and Harry thrived on the sport, but Percy's inclinations were of a less robust nature. He adored the ladies—from a distance. In his estimation, his present style of life was infinitely preferable to the racy existence enjoyed by his companions.

However, as both Jack and Harry were well aware, his present lifestyle left him woefully adrift when it came to matters of strategy in handling the female of the species, particularly those dragons who menaced all rakes—the matrons of the *ton.*

And, naturally, with his mild manners and retiring ways, he was hardly the sort of gentleman who inhabited the debutantes' dreams. All the Lester men—Jack, at thirty-six, with his dark good looks and powerful athlete's physique, and Harry, younger by two years, his lithe figure forever graceful and ineffably elegant—and even twenty-four-year-old Gerald, with his boyish charm—were definitely the stuff of which females' dreams were made.

"Actually, Percy, old man," Harry said. "I rather suspect Jack thinks he can have his pick regardless."

Jack shot a supercilious glance at his sibling. "As a matter of fact, I've not previously considered the point."

Harry's lips lifted; gracefully, he inclined his head. "I have infinite confidence, oh brother mine, that if and when you find your particular golden head, you won't need the aid of our disgusting wealth in persuading her to your cause."

"Yes—but *why* the secrecy?" Percy demanded.

"Because," Jack explained, "while the matrons have considered my fortune, as you so succinctly put it, as barely well-to-do, they've been content to let me stroll among their gilded flowers, letting me look my fill without undue interference."

With three profligate sons in the family and an income little more than a competence, it was commonly understood that the scions of Lester Hall would require wealthy brides. However, given the family connections and the fact that Jack, as eldest, would inherit the Hall and principal estates, no one had been surprised when, once he had let it be known he was seriously contemplating matrimony, the invitations had rolled in.

"Naturally," Harry suavely put in. "With all Jack's years of…worldly experience, no one expects him to fall victim to any simple snares and, given the lack of a Lester fortune, there's insufficient incentive for the dragons to waste effort mounting any of their more convoluted schemes."

"So I've been free to view the field." Jack took back the conversational reins. "However, should any whiff of our changed circumstances begin circulating through the *ton,* my life of unfettered ease will be over. The harpies will descend with a vengeance."

"Nothing they like better than the fall of a rake," Harry confided to Percy. "Brings out their best efforts—never more hellishly inventive than when they've a rich rake with a declared interest in matrimony firmly in their sights. They relish the prospect of the hunter being the hunted."

Jack threw him a quelling glance. "Sufficient to say that my life will no longer be at all comfortable. I won't be able to set foot outside my door without guarding against the unimaginable. Debs at every turn, hanging on a fellow's arm, forever batting their silly lashes. It's easy to put one off women for life."

Harry shut his eyes and shuddered.

The light of understanding dawned on Percy's cherubic countenance. "Oh," he said. Then, "In that case, you'd better accept Lady Asfordby's invitation."

Jack waved a languid hand. "I've all the Season to go yet. No need to get in a pother."

"Ah, yes. But will you? Have all the Season, I mean?" When both Jack and Harry looked lost, Percy explained, "This fortune of yours was made on 'Change, wasn't it?"

Jack nodded. "Lenore took the advice of one of the pater's acquaintances and staked a fleet of merchantmen to the Indies. The company was formed through the usual channels and is listed in London."

"Precisely!" Percy came to a flourishing halt by the fireplace. "So any number of men with an interest at the Exchange know the company was wildly successful. And lots of them must know that the Lesters were one of the major backers. That sort of thing's not secret, y'know. M'father, for one, would be sure to know."

Jack and Harry exchanged looks of dawning dismay.

"There's no way to silence all those who know," Percy continued. "So you've only got until one of those men happens to mention to his wife that the Lesters' fortunes have changed and the whole world will know."

A groan escaped Harry.

"No—wait." Jack straightened. "It's not that simple, thank God." The last was said with all due reverence. "Lenore organized it, but naturally she could hardly act for herself in the matter. She used our broker, old Charters, a terribly stuffy old soul. *He* has never approved of females being involved in business—the old man had to lean on him to accept instructions from Lenore years ago. Charters only agreed on the understanding of secrecy all round—he didn't want it known that he took orders from a woman. Which probably means he won't admit it was us he was working for, as it's fairly well known Lenore was in charge of our finances. If Charters doesn't talk, there's no reason to imagine our windfall will become common knowledge overnight."

Percy frowned and pursed his lips. "Not overnight, maybe. But dashed if I think it'll be all that long. These things filter through the cracks in the mortar, so my old man says."

A sober silence descended on the room as the occupants weighed the situation.

"Percy's right." Harry's expression was grim.

Glumly resigned, Jack held up Lady Asfordby's invitation. "In more ways than one. I'll send round to Lady Asfordby to expect us."

"Not me." Harry shook his head decisively.

Jack's brows rose. "You'll get caught in the storm, too."

Stubbornly, Harry shook his head again. He drained his glass and placed it on a nearby table. "*I* haven't let it be known

I'm in the market for a wife, for the simple reason that I'm not." He stood, stretching his long, lean frame. Then he grinned. "Besides, I like living dangerously."

Jack returned the grin with a smile.

"Anyway, I'm promised at Belvoir tomorrow. Gerald's there— I'll tip him the wink over our desire for silence on the subject of our communal fortune. So you can proffer my regrets to her ladyship with a clear conscience." Harry's grin broadened. "Don't forget to do so, incidentally. You might recall she was an old friend of our late lamented aunt and can be a positive dragon—she'll doubtless be in town for the Season, and I'd rather not find myself facing her fire."

With a nod to Percy, Harry made for the door, dropping a hand on Jack's shoulder in passing. "I should inspect Prince's fetlock—see if that poultice has done any good. I'll be off early tomorrow, so I'll wish you good hunting." With a commiserating grin, he left.

As the door closed behind his brother, Jack's gaze returned to Lady Asfordby's invitation. With a sigh, he put it in his pocket, then took a long sip of his brandy.

"So, are we going?" Percy asked around a yawn.

Grimly, Jack nodded. "We're going."

While Percy went up to bed and the house settled to slumber around him, Jack remained in his chair by the fire, blue eyes intent on the flames. He was still there when, an hour later, Harry re-entered the room.

"What? Still here?"

Jack sipped his brandy. "As you see."

Harry hesitated for a moment, then crossed to the sideboard. "Musing on the delights of matrimony?"

Head back, Jack let his eyes track his brother's movements. "On the inevitability of matrimony, if you really want to know."

Sinking onto the chaise, Harry lifted a brow. "Doesn't have to be you, you know."

Jack's eyes opened wide. "Is that an offer—the ultimate sacrifice?"

Harry grinned. "I was thinking of Gerald."

"Ah." Jack let his head fall back and stared at the ceiling. "I have to admit I've thought of him, too. But it won't do."

"Why not?"

"He'll never marry in time for the pater."

Harry grimaced but made no answer. Like Jack, he was aware of their sire's wish to see his line continue unbroken, as it had for generations past. It was the one last nagging worry clouding a mind otherwise prepared for death.

"But it's not only that," Jack admitted, his gaze distant. "If I'm to manage the Hall as it should be managed, I'll need a chatelaine—someone to take on the role Lenore filled. Not the business side, but all the rest of it. All the duties of a well-bred wife." His lips twisted wryly. "Since Lenore left, I've learned to appreciate her talents as never before. But the reins are in my hands now, and I'll be damned if I don't get my team running in good order."

Harry grinned. "Your fervour has raised a good few brows. I don't think anyone expected such a transformation—profligate rakehell to responsible landowner in a matter of months."

Jack grunted. "You'd have changed, too, if the responsibility had fallen to you. But there's no question about it, I need a wife. One like Lenore."

"There aren't many like Lenore."

"Don't I know it." Jack let his disgruntlement show. "I'm seriously wondering if what I seek exists—a gentlewoman with charm and grace, efficient and firm enough to manage the reins."

"Blond, well-endowed and of sunny disposition?"

Jack shot his brother an irritated glance. "It certainly wouldn't hurt, given the rest of her duties."

Harry chuckled. "No likely prospects in sight?"

"Nary a one." Jack's disgust was back. "After a year of looking, I can truthfully inform you that not one candidate made me look twice. They're all so alike—young, sweet and innocent—and quite helpless. I need a woman with backbone and all I can find are clinging vines."

Silence filled the room as they both considered his words.

"Sure Lenore can't help?" Harry eventually asked.

Jack shook his head. "Eversleigh, damn his hide, was emphatic. His duchess will not be gracing the *ton's* ballrooms this Season. Instead," Jack continued, his eyes gently twinkling, "she'll be at home at Eversleigh, tending to her first-born and his father, while increasing under Jason's watchful eye. Meanwhile, to use his words, the *ton* can go hang."

Harry laughed. "So she's really indisposed? I thought that business about morning sickness was an excuse Jason drummed up to whisk her out of the crowd."

Grimacing, Jack shook his head. "All too true, I fear. Which means that, having ploughed through last Season without her aid, while she was busy presenting Eversleigh with his heir, and frittered away the Little Season, too, I'm doomed to struggle on alone through the shoals of the upcoming Season, with a storm lowering on the horizon and no safe harbour in sight."

"A grim prospect," Harry acknowledged.

Jack grunted, his mind engrossed once more with marriage. For years, the very word had made him shudder. Now, with the ordeal before him, having spent hours contemplating the state, he was no longer so dismissive, so uninterested. It was his sister's marriage that had altered his view. Hardly the conventional image, for while Jason had married Lenore for a host of eminently conventional reasons, the depth of their love was apparent to all. The fond light that glowed in Jason's grey eyes whenever he looked at his wife had assured Jack that all was well with his sister—even more than Lenore's transparent joy. Any notion that his brother-in-law, ex-rake, for years the bane of the dragons, was anything other than besotted with his wife was simply not sustainable in the face of his rampant protectiveness.

Grimacing at the dying fire, Jack reached for the poker. He was not at all sure he wanted to be held in thrall as Jason, apparently without a qualm, was, yet he was very sure he wanted what his brother-in-law had found. A woman who loved him. And whom he loved in return.

Harry sighed, then stood and stretched. "Time to go up. You'd best come, too—no sense in not looking your best for Lady Asfordby's young ladies."

With a look of pained resignation, Jack rose. As they crossed to the sideboard to set down their glasses, he shook his head. "I'm tempted to foist the whole business back in Lady Luck's lap. She handed us this fortune—it's only fair she provide the solution to the problem she's created."

"Ah, but Lady Luck is a fickle female." Harry turned as he opened the door. "Are you sure you want to gamble the rest of your life on her whim?"

Jack's expression was grim. "I'm already gambling with the rest of my life. This damned business is no different from the turn of a card or the toss of a die."

"Except that if you don't like the stake, you can decline to wager."

"True, but finding the right stake is my problem."

As they emerged into the dark hall and took possession of the candles left waiting, Jack continued, "My one, particular golden head—it's the least Lady Luck can do, to find her and send her my way."

Harry shot him an amused glance. "Tempting Fate, brother mine?"

"Challenging Fate," Jack replied.

WITH A SATISFYING SWIRL of her silk skirts, Sophia Winterton completed the last turn of the Roger de Coverley and sank gracefully into a smiling curtsy. About her, the ballroom of Asfordby Grange was full to the seams with a rainbow-hued throng. Perfume wafted on the errant breezes admitted through the main doors propped wide in the middle of the long room. Candlelight flickered, sheening over artful curls and glittering in the jewels displayed by the dowagers lining the wall.

"A positive pleasure, my dear Miss Winterton." Puffing slightly, Mr. Bantcombe bowed over her hand. "A most invigorating measure."

Rising, Sophie smiled. "Indeed, sir." A quick glance around located her young cousin, Clarissa, ingenuously thanking a youthful swain some yards away. With soft blue eyes and alabaster skin, her pale blond ringlets framing a heart-shaped face, Clarissa was a hauntingly lovely vision. Just now, all but quivering with excitement, she forcibly reminded Sophie of a highly strung filly being paraded for the very first time.

With an inward smile, Sophie gave her hand and her attention to Mr. Bantcombe. "Lady Asfordby's balls may not be as large as the assemblies in Melton, but to my mind, they're infinitely superior."

"Naturally, naturally." Mr. Bantcombe was still short of breath. "Her ladyship is of first consequence hereabouts—and she always takes great pains to exclude the *hoi polloi*. None of the park-saunterers and half-pay officers who follow the pack will be here tonight."

Sophie squelched a wayward thought to the effect that she would not really mind one or two half-pay officers, just to lend colour to the ranks of the gentlemen she had come to know suffocatingly well over the last six months. She pinned a bright smile to her lips. "Shall we return to my aunt, sir?"

She had joined her aunt and uncle's Leicestershire household last September, after waving her father, Sir Humphrey Winterton, eminent paleontologist, a fond farewell. Departing on an expedition of unknown duration, to Syria, so she believed, her father had entrusted her to the care of her late mother's only sister, Lucilla Webb, an arrangement that met with Sophie's unqualified approval. The large and happy household inhabiting Webb Park, a huge rambling mansion some miles from Asfordby Grange, was a far cry from the quiet, studious existence she had endured at the side of her grieving and taciturn sire ever since her mother's death four years ago.

Her aunt, a slender, ethereal figure draped in cerulean-blue silk, hair that still retained much of its silvery blond glory piled high on her elegant head, was gracefully adorning one of the chaises lining the wall, in earnest conversation with Mrs. Haverbuck, another of the local ladies.

"Ah, there you are, Sophie." Lucilla Webb turned as, with a smile and a nod for Sophie, Mrs. Haverbuck departed. "I'm positively in awe of your energy, my dear." Pale blue eyes took in Mr. Bantcombe's florid face. "Dear Mr. Bantcombe, perhaps you could fetch me a cool drink?"

Mr. Bantcombe readily agreed. Bowing to Sophie, he departed.

"Poor man," Lucilla said as he disappeared into the crowd. "Obviously not up to your standard, Sophie dear."

Sophie's lips twitched.

"Still," Lucilla mused in her gentle airy voice, "I'm truly glad to see you so enjoying yourself, my dear. You look very well, even if 'tis I who say so. The *ton* will take to you—and you to it, I make no doubt."

"Indeed the *ton* will, if your aunt and I and all your mother's old friends have anything to say about it!"

Both Sophie and Lucilla turned as, with much rustling to stiff bombazine, Lady Entwhistle took Mrs. Haverbuck's place.

"Just stopped in to tell you, Lucilla, that Henry's agreed—we're to go up to town tomorrow." Lifting a pair of lorgnettes from where they hung about her neck, Lady Entwhistle embarked on a detailed scrutiny of Sophie with all the assurance of an old family friend. Sophie knew that no facet of her appearance—the style in which her golden curls had been piled upon her head, the simple but undeniably elegant cut of her rose-magenta silk gown, her long ivory gloves, even her tiny satin dancing slippers—would escape inspection.

"Humph." Her ladyship concluded her examination. "Just as I thought. You'll set the *ton*'s bachelors back on their heels, m'dear. Which," she added, turning to Lucilla, a conspiratorial gleam in her eye, "is precisely to my point. I'm giving a ball on Monday. To introduce Henry's cousin's boy to our acquaintance. Can I hope you'll be there?"

Lucilla pursed her lips, eyes narrowing. "We're to leave at the end of the week, so I should imagine we'll reach London by Sunday." Her face cleared. "I can see no reason not to accept your invitation, Mary."

"Good!" With her habitual bustle, Lady Entwhistle stood, improbable golden ringlets bouncing. Catching sight of Clarissa through the crowd, she added, "It'll be an informal affair, and it's so early in the Season I see no harm in Clarissa joining us, do you?"

Lucilla smiled. "I know she'll be delighted."

Lady Entwhistle chuckled. "All wound tight with excitement, is she? Ah, well—just remember when we were like that, Lucy—you and I and Maria." Her ladyship's eyes strayed to Sophie, a certain anticipation in their depths. Then, with determined briskness, she gathered her reticule. "But I must away—I'll see you in London."

Sophie exchanged a quiet smile with her aunt, then, lips curving irrepressibly, looked out over the crowded room. If she were asked, she would have to admit that it was not only Clarissa, barely seventeen and keyed up to make her come-out, who was prey to a certain excitement. Beneath her composure, that of an experienced young lady of twenty-two years, Sophie was conscious of a lifting of her heart. She was looking forward to her first full Season.

She would have to find a husband, of course. Her mother's friends, not to speak of her aunt, would accept nothing less. Strangely, the prospect did not alarm her, as it certainly had years ago. She was more than up to snuff—she fully intended to look carefully and choose wisely.

"Do my eyes deceive me, or has Ned finally made his move?"

Lucilla's question had Sophie following her aunt's gaze to where Edward Ascombe, Ned to all, the son of a neighbour, was bowing perfunctorily over her cousin's hand. Sophie saw Clarissa stiffen.

A little above average height, Ned was a relatively serious young man, his father's pride and joy, at twenty-one already absorbed in caring for the acres that would, one day, be his. He was also determined to have Clarissa Webb to wife. Unfortunately, at the present moment, with Clarissa full of nervy excitement at the prospect of meeting unknown gentlemen up from London for the hunting, Ned was severely handicapped, suffering as he did from the twin disadvantages of being a blameless and worthy suitor and having known Clarissa all her life. Worse, he had already made it plain that his heart was at Clarissa's tiny feet.

Her sympathy at the ready, Sophie watched as he straightened and, all unwitting, addressed Clarissa.

"A cotillion, if you have one left, Clary." Ned smiled confidently, no premonition of the shaky ground on which he stood showing in his open countenance.

Eyes kindling, Clarissa hissed, "Don't call me that!"

Ned's gentle smile faded. "What the d-deuce *am* I to call you? *Miss Webb?*"

"Exactly!" Clarissa further elevated her already alarmingly tilted chin. Another young gentleman hovered on her horizon; she promptly held out her hand, smiling prettily at the newcomer.

Ned scowled in the same direction. Before the slightly shaken young man could assemble his wits, Ned prompted, "My dance, *Miss Webb?*" His voice held quite enough scorn to sting.

"I'm afraid I'm not available for the cotillion, *Mr. Ascombe.*" Through the crowd, Clarissa caught her mother's eyes. "Perhaps the next country dance?"

For a moment, Sophie, watching, wondered if she and Lucilla would be called upon to intervene. Then Ned drew himself up stiffly. He spoke briefly, clearly accepting whatever Clarissa had offered, then bowed and abruptly turned on his heel.

Clarissa stood, her lovely face blank, watching his back until he was swallowed up by the crowd. For an instant, her lower lip softened. Then, chin firming, she straightened and beamed a brilliant smile at the young gentleman still awaiting an audience.

"Ah." Lucilla smiled knowingly. "How life does go on. She'll marry Ned in the end, of course. I'm sure the Season will be more than enough to demonstrate the wisdom of her heart."

Sophie could only hope so, for Clarissa's sake as well as Ned's.

"Miss Winterton?"

Sophie turned to find Mr. Marston bowing before her. A reserved but eminently eligible gentleman of independent means, he was the target of more than a few of the local matchmaking mamas. As she dipped in a smooth curtsy, Sophie inwardly cursed her guilty blush. Mr. Marston was enamoured—and she felt nothing at all in response.

Predictably interpreting her blush as a sign of maidenly awareness, Mr. Marston's thin smile surfaced. "Our quadrille, my dear." With a punctilious bow to Lucilla, who regally inclined her head, he accepted the hand Sophie gave him and escorted her to the floor.

Her smile charming, her expression serene, Sophie dipped and swayed through the complicated figures, conscious of treading a very fine line. She refused to retreat in confusion before Mr. Marston's attentions, yet she had no wish to encourage him.

"Indeed, sir," she replied to one of his sallies. "I'm enjoying the ball immensely. However, I feel no qualms about meeting those gentlemen up from London—after all, my cousin and I will shortly be in London ballrooms. Acquaintances made tonight could prove most comforting."

From her partner's disapproving expression, Sophie deduced that the thought of her gaining comfort from acquaintance with any other gentleman, from London or elsewhere, was less than pleasing. Inwardly, she sighed. Depressing pretensions gently was an art she had yet to master.

About them, Lady Asfordby's guests swirled and twirled, a colourful crowd, drawn primarily from the local families, with here and there the elegant coats of those London swells of whom her ladyship approved. This distinction did not extend to all that many of the small army of *ton*-ish males who, during the hunting season, descended on the nearby town of Melton Mowbray, lured by the attraction of the Quorn, the Cottesmore and the Belvoir packs.

Jack realized as much as, with Percy hovering in his shadow, he paused on the threshold of her ladyship's ballroom. As he waited for his hostess, whom he could see forging her way through the crowd to greet him, he was conscious of the flutter his appearance had provoked. Like a ripple, it passed down the dark line of dowagers seated around the room, then spread in ever widening circles to ruffle the feathers of their charges, presently engaged in a quadrille.

With a cynical smile, he bowed elegantly over her ladyship's beringed fingers.

"So glad you decided to come, Lester."

Having smoothly introduced Percy, whom Lady Asfordby greeted with gratified aplomb, Jack scanned the dancers.

And saw her.

She was immediately in front of him, in the set nearest the door. His gaze had been drawn to her, her rich golden curls shining like a beacon. Even as realization hit, his eyes met hers. They were blue, paler than his own, the blue of cloudless summer skies. As he watched, her eyes widened, her lips parted. Then she twirled and turned away.

Beside him, Percy was filling Lady Asfordby's ears with an account of his father's latest illness. Jack inhaled deeply, his eyes on the slim figure before him, the rest of the company a dull haze about her.

Her hair was true gold, rich and bountiful, clustered atop her neat head, artfully errant curls trailing over her small ears and down the back of her slender neck. The rest of her was slender, too, yet, he was pleased to note, distinctly well-rounded. Her delectable curves were elegantly gowned in a delicate hue that was too dark for a debutante; her arms, gracefully arching in the movements of the dance, displayed an attractive roundness not in keeping with a very young girl.

Was she married?

Suavely, Jack turned to Lady Asfordby. "As it happens,

I have not met many of my neighbours. Could I impose on your ladyship to introduce me?"

There was, of course, nothing Lady Asfordby would have liked better. Her sharp eyes gleamed with fanatical zeal. "Such a loss, your dear aunt. How's your father getting on?"

While replying to these and similar queries on Lenore and his brothers, all of whom her ladyship knew of old, Jack kept his golden head in sight. Perfectly happy to disguise his intent by stopping to chat with whomever Lady Asfordby thought to introduce, he steered his hostess by inexorable degrees to the chaise beside which his goal stood.

A small knot of gentlemen, none of them mere youths, had gathered about her to pass the time between the dances. Two other young ladies joined the circle; she welcomed them graciously, her confidence as plain as the smile on her lips.

Twice he caught her glancing at him. On both occasions, she quickly looked away. Jack suppressed his smile and patiently endured yet another round of introductions to some local squire's lady.

Finally, Lady Asfordby turned towards the crucial chaise. "And, of course, you must meet Mrs. Webb. I dare say you're acquainted with her husband, Horatio Webb of Webb Park. A financier, you know."

The name rang a bell in Jack's mind—something to do with horses and hunting. But they were rapidly approaching the chaise on which an elegant matron sat, benignly watching over a very young girl, unquestionably her daughter, as well as his golden head. Mrs. Webb turned as they approached. Lady Asfordby made the introduction; Jack found himself bowing over a delicate hand, his eyes trapped in a searching, ice-blue stare.

"Good evening, Mr. Lester. Are you here for the hunting?"

"Indeed yes, ma'am." Jack blinked, then smiled, careful not to overdo the gesture. To him, Mrs. Webb was instantly recognizable; his golden head was protected by a very shrewd dragon.

A lifted finger drew the younger girl forward.

"Allow me to present my daughter, Clarissa." Lucilla looked on as Clarissa, blushing furiously, performed the regulation curtsy with her customary grace. Speech, however, seemed beyond her. Lifting one sceptical brow, Lucilla spared a glance for the magnificence before her, then slanted a quick look at Sophie. Her niece was studiously absorbed with her friends.

An imperious gesture, however, succeeded in attracting her attention.

Her smile restrained, Lucilla beckoned Sophie forward. "And, of course," she continued, rescuing Jack from Clarissa's tongue-tied stare, "you must let me introduce my niece, Miss Sophia Winterton." Lucilla halted, then raised her fine brows. "But perhaps you've met before—in London? Sophie was presented some years ago, but her Season was cut short by the untimely death of her mother." Switching her regal regard to Sophie, Lucilla continued, "Mr. Jack Lester, my dear."

Conscious of her aunt's sharply perceptive gaze, Sophie kept her expression serene. Dipping politely, she coolly extended her fingers, carefully avoiding Mr. Lester's eye.

She had first seen him as he stood at the door, darkly, starkly handsome. In his midnight-blue coat, which fitted his large lean frame as if it had been moulded to him, his thick dark hair falling in fashionable dishevelment over his broad brow, his gaze intent as he scanned the room, he had appeared as some predator—a wolf, perhaps—come to select his prey. Her feet had missed a step when his gaze had fallen on her. Quickly looking away, she had been surprised to find her heart racing, her breath tangled in her throat.

Now, with his gaze, an unnervingly intense dark blue, full

upon her, she lifted her chin, calmly stating, "Mr. Lester and I have not previously met, Aunt."

Jack's gaze trapped hers as he took her hand. His lips curved. "An accident of fate which has surely been my loss."

Sophie sternly quelled an instinctive tremor. His voice was impossibly deep. As the undercurrent beneath his tones washed over her, tightening the vice about her chest, she watched him straighten from an ineffably elegant bow.

He caught her glance—and smiled.

Sophie stiffened. Tilting her chin, she met his gaze. "Have you hunted much hereabouts, sir?"

His smile reached his eyes. A small shift in position brought him closer. "Indeed, Miss Winterton."

He looked down at her; Sophie froze.

"I rode with the Quorn only yesterday."

Breathless, Sophie ignored the twinkle in his eye. "My uncle, Mr. Webb, is a keen adherent of the sport." A quick glance about showed her aunt in deep conversation with Lady Asfordby; her court was hidden by Mr. Lester's broad shoulders. He had, most effectively, cut her out from the crowd.

"Really?" Jack lifted a polite brow. His gaze fell to her hands, clasped before her, then rose, definite warmth in the deep blue. "But your aunt mentioned you had been in London before?"

Sophie resisted the urge to narrow her eyes. "I was presented four years ago, but my mother contracted a chill shortly thereafter."

"And you never returned to grace the ballrooms of the *ton*? Fie, my dear—how cruel."

The last words were uttered very softly. Any doubts Sophie had harboured that Mr. Lester was not as he appeared vanished. She shot him a very straight glance, irrelevantly noting how the hard line of his lips softened when he smiled. "My father was much cut up by my mother's death. I remained with him, at home in Northamptonshire, helping with the household and the estate."

His response to that depressing statement was not what she had expected. A gleam of what could only be intrigued interest flared in his dark eyes.

"Your loyalty to your father does you credit, Miss Winterton." Jack made the statement with flat sincerity. His companion inclined her head slightly, then glanced away. The perfect oval of her face was a delicate setting for her regular features: wide blue eyes fringed with long, thick lashes, golden brown as were her arched brows, a straight little nose and full bowed lips the colour of crushed strawberries. Her chin was definite, yet gently rounded; her complexion was like thick cream, rich and luscious, without flaw. Jack cleared his throat. "But did you not yearn to return to the *ton*'s ballrooms?"

The question took Sophie by surprise. She considered, then answered, "No. Indeed, the thought never arose. I had more than enough to occupy myself. And I frequently visited with my father's sisters at Bath and Tonbridge Wells." She glanced up—and laughed at the comical grimace that contorted her companion's face.

"Tonbridge Wells?" he uttered, dramatically faint. "My dear Miss Winterton, you would be *wasted* there, smothered beneath the weight of ageing propriety."

Sophie sternly suppressed a giggle. "Indeed, it wasn't very lively," she conceded. "Luckily, my mother had many friends who invited me to their house parties. However, at home, I must admit I oftimes pined for younger company. My father lived very much retired through that time."

"And now?"

"My aunt—" she nodded at Lucilla on the chaise which by some magic was now a step away "—persuaded Papa to take an interest in an expedition. He's a paleontologist, you see."

From beneath her lashes, she glanced up, waiting.

Jack met her innocent gaze, his own inscrutable. Despite her best efforts, Sophie's lips twitched. With a resigned air, Jack raised a languidly interrogatory brow.

This time, Sophie did giggle. "Old bones," she informed him, her voice confidingly low. Despite the fact he had just sidestepped a trap guaranteed to depress the pretensions of any overly confident rake, Sophie could not stop her smile. As her eyes met his, warmly appreciative, the suspicion that while Mr. Lester might be demonstrably confident, he was not overly so, broke over her. Her breath became tangled again.

His gaze sharpened. Before she could react, and retreat, he lifted his head, then glanced down at her, his brows lightly lifting.

"Unless my ears are at fault, that's a waltz starting up. Will you do me the honour, Miss Winterton?"

The invitation was delivered with a calm smile, while his eyes stated, very clearly, that no feeble excuse would suffice to deflect him.

Nerves aquiver, Sophie surrendered to the inevitable with a suffocatingly gracious inclination of her head.

Her determinedly calm composure very nearly cracked when he swept her onto the floor. His arm about her felt like iron; there was such strength in him it would be frightening if it was not so deliberately contained. He whirled her down the floor; she felt like thistledown, lighter than air, anchored to reality only by his solidity and the warm clasp of his hand.

She had never waltzed like this before, precessing without conscious thought, her feet naturally following his lead, barely touching the floor. As her senses, stirred by his touch, gradually settled, she glanced up. "You dance very well, Mr. Lester."

His eyes glinted down at her from under heavy lids. "I've had lots of practice, my dear."

His meaning was very clear; she should have blushed and

looked away. Instead, Sophie found enough courage to smile serenely before letting her gaze slide from his. Aware of the dangerous currents about her, she made no further attempt to converse.

For his part, Jack was content to remain silent; he had learned all he needed to know. Freed of the burden of polite conversation, his mind could dwell on the pleasure of having her, at long last, in his arms. She fitted perfectly, neither too tall nor, thankfully, too short. If she were closer, her curls would tickle his nose, her forehead level with his chin. She was not completely relaxed—he could not expect that— yet she was content enough in his arms. The temptation to tighten his hold, to draw her closer, was very real, yet he resisted. Too many eyes were upon them, and she did not yet know she was his.

The last chord sounded; he whirled them to a flourishing halt. He looked down, smiling as he drew her hand through his arm. "I will return you to your aunt, Miss Winterton."

Sophie blinked up at him. Could he hear her heart thudding? "Thank you, sir." Retreating behind a mask of cool formality, she allowed him to lead her back to the chaise. However, instead of leaving her by her aunt's side, her partner merely nodded at Lucilla, then led her to where her circle of acquaintances was once again forming. Larger than life, he stood beside her, acknowledging her introductions with a coolly superior air which, she suspected, was innate. Feeling her nerves stretch and flicker, Sophie glanced up as the musicians once more laid bow to string.

His eyes met hers. Suddenly breathless, Sophie looked away. Her gaze fell on Lady Asfordby, bustling up.

"Glad to see, Lester, that you're not one of those London dandies who think they're above dancing in country ballrooms."

Stifling a resigned sigh, Jack turned to his hostess, an amiable smile on his lips.

Her ladyship's gimlet gaze swept the assembled company, fixing on a bright-faced young lady. "Dare say Miss Elderbridge will be pleased to do you the honour."

Thus adjured, Jack bent a practiced smile on Miss Elderbridge, who assured him, somewhat breathlessly, that she would be delighted to partner him in the country dance about to begin. Hearing a murmur to his left, Jack glanced back to see Sophie place her hand on another gentleman's sleeve. They were both poised to move away, their partners by their sides. Jack grasped the moment, trapping Sophie's gaze in his, lowering his voice to say, "Until next we meet, Miss Winterton."

Sophie felt her eyes widen. Lowering her lashes, she inclined her head. As she moved to her place in the set, she felt his words reverberate deep within her. Her heart thudded; it was an effort to concentrate on Mr. Simpkins's conversation.

There had been a wealth of meaning hidden in Jack Lester's subtle farewell—and she had no idea whether he meant it or not.

CHAPTER TWO

HE DID MEAN IT.

That was the only logical conclusion left to Sophie when, poised to alight from the Webb family carriage in the shadow of the lych-gate the next morning, she caught sight of a pair of powerful shoulders, stylishly encased in the best Bath superfine, and then their owner, wending his way aimlessly through the gravestones. As if sensing her regard, he looked around and saw her. White teeth flashed as he smiled. Recalled to her surroundings by Clarissa's finger in her ribs, Sophie abruptly gathered her wits and descended.

In the protective confines of the lych-gate, she fussed with her reticule and the skirts of her cherry-red pelisse while her cousins, Jeremy, George and Amy, as well as Clarissa—at just six years old, the twins, Henry and Hermione, were too young to be trusted in church—descended and straightened their attire under their mother's eagle eye. Finally satisfied, Lucilla nodded and they fell into line, Amy beside her mother in the lead, Sophie and Clarissa immediately behind, followed by the two boys, their boots on the paving stones.

As they ascended the steps leading up from the gate, Sophie carefully avoided glancing at the graveyard to their left, looking up, instead, at the sharp spire that rose into the wintry sky. March had arrived, unexpectedly mild. The chill blue of the heavens was dotted with puffs of white cloud, scudding along before the brisk breeze.

"Good morning, Mrs. Webb."

The cavalcade stopped. Although she could only see her aunt's back, Sophie had the distinct impression that even that redoubtable matron was taken aback by the sight of Jack Lester bowing elegantly before her just yards from the church door. His ambling peregrination had, most conveniently, converged with their route at that spot.

Regardless of her surprise, there was no doubt of her aunt's pleasure. Her "Mr. Lester, how fortunate. We had not looked to see you thus soon" positively purred with satisfaction. "Would you care to join us in our pew, sir?"

"I'd be delighted, ma'am." Until then, Jack had not looked Sophie's way. Now, smiling, he turned to her. "Good morning, Miss Winterton." He briefly nodded at Clarissa. "Miss Webb."

Sophie dipped and gave him her hand.

"Sophie dear, perhaps you would show Mr. Lester the way while I take care of this brood." Her aunt waved an airy hand at her offspring, who, of course, could very well have found their way unaided to the pew they occupied every Sunday.

"Of course, Aunt." Sophie knew better than to argue.

As Lucilla swept her children into the church, Sophie risked a glance upwards, only to meet a pair of dark blue eyes that held a very large measure of amused understanding. Her own eyes narrowed.

"Miss Winterton?" With a gallant gesture, Jack offered his arm. When she hesitated, his brows rose slightly.

Head high, Sophie placed her fingers on his sleeve and allowed him to lead her to the door. As they entered the dim nave, she noted the smothered stir as their neighbours noticed her escort. It was close to eleven and the church was full. Hiding her consciousness behind a calm mask, she indicated the pair of pews, close to the front on the left, where her cousins were already settling. Glancing down as they passed the pew two rows behind, she encountered a malevolent stare from

Mrs. Marston and a sternly disapproving one from her son, seated supportively beside her.

Suppressing a sudden grin, Sophie reflected that, as this was God's house, perhaps Mr. Lester was the Almighty's way of assisting her in the difficult task of rejecting Mr. Marston. She had no time to dwell on that unlikely prospect, however, for, gaining the second of the Webb pews, she found herself seated between Lucilla and Mr. Lester. Luckily, the vicar, Mr. Snodgrass, entered almost immediately.

To her relief, Mr. Lester behaved impeccably, as if going to church on Sunday were his normal habit.

Beside her, Jack bided his time.

When the congregation rose for the first hymn, he reached out and touched Sophie's gloved wrist. Leaning closer, he whispered, "I'm afraid, Miss Winterton, that I did not anticipate attending church during my stay in Leicestershire."

She blinked up at him, then glanced down at the slim volume covered in tooled blue leather that she had extracted from her reticule.

"Oh." With an effort, Sophie dragged her mind from the disturbing thought of what, exactly, *had* brought him to the tiny church of Allingham Downs. Her fingers busy flicking through the pages, she glanced up at him and hoped her distrust was evident. "Perhaps, sir, if I hold it between us, we could share my book?"

He smiled, so very sweetly that, if she had not known better, she would have thought his predicament an innocent oversight. Raising her chin, she held her hymnal between them, up and slightly to her right.

The organ swelled into the introduction. Even as she drew breath for the first note of the first verse, Sophie experienced an inner quake. He had moved closer, an action excused by the fine print of the hymnal. His shoulder was behind her, her shoulder close to his chest. She could sense the warmth of his large body, now so near—and feel the dagger glances of the Marstons, mother and son, on her back.

Her hand shook; his came up to steady the hymnal. She quelled the impulse to glance sideways—he was so close, his head bent, his eyes would be very near, his lips a potent distraction. With an effort, she concentrated on the music, only to be thoroughly distracted by the sound of his warm baritone, rich and strong, effortlessly supporting her soprano.

The hymn was one of praise—and an unexpected joy.

At its conclusion, Sophie felt slightly dizzy. She forced herself to breathe deeply.

Her companion hesitated; she knew his gaze was on her. Then he lifted the hymnal from her hand, gently closed it and presented it to her.

"Thank you, Miss Winterton."

It was impossible; she had to glance up. His eyes, darkly blue, warm and gently smiling, were every bit as close as she had imagined; his lips, softened by his smile, drew her gaze.

For a moment, time stood still.

With an enormous effort, Sophie dragged in a breath and inclined her head.

They were the last to sit down.

The sermon brought her no peace; indeed, Mr. Snodgrass would have needed to be inspired to compete with her thoughts, and the subtle tug of the presence beside her. She survived the second hymn only because she now understood the danger; she kept her mind totally focused on the lyrics and melody, ignoring her companion's harmony as best she could. Ignoring *him* proved even more difficult.

It was something of a relief to stroll slowly up the aisle, her hand on his sleeve. They were among the last to quit the church. Lucilla and her children preceded them; her aunt stopped on the porch steps to exchange her usual few words with the vicar.

"Sophia you know, of course." Lucilla paused as the vicar nodded, beamed and shook Sophie's hand. "But I'm not sure if you've met Mr. Lester. From Rawling's Cottage." Lucilla gestured at Jack, immediately behind Sophie.

"Indeed?" Mr. Snodgrass was an absent-minded old soul. "I don't recall ever having met anyone from there." He blinked owlishly up at Jack.

Sophie looked up in time to catch the reproachful glance that Jack bent on her aunt, before, with ready courtesy, he greeted the vicar.

"I'm rarely to be found in these parts, I'm afraid."

"Ah." The vicar nodded his head in complete understanding. "Up for the hunting."

Jack caught Sophie's eye. "Just so."

Sternly quelling a shiver, Sophie turned away. Her aunt had stopped to chat with Mrs. Marston farther along the path. Clarissa stood slightly to one side, cloaked in fashionable boredom. This last was attributable to Ned Ascombe, standing some yards away, his expression similarly abstracted. Noting the quick, surreptitious glances each threw the other, Sophie struggled not to smile. Feeling immeasurably older than the youthful pair, she stepped off the church steps and strolled slowly in her aunt's wake.

Jack made to follow but was detained by the vicar.

"I often used to ride with the Cottesmore, you know. Excellent pack, excellent. Major Coffin was the Master, then." Launched on reminiscence, the old man rambled on.

From the corner of his eye, Jack watched Sophie join her aunt, who was deep in discussion with a country matron, a large figure, swathed in knitted scarves.

"And then there was Mr. Dunbar, of course..."

Jack stiffened as a dark-coated gentleman stepped around the country dame to accost Sophie. Abruptly, he turned to the vicar, smoothly breaking into his monologue. "Indeed, sir. The Cottesmore has always been a most highly qualified pack. I do hope you'll excuse me—I believe Miss Winterton has need of me."

With a nod, Jack turned and strode briskly down the path. He reached Sophie's side just in time to hear the unknown gentleman remark, in a tone that, to Jack, sounded a great deal too familiar, "Your aunt mentioned that she expected to remove to London at the end of the week. Dare I hope I may call on you before you depart?"

Inwardly, Sophie grimaced. "I'm sure, Mr. Marston, that my aunt will be delighted, as always, to entertain Mrs. Marston and yourself. However, I'm not certain of her plans for this week. It's so very complicated, transferring the whole family up to town."

Sensing a presence by her side, she turned and, with inexplicable relief, beheld her late companion. He was not looking at her, however, but at Mr. Marston, with a frown in his eyes if not on his face.

"I believe I introduced you to Mr. Marston last evening, Mr. Lester."

The dark blue gaze momentarily flicked her way. "Indeed, Miss Winterton." Apparently a distant nod was all the recognition Mr. Marston rated.

For his part, Phillip Marston had drawn himself up, his thin lips pinched, his long nose elevated, nostrils slightly flaring. He returned Jack's nod with one equally curt. "Lester." He then pointedly turned back to Sophie. "I have to say, Miss Winterton, that I cannot help but feel that Mrs. Webb is being far too soft-hearted in allowing the younger children to accompany the party." His gaze grew stern as it rested on Jeremy and George, engaged in an impromptu game of tag about the gravestones. "They would be better employed at their lessons."

"Oh, no, Mr. Marston—just think how educational the

trip will be." Sophie did not add that 'soft-hearted' was a singularly inappropriate adjective when used in conjunction with her aunt. Lucilla might appear as fragile as glass, but her backbone was pure steel. Sophie knew the combination well; her own mother had been just the same. "The children have been so looking forward to it."

"I should think, Marston, that Mr. and Mrs. Webb are well able to decide the right of such matters."

Sophie blinked. The coldly superior edge of Mr. Lester's deep voice was distinctly dismissive. She turned, only to find an elegant sleeve cloaking an arm she already knew to be steel before her.

"If I may, I'll escort you to your carriage, Miss Winterton. Your aunt has moved on."

Sophie looked up; his expression was not what she had expected. Superficially assured, fashionably urbane, there was an underlying tension, a hint of hardness in the patriarchal features; she was at a loss to account for it. However, she was not about to decline an opportunity to escape Mr. Marston, particularly in his present, officiously disapproving mood. Nevertheless, she kept her answering smile restrained. Mr. Lester, regardless of his mood, needed no encouragement. "Thank you, sir." Placing her hand on his sleeve, she looked back—and surprised a look of distinct chagrin on Phillip Marston's face. "Good day, Mr. Marston."

With a nod, she turned away, and found herself very close to Jack Lester at the top of the steps above the lych-gate. Sophie's heart hiccoughed. She glanced up.

His dark eyes met hers, his expression mellow. "Helping you down the steps is the least I can do to repay you for your…company this morning, my dear."

Sophie did not need to look to know Phillip Marston and his mother were close behind; all the confirmation she needed was contained in Jack Lester's smooth, deep and thoroughly reprehensible tone. Incensed, unable to contradict his subtle suggestion, she glared at him. "Indeed, Mr. Lester, you are *certainly* in my debt."

His slow smile softened his lips. "I'll look forward to repaying your kindness, Miss Winterton—when I see you in London."

He made it sound like a promise—one her aunt made certain of as he handed her into the carriage.

"I would invite you to call, Mr. Lester," Lucilla declared. "Yet with our departure imminent, I fear it would be unwise. Perhaps you might call on us when you return to the capital?"

"Indeed, Mrs. Webb, nothing would give me greater pleasure." The carriage door was shut; he bowed, a gesture compounded of strength and grace. "I shall look forward to seeing you in London, Mrs. Webb. Miss Webb." His blue eyes caught Sophie's. "Miss Winterton."

Outwardly calm, Sophie nodded in farewell. The carriage jolted forward, then the horses found their stride. The last view she had was of an elegant figure in pale grey morning coat, tightly fitting inexpressibles and highly polished Hessians, his dark hair slightly ruffled by the breeze. He dominated her vision; in contrast, in his severe, if correct, garb, Mr. Marston seemed to fade into the shadows of the lych-gate. Sophie laid her head back against the squabs, her thoughts in an unaccustomed whirl.

Her aunt, she noticed, smiled all the way home.

SUNDAY AFTERNOON WAS a quiet time in the Webb household. Sophie habitually spent it in the back parlour. In a household that included five boisterous children, there was always a pile of garments awaiting mending and darning. Although the worst was done by her aunt's seamstress, Lucilla had always encouraged both Clarissa and herself to help with the more delicate work.

Her needle flashing in the weak sunshine slanting through the large mullioned windows, Sophie sat curled in one corner of the comfortable old chaise. While a small part of her mind concentrated on the work in her hands, her thoughts were far away.

The click of the latch brought her head up.

"Melly's here." Clarissa came through the door, followed by her bosom bow, Mellicent Hawthorne, commonly known as Melly.

Sophie smiled a ready welcome at Melly, a short, plump figure, still slightly roly-poly in the manner of a young puppy, an impression enhanced by her long, floppy, brown ringlets and huge, spaniel-like eyes. These were presently twinkling.

"Mama's talking to Mrs. Webb, so I'm here for at least an hour. Plenty of time for a comfortable cose." Melly curled up in the armchair while Clarissa settled on the other end of the chaise. Seeing Clarissa reach for a needle and thread, Melly offered, "Would you like me to help?"

Sophie exchanged a quick glance with Clarissa. "No need," she assured Melly. "There's really not that much to do." She blithely ignored the huge pile in the basket.

"Good." Melly heaved a sigh of relief. "I really don't think I'm much good at it."

Sophie bit her lip. Clarissa, she saw, was bent over her stitching. The last time Melly had "helped" with the mending, at least half the garments had had to be rewashed to removed the bloodstains. And if there was one task worse than darning, it was unpicking a tangled darn.

"Still, I don't suppose Mrs. Webb will have you darning in London. Oooh!" Melly hugged herself. "*How* I envy you, Clarissa! Just imagine being in the capital, surrounded by beaux and London swells—just like Mr. Lester."

Clarissa lifted her head, blue eyes alight. "Indeed, I really can't wait! It will be beyond anything great—to find oneself in such company, solicited by elegant gentlemen. I'm sure they'll eclipse the country gentlemen—well—" she shrugged "—how could they not? It will be *unutterably* thrilling."

The fervour behind the comment made Sophie glance up. Clarissa's eyes shone with innocent anticipation. Looking down at the tiny stitches she was inserting in a tear in one of Jeremy's cuffs, Sophie frowned. After a moment, she ventured, "You really should not judge all London gentlemen by Mr. Lester, Clarissa."

Unfortunately, her cousin mistook her meaning.

"But there *can't* be many more elegant, Sophie. Why, that coat he wore to the ball was top of the trees. And he did look so dashing this morning. And you have to admit he has a certain air." Clarissa paused for breath, then continued, "His bow is very graceful—have you noticed? It makes one wonder at the clumsiness of others. And his speech is very refined, is it not?"

"His voice, too," put in Melly. She shivered artistically. "So deep it reaches inside you and sort of rumbles there."

Sophie pricked her finger. Frowning, she put it in her mouth.

"And his waltzing must just be divine—so…so powerful, if you take my meaning." Clarissa frowned as she considered the point.

"We didn't hear much of his conversation, though," Melly cautioned.

Clarissa waved a dismissive hand. "Oh, that'll be elegant, too, I make no doubt. Why, Mr. Lester clearly moves in the best circles—good conversation would be essential. Don't you think so, Sophie?"

"Very likely." Sophie picked up her needle. "But you should remember that one often needs to be wary of gentlemen of manifold graces, like Mr. Lester."

But Clarissa, starry-eyed and rosy-cheeked, refused to accept the warning. "Oh, no," she said, shaking her head. "I'm sure you're wrong, Sophie. Why, with all his obvious experience, I'm sure one could trust Mr. Lester, or any gentleman like him. I'm sure they'd know just how things should be done."

Mentally Sophie goggled. She was quite sure Jack Lester, for one, would know just how "things" were done—but they certainly weren't the "things" Clarissa imagined. "Truly, Clarissa, trust me when I say that you would be very much safer with a gentleman *without* Mr. Lester's experience."

"Oh, come now, Sophie." Puzzled, Clarissa eyed her curiously. "Have you taken him in aversion? How could you? Why, you'll have to admit he's most terribly handsome."

When it became clear neither Clarissa nor Melly was going to be satisfied with anything short of an answer, Sophie sighed. "Very well. I'll concede he's handsome."

"And elegant?"

"And elegant. But—"

"And he's terribly…" Melly's imagination failed. "Graceful," she finally said.

Sophie frowned at them both. "And graceful. Yet—"

"And his conversation is elegant, too, is it not?"

Sophie tried a scowl. "Clarissa…"

"Is it not?" Clarissa was almost laughing, her natural exuberance bubbling through her recently acquired veneer of sophistication.

In spite of herself, Sophie could not restrain her smile. "Very well," she capitulated, holding up one hand. "I will admit that Mr. Lester is a paragon of manly graces. There—are you satisfied?"

"And you did enjoy your waltz with him, didn't you? Susan Elderbridge was in transports, and *she* had only a country dance."

Sophie didn't really want to remember that waltz, or any

other of her interactions with Jack Lester. Unfortunately, the memories glowed bright in her mind, crystal clear, and refused to wane. As for his eyes, she had come to the conclusion that their image had, somehow, impinged on her brain, like sunspots. Whenever she closed her eyes, she could see them, that certain light which she trusted not at all in their deep blue depths.

She blinked and refocused on Clarissa's face, suffused with ingenuous curiosity. "Mr. Lester is very...skilled in such matters."

With that global statement, Sophie took up her needle, hoping her cousin would take the hint.

But Clarissa was not finished. Her arms sweeping wide to encompass all they had discussed, she concluded, her voice dramatic, her expression that of one convinced beyond doubt, "So we are agreed: Mr. Lester is a paragon, a maiden's dream. How then, Sophie can you not *yearn* to find happiness in his arms?"

"Well—his, or someone like him," Melly added, forever prosaic.

Sophie did not immediately raise her head. Her cousin's question was, indeed, very like the one she had been asking herself before Clarissa and Melly had entered. Was what she felt simply the inevitable response to such as Jack Lester? Or was it— Abruptly, she cut off the thought. "Indeed, Clarissa," she replied, shaking out Jeremy's shirt and folding it up, "Mr. Lester is the sort of gentleman of whom it's most unwise to have such thoughts."

"But why?"

Sophie looked up and saw genuine bewilderment in Clarissa's lovely face. She grimaced. "Because he's a rake."

There. It was said. Time and more that she brought these two down to earth.

Their reaction was immediate. Two pairs of eyes went round, two mouths dropped open.

Clarissa was the first to recover. "Really?" Her tone was one of scandalized discovery.

"No!" came from Melly. Then, "How can you tell?"

Clarissa's expression stated that was her question, too.

Sophie stifled her groan. How could she explain? A subtle something in his eyes? An undertone in his deep voice? Something in his suave manner? Then she recalled she had known instantly, in the moment she had seen him framed in Lady Asfordby's doorway. "His arrogant air. He carried himself as if the world were his oyster, the women in it his pearls."

His to enjoy at his whim. Sophie had surprised even herself with her words.

Both Clarissa and Melly fell silent. Then, frowning slightly, Clarissa glanced up. "I don't mean to doubt you, Sophie, but, you know, I don't think you can be right—at least, not in this instance."

Resigned to resistance, Sophie merely raised her brows.

Encouraged, Clarissa ventured, "If Mr. Lester *were* a rake, then surely Mama would not be encouraging him. And she is, you know. Why, she was perfectly thrilled to see him this morning—you know she was. And it was her suggestion he sit with us, beside you."

That, of course, had been the other niggling concern that had been inhabiting Sophie's mind. All Clarissa said was true; the only point Sophie was yet unsure of was what, exactly, her aunt was about. And that, as she well knew, could be just about anything. Given that Mr. Lester was a rake, one of the more dangerous of the species if her instincts were any guide, then Lucilla might just be grasping the opportunity to have her, Sophie, brush up on the social skills she would doubtless need once they were established in London. In the present circumstances, safe in the bosom of her family in their quiet country backwater, there was no real danger involved.

"Anyway," Clarissa said, drawing Sophie from her thoughts, "what I said at first is still undeniably true. Experienced London gentlemen are *much* more interesting than country gentlemen."

Knowing there was one particular country gentleman Clarissa had in mind, Sophie felt compelled to point out, "But young country gentlemen do grow older, and gain experience in so doing. Even experienced gentlemen must once have been young."

The comment drew a spurt of laughter from Melly. "Can you imagine Mr. Marston young?"

Clarissa giggled. Sophie knew she should chide them but did not; she agreed far too well to make a rebuke sound sincere. As Clarissa and Melly fell to chattering, comparing various older men of their acquaintance and speculating on their younger incarnations, Sophie tried to visualize a younger Jack Lester. It was, she found, a very difficult task. She couldn't imagine his eyes without that certain gleam. With an inward snort, she banished such foolish thoughts and reached for the next garment to be mended.

Doubtless, Jack Lester had been born a rake.

CHAPTER THREE

FATE WAS DEFINITELY smiling upon him.

Tooling his curricle along the lane to the village, Jack squinted against the glare of the brittlely bright morning sunshine, his gaze locked on the group slowly making its way down the lane on the other side of the narrow valley, also bound for the village. A female figure in a familiar cherry-red pelisse was walking a horse of advanced years, hitched to the poles of a gig. A young girl skipped about, now beside the woman, now on the other side of the horse.

"Looks like a problem, Jigson." Jack threw the comment over his shoulder to his groom, perched on the box behind him.

"Aye," Jigson replied. "Likely a stone from the way he's favouring that hoof."

A tiny track joining the two main lanes across the narrow valley came into sight just ahead. Jack smiled and checked his team.

"Be we a-going that way, guv'nor? I thought we was for the village?"

"Where's your sense of chivalry, Jigson?" Jack grinned as he steered his highly strung pair onto the hedged track, then steadied them down a steep incline. "We can't leave a lady in distress."

Especially not *that* lady.

He should, of course, have left for London by now—or, at the very least, quit the scene. His experienced brother-in-law, for one, would certainly have recommended such a strategic retreat. "Women should never be crammed, any more than one's fences" had been a favourite saying of Jason's. He had, of course, been speaking of seduction, a fact that had given Jack pause. Given that he was, to all intents and purposes, wooing his golden head, he had elected to ignore the voice of experience, choosing instead to take heed of a new and unexpectedly strong inner prompting, which categorically stated that leaving the field free to Phillip Marston was not a good idea.

As he feathered his leader around a tight curve, Jack felt his expression harden.

According to Hodgeley, his head groom at the cottage, Marston was a gentleman farmer, a neighbour of the Webbs. He was commonly held to be a warm man, comfortably circumstanced. Village gossip also had it that he was on the lookout for a wife, and had cast his eye in Miss Winterton's direction.

Jack gritted his teeth. He took the tiny bridge at a smart clip, surprising a startled expletive from Jigson, but not so much as scratching the curricle's paintwork. Frowning, he shook aside the odd urge that had gripped him. For some reason, his mind seemed intent on creating monsters where doubtless none lurked. Fate wouldn't be so cruel as to parade his golden head before him, only to hand her to another. Besides, Jigson, who frequented the local tap, had heard no whispers of Mr. Marston heading south for the Season.

Deftly negotiating the tight turn into the lane, Jack relaxed. He came upon them around the next bend.

Sophie glanced up and beheld a team of matchless bays bearing down upon them. She grabbed Amy, then blinked as the team swung neatly aside, pulling up close by the ditch. Only then did she see the driver.

As he tossed the reins to his groom and swung down from

the elegant equipage, she had ample time to admire the sleek lines of both carriage and horses. He strode across the narrow lane, his many-caped greatcoat flapping about the tops of his glossy Hessians, the cravat at his throat as neat and precise as if he were in Bond Street. His smile, unabashed, stated very clearly how pleased he was to see her. "Good day, Miss Winterton."

Stifling her response was impossible. Her lips curving warmly, Sophie countered, "Good morning, Mr. Lester. Dobbin has loosed a shoe."

He put a hand on the old horse's neck and, after casting an improbably apologetic glance her way, verified that fact. Releasing the horse's leg, he asked, "I can't remember—is the blacksmith in the village?"

"Yes, I was taking him there."

Jack nodded. "Jigson, walk Miss Winterton's horse to the blacksmith's and have him fix this shoe immediately. You can return the gig to Webb Park and wait for me there."

Sophie blinked. "But I was on my way to see my mother's old nurse. She lives on the other side of the village. I visit her every Monday."

A flourishing bow was Jack's reply. "Consider me in the light of a coachman, Miss Winterton. And Miss Webb," he added, his gaze dropping to Amy, who was staring, open-mouthed, at his curricle.

"Oh, but we couldn't impose...." Sophie's protest died away as Jack lifted his head. The glance he slanted her brimmed with arrogant confidence.

Jack looked down at Amy. "What say you, Miss Webb? Would you like to complete your morning's excursion atop the latest from Long Acre?"

Amy drew in a deep breath. "*Oooh,* just wait till I tell Jeremy and George!" She looked up at Jack's face—a long way up from her diminutive height—and smiled brilliantly.

She reached out and put her small hand in his. "My name is Amy, sir."

Jack's smile was equally brilliant. "Miss Amy." He swept her an elegant bow, and Amy's expression suggested he had made a friend for life. As he straightened, Jack shot Sophie a victorious grin.

She returned it with as much indignation as she could muster, which, unfortunately, was not much. The prospect of being driven in his curricle was infinitely more attractive than walking. And, after his conquest of Amy, nothing would suffice but that they should travel thus. The decision was taken out of her hands, though Sophie wasn't sure she approved.

His groom had already taken charge of old Dobbin. The man nodded respectfully. "I'll see the blacksmith takes good care of him, miss."

There was nothing to do but incline her head. "Thank you." Sophie turned and followed as Jack led Amy, skipping beside him, to the curricle. Abruptly, Sophie quickened her stride. "If you'll hand me up first, Mr. Lester, Amy can sit between us."

Jack turned, one brow slowly lifting. The quizzical laughter in his eyes brought a blush to Sophie's cheeks. "Indeed, Miss Winterton. A capital notion."

Relieved but determined not to show it, Sophie held out her hand. He looked at it. An instant later, she was lifted, as if she weighed no more than a feather, and deposited on the curricle's padded seat. Sophie sucked in a quick breath. He held her firmly, his fingers spread about her waist, long and strong. In the instant before his hands left her, his eyes locked with hers. Sophie gazed into the deep blue and trembled. Then blushed rosy red. She looked down, fussing with her skirts, shuffling along to make room for Amy.

He had taken up the reins and half turned the curricle before she recalled the purpose of her trip.

"The basket." Sophie looked back at the gig. "For Mildred. It's under the seat."

Jack smiled reassuringly. In a trice, Jigson had the basket out and transferred to the curricle's boot. "Now," Jack said, "whither away?"

Sophie bestowed a smile of thanks on Jigson. "The other side of the village and out along the road to Asfordby, a mile or so. Mildred lives very quietly; she's quite old."

Jack gave his horses the office. "Your mother's nurse, you said. Did your mother's family come from hereabouts?"

"No, from Sussex. Mildred came to Webb Park with Aunt Lucilla on her marriage. My aunt was the younger, so Mildred stayed with her."

Jack slanted a glance at the pure profile beside him—Amy's head was too low to interfere with his view. "Do you often do the duty visits for your aunt?"

Sophie considered the question. "I've often done so whenever I've stayed." She shrugged. "Aunt Lucilla is frequently very busy. She has twins younger than Amy—they're just six."

Jack grinned. "And quite a handful?"

"That," declared Sophie, "is a description insufficient to adequately convey the full glory of the twins."

Jack chuckled. "So you help out by taking on the role of the lady of the manor?"

"It's hardly an arduous task," Sophie disclaimed. "I've been doing much the same on my father's estate ever since my mother died."

"Ah, yes. I recall you mentioned helping your father."

Sophie threw him a quick frown. "That's not what I meant. Performing one's duty is hardly doing anything out of the ordinary." There had been something in his tone, a note of dismissal, which compelled her to explain. "I acted as his amanuensis in all matters concerning the estate and also for his studies. And, of course, since my mother's death, I've had charge of the house." It sounded like a catalogue of her talents, yet she couldn't help adding, "House parties, naturally, were impossible, but even living retired as we did, my father could not escape some degree of local entertaining. And the house, being so old and rambling, was a nightmare to run with the small staff we kept on." Sophie frowned at the memory.

Jack hid his keen interest behind an easy expression. "Who's running the house now?"

"It's closed up," Sophie informed him, her tone indicating her satisfaction. As the curricle rounded a corner, she swayed closer. "My father would have left it open—but for what? I finally managed to persuade him to leave just a caretaker and his agent and let the others go on leave. He may be away for years—who can tell?"

Jack slanted a curious glance at her. "If you'll forgive the impertinence, you don't seem overly troubled by the prospect."

Sophie grinned. "I'm not. Indeed, I'm truly glad Papa has gone back to his 'old bones.' He was so abjectly unhappy after my mother's death that I'd be a truly ungrateful wretch were I to begrudge him his only chance at contentment. I think his work carries him away from his memories, both physically and mentally." Her lips curved wryly; her gaze swung to meet Jack's. "Besides, even though I managed affairs for his own good, he could be a crusty old devil at times."

Jack's answering smile was broad. "I know exactly what you mean. My own father's in much the same case."

Sophie grasped the opportunity to turn the conversation from herself. "Are you his only son?"

"Oh, no." Jack turned his head to glance at her. "There are three of us." He was forced to look to his horses but continued, "I'm the eldest, then Harry. My sister, Lenore, came next; she's now married to Eversleigh. And the baby of the family is Gerald. Our mother died years ago but m'father's held on pretty well. Our Aunt Harriet used to watch over us, but Lenore did most of the work." He threw another glance at Sophie. "My sister is one of those women who shuns the bright lights of the *ton;* she was perfectly content to remain at home in Berkshire and keep the Hall going and the estates functioning. I'm ashamed to confess that, when she married two years ago, I was totally unprepared to take on the burden."

Noting the wry grimace that twisted his lips, Sophie ventured, "But you've managed, have you not?"

Jack's lips lifted. "I learn quickly." After a moment, he went on, his gaze still on the road, "Unfortunately, Aunt Harriet died last year. The estate I can manage—the house…that's something else altogether. Like your father's, it's a rambling old mansion—heaps of rooms, corridors everywhere."

To Jack's surprise, he heard a soft sigh.

"They're terribly inconvenient, but they *feel* like home, don't they?"

Jack turned his head to look at Sophie. "Exactly."

For a long moment, Sophie held his gaze, then, suddenly breathless, looked ahead. The first houses of the village appeared on their right. "The fork to the left just ahead leads to Asfordby."

Their passage through the small hamlet demanded Jack's full attention, his bays taking well-bred exception to the flock of geese flapping on the green, the alehouse's dray drawn up by the side of the road and the creak of the tavern's weatherbeaten sign.

By the time they were passing the last straggling cottages, Sophie had herself in hand. "Mildred's cottage is just beyond the next corner on the right."

Jack reined in the bays by the neat hedge, behind which a small garden lay slumbering in the sunshine. A gate gave on to a narrow path. He turned to smile ruefully at Sophie.

"I'd come and lift you down, but these brutes are presently too nervy to be trusted on loose reins. Can you manage?"

Sophie favoured him with a superior look. "Of course." Gathering her skirts, she jumped down to the lane. Collecting her basket from the boot, she turned to Amy.

"I'll stay here with Mr. Lester," her cousin promptly said. "Old Mildred always wants to tidy my hair." Her face contorted in a dreadful grimace.

Sophie struggled to keep her lips straight. She glanced up at Jack, a questioning look in her eyes.

He answered with a smile. "I can manage, too."

"Very well. But don't be a nuisance," she said to Amy, then, unconsciously smoothing her curls, Sophie went to the gate.

The door opened hard on her knock; Mildred had obviously been waiting. The old dame peered at the curricle and all but dragged Sophie over the threshold. Mildred barely waited for Sophie to shut the door before embarking on a catechism. In the end, Sophie spent more time reassuring Mildred that Mr. Lester was perfectly trustworthy than in asking after Mildred herself, the actual purpose of her visit.

Finally taking her leave, Sophie reached the curricle to find Jack busy teaching Amy how to hold the reins. Depositing the empty basket in the boot, she climbed aboard.

Jack reached across Amy to help her up, then lifted a brow at her. "Webb Park?"

Sophie smiled and nodded. Amy relinquished the reins with sunny good humour, prattling on happily as the horses lengthened their stride.

About them, the March morning sang with the trills and warbles of blackbirds and thrush. The hedges had yet to unfurl their buds, but here and there bright flocks of daffodils nodded their golden heads, trumpeting in the spring.

"So tell me, Miss Winterton, what expectations have you of your stay in the capital?" Jack broke the companionable silence that had enveloped them once Amy had run her course. He flicked a quizzical glance at Sophie. "Is it to be dissipation until dawn, dancing until you drop, Covent Garden and the Opera, Drury Lane and the Haymarket, with Almack's every Wednesday night?"

Sophie laughed, and ducked the subtle query in his last words. "Indeed, sir. That and more."

"More?" Jack's brows rose. "Ah, then it'll be three balls every night, the Park and two teas every afternoon and more gossip than even Silence knows."

"You've forgotten the modistes."

"And the milliners. And we shouldn't forget the boot-makers, glovers and assorted emporia, the ribbon-makers and mantua-makers."

"Then there are the intellectual pursuits."

At that Jack turned to gaze at her, his expression one of stunned dismay. "Good heavens, Miss Winterton. You'll show us all up for the fribbles we are. No, no, my dear—*not* museums."

"Indeed," Sophie insisted, tossing her head, "I fully intend to view Lord Elgin's marbles."

"Oh, those. They don't count." When Sophie stared at him, Jack explained, "They're fashionable."

Sophie laughed again, a silvery sound. Jack smiled. He waited for a moment, then asked, "Will you be riding in the Park?"

"I should think nothing's more likely." Sophie glanced at him over Amy's head. "My cousins all rode before they could walk—literally. My uncle is a very keen horseman and I'm sure he'll be sending mounts down for us."

"So you won't be cutting a dash in a high-perch phaeton?"

"Alas," Sophie sighed. "Although I have always yearned to handle the ribbons, I've never had the opportunity to learn."

Immediately, the curricle slowed. As it came to a halt, she turned to look at Jack.

His slow smile greeted her. "That sounded like a cry from the heart. Never let it be said that a Lester failed to respond to a damsel's plight."

Sophie blinked.

Jack's smile broadened. "I'll teach you."

"Here?"

"Now." He leaned across Amy. "Here, hold the reins like this."

Bemused, Sophie did as he said, taking the leather ribbons in her gloved fingers, looping them in accordance with his directions. It was a fiddle, with Amy between them.

"This will never work," Jack said, echoing Sophie's sentiments. Leaving the reins in her hands, he sat back, his gaze considering. "Just hold them a moment. They won't bolt as long as they sense some weight on the reins." He swung down from the carriage as he spoke. "They're not particularly frisky now; they've been out for over an hour."

Sophie just hoped he knew what he was talking about. Her heart was in her mouth as the leader tossed his head.

Jack rounded the horses and came up beside her. "Shuffle up, Miss Amy, so I can give your cousin her first lesson."

Startled, Sophie glanced down at him. The leader immediately tugged on the loosened reins.

"Hoa, there."

One strong hand closed about her fingers, tightening the rein, steadying the restive horse.

Sophie knew she was blushing. With no alternative offering, she shuffled over, followed a delighted Amy across the seat, allowing her rakish mentor to sit beside her. Her first lesson—in what?

She risked a glance up from beneath her lashes; his eyes held a mocking gleam.

"Fie, Miss Winterton." His voice was low. One dark brow rose. "If I offered a guinea for your thoughts, would you take it?"

Sophie blushed even more. She abruptly transferred her gaze to the horses, thus missing Jack's smile.

"Now, the first thing to remember…"

To Sophie's surprise, despite the distraction of his nearness, she quickly mastered the reins, keeping the thoroughbreds well up to their bits. Even more amazingly, he kept strictly to his role of tutor; doubtless, she rationalized, he was sufficiently concerned over the welfare of his horses—and their sensitive mouths—to keep his mind on their safety. Whatever, her suspicions proved unfounded; caution evaporating, she quickly dropped her guard, absorbed in practising the skills he imparted.

Webb Park appeared far too soon.

Exhilarated, Sophie tooled the curricle up the drive, slowing to effect a sedate halt in the gravel forecourt. Her eyes were bright, her cheeks pink as she turned to her companion and, with real reluctance, handed back the reins.

"A most commendable first outing, my dear." Jack met her shy smile with a smile of his own, his eyes searching hers.

A groom came running to hold the horses. Recalled to his surroundings, Jack tied off the reins and leapt down. Amy scrambled from her perch on the other side and went to natter to the groom.

Sophie slid to the side of the carriage. She made no demur when Jack reached for her and lifted her down. Her feet touched solid earth; she glanced up, and was overcome by flustered shyness. Sternly subduing the sensation, she accepted her empty basket and held out one gloved hand. "Thank you, Mr. Lester. You have indeed proved yourself a knight errant this day. Not only must I thank you for your timely rescue, but also for your excellent tuition."

Smiling down at her, Jack took her hand. "On the contrary, Miss Winterton, the gain was mine. I've rarely had the pleasure of an outing with a lady of such manifold talents."

Squelching the inner glow that rose in response to that compliment, Sophie shot him a sceptical glance. "Indeed, sir, I fear I'm no different from many another."

Jack's slow smile softened his features. "Now, there you are wrong, my dear." He trapped her gaze with his. "You are quite unique." Sophie's eyes widened; he felt her quiver.

Letting his lids veil his eyes, Jack lifted her hand, studying the slender palm, the long, slim fingers. Then his lids rose, his dark gaze again holding hers. Smoothly, he raised her hand and placed a kiss on her inner wrist, exposed above the edge of her glove. "You take the shine out of all the London belles, my dear."

Sophie's skin burned where his lips had touched. Her breathing suspended; light-headedness threatened. It took all the experience she possessed to summon an unaffected smile. "Why, thank you, sir. Will you come in and meet my aunt? I know she'll want to thank you for your help."

He accepted the dismissal without a blink, although the expression in his eyes was amused. "No, I thank you. I know your aunt will be busy; I will not press my presence on her at this time."

Holding hard to her composure, Sophie inclined her head. "Then I'll bid you a very good day, Mr. Lester."

He smiled then, his slow, teasing smile. "*Au revoir,* Miss Winterton."

Sophie turned and climbed the steps. On the threshold, she paused and looked back. He had climbed to the curricle's seat; as she watched, he flicked the reins. With a last wave, he was away, the carriage sweeping down the drive.

She watched until his dark head was no longer in sight. Then, lowering the hand she had automatically raised in farewell, Sophie frowned and turned indoors. She eventually located Amy in the kitchens, munching on a fresh-baked bun.

"Come, Amy. You should change."

Bustling the exuberant child, full of prattle, up the back stairs, Sophie was jolted from her thoughts by her cousin's bright voice, raised in innocent query.

"Is Mr. Lester courting you, Sophie?"

The breath caught in Sophie's throat. For an instant, she felt as if the world had lurched. She coughed. "Good heavens, Amy!" The dimness of the stairs hid her furious blush. "Of course not—he was just funning." She sought for more words—more convincing words—to deny the possibility; none were forthcoming. In desperation, she flapped her hands at Amy. "Come on now, up you go."

As she followed the little girl up the stairs, Sophie frowned. From the mouth of an innocent babe..?

CHAPTER FOUR

NOT CONTENT WITH her efforts thus far, Fate seemed intent on assisting him at every turn.

As he sat his black hunter in the shadows of a wind-break and watched the small cavalcade come thundering up Ashes' Hill, Jack couldn't keep the smile from his face.

Jigson, ever mindful of his place in the scheme of things, had been assiduous in his visits to the tap. Thus Jack had learned that the junior Webbs, accompanied by Miss Winterton and Miss Webb, were to be found on horseback most afternoons. Weather permitting, they would hack about the lanes and fields, but, according to one of the Webb grooms, the track over Ashes' Hill was currently their favoured route.

As he watched them canter up onto the green swath before him, Jack's smile broadened. His golden head was a delight in moss-green velvet, the long skirts of her habit brushing tan boots. On her guinea-gold curls perched a typically feminine contraption; he knew she'd call it a hat, but to his mind the wisp of fabric anchoring a pheasant's feather hardly qualified for the title. Turning, he lifted a brow at Percy mounted on a bay gelding beside him. "Shall we?"

Percy started; his abstracted gaze, very likely visualizing the rival merits of herringbone and country plaid, rapidly refocused. "What? Oh, yes. 'Bout time."

Jack smiled and led the way forward, out of the shadows of the firs.

Pulling up on the crest of the hill, then wheeling her horse to view her cousins, straggling up in her wake, Sophie did not immediately see him. Clarissa, who had reached the spot some moments ahead of her, had likewise turned to view the vista spread below them. Stone walls and still-dormant hedges divided the brown fields, their colour just tinged with the first hint of green. Jeremy and George, fourteen and twelve respectively, were but yards from the top; Amy, bouncing along on her placid cob, brought up the rear. The twins, yet to graduate from plodding ponies, were not included in these afternoon expeditions.

Reassured that all was well, Sophie relaxed her reins. Eyes bright, cheeks aglow, she drew in a deep breath, savouring the crisp freshness.

"Well met, Miss Winterton!"

The hail brought her head round; the deep voice sent the colour to her cheeks even before her eyes found him. He was mounted on a raking black hunter, sleek and powerful. As the animal walked towards her, neck proudly arched, black withers rippling, Sophie was struck by its harnessed power. Then her eyes lifted to its owner.

Broad shoulders encased in a hacking jacket of soft tweed, his powerful thighs, clad in buckskin breeches, effortlessly controlling the horse, he appeared the very epitome of a wealthy country gentleman. His face, features stamped with that coolly arrogant cast which identified his antecedents more definitively than his name. His eyes were very blue, dark, his gaze intent.

There was power there, too. As he brought his horse alongside hers, Sophie felt it reach for her.

"Good afternoon, Mr. Lester." She forced herself to extend a gloved hand, disconcerted by the warmth that caressed her cheeks and the breathlessness that had assailed her.

He took her hand and bowed over it, a difficult feat he performed with rare grace. His eyes quizzed her. "We saw you riding up and wondered if we might join you?"

"What a splendid idea!" From beside Sophie, Clarissa beamed ingenuously.

Feeling slightly helpless, Sophie could not resist the subtle laughter lurking in the blue eyes holding hers. Very much on her dignity, she retrieved her hand and indicated the track leading on over the hill. "If it pleases you, sir."

The smile she received in reply warmed her through and through.

Jack gestured to Percy, hanging back on his other side. "If you'll permit me to introduce Lord Percy Almsworthy?"

"Pleased to make your acquaintance, Miss Winterton."

Prepared to be wary, Sophie saw at a glance that Lord Percy was sprung from a mould quite different from his companion. Reassured, she smiled and held out a hand.

As he leant from the saddle to shake it, she thought she detected a look of keen appraisal in Lord Percy's mild gaze. "M'father's Carlisle," he said, giving her a peg on which to hang his hat.

Sophie dutifully introduced her cousins, in strict order of precedence. Jeremy and George barely waited for Amy's shy "Hello," before pouncing.

"What a bang-up set of blood and bones, sir!"

"Splendid hocks!"

"What stable does he hail from?"

"Is he a Thoroughbred?"

Jack laughed. "My brother bred him out of Jack Whistle."

"The winner of the Derby?" Jeremy's expression mirrored his awestruck tone.

Jack's eyes touched Sophie's. "The very same."

"Is your brother staying with you?" Gerald asked breathlessly.

Jack couldn't help his smile. "He was, but he's gone on to Belvoir."

"Oh." Both boys appeared crestfallen that they had missed the opportunity to badger a breeder who could turn out such a horse as the black.

"Never mind," Jack said. His eyes again met Sophie's. "I'll mention to him that you're interested in speaking with him, it's perfectly possible you may meet in him in Hyde Park."

"On Rotten Row?" George's eyes were round.

When Jack nodded, Jeremy put their seal of approval firmly on the plan. He breathed out in a great sigh, his face alight. "Capital!"

Then, with the rapid change of direction that characterised the young, Jeremy turned to George. "Race you to the oak." They were off on the words, thundering down the slope towards the distant tree.

As by unvoiced consent they set their horses ambling after the two boys, Sophie glanced up at Jack. "You'll have to excuse them—they're rather single-minded when it comes to horses."

Jack slanted her a smile. "Harry and I were the same."

Sophie let her glance slide away. She could hear Clarissa and Lord Percy conversing; they were only a step or so behind. It was true they had no real chaperon, yet she could not imagine there was any impropriety in the situation; the presence of the children lent a certain innocence to the gathering.

Jack had only just registered the absence of a groom. He suppressed an instinctive frown. "Tell me, Miss Winterton, do you commonly ride unescorted?"

Glancing up, Sophie caught the frown in his eyes. Her brows rose. "All my cousins are expert riders; there's little chance of calamity in a gentle ride about the lanes."

"The lanes?"

Sophie had the grace to blush. "You can hardly expect

such high spirits—" she indicated Jeremy and George "—to be content with such mild entertainment." Somewhat defensively, she added, "Clarissa and I are experienced riders, and Amy's cob is so ancient it rarely gets above a canter."

That last was self-evident as Amy, not content with their ambling progress, was jigging along ahead of them as fast as the cob would go. Barely a canter, much to Amy's disgust.

"Besides, sir," Sophie added, slanting a glance up at him, "I cannot believe that you and your brother—Harry, was it not?—would have been content with the lanes."

To her surprise, Jack's lips firmed into a distinctly grim line. "Indeed, no, Miss Winterton. Which is why I feel peculiarly well-qualified to express an opinion on what disasters are possible—nay, probable—given two high-couraged youngsters on fine horses." He turned from his contemplation of the boys, now circling the oak ahead, to look down at her. "And," he added, "which is why I think you should most certainly have a groom with you."

A trifle nettled, Sophie reached down to pat the proud neck of her own mount, a raw-boned grey stallion. "You need have no fear of them getting away from me. Few horses can outrun the Sheik."

Her action drew Jack's gaze to her horse; until then, despite his frequent preoccupation with the species, he had not really noticed it. As his gaze took in the large head, the long legs and heavy shoulders and rump, he felt the hairs on his nape rise. Despite the fact he had heard the warning note in her voice, despite knowing she would not welcome his question, he cleared his throat and asked it. "Do you normally ride that beast, Miss Winterton?"

His curiously flat tone had Sophie glancing up, searching his face. "No," she admitted, after a moment's hesitation. "My uncle's stables are extensive. We all take turns helping to exercise the hunters."

Jack's jaw firmed. "And does your uncle know you're riding such a dangerous creature?"

Sophie stiffened. "Mr. Lester," she said, her accents precise, "I have grown up around horses—have been riding since my earliest days. I assure you I am perfectly capable of managing the Sheik, or any other of my uncle's horses."

"That horse is too strong for you." His brows lowered, Jack stated unequivocally, "You should not be riding such an animal."

In the sky above them, the larks swooped and carolled. Their horses, displaying a fine equine imperturbability, trotted on down the hill. Sophie, flags of colour in her cheeks, abruptly retrieved her dropped jaw. Wrenching her gaze from the deeply turbulent blue into which it had fallen, she looked ahead.

The froth of white lace covering her breast rose as she drew in a deep breath. "Mr. Lester," she began, her tone icy, her accents clipped, "I believe we would do well to leave this topic of conversation. I am perfectly capable of managing the Sheik. Now, if you don't mind, I think we should join my cousins."

Resisting the impulse to toss her head, she flicked her reins and the Sheik surged forward. She thought she heard an angry snort, then the black moved up beside her, long fluid strides eating up the turf. Irritation, consternation and something even more unnerving rasped her temper; Sophie kept her gaze fixed forward, ignoring the glowering presence beside her.

Through narrowed eyes, Jack viewed her chilly dignity with very real disapproval.

The two boys and Amy were waiting by the oak. Sophie drew rein and looked back. Clarissa and Lord Percy had followed them down. As his lordship drew up, she heard him remark, "The best bonnets are to be found at Drusilla's, in my opinion. Just off Bruton Street. All the crack at the moment." Her cousin and Lord Percy were clearly deep in fashion. His lordship appeared perfectly content; Clarissa was hanging on his every word. With a smothered snort, Sophie turned to her younger relatives.

"We'll walk along the hedge until we come to the ride. Then back beside the woods."

There was a definite edge to her tone. Jeremy, George and Amy cast her swift glances; without a word, they fell in behind her. Jack remained by her side; Sophie did not waste any effort in trying to dislodge him. Clarissa and Lord Percy brought up the rear, barely glancing up from their sartorial discussion.

Sophie slanted a wary and warning glance at Jack. He met it with a coolly inscrutable expression. With determined calm, Sophie lifted her chin and set off along the hedge.

The silence that engulfed them stretched ominously. She could feel the occasional touch of his glance; she knew there was a frown in his eyes. Sophie wondered why her throat felt so tight, why simply breathing seemed so difficult. Suppressing a grimace, she racked her brains for some suitably innocuous topic of conversation.

Behind her, George was idly threshing the hedge with his whip.

Later, Sophie learned that, entirely inadvertently, George had flushed a hare from the hedge. The animal darted out, straight under the Sheik's hooves.

The stallion reared, screaming.

Sophie fought for control. It was all she could do to keep her precarious seat.

Then the Sheik was off.

Like a steam engine, the huge stallion pounded down the line of the hedge. Sophie clung to his back. Mounted side-saddle, she could not exert sufficient strength to rein in the panicked beast. The wind of their passing whistled in her ears and whipped her breath away. Desperate, she peered ahead through the wisps of hair flattened against her face, through the rough mane that whipped her cheeks. The hedge at the end of the field loomed ahead. Whispering a fervent prayer, Sophie dropped one rein and threw all her weight onto the other. Almost sobbing, she hauled back. The manoeuvre worked. The Sheik's head slewed, responding to the drag on the bit. But the stallion did not slow. Sophie felt herself tipping sideways. A scream stuck in her throat as she flung herself forward to cling once more to the Sheik's glossy neck. The ride they had been making for opened out before them; a single tug of the Sheik's powerful head pulled the rein from her grasp. Snorting, the stallion flew down the green turf.

Rattled, jolted, Sophie struggled to regain the reins. The ride eventually entered the woods, narrowing to a bridle track. She had to control the Sheik before that.

But the horse had the bit firmly between his teeth; even when she had the reins back in her hands, he refused to respond to her puny strength.

A flash of black to her left was her first intimation that help was at hand. Then Jack was beside her, the heavier black crowding the grey. He leaned across, one hand closing hard over her fingers as he added his weight to hers. Sophie felt him exert an increasing pressure, not jerking, as less experienced riders might. The Sheik felt the inexorable command.

Gradually, the grey slowed, finally stopping by the side of the ride.

Dragging in a ragged breath, Sophie sat up. Immediately the world tilted and spun. A ripe curse fell on her ears; it seemed to come from a long way away. Then strong hands fastened about her waist and weightlessness was added to the disconcerting sensations buffeting her.

Her feet touched firm earth. Shudder upon shudder racked her; she was trembling like a leaf.

The next instant she was enveloped in a warm embrace,

locked against a hard frame. A large hand cradled her head, pressing her cheek against a firm male chest. The earthy scent of tweed and leather surrounded her, inexplicably comforting. With a gasp, stifled against his coat, Sophie clung to him, a solid anchor in her suddenly perilous world.

"*My God!* Are you all right?"

He sounded as shaken as she felt. Her throat was still closed; dumb, Sophie nodded. Dimly recalling the proprieties, she reluctantly drew away.

Hard fingers gripped her upper arms; abruptly Jack put her from him. Gasping, Sophie looked up, only to be subjected to a merciless shake.

"I thought you said you could handle that beast!"

Numb, Sophie stared at him, at the fury that flamed in his eyes. A chill trickled through her veins, then spread; she felt the blood drain from her face. Cold blackness drew in; she blinked groggily.

Jack paled as she drooped in his hands. With a muttered curse, he gathered her to him.

Sophie didn't resist. Supporting her against him, Jack guided her to a fallen log. "Sit down!"

The harshness in his tone brought Sophie's head up. Simultaneously, her legs gave way and she complied with more haste than grace.

Jack stood over her, his face an icy mask. "You're white as a sheet. Put your head down."

Dizzy, disorientated, Sophie simply stared at him.

Jack cursed again.

The next thing Sophie knew her head was descending towards her knees, yielding to the insistent pressure of a large hand. He didn't let up until her forehead rested on her knees. As another wave of black nothingness swept over her, Sophie jettisoned any thought of resistance. She set her mind on breathing deeply, calming the turmoil inside. The world and her senses slowly returned to her. Only then did she become aware of the long fingers that had insinuated themselves beneath the collar of her habit and blouse, pushing aside her curls to gently caress her nape. Cool, firm, they traced sorcerous patterns on her sensitive skin. Faintness threatened again; his touch drew her back, anchoring her to reality, soothing her frayed nerves, promising security and safety.

They remained thus for what seemed like an age. Eventually, Sophie drew in a deep breath and sat up. The hand at her nape fell away. She glanced up through her lashes. His expression was closed, shuttered. Dragging in another breath, she gathered her skirts.

His hand appeared before her. After a moment's hesitation, she placed her hand in his and allowed him to assist her to her feet.

"I have to thank you, Mr. Lester, for your assistance." She managed the words creditably but could not look at him. Instead, eyes downcast, she fussed with her skirts, smoothing down the moss velvet.

"I would infinitely prefer, Miss Winterton, if, instead of your thanks, you would give me your promise not to ride that animal, or any like him, again."

The coolly arrogant tones left no doubt of the nature of that request. Slowly straightening, Sophie met his gaze. Inscrutable, distant, it told her little, as if he had brought a curtain down across his feelings, shutting her out. Lifting her head, she stated, "What befell, Mr. Lester, was purely an accident."

Jack bit back a caustic response. "The fact you were riding that horse, Miss Winterton, was no accident." His accents clipped, he viewed her through narrowed eyes. "He's too strong for you—and you knew it."

Sophie folded her lips, and gave him back stare for stare, her expression as remote as his.

Jack felt his temper slowly slip its leash. His expression

hardened from mere flint to granite. "Before we leave here, Miss Winterton," he said, his voice low and commendably even, "I want your promise that you will not, in future, engage in such wanton recklessness." He saw her blink; he kept his gaze on hers. "Furthermore, I give you fair warning that should I ever find you on such a horse's back again, you have *my* promise you'll not sit a saddle for a sennight." He watched as her eyes widened, stunned disbelief in their depths. He raised one brow. "Is that perfectly clear, my dear?"

Sophie suppressed a shiver. Unable to hold his relentless gaze, her own dropped to his lips, compressed to a mere line in his ruggedly handsome face.

There was no more than a foot between them. Luckily, the shock of her recent terror was fading; Sophie felt her strength, her normal independence, returning, flooding back, stiffening her resolve. She raised her eyes once more to his. "You have no right to make such a demand of me, Mr. Lester—nor yet threaten me."

Her words were cool, her composure fragile but intact.

Gazing down at her, Jack made no answer, too engrossed in a ferocious inner struggle to subdue the tumultuous emotions raging through him. Every ounce of determination he possessed was required to keep his body still, his muscles locked against the impulse to sweep her into his arms, to demonstrate the validity of his claim on her.

Sophie sensed his turmoil. The odd flicker of the muscle along his jaw, his tightly clenched fists, the tension that gripped his whole frame bespoke her danger. The dark blue of his eyes had deepened, his gaze compelling, flames flickering elusively in the darkened depths. The hard line of his lips had not eased. His physical presence was overwhelming; even more than that, she sensed his strength, a tangible entity, emanating from his large, hard, masculine frame, an aura that reached out, surrounding her, threatening to engulf her, to trap her, to conquer her wilfulness and make her his.

"Sophie?" Clarissa's voice cut across her thoughts. "Sophie? Are you all right?"

A shiver slithered down Sophie's spine. She blinked and realized her heart was racing, her breasts rising and falling rapidly. For one last instant, she met that intense blue gaze. Then, with an effort, she looked away to where Clarissa, with the others in tow, was approaching. Struggling to reassemble her disordered wits, Sophie moved, walking the few feet to the side of her horse. "I'm all right. No harm done."

Jack moved with her, not touching her but ready to support her if needed. Sophie was aware of his protective presence. Recalling how much she owed him, for she was too honest not to acknowledge that it had, indeed, been a very near-run thing, she glanced up through her lashes.

Jack caught her gaze. "Are you able to ride home?"

Sophie nodded. His expression was hard, shuttered, concern the only emotion visible. She drew a shaky breath and raised her head. "I do thank you for your assistance, sir."

Her voice was low, soft, a quaver of awareness running beneath her words.

Jack acknowledged her thanks with a curt nod. Holding fast to the frayed reins of his control, he reached for her, lifting her effortlessly to the grey's back.

Unnerved by the streak of sensation that speared through her at his touch, Sophie made a production of arranging her skirts, using the time to draw every last shred of her experience about her.

As the party reformed, she was grateful to find Clarissa, openly concerned, between herself and Mr. Lester. Lord Percy, on her left, proved an unthreatening companion, chatting on a wide variety of subjects as they wended their way homeward through the golden afternoon.

No further words passed between herself and her rescuer, yet all the way back to the gates of Webb Park, Sophie was conscious of the touch of his brooding gaze.

ONCE SHE WAS SAFELY returned to the bosom of her family, circumstance conspired to afford Sophie no peace in which to ponder. As there were no guests that evening, dinner was served at the earlier hour of five o'clock, *en famille*. All the Webbs barring the twins sat down about the long table in the dining room.

Naturally, her aunt and uncle were immediately regaled with the details of her thrilling rescue. It was all Sophie could do to erase the embellishments with which the younger Webbs enthusiastically embroidered the tale. From their glowing faces and excited voices it was clear that Jack Lester, modern-day hero, could have no fault in their youthful eyes.

"Dear Sophie," Lucilla said, her customary calm intact. "You took no hurt of any kind, I hope?"

"None, aunt." Sophie laid down her soup-spoon. "It was an unfortunate accident but I was not in any way harmed."

"Thanks to Mr. Lester!" piped up Amy.

"You should have seen that black go, sir!" Jeremy addressed himself to his father. "A prime 'un—a real stayer."

"Indeed?' From the head of the table, Horatio Webb beamed his deceptively gentle smile upon them all. A short-ish, distinctly rotund gentleman, with a face that somehow combined elements of both youth and wisdom, many, at first glance, relegated him to the rank of a genial country squire with few thoughts beyond his fields. Only those who looked closer, into his fine grey eyes, twinkling now as Sophie's delicately flushed cheeks assured him she had taken no hurt but was being made more than a little uncomfortable by the continuing fuss, saw a glimmer of the quick-silver intelligence that lurked behind his outward appearance. The very intelligence that had made Horatio Webb a byword in certain rarefied financial circles and was, at some deeper level, part of the reason the beautiful and talented Lucilla Carstairs, capable of landing a dukedom with her smiles, had, instead, very happily married him. Peering at Jeremy over the top of his ever-present spectacles, Horatio replied, "I must say I would not mind getting a look at any horse that could run the Sheik down."

"Mr. Lester is staying in the neighbourhood, I believe," Clarissa volunteered.

Horatio nodded. "Rawling's Cottage, I expect." With bland calm, he picked up the carving implements and fell to carving the roast which had, that moment, been ceremonially placed before him.

To Sophie's relief, the healthy appetites of the younger Webbs thrust her adventure temporarily from their minds.

Dinner was followed by a noisy game of Speculation, after which, feeling positively exhausted, mentally and physically, Sophie took herself off to bed. She had expected to find time, in the quiet of her chamber, to review the afternoon's happenings—not the stirring events her cousins had described, but the far more unnerving moments she had spent alone with Jack Lester, a rescued damsel with her knight. Indeed, with her inner peace in disarray, she climbed the stairs determined to place the episode in proper perspective.

Instead, she fell deeply asleep, her dreams haunted by a pair of midnight-blue eyes.

THE FOLLOWING MORNING was filled to overflowing with the first of the tasks needed to be completed to allow them to remove to the capital at the end of the week as planned. Lucilla had the entire event organized, down to the last bottle of elderflower lotion needed to preserve their complexions against any breeze that might be encountered while being driven in gentlemen's curricles in the Park.

Excused from the first round of packing for a light luncheon, both Sophie and Clarissa were commanded to appear before the family's seamstress for a final fitting of the walking gowns, morning gowns, chemises and petticoats they had all agreed could be perfectly adequately supplied from home. The rest of their wardrobes, Lucilla had declared, must come from Bruton Street. As, after four years' absence from London, none of the gowns Sophie currently possessed could be considered presentable, she was as much in need of the modistes as Clarissa. Even Lucilla had murmured her intention of taking advantage of their time in the capital to refurbish her own extensive wardrobe.

It was midafternoon before Sophie was free. She had barely had time to wander down to the front hall before the younger Webbs found her. With the single-mindedness of the young, they claimed her for their accustomed ride. With an inward sigh, Sophie surveyed the bright faces upturned to hers, eyes glowing, eager to be off. "Very well," she said. "But I think we'll take a groom with us today. Jeremy, please tell John he's to accompany us. I'll get Clarissa and meet you at the stables."

To her relief, none of them commented on her departure from their established norm. Jeremy merely nodded, and all three departed with alacrity.

Glancing down at her morning gown, Sophie turned and started back up the stairs, refusing to dwell on what had prompted her caution, reflecting instead that, given that her aunt relied on her to ensure her cousins were exposed to no untoward occurrences, it was the least she should do.

When she appeared at the stables, Clarissa in tow, Old Arthur, the head groom, raised a questioning brow at her. Pulling on her gloves, Sophie nodded a greeting. "I'll take Amber out today. She hasn't had a run for some time, I believe."

Arthur blinked. Then, with a shrug which stated louder than words that it was not his place to question the vagaries of his betters, he went to fetch the mare. To Sophie's surprise, Clarissa, busy mounting her own high-bred chestnut, refrained from questioning her choice. Amber was as close to docile as any horse in the Webb stables. Taking her cue from her cousin, Sophie steadfastly ignored the niggling little voice which harped in her ear. Her choice of mount had nothing to do with Mr. Lester—and even less with that gentleman's too strongly stated opinions.

The tenor of his comments, both before and after dragging her from the Sheik's back, had stunned her. She had not before encountered such arrogantly high-handed behaviour, but she was quite certain what she thought of it. Yet her lingering reaction to the entire episode was equivocal, ambivalent, no help at all in restoring her equanimity.

Setting placid Amber to the task of catching up with the boys and Amy, already well ahead, Sophie frowned.

Until yesterday, she had been inclined to suspect Jack Lester of harbouring some romantic interest in her. Her conscience stirred, and Sophie blushed delicately. Irritated, she forced herself to face the truth: she had started to hope that he did. But his reactions yesterday afternoon had given her pause; whatever it was that had stared at her from the depths of his dark blue eyes—some deeply felt emotion that had disturbed his sophisticated veneer and wreaked havoc on her calm—it was not that gentle thing called love.

Sophie acknowledged the fact with a grimace as, with a wave and a whooping "halloo," Clarissa shot past. Twitching the reins, Sophie urged Amber into the rolling gait which, with her, passed for a gallop. Clarissa, meanwhile, drew steadily ahead.

Trapped in her thoughts, Sophie barely noticed. Love, as she understood it, was a gentle emotion, built on kindness, consideration and affection. Soft glances and sweet smiles was her vision of love, and all she had seen, between her uncle and aunt and her mother and father, had bolstered that image. Love was calm, serene, bringing a sense of peace in its wake.

What she had seen in Jack Lester's eyes had certainly not been peaceful.

As the moment lived again in her mind, Sophie shivered. What was it she had stirred in him? And how did he really view her?

HER FIRST QUESTION, had she but known it, was also exercising Jack's mind, and had been ever since he had returned from Webb Park the afternoon before. As soon as his uncharacteristically violent emotions had eased their grip on his sanity, he had been aghast. Where had such intense impulses sprung from?

Now, with the afternoon bright beyond the windows, he restlessly paced the parlour of Rawling's Cottage, inwardly still wrestling with the revelations of the previous day. He was deeply shocked, not least by the all but ungovernable strength of the emotion that had risen up when he had seen Sophie's slender figure, fragile against the grey's heaving back, disappear in the direction of the woods and possible death.

And he was shaken by what the rational part of his brain informed him such feelings foretold.

He had innocently supposed that courting the woman he had chosen as his wife would be a mild process in which his emotions remained firmly under his control while he endeavoured, through the skill of his address, to engage hers. A stranger, as he now realized, to love, he had imagined that, in the structured society to which they belonged, such matters would follow some neatly prescribed course, after which they could both relax, secure in the knowledge of each other's affections.

Obviously, he had misjudged the matter.

A vague memory that his brother-in-law had not surrendered to love without a fight glimmered at the back of his mind. Given Jason's undoubted conversion, and his equally undoubted acumen, Jack had always wondered what had made him hesitate—on the brink, as it were.

Now he knew.

Emotions such as he had felt yesterday were dangerous.

They boded fair to being strong enough to overset his reason and control his life.

Love, he was fast coming to understand, was a force to be reckoned with.

A knock on the front door interrupted his reverie. Glancing out of the window, he saw his undergroom leading a handsome bay around to the stables. The sight piqued Jack's interest.

A scrape on the parlour door heralded his housekeeper. "Mr. Horatio Webb to see you, sir."

Intrigued, Jack lifted a brow. "Thank you, Mrs. Mitchell. I'll receive him here."

A moment later, Horatio Webb was shown into the room. As his calm gaze swept the comfortable parlour, warm and inviting with its wealth of oak panelling and the numerous sporting prints gracing the walls, a smile of ineffable good humour creased Horatio's face. Rawling's Cottage was much as he remembered it—a sprawling conglomeration of buildings that, despite its name, constituted a good-sized hunting lodge with considerable stabling and more than enough accommodation for guests. Approaching his host, waiting by the fireplace, he was pleased to note that Jack Lester was much as he had imagined him to be.

"Mr. Webb?" Jack held out a hand as the older man drew near.

"Mr. Lester." Horatio took the proffered hand in a strong clasp. "I'm here, sir, to extend my thanks, and that of Mrs. Webb, for the sterling service you rendered in averting misadventure yesterday afternoon."

"It was nothing, I assure you, sir. I was there and merely did what any other gentleman, similarly circumstanced, would have done."

Horatio's eyes twinkled. "Oh, I make no doubt any other gentleman would have *tried,* Mr. Lester. But, as we both know, few would have succeeded."

Jack felt himself falling under the spell of the peculiarly engaging light in his visitor's eye. His lips twitched appreciatively. "A glass of Madeira, sir?" When Horatio inclined his head, Jack crossed to pour two glasses, then returned, handing one to his guest. "Phoenix is, perhaps, one of the few horses that could have caught your Sheik. I'm just dev'lish glad I was on him."

With a wave, he invited Sophie's uncle to a chair, waiting until the older man sat before taking a seat facing him.

With the contemplative air of a connoisseur, Horatio sipped the Madeira, savouring the fine wine. Then he brought his grey gaze to bear on Jack. "Seriously, Mr. Lester, I do, as you must understand, value your intervention of yesterday. If it weren't for the fact we'll be shortly removing to town, I'd insist you honour us for dinner one night." His words came easily, his eyes, calmly perceptive, never leaving Jack's face. "However, as such is the case, and we will depart on Friday, Mrs. Webb has charged me to convey to you her earnest entreaty that you'll call on us once we're established in Mount Street. Number eighteen. Naturally, I add my entreaty to hers. I take it you'll be removing to the capital shortly?"

Jack nodded, discarding the notion of urging Sophie's

uncle to forbid her his more dangerous steeds. The shock she had so recently received should, with luck, suffice to keep her from the backs of murderous stallions, at least until the end of the week. "I intend quitting Melton any day, as it happens. However, as I must break my journey in Berkshire, I don't expect to reach the metropolis much in advance of your party."

Horatio nodded approvingly. "Please convey my greetings to your father. We were once, if not close friends, then certainly good acquaintances."

Jack's eyes widened. "You're *that* Webb!" Blinking, he hastily explained, "Forgive me—I hadn't realized. With so many Webbs in these parts, I wasn't sure which one had been my father's crony. I understand you and he shared many interests. He has told me of your devotion to the field."

"Ah, yes." Horatio smiled serenely. "My one vice, as it were. But I think you share it, too?"

Jack returned the smile. "I certainly enjoy the sport, but I feel my interest does not reach the obsessive heights of my father's."

"Naturally," Horatio acceded. "You younger men have other obsessions to compete with the Quorn, the Cottesmore and the Belvoir. But the Lester stud is still one of the best in the land, is it not?"

"Under my brother Harry's management," Jack replied. "Our kennels still produce some of the strongest runners, too."

While their conversation drifted into a discussion of the latest trends in breeding both hunters and hounds, Jack sized up Sophie's uncle. Horatio Webb, while younger than his own father, had been a long-time acquaintance of the Honorable Archibald Lester. More specifically, it had been he who had dropped that quiet word in his father's ear which had ultimately led to the resurrection of the family fortunes.

Taking advantage of a natural lull in the conversation,

Jack said, "Incidentally, I must make you all our thanks for your timely advice in the matter of the Indies Corporation."

Horatio waved a dismissive hand. "Think nothing of it. What friends are for, after all." Before Jack could respond with a further expression of gratitude, Horatio murmured, "Besides, you've cleaned the slate. I assure you I would not have liked to have had to face my brother-in-law, eccentric though he is, with the news that his Sophie had broken her neck on one of my stallions. As far as I can see, the scales between the Webbs and the Lesters are entirely level."

Just for an instant, Jack glimpsed the reality behind Horatio Webb's mask. Understanding, then, that this visit had many purposes, perhaps even more than he had yet divined, Jack could do no more than graciously accept the older man's edict. "I'm pleased to have been able to be of service, sir."

Horatio smiled his deceptive smile and rose. "And now I must be off." He waited while Jack rang and gave orders for his horse to be brought round, then shook hands with his host. His eyes roving the room once more, he added, "It's nice to see this place kept up. It's been in your family for some time, has it not?"

Escorting Sophie's amazing uncle to the door, Jack nodded. "Five generations. All the Lester men have been bred to hunting."

"As it should be," Horatio said, and meant far more than the obvious. "Don't forget," he added, as he swung up to the back of his bay. "We'll look to see you in London."

Horatio nodded a last farewell and turned his horse's head for home. As he urged the bay to a canter, a subtle smile curved his lips. He was well pleased with what he had found at Rawling's Cottage. Aside from all else, the Lesters were obviously planning on remaining a part of the landscape, here as much as in Berkshire.

Lucilla would be pleased.

By THE TIME she returned from their ride, Sophie had a headache. As she was not normally prey to even such minor ailments, she felt the constraint deeply. As she preceded Clarissa into the back parlour, she massaged her temples in an effort to ease the throbbing ache behind them.

It was, of course, all Jack Lester's fault. If she hadn't spent half her time worrying about how she would respond if he joined them, and the other half scanning the horizon for his broad-shouldered frame, metaphorically looking over her shoulder all the way, she would doubtless have taken her customary enjoyment in the ride. Instead, she felt dreadful.

Throwing her riding cap onto a chair, she sank gratefully into the overstuffed armchair in the shadows by the hearth.

"A pity Mr. Lester and Lord Percy didn't join us." Clarissa dropped onto the chaise, obviously ready to chat. "I was sure that, after yesterday, they would be waiting at Ashes' Hill."

"Perhaps they've already returned to London," Sophie suggested. "The ground's certainly soft enough to send the tail-chasers back to town."

"Tail-chasers" was the family term for those gentlemen whose only purpose in coming to Melton Mowbray was to chase a fox's tail. At the first sign of the thaw, such gentlemen invariably deserted the packs for the more refined ambience of the *ton*'s gaming rooms.

"Oh, but I don't think Mr. Lester and Lord Percy are tail-chasers, exactly. Not when they both ride such superb horses."

Sophie blinked and wondered if her headache was affecting her reason. "What have their horses to do with it?" she felt compelled to ask. "All tail-chasers, *ipso facto,* must have horses."

But Clarissa's mind was on quite a different track. "They're both terribly *elegant,* aren't they? Not just in the ballroom— well, everyone *tries* to be elegant there. But they both have that indefinable London polish, don't they?"

Sophie openly studied her cousin's lovely face. At the sight of the glowing expression inhabiting Clarissa's clear eyes, she stifled a groan. "Clarissa—please believe me—not all London gentlemen are like Lord Percy and Mr. Lester. Some of them are no better than…than any of the young gentlemen you've met at the local balls. And many are a great deal worse."

"Maybe so," Clarissa allowed. "But it's an indisputable fact that both Mr. Lester and Lord Percy put *all* the gentlemen hereabouts to shame."

Sophie closed her eyes and wished she could argue.

Clarissa rose, eyes shining, and twirled about the room. "Oh, Sophie! I'm so looking forward to being surrounded by all the swells—the dandies, the town beaux, even the fops. It will be so *thrilling* to be sought after by such gentlemen, to be twitted and teased—in a perfectly acceptable way, of course." Clarissa dipped and swirled closer. "And I know," she continued, lowering her voice, "that one is not supposed to say so, but I can't wait to at least try my hand at flirting, and I positively can't *wait* to be ogled."

As she squinted against the glare of the late afternoon sun, her narrowed vision filled with Clarissa's svelte form, Sophie didn't think her cousin would have all that long to wait. She should, she supposed, make a push to bring Clarissa back to earth, and defend the local young gentlemen, Ned in particular. If she hadn't been feeling so ill, she would have. But with her head throbbing so, and her mind still tangled in her own confusion, she doubted she could find sufficient words to succeed.

"But what of you, Sophie?" Abruptly, Clarissa turned from rapt contemplation of her rosy future and plumped down on the chaise close by. "After his dramatically chivalrous rescue yesterday, aren't you just a *little* bit taken with Mr. Lester?"

Sophie let her lids fall; Clarissa, when she put her mind to it, could be quite as perspicacious as her mother. "Indeed," she forced herself to say. "Mr. Lester was everything that is gallant. However, that's hardly the only criterion I have for choosing a husband."

"So, what are your other criteria?"

Squinting through her lashes, Sophie studied Clarissa's grin. Her cousin, she reluctantly concluded, was unlikely to be diverted by any prevarication. "A liking for children," she stated. An obvious test; one, she suspected, Jack Lester would pass. He had handled Amy very well, and the boys, too. "And a sense of humour." He had that, too, reprehensible though it might sometimes be.

"And I would want a man who was steady and reliable, not given to fits of temper." Now *that* was a prerequisite her knight in shining armour might have trouble complying with. Rakes, she had always understood, were totally *un*reliable. Becoming absorbed with her catalogue, Sophie frowned. "Sufficiently handsome, although he needn't be an Adonis. Not mean or stingy. And he'd have to be able to waltz. There," she concluded, opening her eyes fully and fixing Clarissa with a mock glare. "Are you satisfied?"

Clarissa laughed and clapped her hands, making Sophie wince. "But that's famous! Mr. Lester might be just the man for you."

Abruptly, Sophie stood, disguising the sudden movement with a little laugh. "I pray you, Clarissa, don't let your imagination fly away with you. Mr. Lester's presence here—and our meetings—have been occasioned by nothing more than coincidence."

Clarissa looked slightly surprised by her vehemence but, to Sophie's intense relief, she forbore to argue. "I expect something must have detained them today." Clarissa's tone suggested she could see no other likelihood. As she fell to neatly folding the ribbons of her hat, she added, "I wonder when next we'll meet?"

As HE SAT DOWN to dinner that evening in the dining room of the cottage, Jack could have answered Clarissa's question without further thought. He was leaving Leicestershire on the morrow. Early.

He said as much to Percy, taking his seat on his right hand.

"What brought that on? Thought you were fixed here for another few weeks?"

"So did I," Jack returned. "But something's come up." Before Percy could ask what, he added, "And the weather's turned, so I think I'll do better to look in at Lester Hall before hying up to town."

"There is that," Percy agreed knowledgeably. "Ground's softening up. Not many good runs left in the season."

Jack nodded, unexpectedly grateful for the thaw. As he rode very heavy, the going for his mounts would become noticeably harder in the coming weeks.

"Think I'll take a look in on the old man," Percy mused, his expression distant. "Gets a bit obstreperous if we forget him. I'll go and do my filial duty, then meet you in town."

Jack nodded again, his mind busy with his plans. There was no need to hurry up to town. The Webbs would not be receiving for at least another week.

His decision to quit the field in Leicestershire was prompted by a firm conviction that such a scene as had occurred when he'd hauled Sophie from her stallion's back could not be repeated. However, thanks to the incident, he was now on good terms with the Webbs and had been all but commanded to call, once in town. Assuming Mrs. Webb approved, there would, he felt sure, be no impediment placed in his path should he desire to further his interest with Sophie in the usual way.

It was his first, albeit small, advance.

However, given his turbulent and presently unpredictable reactions, it seemed the course of wisdom to suspend all further activity until his golden head was safe in the bosom of the *ton*. His home ground, as it were.

The strictures of Society reached a pinnacle of stringency in London—the strict mores and unwavering practices would undoubtedly prove sufficiently rigid to ensure his wooing followed acceptable paths.

So, for her sake, and, he reluctantly admitted, his own, he had determined to forgo the sight of Sophie's fair face until she appeared in London.

It would be safer for everyone that way.

CHAPTER FIVE

CLIMBING THE STAIRS of Entwhistle House, Sophie looked about
her, at the silks and satins, the jewels and curls, and knew she
was back in the *ton*. About her, the refined accents and dramatic tones of the elite of society, engaged in their favourite
pastime, drowned out the plaintive strains of a violin, struggling through from the ballroom ahead. Immediately in front
of her, Lucilla, clad in an exquisite gown of deep blue silk
overlaid with figured lace, forged steadily onward, stopping
only to exchange greetings with the acquaintances, both close
and distant, who constantly hailed her.

Close beside Sophie, Clarissa frankly stared. "Isn't it *wonderful?*" she breathed. "So many beautiful gowns. And the
men look just as I imagined—precise to a pin. Some are very
handsome, are they not?"

As she whispered the words, Clarissa caught the eye of an
elegant buck, who, noticing her wide-eyed stare, ogled her
shamelessly. Clarissa blushed and retreated behind her fan.

Following her gaze, Sophie caught the gentleman's eye,
and raised a coolly superior brow. The man smiled and bowed
slightly, then turned back to his companions. Sophie slipped
an arm through Clarissa's. "Indeed, and you look very handsome, too, so you must expect to be ogled, you know. The best
way to deal with such attentions is to ignore them."

"Is it?" Clarissa sent a cautious glance back at the gentleman, now fully engaged with his friends. Relieved, she relaxed and looked down at her gown, a delicate affair in palest

aquamarine muslin, a demure trim of white lace about the neckline and tiny puffed sleeves. "I must admit, I did wonder at Madame Jorge's choice, but it really does suit me, doesn't it?"

"As that gentleman has just confirmed," Sophie replied. "I told you you should never argue with Madam Jorge. Aside from anything else, it's wasted breath."

Clarissa giggled. "I never imagined she would be like that."

Looking ahead, Sophie smiled. They had quit Leicestershire on Friday, spending two nights on the road in a stately progress that had delivered them up in Mount Street on Sunday afternoon. The rest of that day had gone in the predictable chaos of unpacking and installing the family in their home for the Season. Lucilla had shooed them all off to bed early, warning both Sophie and Clarissa, "We'll be out first thing, off to Madame Jorge. I refuse to permit either of you to step into a *ton* ballroom unsuitably gowned. We shall have to hope Jorge can come to our aid, for we're promised to Lady Entwhistle tomorrow night if you recall."

And so, that morning, immediately after breakfast at the unheard-of hour of ten, they had arrived before the small door on Bruton Street that gave on to Madame Jorge's salon.

"I only hope she can help us at such short notice," Lucilla had said as she led the way up the stairs.

Her aunt needn't have worried; Madame Jorge had fallen on her neck with unfeigned delight.

Madame Jorge was the modiste who for years had been her mother's and aunt's favourite; her own wardrobe for her ill-fated first Season had come from Madame Jorge's salon. But Madame Jorge was definitely not what one expected of a modiste who made for a very select clientele amongst the *ton*.

For a start, she was huge, a massive bosom balanced by immense hip and brawny arms. But her small hands and thick, short fingers were remarkably nimble. She had almost no neck that one could see; her neat grey hair was perennially coiled in a tight bun upon her round head. Small blue eyes twinkled in a rosy-cheeked face. Only the shrewd gaze and the determined set of Madame Jorge's mouth gave her away.

"And Miss Sophie, too!" she had exclaimed, once she had finished greeting Lucilla. "*Ma pauvre* little one, how good it is to see you again."

Jorge had hugged her to her massive bosom, neatly covered in black bombazine, and then held her at arm's length, the better to survey her. "But, yes! This is wonderful—*wunderbar!*" Jorge had never settled entirely into any one language. She was a polyglot and spoke at least three, often all at once. She took a step back, eyes narrowing, then whipped the tape measure which always hung about her neck into her hands. "For you, my *liebschen,* we will have to retake the measurements." Jorge's eyes had gleamed. "You will turn the gentlemen on their heads, no?"

She had murmured that she hoped not, but was not sure Jorge heard. The modiste had spied Clarissa, hanging back, a little overwhelmed. Her cousin had promptly been even more overwhelmed by Jorge's bear-like embrace.

"Oh—the *petit chou!* You are your mother's daughter, but yes! Very young—but the bloom is worth something, *hein?*"

Utterly bewildered, Clarissa had glanced at her mother. Lucilla had taken Jorge in hand, rapidly explaining their requirements and the need for haste.

Jorge had understood immediately. "*Quelle horreur!* To go to the ball without a gown—it is not to be thought of! No, no, somehow we will contrive."

Contrive she certainly had.

Glancing down at her own silk skirts, in a delicate pale-green hue that was the perfect foil for her colouring, making the blue of her eyes more intense and setting off the true gold of her curls, Sophie felt more than content. The long lines of the skirts, falling from the high waist beneath an unusual square-cut neckline, displayed her slender figure to perfection. Jorge, as always, had come to the rescue; she was a wizard and had waved her magic wand. Their new ball gowns had been delivered at six that evening, the first of their day gowns would be on the doorstep by nine the next morn.

"Sophie! Look!"

Following Clarissa's gaze, Sophie beheld another young girl, weighed down by a gown in frothy pink muslin, a heavy flounce about the neckline repeated twice about the hem making her appear wider than she was tall. The gown was precisely what Clarissa had gone to Madame Jorge's salon determined to have for her first ball.

"Oh, dear." Clarissa viewed the apparition with empathetic dismay. "Would I have looked like that?"

"Very likely," Sophie replied. "Which all goes to show that one should never, ever, argue with Madam Jorge."

Clarissa nodded, carefully averting her gaze from the unfortunate young lady to study, somewhat nervously, the crowd still separating them from their hostess. "I'd never imagined to see so many elegant people in one place at one time."

Sophie felt her lips twitch. "I hesitate to mention it, but this is only a small gathering by *ton* standards, and an informal one at that. There could only be a hundred or so present."

The look Clarissa sent her did not exactly glow with anticipation. They had gained the top of the stairs and were now slowly shuffling across the upper foyer. Then the curtain of bodies before them parted and they found themselves facing Lady Entwhistle.

"Lucilla dear, so glad you could come." Her ladyship and Lucilla touched scented cheeks. Casting a knowledgeable eye over Lucilla's gown, Lady Entwhistle raised a brow. "Dashed if you aren't capable of giving these young misses a run for their money."

Lucilla's eyes flew wide. "*Run,* Mary? Gracious heavens, my dear—*so* enervating!" With a smile that was almost mischievous, Lucilla passed on to greet the young gentleman next in line—Lord Entwhistle's cousin's boy, Mr. Millthorpe—leaving both Sophie and Clarissa to make their curtsies to her ladyship.

Rising, Sophie once more found herself subjected to her ladyship's lorgnette. As before, no item of her appearance escaped Lady Entwhistle's scrutiny, from the green ribbon in her curls to her beaded satin dancing slippers.

"Hmm, yes," Lady Entwhistle mused, her expression brightening. "*Excellent,* my dear. No doubt but that you'll have a truly *wonderful* Season this time."

Her ladyship's tone left little doubt as to what, in her mind, constituted a "wonderful" Season. Having known what to expect from her mother's old friends, Sophie smiled serenely. Together with Clarissa, she moved on to Mr. Millthorpe.

A young gentleman of neat and pleasant aspect, Mr. Millthorpe was clearly overawed at finding himself thus thrust upon the notice of the *ton.* He replied to Sophie's calm greeting with a nervously mumbled word; she saw him fight to keep his hand from tugging his cravat. Then he turned to Clarissa, who was close on her heels. Mr. Millthorpe's colour promptly fled, then returned in full measure.

"Indeed," he said, his bow rendered awkward by his determination to keep Clarissa's face in view. "I'm very glad to meet you Miss…Miss…." Mr. Millthorpe's eyes glazed. "Miss Webb!" Triumph glowed in his smile. "I hope you won't mind…that is, that you might have a few minutes to spare later, Miss Webb. Once I get free of this." His expression earnest, he gestured ingenuously at his aunt.

A little taken aback, Clarissa sent him a shy smile.

That was more than enough encouragement for Mr. Millthorpe. He beamed, then was somewhat peremptorily recalled to his duties.

Bemused, Clarissa joined Sophie where she waited at the top of the shallow flight of steps leading down into the ballroom.

Poised above the room, Sophie resisted the impulse to send a questing glance out over the sea of heads. Looking down, she raised her skirts and commenced the descent in her aunt's wake. Beside her, Clarissa was tensing with excitement, her eyes, bright and wide, drinking in every sight. The sensation of tightness about her own lungs informed Sophie that she, too, was not immune to expectation. The realization brought a slight frown to her eyes.

The odds were that Mr. Lester would not be present. Even if he was, there was no reason to imagine he would seek her out.

With an inward snort, Sophie banished the thought. Jack Lester was a rake. And rakes did not dance attendance on young ladies—not, that is, without reason. She, however, was in town to look for a husband, the perfect husband for her. She should devote her thoughts to that goal, and forget all about engaging rakes with dark blue eyes and unnerving tempers.

Determination glimmered in her eyes as she lifted her head—only to have her gaze fall headlong into one of midnight blue.

Sophie's heart lurched; an odd tremor shook her. He filled her vision, her senses, tall and strong, supremely elegant in black coat and pantaloons, his dark locks in fashionable disarray, the white of his cravat a stark bed on which a large sapphire lay, winking wickedly.

Jack watched as, her surprise at seeing him plainly writ in her large eyes, Sophie halted on the second-last stair, her lips parting slightly, the gentle swell of her breasts, exposed by her gown, rising on a sharp intake of breath.

His eyes on hers, he slowly raised a brow. "Good evening, Miss Winterton."

Sophie's heart stuttered back to life. Large, dark and handsome, he bowed gracefully, his gaze quizzing her as he straightened. Giving her wits a mental shake, she descended the last step, dipping a curtsy, then extending her hand. "Good evening, Mr. Lester. I had not expected to see you here, sir."

His brow lifted again; to her relief, he made no direct reply. "Might I request the pleasure of a waltz, my dear? The third, if you have it to spare."

She had not even had time to look at her dance card. Shooting him a cool glance, Sophie opened it, then, meeting his eyes briefly, she lifted the tiny pencil and marked his name in the appropriate spot.

The answer to the question in her mind came with his smooth, "And, perhaps, if you're not already bespoken, I might escort you to supper at the conclusion of the dance?"

Blinking, Sophie found she had unthinkingly surrendered her hand to his. Her gaze flew to his as he drew her gently to his side. Her heart leapt to her throat and started beating erratically there. "That will be most pleasant, Mr. Lester," she murmured, looking away.

"It will, you know."

His tone was gently teasing, on more levels than one. Elevating her chin, Sophie drew her composure more firmly about her. Ahead of them, her aunt was strolling through the crowd, Clarissa by her side.

To Sophie's surprise, having escorted her as far as the chaise where her aunt finally deigned to rest, Mr. Lester exchanged a few pleasantries with Lucilla, then, with an elegant bow, excused himself, leaving her to weather a spate of introductions as a small host of gentlemen gravitated to her side.

Despite the nature of Lady Entwhistle's little ball, despite the fact that the *ton* was only just beginning to desert its winter playgrounds to return to the capital, there were sufficient eligible bachelors present to fill her card long before the first dance began.

Clarissa, by her side, proved a potent attraction for the younger gentlemen. She was soon casting anxious glances at Sophie.

Keeping her voice firm and clear, Sophie calmly apologized to Mr. Harcourt. "Indeed, sir, I'm most sorry to disappoint you but I fear my card is full."

Minutes later, she heard Clarissa copy her words, prettily turning Lord Swindon away.

As her equilibrium, momentarily undermined, returned, Sophie became conscious of a niggling disquiet, a sense that something was not entirely right. Only when, for the third time, she found her gaze scanning the room, searching automatically, did she realize just what it was she felt.

Feeling very like muttering a curse, she instead pinned a bright smile on her lips and, with renewed determination, gave her attention to her court. "Will your sister be coming up to London, Lord Argyle? I should be delighted to meet her again."

She was here to find a husband, not to fall victim to a rake's blue eyes.

By dint of sheer determination, Jack managed to keep himself occupied until the country dance preceding the supper waltz was in progress. He was, he kept reminding himself, far too experienced to cram his leaders. Instead, he had forced himself to circulate, artfully sidestepping subtle invitations to lead other young ladies onto the floor. Now, as the last strains of the music died, he threaded his way through the crowd to come up by Sophie's side. Fate was smiling on him again; she had just finished thanking her partner, Lord Enderby.

"Miss Winterton." With a slight bow, Jack reached for Sophie's hand. "Evening, Enderby." A nod was enough to distract her recent partner.

"Eh?" Squinting slightly, Lord Enderby switched his near-sighted stare from Sophie to Jack. "Oh, it's you, Lester. Surprised to see *you* here. Thought you'd be at Newmarket."

Jack smiled—into Sophie's eyes. "I discovered that, this Season, there was to be an unlooked-for distraction in London."

"Really?" Lord Enderby's eyes were too weak to appreciate the action taking place before them. "What's that?"

Feeling the warmth rise to her cheeks, Sophie held her breath, her gaze daring her next partner to say anything untoward.

Jack's gaze grew more intent. "Far be it from me to reveal any secrets," he said. "You'll learn the truth soon enough." His gaze remained on Sophie's face. "But I'm come to steal Miss Winterton from you, Enderby. My dance is next, I believe, my dear?" With a calmly proprietorial air, Jack tucked Sophie's hand into the crook of his elbow and, with the barest of nods for Lord Enderby, now thoroughly bemused, turned her down the room.

Sophie blinked and grabbed her wandering wits. "I believe you're right, Mr. Lester. But shouldn't we return to my aunt?"

"Why?"

She glanced up to find an improbably mild expression inhabiting her companion's patrician features as, undeterred by her remonstrance, he led her further and further from her aunt. "Because it's expected," she replied.

He smiled then, a slow, devilish smile, and looked down, meeting her gaze. "You're not a deb, my dear." His voice had deepened; she felt as well as heard it. Then his intent look softened and he looked ahead. "And, despite the throng, the room is not so crowded your aunt cannot keep you in view, if she's so inclined."

That, Sophie realized as she calmed her leaping heart, was true. A quick glance over her shoulder revealed Lucilla, with Clarissa beside her, almost at the other end of the room. There were many bodies between, but the crowd was not so thick it blocked them off.

"I don't intend to kidnap you, you know."

The soft statement pulled her gaze back to his face.

Jack smiled and tried his best to make the gesture reassuring. "I merely thought you might like to see who else is here tonight."

Her "Oh," was there in her eyes. Then, with a last, still-suspicious glance, she gave up her resistance, her hand settling on his arm.

He did as he had indicated, embarking on a gentle perambulation of the room. "Lady Entwhistle's lucky to see so many here so early in the Season. Lord Abercrombie," Jack indicated that well-known huntsman. "Have you met him before?" Sophie nodded. "He, for one, rarely leaves Northamptonshire until late April. The thaw must be extensive to have driven him south this early."

Sophie had, indeed, been surprised to find so many of the *ton*'s more mature yet eligible bachelors present. "I hadn't realized that the weather was to blame."

Again, she was aware of his gaze. "For some," he said, his voice low. Sternly quelling a shiver, Sophie pretended to look about.

"So, how do you find Society after four years away? Does it still hold some allure?"

Sophie glanced up at the question; a cynical ripple in his smooth tones gave her pause. "Allure?" she repeated, putting her head on one side. "I do not know that that is the right term, Mr. Lester." She frowned slightly. "There's glamour, perhaps." With one hand, she gestured about them. "But any with eyes must see it is transitory, an illusion with no real substance." They strolled on and Sophie smiled wryly. "I have long thought the Season society's stage, where we all come together to impress each other with our standing before summer draws us back to our true professions, to the management of our estates."

His gaze on her face, Jack inclined his head, his expression enigmatic. "You are wise beyond your years, my dear."

Sophie met his gaze; she arched a sceptical brow. "And you, sir?" She let her gaze slide away. Greatly daring, she continued, "I find it hard to believe that your view of the Season agrees with mine. I have always been told that gentlemen such as yourself pursue certain interests for which the Season is indispensible."

Jack's lips twitched. "Indeed, my dear." He let a moment stretch in silence before adding, "You should not, however, imagine that such interests are behind my presence here in town this early in the year."

Resisting the urge to look up at him, Sophie kept her gaze on those surrounding them. "Indeed?" she replied coolly. "Then it was boredom that fetched you south?"

Jack glanced down at her. "No, Miss Winterton. It was not boredom."

"Not boredom?" Determination not to allow him to triumph, Sophie swung about and, disregarding the crazed beating of her heart and the constriction which restricted her breathing, met his blue gaze. "Indeed, sir?"

He merely raised an arrogant brow at her, his expression unreadable.

She met his gaze coolly, then allowed hers to fall, boldly taking in his large, immaculately clad frame. The sapphire glinted in the white folds of his cravat; he wore no fobs or other ornament, nothing to detract from the image created by lean and powerful muscles. "Ah," she declared, resisting the urge to clear her throat. Settling her hand once more on his sleeve, she fell in by his side. "I see it now. Confess, sir, that it is the prospect of your mounts having to wade through the mire that has driven you, in despair I make no doubt, from Leicestershire."

Jack laughed. "Wrong again, Miss Winterton."

"Then I greatly fear it is the lure of the gaming rooms that has brought you to town, Mr. Lester."

"There's a lure involved, I admit, but it's not one of green baize."

"What, then?" Sophie demanded, pausing to look up at him.

Jack's gaze rose to touch her curls, then lowered to her eyes, softly blue. His lips lifted in a slow smile. "The lure is one of gold, my dear."

Sophie blinked and frowned slightly. "You've come seeking your fortune?"

Jack's gaze, darkly blue, became more intent. "Not my fortune, Miss Winterton." He paused, his smile fading as he looked into her eyes. "My future."

Her gaze trapped in his, Sophie could have sworn the polished parquetry on which she stood quivered beneath her feet. She was dimly aware they had halted; the crowd about them had faded, their chattering no longer reaching her. Her heart was in her throat, blocking her breath; it had to be that that was making her so lightheaded.

The midnight blue gaze did not waver; Sophie searched his eyes, but could find no hint, in them or his expression, to discount the wild possibility that had leapt into her mind.

Then he smiled, his mouth, his expression, softening, as she had seen it do before.

"I believe that's our waltz starting, Miss Winterton." Jack paused, then, his eyes still on hers, his voice darkly deep, he asked, "Will you partner me, my dear?"

Sophie quelled a shiver. She was not a green girl; she was

twenty-two, experienced and assured. Ignoring her thudding heart, ignoring the subtle undertones in his voice, she drew dignity about her and, calmly inclining her head, put her hand in his.

His fingers closed strongly over hers; in that instant, Sophie was not at all sure just what question she had answered. Yet she followed his lead, allowing him to seep her into his arms. With a single deft turn, he merged them with the circling throng; they were just one couple among the many on the floor.

Time and again, Sophie told herself that was so, that there was nothing special in this waltz, nothing special between them. One part of her mind formed the words; the rest wasn't listening, too absorbed in silent communion with a pair of dark blue eyes.

She only knew the dance was over when they stopped. They had spoken not a word throughout; yet, it seemed, things had been said, clearly enough for them both. She could barely breathe.

Jack's expression was serious yet gentle as he drew her hand once more through his arm. "It's time for supper, my dear."

His eyes were softly smiling. Sophie basked in their glow. Shy yet elated, off balance yet strangely assured, she returned the smile. "Indeed, sir. I rely on you to guide me."

His lips lifted lightly. "You may always do so, my dear."

He found a table for two in the supper room and secured a supply of delicate sandwiches and two glasses of champagne. Then he settled back to recount the most interesting of the past year's *on-dits,* after which they fell to hypothesizing on the likely stance of the various protagonists at the commencement of this Season.

Despite her blithe spirits, Sophie was grateful for the distraction. She felt as if she was teetering on some invisible brink; she was not at all sure it was wise to take the next step. So she laughed and chatted, ignoring the sudden moments when breathlessness attacked, when their gazes met and held for an instant too long.

Her elation persisted, that curious uplifting of her spirits, as if her heart had broken free of the earth and was now lighter than air. The sensation lingered, even when Jack, very dutifully, escorted her back to Lucilla's side.

With what was, she felt, commendable composure, Sophie held out her hand. "I thank you for a most enjoyable interlude, sir." Her voice, lowered, was oddly soft and husky.

A small knot of gentlemen hovered uncertainly, awaiting her return.

Jack eyed them, less than pleased but too wise to show it. Instead, he took Sophie's hand and bowed elegantly. Straightening, for the last time that evening he allowed his gaze to meet hers. "Until next we meet, Miss Winterton."

His eyes said it would be soon.

TO SOPHIE'S CONSTERNATION, he called the next morning. Summoned to join her aunt in the drawing-room, she entered to find him, garbed most correctly for a morning about town in blue Bath superfine and ivory inexpressibles, rising from a chair to greet her, a faint, challenging lift to his dark brows.

"Good morning, Miss Winterton."

Determined to hold her own, Sophie bludgeoned her wits into order and plastered a calm, unflustered expression over her surprise. "Good day, Mr. Lester."

His smile warmed her before he released her hand to greet Clarissa, who had entered in her wake.

Aware that her aunt's deceptively mild gaze was fixed firmly upon her, Sophie crossed to the chaise, cloaking her distraction with a nonchalant air. As she settled her skirts, she noted that susceptibility to Mr. Lester's charms appeared strangely restricted. Despite her inexperience, Clarissa showed no sensitivity, greeting their unexpected caller with unaffected delight. Released, her cousin came to sit beside her.

Jack resumed his seat, elegantly disposing his long limbs in a fashionably fragile white-and-gilt chair. He had already excused his presence by turning Lucilla's edict to call on them to good account. "As I was saying, Mrs. Webb, it is, indeed, pleasant to find oneself with time to spare before the Season gets fully under way."

"Quite," Lucilla returned, her pale gaze open and innocent. In a morning gown of wine-red cambric, she sat enthroned in an armchair close by the hearth. "However, I must confess it took the small taste of the *ton* that we enjoyed last night to refresh my memories. I had quite forgotten how extremely fatiguing it can be."

From behind his urbane facade, Jack watched her carefully. "Indeed." He gently inclined his head. "Coming direct from the country, the *ton*'s ballrooms can, I imagine, take on the aspect of an ordeal."

"A very stuffy ordeal," Lucilla agreed. Turning to the chaise, she asked, "Did you not find it so, my dears?"

Clarissa smiled brightly and opened her mouth to deny any adverse opinion of the previous evening's entertainment.

Smoothly, Sophie cut in, "Indeed, yes. It may not have been a crush, yet the crowd was not inconsiderable. Towards the end, I found the atmosphere positively thick."

It was simply not done to admit to unfettered delight, nor to dismiss a kindly hostess's entertainments as uncrowded.

Jack kept his smile restrained. "Just so. I had, in fact, wondered, Miss Winterton, if you would like to blow away any lingering aftertaste of the crowd by taking a turn in the Park? I have my curricle with me."

"What a splendid idea." Lucilla concurred, turning, wide-eyed, to Sophie.

But Sophie was looking at Jack.

As she watched, he inclined his head. "If you would care for it, Miss Winterton?"

Slowly, Sophie drew in a breath. And nodded. "I..." Abruptly, she looked down, to where her hands were clasped in the lap of her morning gown, a concoction of lilac mull-muslin. "I should change my gown."

"I'm sure Mr. Lester will excuse you, my dear."

With a nod to her aunt, Sophie withdrew, then beat a hasty retreat to her chamber. There, summoning a maid, she threw open the doors of her wardrobe and drew forth the carriage dress Jorge had sent round that morning. A golden umber, the heavy material was shot with green, so that, as she moved, it appeared to bronze, then dull. Standing before her cheval-glass, Sophie held the gown to her, noting again how its colour heightened the gold in her hair and emphasized the creami-ness of her complexion. She grinned delightedly. Hugging the dress close, she whirled, waltzing a few steps, letting her heart hold sway for just a moment.

Then she caught sight of the maid staring at her from the doorway. Abruptly, Sophie steadied. "Ah, there you are, Ellen. Come along." She waved the young girl forward. "I need to change."

Downstairs in the drawing-room, Jack made idle conver-sation, something he could do with less than half his brain. Then, unexpectedly, Lucilla blandly declared, "I hope you'll excuse Clarissa, Mr. Lester. We're yet very busy settling in." To Clarissa, she said, "Do look in on the twins for me, my love. You know I never feel comfortable unless I know what they're about."

Clarissa smiled in sunny agreement. She rose and bobbed

a curtsy to Jack, then departed, leaving him wondering about the twins.

"They're six," Lucilla calmly stated. "A dreadfully *imaginative* age."

Jack blinked, then decided to return to safer topics. "Allow me to congratulate you on your daughter, Mrs. Webb. I've rarely seen such beauty in conjunction with such a sweet disposition. I prophesy she'll be an instant success."

Lucilla glowed with maternal satisfaction. "Indeed, it seems likely. Fortunately for myself and Mr. Webb, and I dare say Clarissa, too, her Season is intended purely to—" Lucilla gestured airily "—broaden her horizons. Her future is already all but settled. A young gentleman from Leicestershire—one of our neighbours—Ned Ascombe."

"Indeed?" Jack politely raised his brows.

"Oh, yes," his redoubtable hostess continued in a comfortably confiding vein. "But both my husband and I are firmly of the opinion that it does no good for a young girl to make her choice before…surveying the field, as it were." With every appearance of ingenuousness, Lucilla explained, "The chosen suitor may be the same as before she looked but she, certainly, will feel much more assured that her choice is the right one if she's given the opportunity to convince herself it is so." Lucilla's pale eyes swung to Jack's face. "That's why we're so keen to give Clarissa a full Season—so that she'll know her own mind."

Jack met her level gaze. "And your niece?"

Lucilla frowned delicately but approval glimmered in her eyes. "Indeed. Sophie's first Season was cut so very short it hardly signified. She was presented, and had her comeout and even braved the trial of Almack's, but it was barely three weeks in all before my sister succumbed to a chill. So very tragic."

Her sigh was sorrowful; Jack inclined his head and waited.

"So, you see, Mr. Lester," Lucilla continued, raising her head to look him in the eye. "Both Mr. Webb and I hope very much that any gentleman who truly appreciates dear Sophie will allow her to have her Season this time."

Jack held her coolly challenging gaze for what seemed like an age. Then, reluctantly, he inclined his head. "Indeed, ma'am," he replied, his tone even. "Your arguments are hard to deny." When it became clear his hostess was waiting for more, he added, his expression impassive, "Any gentleman who valued your niece would, I feel sure, abide by such wisdom."

Gracious as ever, Lucilla smiled her approbation, then turned as the latch lifted. "Ah, there you are, Sophie."

Smoothly, Jack rose and went forward, his eyes feasting on the vision hovering on the threshold. She had donned a forest green half-cape over her carriage dress, which was of a strange bronzy-gold shade with piping of the same dark green at collar and cuffs. Green gloves and green half-boots completed her outfit. Jack felt his lips soften in a smile; his Sophie was fashionable elegance incarnate.

Reassured by his smile, and the appreciative light in his eyes, Sophie smiled back and gave him her hand. Together, they turned to Lucilla.

"I will engage to take all care of your niece, Mrs. Webb." Jack sent an arrogantly questioning glance across the room.

Lucilla studied the picture they made, and smiled. "I trust you will, Mr. Lester. But do not be too long; Lady Cowper is to call this afternoon, and we must later attend Lady Allingcott's at-home." With a graciously benevolent nod, she dismissed them.

It was not until they reached the Park and Jack let his horses stretch their legs that Sophie allowed herself to believe it was real. That she was, in truth, bowling along the well-tended carriageway with Jack Lester beside her. The brisk breeze, cool and playful, twined in her curls and tugged little wisps free to wreath about her ears. Above and about them, arched branches were swelling in bud; the sky, a clear, crisp blue, formed a backdrop for their nakedness. Slanting a glance at her companion, she wondered, not for the first time, just what he intended.

He had, most correctly, escorted her down the steps of her aunt's house, then blotted his copybook by ignoring her hand and lifting her instead to his curricle's seat. On taking his own seat beside her and being assured she was comfortable, he had smiled, a slow, proudly satisfied smile, and clicked the reins. The bustle in the streets had made conversation unwise; she had held her peace while they travelled the short distance to the gates of the Park.

Now, with the first fashionable carriages looming ahead, she said, her tone merely matter-of-fact, "I had not looked to see you so soon, sir."

Jack glanced down at her. "I couldn't keep away." It was, he somewhat ruefully reflected, the literal truth. He had fully intended to allow the Webbs reasonable time to settle in the capital; instead, he had not been able to resist the compulsion to take Sophie for a drive, to show her the *ton,* and display her to them, safely anchored by his side. Staking his claim— and in such uncharacteristically blunt fashion that Sophie's aunt had seen fit to metaphorically wag her finger at him. Even the weather was conspiring to make him rush on with his wooing, the bright sunshine more redolent of April and May than chilly March.

He had expected some confusion in response to his forth-right answer. Instead, to his delight, Sophie raised her chin and calmly stated, "In that case, you may make yourself use-ful and tell me who all these people are. My aunt has had lit-tle time to fill me in, and there are many I don't recognize."

Jack grinned. It was close on noon, a most fashionable

time to be seen driving in the Park. "The Misses Berry you must recall," he said as they swept down on an ancient landau drawn up by the verge. "They're always to be found at precisely that spot, morning and afternoon throughout the Season."

"Of course I remember them." With a gay smile, Sophie nodded to the two old dames, bundled up in scarves and shawls on the seat of the landau. They nodded back. As the curricle swept past, Sophie saw the gleam in their bright eyes.

"Next we have Lady Staunton and her daughters. You don't need to know them, although doubtless your cousin will make the younger girls' acquaintance."

Sophie bestowed a distant smile on the bevy of girlish faces turned to stare in open envy as she went by. Despite Jorge's undoubted expertise, she doubted it was her new carriage dress that had excited their interest.

As she looked ahead once more, she saw a tall woman, modishly gowned in bright cherry-red, strolling the lawns just ahead. Her hand rested on the arm of a rakishly handsome buck. Both looked up as the carriage neared. The woman's face lit up; she raised her hand in what appeared, to Sophie, a distinctly imperious summons.

The reaction on her right was immediate; Jack stiffened. As it became clear the carriage was not about to stop, nor even slow, Sophie glanced up. Chilly reserve had laid hold of Jack's features; as Sophie watched, he inclined his head in the most remote of greetings.

The carriage swept on, leaving the couple behind. Relaxing against the padded seat, Sophie forced her lips to behave. "And that was?" she prompted.

The glance she received was dark with warning. She met it with a lifted brow—and waited.

"Harriette Wilson," came the answer. "Someone you definitely do *not* need to know."

His repressive tone evoked a gurgle of laughter; Sophie swallowed it and airily looked around. Lady Cowper's barouche was drawn up in a curve of the carriageway; Sophie waved as they passed, pleased to note her ladyship's answering smile. Lady Cowper was yet another old friend of her late mama's.

They passed many others; Jack knew them all. His running commentary kept Sophie amused and distracted. She was content to enjoy his company and his apparent liking for hers; she would dwell on what it might mean later. So she smiled and laughed up at him, basking in the glow of his very blue eyes.

"Jack!"

The hail jolted them from their absorption.

It emanated from a young, dark-haired gentleman, clearly of the first stare, who, together with his similarly well-turned-out companion, was perched on the driving seat of a swan-necked phaeton, approaching at a clipping pace. Jack reined his horses to the side of the track; the elegant equipage executed a neat turn and came to a swooping stop beside them.

"Been searching for you forever," the young gentleman declared, his eyes, also deeply blue, passing from Jack to Sophie. He smiled with cheery good-humour. "Dashed if I'd thought to find you here!"

Glancing up at her escort's face, Sophie saw a whimsical smile soften his hard features.

"Gerald." Jack nodded to his brother, his knowledgeable gaze roving over the finer points of the pair of high-bred horses harnessed between the long shafts of the phaeton, itself spanking new if its gleaming paintwork was to be believed. "Where'd you get this rig?"

"The phaeton's fresh out of old Smithers's workshop. The nags are Hardcastle's. He'll let me have them for a tithe their true value—five hundred the pair. The phaeton'll be full price, though, and you know what Smithers is like."

Brows lifting, Jack nodded. With a deft twirl of his wrist, he looped his reins and offered them to Sophie. "Will you do me the honour, my dear?"

Scrambling to hide her surprise, greatly pleased for she well knew that few gentlemen would entrust their horses to a mere female, Sophie graciously nodded and took the reins. With a reassuring smile, Jack climbed down. The horses shifted slightly; determined to keep them in line, Sophie kept her eyes firmly on them, her brow furrowing in concentration.

Hiding his grin, Jack paced slowly around Gerald's carriage and horses, his blue eyes shrewdly assessing. Gerald and his friend watched with bated breath, their eagerness barely suppressed. Then, rejoining Sophie and retaking possession of the reins with a warm smile, Jack nodded at his brother. "Not a bad set-up."

Gerald grinned delightedly.

"But allow me to make you known to Miss Winterton." Jack paused to allow Gerald to bow, lithely graceful. "My youngest brother, Gerald Lester."

Having had time to note the similarity between Jack and the youthful gentleman, also dark-haired, blue-eyed and broad-shouldered, but without the heavy musculature that characterized her escort's more mature frame, Sophie showed no surprise.

While his brother introduced Lord Somerby, his companion, Jack cast a last glance over the phaeton and pair. His lips quirked. Turning to Gerald, he smoothly said, "And now you'll have to excuse us. I'm overdue to return Miss Winterton to her home."

"Jack!" Gerald's pained exclamation was heartfelt. "Dash it all—don't tease. May I have them or not?"

Jack chuckled. "You may. But make sure you get an account from Smithers. Drop by this evening and I'll give you a draft." Although it was his own money Gerald would be spending, as his trustee until his twenty-fifth birthday, Jack had to approve all his youngest brother's transactions.

Gerald's smile was ecstatic. "I'll be around at seven." With an insouciant wave of his whip, he touched his horses' ears. As the phaeton disappeared along the avenue, his gay carolling rolled back to them.

Smiling at Jack's exuberance, a sort of boundless *joie de vivre,* Sophie glanced up at her companion.

As if sensing her regard, Jack's smile, distant as he contemplated his brother's delight, refocused on her face. "And now, I fear, I really should return you to Mount Street, my dear."

So saying, he whipped up his horses; they took the turn into the main avenue in style. As they bowled along, a stylish matron chatting idly with an acquaintance in her carriage, glanced up, then waved them down. Jack politely drew in beside the lady's barouche.

"Sophia, my dear!" Lady Osbaldestone beamed at her. "I take it your aunt has finally arrived in town?"

"Indeed, ma'am." Sophie leant from the curricle to shake her ladyship's hand. "We'll be here for the Season."

"And a good thing, too! It's entirely more than time you were amongst us again." Her ladyship's eyes gleamed with a fervour to which Sophie was innured.

Jack was not so fortunate. He exchanged nods with Lady Osbaldestone, wryly resigned to being ignored for at least the next ten minutes. Lady Osbaldestone's lack of concern in finding a young lady with whom she clearly claimed more than a passing acquaintance alone in his presence registered—and made his inner smile even more wry. There had been a time, not so very far distant, when she would not have been so sanguine. However, over the past year, his acknowledged search for a wife had gained him, if not immunity from all suspicion, then at least a certain acceptance amongst the *grandes dames*. He suspected they viewed him as a leopard who, at least temporarily, had changed his spots.

That much, he was willing to concede, might be true. Nevertheless, the underlying temperament remained.

As he heard her ladyship's plans for Sophie's future unfurl, his instincts rose to shake his complacency.

He waited until they had, at last, parted from his ladyship and were once more rolling towards the gates before saying, "Lady Osbaldestone seems quite determined to see you well wed."

Totally unconcerned by her ladyship's grand schemes, which had even stretched as far as the Duke of Huntington, Sophie smiled gaily. "Indeed. They are all of them busy hatching schemes."

"All of them?"

There was something in his flat tones that made her glance up but her companion's expression was inscrutable. Light-hearted still, even light-headed, the aftermath, no doubt, of an uninterrupted hour of his company, Sophie grinned. "All of my mother's old friends," she explained. "They all look upon me as a motherless chick—one and all, they're determined to see me 'properly established'." She uttered the last words in a passable imitation of Lady Osbaldestone's haughty accents.

She glanced up, expecting to see him smiling, laughing with her at the prospect of so many matrons busily scheming on her behalf. Instead, his face remained stony, devoid of expression. Jack felt her glance. His emotions straining at the leash, he looked down.

Sophie met his dark gaze, and felt a vice slowly close about her heart. Avid, eager to find the reason, for that and the force that held them in a curious hiatus, out of time, she searched his face and his deeply glowing eyes. Jack watched as her smile slowly faded, to be replaced with puzzlement—and a clear query.

"Sophie—" He drew in a deep breath and glanced ahead, just in time to avoid colliding with a natty trilby, swung through the gates far too fast.

Jack swore. In the ensuing chaos as he calmed his own horses, then received the shrill and abject apologies of the trilby's owner, a young sprig barely old enough to shave and, in Jack's pithily offered opinion, of insufficient experience to be entrusted with the reins, the purport of Lucilla's words returned to him.

As the trilby crept away, Jack turned to Sophie, his expression carefully blank. "Are you all right?"

"Yes." Sophie smiled brightly up at him, while inwardly she wondered if that was strictly true. The instant before the trilby's advent had left her nerves stretched and quivering.

Jack forced his lips into an easy smile. "I'd better get you back to Mount Street forthwith, or your aunt will doubtless forbid me your company. It's well past our allotted hour."

Sophie kept her own smile light. "My aunt is very understanding."

That, Jack thought, as he eased into the traffic, was undoubtedly the greatest understatement he had ever heard. He made no effort to break the silence until they reached Mount Street. Even then, relinquishing the reins to Jigson, whom he had left awaiting his return, he eschewed comment, reaching up to lift Sophie down to the pavement in what was rapidly becoming a charged silence.

As he expected, she showed no signs of fluster. Instead, she stood before him, her face turned up to his, her query contained in the gentle lift of her delicate brows.

Despite himself, Jack smiled—his slow, sensuous smile, the one he was usually careful to hide from well-bred young ladies.

Sophie didn't disappoint him; she studied his face, openly gauging his smile, then, lifting her eyes to his, merely raised her brows higher.

Jack laughed softly but shook his head. "The time is not yet," was all he dared say. Holding her eyes with his, he raised her gloved hand and, most reprehensibly, placed a kiss on her bare wrist. Then, placing her hand on his sleeve, he covered it with his and strolled with her up the steps. As the door opened to admit her, he bowed. "Once again, my dear—until next we meet."

CHAPTER SIX

FOR SOPHIE, THE rest of Tuesday and all of Wednesday passed in a rosy-hued blur. As expected, Lady Cowper called, promising vouchers for Almack's and her most earnest endeavours. Lucilla and her ladyship spent a full hour with their heads close together; Sophie stared absent-mindedly at the window, her expression distant. Recalled to the present when her ladyship rose, she flashed a bright smile and bade Lady Cowper farewell. The smile lingered, muted but nevertheless present, long after her ladyship's carriage rattled away down the street.

"Well then, my dears." Lucilla swept back into the drawing-room. Clarissa followed with Sophie trailing in the rear. "In the light of Lady Cowper's remarks, we had best reconsider our strategy."

Closing the door, Sophie made for the chaise, a slight blush tinting her cheeks. "How so, aunt?" She could not, in truth, recall all that much of Lady Cowper's conversation.

With a long-suffering air, Lucilla raised her brows. "Because, my dear, if the *ton* is already in town then there's no reason not to steal a march on those who have planned their entertainments to coincide with the usual start of festivities and already sent out their invitations." Reclaiming her seat, she gestured to the pile of white cards upon the mantelshelf. "The list grows every day. I have it in mind to make our mark with a tactical manoeuvre, if I have the phrase correctly."

Sophie tried to concentrate on her aunt's meaning. Yet at every pause, her mind slid sideways, to ponder the subtleties in a certain deep voice, and the light that had glowed in his eyes. Frowning, she struggled to banish her distracting fascination. "So you mean to bring Clarissa's come-out forward?"

Deep in thought, Lucilla nodded. "It seems strategically imperative—if she's not out, she cannot be present at the rush of balls and parties which, as dear Emily pointed out, are this year going to precede the usual commencement." Lucilla pulled a face. "Yet it's not the sort of decision one takes lightly." She pondered a moment, one elegant fingernail tapping on the chair arm. Then she straightened. "We have Lady Allingcott's at-home this afternoon and Lady Chessington's little party tonight, then Almack's tomorrow—even they have started early this year. I pray you both to keep your ears open. Depending on what we all hear, I think we might start with an impromptu party, just for the younger folk, next week. And plan Clarissa's ball for the week after that. My ideas are already well advanced; it will simply be a matter of bringing them forward a trifle." Nodding to herself, Lucilla turned to Clarissa. "What say you to that, my dear?"

"It sounds *wonderful!*" Clarissa's eyes radiated excited relief. "Indeed, I wasn't looking forward to missing the balls in the next weeks."

"And why should you?" Lucilla spread her hands wide. "This is your Season, my love; you're here to enjoy it." She smiled her subtlest smile. "As Madame Jorge said; we will contrive."

Sophie had nothing to say against her aunt's plans. Mr. Lester, of course, would not be present at the small, informal parties and dances held by the families with young girls making their come-out, to help the young ladies gain their social feet. Until Clarissa was officially out, the Webb ladies would be restricted to such tame affairs, which were all very well if there was nothing else on offer. But this year, this Season, was going to be different—and it wasn't only the weather that would make it so for her.

They attended Lady Allingcott's and Lady Chessington's entertainments, and on Wednesday called on Lady Hartford and the Misses Smythe, then danced at Almack's, all the while listening to what their peers had to say of projected entertainments.

Over breakfast the next morning, Lucilla called a council of war. "Now pay attention, Sophie."

Thus adjured, Sophie blinked. And endeavored to obey the injunction.

"I've consulted with your father, Clarissa, and he's in full agreement. We will hold your come-out ball at the end of the week after next."

Clarissa crowed. Her younger brothers pulled faces and taunted.

"In the meantime, however," Lucilla raised her voice only slightly; as her eagle eye swept the table the din subsided. "We'll hold a dance at the end of next week—on Friday. An informal affair—but we need not restrict the guest list solely to those making their come-out. I see no reason not to invite some of those amongst the *ton* with whom you are already acquainted."

Sophie knew her smile was almost as bright as Clarissa's. Her aunt's gaze, pausing meaningfully on her, sent her heart soaring. Ridiculous—but there was no other word for it—the exhilarating excitement that gripped her at the mere thought of seeing him again. She lived for the moment but, given he had not appeared at Almack's—faint hope though that had been—it had seemed likely they would not meet again until Clarissa was out and they could move freely in society's mainstream.

Unless, of course, he called to take her driving again.

She spent all morning with one ear tuned to the knocker.

When the time for luncheon arrived and he had not called, she put her disappointment aside and, her smile still bright, descended to the dining-room. She was determined none of her cousins would guess her true state. As for her aunt, she had directed one or two pointed glances at her niece and once, she had surprised a look of soft satisfaction upon Lucilla's face. That, of course, was inevitable.

It was at Mrs. Morgan-Stanley's at-home later that day that her bubble of happiness was punctured.

On entering the Morgan-Stanleys' large drawing-room, Lucilla immediately joined the circle of fashionable matrons gathered about the fireplace. Clarissa drifted across to the windows, to where the youngest of those present had shyly retreated to trade dreams. With a confident smile, Sophie joined a small group of young ladies for whom this was not their first Season. She was taking tea with them in their corner when, in the midst of a discussion on the many notables already sighted in town, Miss Billingham, a thin young lady with severe, pinched features, cast her an arch glance.

"Indeed! Miss Winterton, I fancy, can testify to the fact. Why, we saw you in the Park just the other morning, my dear, driving with Mr. Lester."

"Mr. Lester?" Miss Chessington, a bright, cheerful soul, short, good-natured and of an indefatigably sunny temperament, blinked in amazement. "But I thought he *never* drove mere females."

"Not previously," Miss Billingham conceded with the air of one who had made a thorough study of the matter and was unshakeably certain of her facts. "But it's clear he has, at last, realized he must change his ways. My mama commented on the point, even last Season." When the others, Sophie included, looked their question, Miss Billingham consented to explain. "Well, it's common knowledge that he must marry well. More than well—real money—for there are his brothers, too, and everyone knows the Lesters have barely a penny to bless themselves with. Good breeding, good estates—it's the blunt that's wanting."

Sophie was not the only one who blinked at the crude term and the hard gleam in Miss Billingham's eyes but, in her case, the action was purely reflex. Her mind was reeling; a horrible sinking feeling had taken up residence in the pit of her stomach. Her features froze in a polite mask, and a sudden chill swept through her.

"My mama has long maintained," Miss Billingham declaimed, "that he'd have to come about. Too high in the instep by half, he spent all last Season searching for some goddess. Likely he's come to the understanding that he cannot look so high."

Miss Billingham looked at Sophie. The others, following her lead, did the same. Caught on a welling tide of despair, Sophie did not notice.

"I suppose, it being so early in the Season, he thought to amuse himself—get his hand in at the practice in safety, so to speak—by squiring you about, Miss Winterton."

It was the rustling of skirts as the others drew back, distancing themselves from the snide remark, that shook Sophie from her trance. As Miss Billingham's words registered, she felt herself pale. A cattish gleam of satisfaction flared in Miss Billingham's eyes. Pride came to Sophie's rescue, stiffening her spine. She drew in a steadying breath, then lifted her chin, looking down at Miss Billingham with chilly hauteur. "I dare say, Miss Billingham." Her tone repressively cool, Sophie continued, "I can only assume that Mr. Lester could find no other to suit his purpose, for, as you say, I hardly qualify as a rich prize."

At first, Miss Billingham missed the allusion; the poorly suppressed grins of the other young ladies finally brought Sophie's words home. Slowly, Miss Billingham's sallow complexion turned beet-red, an unhappy sight. She opened her mouth, casting a glance around for support. As she found none, her colour deepened. With a few muted words, she excused herself to return to the safer precincts close by her mother, a woman of battleship proportions.

"Don't pay any attention to her," Miss Chessington advised as their little circle closed comfortably about Sophie. "She's just furious Jack Lester paid her no heed whatever last year. Set her cap at him, and fell flat on her face."

Valiantly, Sophie struggled to return Miss Chessington's bright smile. "Indeed. But what of your hopes? Do you have anyone in your sights?"

Belle Chessington grinned hugely. "Heavens, no! I'm determined to enjoy myself. All that bother about a husband can come later."

Reflecting that, a few months ago, she, too, would have been as carefree, Sophie dragged her thoughts away from what had focused her mind on marriage. She clung to Miss Chessington's buoyant spirits until it was time to depart.

Once enveloped in the quiet of her aunt's carriage, cool reason returned to hold back the misery that threatened to engulf her. Sophie closed her eyes and laid her head back on the squabs.

"Aren't you feeling quite the thing, my dear?"

Lucilla's calm voice interrupted Sophie's thoughts. Sophie tried to smile, but the result was more like a grimace. "Just a slight headache. I found Mrs. Morgan-Stanley's drawing-room a trifle close." It was the best she could do. To her relief, her aunt seemed to accept the weak excuse.

Lucilla reached over and patted her hand. "Well, do take care. I hope you'll both remember that one never appears to advantage while a martyr to ill health." After a moment, Lucilla mused, "I don't think our schedule is overly full, but if you do feel the need, you must both promise me you'll rest."

Together with Clarissa, Sophie murmured her reassurances.

As the carriage rolled steadily onward, she kept her eyes closed, hiding her frown. Despite her often outrageous machinations, Lucilla was ever supportive, always protective. If Jack Lester was, indeed, totally ineligible as a suitor for her hand—or, more specifically, if, as a mere lady of expectations, *she* was ineligible to be his bride, then Lucilla would not have allowed him to draw so close. Her aunt was as clever as she could hold together. Surely she could trust in Lucilla's perspicacity?

Perhaps Miss Billingham had it wrong?

That possibility allowed Sophie to meet the rest of her day with equanimity, if not outright enthusiasm. Until the evening, when Lady Orville's little musical gathering brought an end to all hope.

It was, most incongruously, old Lady Matcham who squashed the bubble of her happiness flat. A tiny little woman, white-haired and silver-eyed with age, her ladyship was a kindly soul who would never, Sophie knew, intentionally cause anyone harm.

"I know you won't mind me mentioning this, Sophia, my dear. You know how very close I was to your mother—well, she was almost a daughter to me, you know. So sad, her going." The old eyes filled with tears. Lady Matcham dabbed them away with a lace-edged handkerchief. "Silly of me, of course." She smiled with determined brightness up at Sophie, sitting beside her on a chaise along the back wall of the music room.

Before them, the very select few whom Lady Orville had invited to air their musical abilities along with her two daughters were entertaining the gathering, seated in rows of little chairs before the pianoforte. Now, to the sound of polite applause, Miss Chessington took her seat at the instrument and laid her hands upon the keys.

Expecting a comment on the colour of her ribbons, or something in similar vein, Sophie smiled reassuringly at Lady Matcham, returning the squeeze of one birdlike claw.

"But that's why I feel I have to say something, Sophia," Lady Matcham continued. "For I would not rest easy thinking you had got hurt when I could have prevented it."

An icy hand closed about Sophie's heart, all expression leached from her face. Numb, paralyzed, she gazed blankly at Lady Matcham.

"I must say," her ladyship went on, her washed-out eyes widening, "I had thought Lucilla would have warned you but, no doubt, having only just returned to the capital, she's not yet up with the latest."

The chill creeping through Sophie had reached her mind; she couldn't think how to interrupt. She didn't want to hear any more, but her ladyship pressed on, her soft, gentle, undeniably earnest tones a death-knell to all hope.

"It's about Mr. Lester, my dear. Such a handsome man—quite the gentleman and so very well-connected. But he needs a rich wife. A very rich wife. I know, for I am acquainted with his aunt, dear soul—she's passed on now. But it was always understood the Lester boys would have to marry money, as the saying goes." Lady Matcham's sweet face grimaced with distaste. "Such a disheartening thought."

Sophie could only agree. Her heart was a painful lump in her breast; her features felt frozen. She couldn't speak; she could only gaze blankly as Lady Matcham lifted her wise old eyes to her face.

Lady Matcham patted her hand. "I saw you in the Park, in his curricle. And I just had to say something, my dear, for it really won't do. I dare say he's everything a gal like you might wish for. But indeed, Sophia dear, he's not for you."

Sophie blinked rapidly and sucked in a quick breath. Her heart was aching; all of her hurt. But she could not give way to her pain in the middle of Miss Chessington's sonata. Sophie swallowed; with an effort, she summoned a weak smile. "Thank you for the warning, ma'am." She couldn't trust herself to say more.

Her ladyship patted her hand, blinking herself. "There, there. It's not the end of the world, although I know it may feel that way. Such unfortunate happenings are best nipped in the bud—before any lasting damage can be done. I know you're too wise, my dear, not to know that—and to know how to go on. Why, you've all the Season before you. Plenty of opportunity to find a gentleman who suits you."

Sophie would have given the earth to deny it, all of it, but nothing could gainsay the sincerity in Lady Matcham's old eyes. With a wavering smile, Sophie gave the old lady a brief hug, then, with a mute nod, rose. Dragging in a steadying breath, she drifted to a corner of the room.

By dint of sheer will-power, she did not allow herself to dwell on Lady Matcham's revelations until, together with her aunt and Clarissa, she was enclosed in the protective shadows of the carriage and bound for home.

Then misery engulfed her, tinged with black despair.

As they alighted in Mount Street, the light from a street flare fell full on her face. Lucilla glanced around; her eyes narrowed. "Sophie, you will lie in tomorrow. I will not have you coming down with any ailment at this time of year."

Fleetingly, Sophie met her aunt's gaze, sharp and concerned. "Yes, Aunt," she acquiesced, meekly looking down. Ignoring Clarissa's concerned and questioning glance, Sophie followed her aunt up the steps.

THE NEXT DAY dawned but brought with it no relief. From behind the lace curtain at her bedchamber window, Sophie watched as Jack Lester descended the steps to the street. He climbed up into his waiting curricle and, as his groom scrambled up behind, deftly flicked his whip and drove away. Sophie watched until he disappeared around the corner, then, heaving a heavy sigh, turned back into the room.

He had called to take her for a drive, only to be met with the news of her indisposition.

Sophie sniffed. Aimless, she drifted across the room towards her bed, her sodden handkerchief wadded in her fist. As she passed her dressing-table, she caught a glimpse of her face in the mirror. Dark shadows circled her eyes; her cheeks were wan, her lips dry. Her head felt woosy and throbbed uncomfortably; her limbs seemed heavy, listless.

Lady Matcham's warning had come too late. In the dark hours of the night, she had faced the dismal fact: the delicate bud rooted in her heart, influenced by the weather and the warmth of his smile, had already flowered. Now it lay crushed, slain by the weight of circumstance. Soon, she supposed, it would wither.

She was not a wealthy catch, a bride who would bring as her dower the ready cash necessary to rescue a gentleman's estates. Nothing could change that cold, hard fact. She was her father's heiress, a lady of expectations, possessed of no more than moderate fortune, and even that was prospective, not immediately accessible as capital.

Sophie sniffed again, then determinedly blew her nose. She had spent too much of the night weeping, not an occupation she had had much experience of, not since her mother's death. Now, she felt emptied, desolate, as she had then. But she knew she would recover. She would allow herself one day in which to mope, and by tonight, she would be back on her feet, her smile bright. As the Season unfolded, she would devote herself to her search for a husband with all due diligence. And forget about a handsome rake with dark blue eyes.

That was the way things were in her world; she knew it well enough. And after all Lucilla's and Clarissa's kindnesses, she would not allow her unhappiness to cloud Clarissa's Season. She would do her best to ensure it did not sink her own, either.

Feeling oddly better to have such clear goals before her, Sophie perched on the end of her bed. Her fingers pulled at her wrinkled handkerchief; her gaze grew abstracted. There was one point she had yet to consider: how best to deal with him when they met, as, inevitably, they would.

After deep and lengthy cogitation, she had absolved him of all blame. She could not believe he had sought to cause her pain. She it was who had misread his purpose; she was, in reality, no more experienced in such matters than Clarissa. It was, very likely, as Miss Billingham had said—to him, she was a safe and agreeable companion, one with whom to pass the time until the Season was fully under way and he could set about choosing his bride. Indeed, Lady Matcham's observations left little room for any other interpretation.

There were, admittedly, his curious words when he had last left her. *The time is not yet.* She had thought he had meant.... Abruptly, Sophie cut off the thought, setting her teeth against the pain. What he *had* probably meant was to propose some outing, some excursion which their present early stage of friendship would not stretch to encompass. She had read more—much more—into his innocent words than he could ever have intended.

Which meant that, given his innocence, she would have to treat him as if nothing was wrong. Pride dictated she do so. Any awkwardness she felt must be suppressed, hidden, for she couldn't bear him to know what she had thought—hoped.

Somehow, she would cope. Like Madame Jorge, like Lucilla, she could contrive.

With a sigh, Sophie climbed onto her bed and tugged the

covers over her. She snuggled down, settling her head on the pillows; calmly determined, she closed her eyes. She forced herself to relax, to allow the furrows in her forehead to ease away. If she was going to contrive, she would need some sleep.

The days ahead would not be easy.

CHAPTER SEVEN

EVEN PICCADILLY WAS CROWDED. Jack frowned as, leaving the shady avenues of the Park behind him, he was forced to rein in his horses by the press of traffic, vehicular and pedestrian, that thronged the wide street. Manoeuvring his curricle into the flow, he sat back, resigned to the crawling pace. To his right, Green Park luxuriated in the unseasonable heat, green buds unfurling as the fashionable strolled its gentle paths. Its calm beckoned, but Jack ignored it. The clamour of the traffic more suited his mood.

Grimacing at his inching progress, he kept his hands firm on his horses' reins. Just as he did on his own. He supposed his wooing of Sophie Winterton was progressing satisfactorily, yet this snail's pace was hardly what he had had in mind when he had exchanged the informality of the country for the *ton*'s structured delights. Lady Entwhistle's small ball had raised his hopes; at its conclusion he had felt decidedly smug. Thus, he felt sure, should a lady be wooed.

That success had been followed by his admittedly precipitous invitation to go driving, prompted by the unexpectedly tempestuous feelings which lay beneath his reasoned logic. He could justify to his own and anyone else's satisfaction just why Sophie Winterton would make him an excellent wife but, underneath it all, that peculiarly strong emotion which he hesitated to name simply insisted she was his.

Which was all very well, but Sophie's aunt, while not disputing his claim, had made it clear she would not assist him in sweeping Sophie off her feet.

Which, given his present state, was a serious set-back.

His horses tossed their heads impatiently, tugging at the reins. Reining them in, Jack snorted, very much in sympathy.

That drive in the Park, that gentle hour of Sophie's company, had very nearly tripped him up. If he was to obey her aunt's clear injunction and allow her to enjoy her Season unencumbered by a possessive fiancé—he had few illusions about that—then he would have to keep a firmer grip on himself. And on his wayward impulses.

Not that that was presently proving a problem; he had not set eyes on Sophie since that morning nearly a week ago. After her aunt's warning, he had held off as long as he could—until Friday, when he had called only to learn she was ill. That had shaken him; for an instant, he had wondered if her indisposition was real or just one of those tricks ladies sometimes played, then had dismissed the thought as unworthy—of Sophie and himself. He knew she liked him; it was there in her eyes, a warm, slightly wary but nonetheless welcoming glow that lit up her face whenever they met. Chiding himself for his ridiculous sensitivity, he had dispatched his man, Pinkerton, to scour the town for yellow roses. As always, Pinkerton, despite his perennial gloom, had triumphed. Three massive sprays of yellow blooms had duly been delivered in Mount Street with a card, unsigned, wishing Miss Winterton a speedy recovery.

He had looked for her in the Park, morning and afternoon, on both Saturday and Sunday but had failed to come up with the Webb carriage.

So, feeling distinctly edgy, all but champing on his metaphorical bit, he had called in Mount Street this morning—only to be informed that Miss Winterton had gone walking with her cousins.

Fate, it seemed, had deserted him. Despite the bright sunshine, his view of the Season was growing gloomier by the minute.

Lord Hardcastle, driving his greys, hailed him; they spent a few minutes exchanging opinions on the unusual press of traffic before said traffic condescended to amble onward, parting them. An organ-grinder, complete with monkey, was playing to an attentive crowd, blocking the pavement, much to the disgust of merchants and those less inclined to dally. Jack smiled and returned his attention to his horses. As he did so, a flash of gold caught his eye.

Turning, he searched the throng bustling along the pavement—and saw Sophie with Clarissa beside her, the two boys and Amy reluctantly following, casting longing glances back at the organ-grinder. As he watched, the little cavalcade halted before a shop door, then, leaving the maid and groom who had brought up the rear outside, Sophie led the way in.

Jack glanced up and read the sign above the shop, and smiled. He pulled his curricle over to the kerb. "Here—Jigson! Take charge of 'em. Wait here." Tossing the reins in Jigson's general direction, Jack leapt down and, threading his way through the traffic, entered the door through which Sophie had passed.

The door shut behind him, abruptly cutting off the noisy bustle outside. Calm and well-ordered, the refined ambience of Hatchard's Book Shop and Circulating Library enfolded him. No raised voices here. A severely garbed man behind a desk close to the door eyed him, disapproval withheld but imminent. Jack smiled easily and walked past. Despite its relative peace, the shop was quite crowded. He scanned the heads but could not find the one he sought. An eddy disturbed the calm; Jack spotted Jeremy, George and Amy huddling in a nook by the window, noses pressed to the pane, gazes locked on the entertainment on the pavement opposite.

Glancing around, Jack discovered that the disapproving man had been joined by an equally severely garbed woman. They were now both regarding him askance. With another urbane smile, he moved into the first aisle and pretended to scan the spines until he was out of their sight.

At the end of the third aisle, Sophie frowned up at the novel she most expressly wished to borrow. It was wedged tightly between two others on the topmost shelf, barely within reach. She thought of summoning the clerk to retrieve it for her, and grimaced; he was, she had discovered, quite cloyingly admiring. Sophie smothered a snort. She would make one last effort to prise the book loose before she surrendered to the attentions of the clerk.

Sucking in a breath, she stretched high, her fingers grappling to find purchase above the leather-covered tome.

"Allow me, my dear."

Sophie jumped. Snatching back her hand, she whirled, her colour draining then returning with a rush. "Oh! Ah…" her eyes widened as they met his. Abruptly, she dropped her gaze and stepped back, determinedly shackling her wayward wits. "Why thank you, Mr. Lester." With all the calm she could command, Sophie raised her head. "This is quite the last place I had thought to meet you, sir."

Tugging the book free of its fellows, Jack presented it to her with a bow. "Indeed. Not even *I* would have thought to find me here. But I saw you enter and was filled with an unquenchable desire—" Jack trapped her gaze, a rakish smile dawning "—to view such apparently attractive premises. Strange, was it not?"

"Indeed." Sophie sent him a cool glance. "Most strange." She accepted the volume, reminding herself of her sensible conclusion, and her determination to view him as he viewed her: as a friendly acquaintance. "I do, most sincerely, thank you for your assistance, sir. But I must not keep you from your business."

"Rest assured you are not doing so, my dear." As he fell in beside her, Jack slanted her a glance. "I have what I came in to find."

The tenor of his deep voice tightened the vice about Sophie's heart. She glanced up, meeting his blue gaze, and abruptly realized that her vision of a "proper distance" might differ considerably from his. A sudden revelation of what that might mean—the effect his warm regard and teasing ways would inevitably have on her—set her chin rising. With commendable hauteur, she bestowed a repressively chilly glance on him. "Indeed? I take it you are not particularly fond of reading?"

Jack grinned. "I confess, my dear, that I'm a man of action rather than introspection. A man of the sword rather than the word."

Sophie ignored his subtle tone. "Perhaps that's just as well," she opined. "Given you have large estates to manage."

"Very likely," Jack conceded, his lips twitching.

"There you are, Sophie. Oh, hello, Mr. Lester." Clarissa appeared around the corner of the aisle. She smiled blithely up at Jack and dropped a slight curtsy.

Jack shook her hand. "Have you found sufficient novels to keep you entertained, Miss Webb?" He eyed the pile of books Clarissa carried in her arms.

"Oh, yes," Clarissa replied ingenuously. "Are you ready, Sophie?"

Sophie considered replying in the negative, but was convinced that, rather than leave, Jack Lester would insist on strolling with her up and down the aisles, distracting her from making any sensible selection. She glanced about; her gaze fell on her younger cousins, glued to the prospect outside. "I suspect we *had* better leave before Jeremy falls through the window."

While Sophie and Clarissa went through the process of borrowing their chosen novels, Jack smiled smugly at the disapproving assistant.

To her relief, Sophie found the assistant disinclined to conversation, a fact for which she gave mute thanks. Clarissa summoned her brothers and sister and they all started for the door. As she stepped over the threshold and paused to get her bearings, Sophie felt her packaged novel lifted from her hands.

"Allow me, my dear." Jack smiled as Sophie glanced up, consternation in her wide, slightly startled gaze. Puzzled, Jack inwardly frowned. "If you have no objection, I'll escort you to Mount Street."

Sophie hesitated, then, her lids veiling her gaze, inclined her head. "Thank you. That would be most kind." With a determinedly light air, she surrendered her hand into his warm clasp and allowed him to settle it on his sleeve. While she waited beside him as he dismissed his groom and, with a simple admonition, succeeded in convincing Jeremy, George and Amy to leave the crowd about the organ-grinder, Sophie prayed that her momentary dismay had not shown; she did not wish to hurt him any more than she wished him to guess how much her heart had been bruised. As their little party got under way, she flashed Jack a bright smile. "Did you see Lady Hemminghurst's new carriage?"

To her relief, his rakish smile appeared. "And those nags she insists are high-steppers?"

With Clarissa beside them, they chatted easily, more easily than she had hoped, all the way back to Mount Street. Indeed, the steps leading up to her uncle's door appeared before them far sooner than she had expected. Jeremy and George bounded up the steps to ring the bell, Amy close behind. With a cheery smile, Clarissa bade their escort farewell and followed her siblings as they tumbled through the door.

Acutely conscious of the gentleman before her, of Ellen and the groom, still standing decorously a few steps behind, and of Minton, the butler, holding open the door, Sophie held firm to her composure and, receiving her book, presented with a flourish, calmly said, "Thank you for your escort, Mr. Lester. No doubt we'll run into each other at the balls once they start."

Jack's slow smile twisted his lips. "I fear, my dear, that I'm not endowed with as much patience as you credit me." He hesitated, his eyes narrowing as he searched her face. "Would you be agreeable if I called to take you driving again?"

Sophie held her breath and wished she could lie. When one dark brow rose, a gentle prompt, his gaze steady on hers, she heard herself say, "That would be most pleasant, sir." His smile was triumphant. *"But,"* she hurried on, "my time is not always my own. My aunt has decided to start entertaining and I must assist her if required."

Jack's smile did not fade. "Indeed, my dear. But I'm sure she'll not wish you to hide yourself away." With smooth authority, he captured her hand. His eyes met hers; he raised her fingers, then turned them.

"No!" As surprised as he by her breathless denial, Sophie stared up at him, her heart thudding wildly. Abruptly, she dropped her gaze, quite unable to meet the startled question in his. Head bowed, she withdrew her hand from his and dropped a slight curtsy. "Good day, Mr. Lester."

The words were barely audible.

Jack felt as if he'd taken a blow to the head. He forced himself to execute a neat bow. Sophie turned and quickly climbed the steps, disappearing inside without a backward glance.

Finding himself standing stock-still, alone in the middle

of the pavement, Jack drew in a ragged breath. Then, his expression stony, he turned and strode briskly away.

WHAT IN THE NAME of all creation had gone wrong?

The question haunted Jack through the next three days and was still revolving incessantly in his brain as, the evening chill about him, he climbed the steps to knock on the Webbs' oak-panelled door. Despite his initial intentions, it was the first time he had called in Mount Street since his unexpected expedition to Hatchard's. He had returned home in a most peculiar mood, a mood that had been only slightly alleviated by the white and gold invitation he had discovered awaiting him.

"Mrs. Horatio Webb takes great pleasure in inviting Mr. Jack Lester to an impromptu dance to be held on Thursday evening."

The words had not dissipated the cloud that had settled over him, but had, at least, given him pause. Thus, he had not pressed the, albeit minor, intimacy of a drive on Sophie but had waited instead to come up with her in her aunt's ballroom, where, surely, she would feel more confident, less likely to take fright at his advances.

Quite clearly he had been too precipitate. He had put a foot wrong somewhere, although he wasn't entirely sure where.

From now on, he would woo her according to the book, without any subtle deviations. He would simply have to conceal his feelings; he would not risk panicking her by heeding them.

Admitted by the butler, who recognized him well enough to greet him by name, Jack climbed the stairs, slightly mollified by the man's cheery demeanour. Not what one was accustomed to in a butler but probably inevitable, given the junior Webbs. They would undoubtedly give any overly stuffed shirt short shrift.

Entering the salon on the first floor, Jack paused on the

threshold and glanced around. A warm, welcoming atmosphere blanketed the room; it was not overly crowded, leaving adequate space for dancing, yet his hostess was clearly not going to be disappointed by the response to her summons. He discovered Sophie immediately, talking with some others. To his eyes, there was none to match her, her slim form sheathed in silk the colour of warm honey. With an effort, he forced his gaze to travel on, searching out his hostess. As he sighted her, Lucilla excused herself from a small knot of guests. She glided forward to greet him, regally gowned in satin and lace.

"Good evening, Mr. Lester." Lucilla smiled benevolently. She watched approvingly as he bowed over her hand.

"Mrs. Webb." Jack straightened. "May I say how honoured I was to receive your invitation?"

Lucilla airily waved her fan. "Not at all, Mr. Lester. It is I who am very glad to see you. I've been a trifle concerned that dear Sophie might be finding our present round of engagements somewhat stale. Dare I hope you might feel inclined to relieve her boredom?"

Jack forced his lips to behave. "Indeed, ma'am, I would be happy to do whatever I may in that endeavour."

Lucilla smiled. "I knew I could rely on you, Mr. Lester." With an imperious gesture, she claimed his arm. "Now you must come and speak with Mr. Webb."

As she led him into the crowd, Jack suppressed the thought that he had been conscripted.

On the other side of the room, Sophie chatted with a small group of not-so-young ladies. Some, like Miss Chessington, her aunt had invited specifically to keep her company, while others, like Miss Billingham, had younger sisters making their come-out this year. Gradually, they had attracted a smattering of the gentlemen present. Most of these were either carefully vetted Webb connections or unexceptionable young men who were the sons of Lucilla's closest cronies. There was no danger lurking among them.

Stifling an inward sigh, Sophie applied herself to keeping the conversation rolling; not a difficult task, supported as she was by the ebullient Miss Chessington.

"I had heard," that ever-bright damsel declared, "that there's to be a duel fought on Paddington Green, between Lord Malmsey and Viscount Holthorpe!"

"Over what?" Miss Billingham asked, her long nose quivering.

Belle Chessington looked round at the gentlemen who had joined them. "Well, sirs? Can no one clear up this little mystery?"

"Dare say it's the usual thing." Mr. Allingcott waved a dismissive hand, his expression supercilious. "Not the sort of thing you ladies want to hear about."

"If *that's* what you think," Miss Allingcott informed her elder brother, "then you know *nothing* about ladies, Harold. The reason for a duel is positively *thrilling* information."

Discomfited, Mr. Allingcott frowned.

"Has anyone heard any further details of the balloon ascension from Green Park?" Sophie asked. In less than a minute, her companions were well launched, effectively diverted. Satisfied, Sophie glanced up—and wished she could tie a bell about Jack Lester's neck. A bell, a rattle, anything that would give her warning so that her heart would not lurch and turn over as it did every time her gaze fell into his.

He smiled, and for an instant she forgot where she was, that there were others standing only feet away, listening and observing intently. An odd ripple shook her, stemming from where his fingers had closed over hers. She must, she realized, have surrendered her hand, for now he was bowing over it, making every other gentleman look awkward.

"Good evening, Mr. Lester," she heard herself say, as if

from a distance. She sincerely hoped her smile was not as revealing as her thoughts.

"Miss Winterton."

His smile and gentle nod warmed her—and made her suspect she had been far too transparent. Taking herself firmly in hand, Sophie turned and surprised an avid gleam in Miss Billingham's eyes. "Have you made the acquaintance of Miss Billingham, sir?"

"Oh, yes!" Augusta Billingham gushed. "Indeed," she said, her expression turning coy. "Mr. Lester and I are *old* acquaintances." She held out her hand, her smile sickly sweet, her eyes half-veiled.

Jack hesitated, then took the proffered hand and curtly bowed over it. "Miss Billingham."

"And Miss Chessington."

Belle's bright smile had nothing in common with Augusta Billingham's. "Sir," she acknowledged, bobbing a curtsy.

Jack smiled more naturally and allowed Sophie to introduce him to the rest of the company. By the time she had finished, he was feeling a trifle conspicuous. Nevertheless, he stuck it out, loath to leave Sophie's side.

When the musicians struck up, he bent to whisper, "I do hope, Miss Winterton, that you'll return. I would be quite overcome—utterly at a loss in such company as this—if it weren't for the reassurance of your presence."

Sophie lifted her head and looked him in the eye. "Gammon," she whispered back. But her lips quirked upward; Jack let her go with a smile.

While she danced the cotillion and then a country reel, he endeavoured to chat to some of the younger gentlemen. They were slightly overawed. His reputation as a devotee of Jackson's and one of Manton's star pupils, let alone his memberships in the Four-in-Hand and Jockey Clubs were well-known; their conversation was consequently stilted. It made Jack feel every one of his thirty-six years—and made him even more determined to bring his dazzling career as a bachelor of the *ton* to a close as soon as might be.

The prospect was still too far distant for his liking. A quadrille had followed hard on the heels of the reel; Sophie had been claimed for it before she had left the floor. With a brief word, Jack excused himself and wandered over to the musicians. The violinist was the leader; a few quick words were all that was needed, and a guinea sealed their bargain.

When the music stopped, Jack was passing the point where Sophie came to rest. She turned towards the end of the room, where her small group was once again gathering, her youthful partner at her side; she was laughing, her expression open and carefree. Her eyes met his—and a subtle change came over her.

Sophie forced a laugh to her lips, denying the sudden tightening about her lungs, the sudden constriction in her throat. She shot Jack a quizzical glance. "Have you survived thus far, sir?"

With a single, fractionally raised brow, Jack dispensed with her companion. Flustered, the young man bowed and murmured something before taking himself off.

Turning from thanking him, Sophie frowned a warning at her nemesis. "That was most unfair, taking advantage of your seniority."

Jack hid a wince. "I fear, my dear, that my…ah, experience marks me irrevocably." Making a mental note to be more careful in future, he took her hand and settled it in the crook of his elbow. "I feel very much like the proverbial wolf amongst the sheep."

His glance left Sophie breathless. Coolly, she raised a brow at him, then fixed her gaze on her friends. He led her in their direction but made no haste. Nor did he make any attempt at conversation, which left her free, not to regain her composure, as she had hoped, but, instead, to acknowledge the truth of his observation.

He did stand out from the crowd. Not only because of his manner, so coolly arrogant and commanding, but by virtue of his appearance—he was precise as always in a dark blue coat over black pantaloons, with a crisp white cravat tied in an intricate knot the envy of the younger men—his undeniable elegance and his expertise. No one, seeing him, could doubt he was other than he was: a fully fledged and potentially dangerous rake.

Sophie frowned, wondering why her senses refused to register what was surely a reasonable fear.

"Why the frown?"

Sophie looked up to find Jack regarding her thoughtfully.

"Would you rather I left you to your younger friends?"

There was just enough hesitation behind the last words to make Sophie's heart contract. "No," she assured him, and knew it was the truth.

A flame flared in his eyes, so deeply blue.

Shaken, Sophie drew her eyes from the warmth and looked ahead to where her friends waited. In her eyes, the younger gentlemen were no more than weak cyphers, cast into deep shade by his far more forceful presence.

After a moment, Jack bent his head to murmur, "I understand there's a waltz coming up. Will you do me the honour of waltzing with me, my dear?"

Sophie fleetingly met his gaze, then inclined her head. Together, they rejoined her little circle, Jack withdrawing slightly to stand by her side, a little behind. He hoped, thus, to feature less in the conversation himself, commendably doing his best not to intimidate the younger sparks who, he kept telling himself, were no real threat to him.

Twenty minutes of self-denial later, he heard the musicians again put bow to string. Sophie, who knew very well that he had not moved from his position behind her, turned to him, shyly offering her hand.

With a smile of relief and anticipation both, Jack bowed and led her to the floor.

His relief was short-lived. A single turn about the small floor was enough to tell him something was seriously amiss. True, there was a smile on his partner's face; now and again, as they turned, she allowed her gaze to touch his. But she remained stiff in his arms, not softly supple, relaxed, as previously. She was tense, and her smile was strangely brittle.

His concern grew with every step. Even the cool glance her aunt directed at him as they glided gracefully past, held no power to distract him.

Eventually, he said, his voice gentle, "I had forgot to ask, Miss Winterton—I sincerely hope you've fully recovered from your indisposition?"

Momentarily distracted from the fight to guard her senses against his nearness, Sophie blinked, then blushed. Guilt washed through her; his tone, his expression, were touchingly sincere. "Indeed," she hastened to reassure him. "I..." She searched for words which were not an outright lie. "It was nothing serious, just a slight headache." She found it hard to meet his eyes.

Jack frowned, then banished the notion that once more popped into his brain. Of course she had been truly ill; his Sophie was not a schemer.

"And indeed, sir, I fear I've been remiss in not thanking you before this for your kind gift." Sophie's words died as she stared up at his face, strangely impassive. "You did send them, did you not? The yellow roses?"

To her relief, he nodded, his smile real but somehow distant. "I only hope they lightened your day." His gaze focused on her face. "As you do mine."

His last words were whispered, yet they clanged like bells

in Sophie's head. She suddenly felt absolutely dreadful. How could she go on pretending like this, trying to hide her heart? It would never work. She was not strong enough; she would trip and he would find out...

Her distress showed very clearly in her eyes. Jack caught his breath. He frowned. "Sophie?"

The music came to an end. He released her only to trap her hand firmly on his sleeve. "Come. We'll stroll a little."

Sophie's eyes flared wide. "Oh, no, really. I'd better get back."

"Your friends will survive without you for a few minutes." Jack's accents were clipped, commanding. "There's a window open at the end of the room. I think you could do with some air."

Sophie knew fresh air would help, yet the fact that he was sensitive enough to suggest it didn't help at all. She murmured her acquiescence, not that he had waited for it, and told herself she should be grateful. Yet being so close to him, and cut off from ready distraction, her senses were being slowly rasped raw. His effect on them, on her, seemed to get worse with every meeting.

"Here. Sit down." Jack guided her to a chair set back by the wall, not far from where a set of fine draperies billowed gently in the breeze.

Sophie sank onto the upholstered seat, feeling the cool wood of the chair back against her shoulders. The sensation helped her think. "Perhaps, Mr. Lester, if I could impose on you to get me a drink."

"Of course," Jack said. He turned and snapped his fingers at a waiter. With a few terse words, he dispatched the man in search of a glass of water. Sophie hid her dismay.

"And now, Sophie," Jack said, turning to look down at her. "You're going to tell me what's wrong."

It was a command, no less. Sophie dragged in a deep breath

and forced herself to meet his gaze calmly. "Wrong?" She opened her eyes wide. "Why, Mr. Lester, nothing's wrong." She spread her hands in a gesture of bewilderment. "I'm merely feeling a trifle…warm." That, she suddenly realized, was the literal truth. He stood over her, his dark brows drawn down, and she was violently reminded of their interlude in the glade in Leicestershire. That same something she had glimpsed then, behind the intense blue of his eyes, was there again tonight. A prowling, powerful, predatory something. She blinked and realized she was breathing rapidly. She saw his lips compress.

"Sophie…"

His eyes locked with hers; he started to lean closer.

"Your glass of water, miss."

Sophie wrenched her gaze away and turned to the waiter. She dragged in a quick breath. "Thank you, John." She took the glass from the man's salver and dismissed him with a weak smile.

It took considerable concentration to keep the glass steady. With her gaze fixed, unfocused, on the couples now dancing a boulanger, Sophie carefully sipped the cool water. An awful silence enfolded them.

After a few minutes, Sophie felt strong enough to glance up. He was watching her, his expression utterly impassive; he no longer seemed so threatening. She inclined her head. "Thank you, sir. I feel much better now."

Jack nodded. Before he could find words for any of his questions, his attention was diverted by a group of younger folk who descended amid gusts of laughter to cluster not ten paces away.

Sophie looked, too, and saw her cousin surrounded by a group of young gentlemen, each vying for Clarissa's attention. Noting the frenetic brittleness that had infused Clarissa's otherwise bright expression, Sophie frowned. She looked up, and met an arrogantly raised brow.

She hesitated, then leaned closer to say, "She doesn't really like having a fuss and flap made over her."

Jack looked again at the fair young beauty. His lips twisted wryly as he watched her youthful swains all but cutting each other dead in an effort to gain her favour. "If that's the case," he murmured, "I fear she'll have to leave town." He turned back to Sophie. "She's going to be a hit, you know."

Sophie sighed. "I know." She continued to watch Clarissa, then frowned as a particularly petulant expression settled firmly over her cousin's features. "What…?" Sophie followed Clarissa's gaze. "Oh, dear."

Following Sophie's gaze, Jack beheld a well-set-up young man, unquestionably recently up from the country if his coat was any guide, bearing determinedly down on the group about Sophie's cousin. The young man ignored the attendant swains as if they didn't exist, an action that won Jack's instant respect. Directly and without preamble, the youngster addressed Clarissa; to Jack's disappointment, they were too far away to hear his words. Unfortunately, the young man's grand entrance found no favour in Clarissa's eyes. As Jack watched, Clarissa tossed her silvery curls, an indignant flush replacing the sparkle of moments before.

"Oh, dear. I do hope he didn't call her 'Clary' again."

Jack glanced down. Sophie was watching the unfolding drama, small white teeth absent-mindedly chewing her lower lip. "Whatever," he said. "It appears that his embassy has failed."

Sophie sent him a worried frown. "They've known each other since childhood."

"Ah." Jack glanced back at the tableau being enacted but yards away. A wisp of remembered conversation floated through his mind. "Is that young sprig by any chance Ned Ascombe?"

"Why, yes." Sophie stared up at him. "The son of one of my uncle's neighbours in Leicestershire."

Jack answered the question in her eyes. "Your aunt mentioned him." Glancing again at the young couple, Jack felt an empathetic twinge for the earnest but callow youth who was, quite obviously, under the impression he held pride of place in the beautiful Clarissa Webb's heart. As he watched, Ned gave up what was undeniably a losing fight and, with a galled but defiant expression, retired from the lists. Looking down at Sophie, Jack asked, "I take it he was not expected in London?"

Sophie considered, then said, "Clarissa didn't expect him."

Jack's brows lifted cynically. "Your aunt gave me to understand that their future was all but settled."

Sophie sighed. "It probably is. Clarissa does not really care for racketing about and she has never been one to enjoy being the centre of attention for very long. My aunt and uncle believe that, by the end of the Season, she'll be only too happy to return to Leicestershire."

"And Ned Ascombe?"

"And Ned," Sophie confirmed.

Considering the colour that still rode Clarissa Webb's cheeks, Jack allowed one brow to rise.

Sophie finished the last of her water. It was time and more to return to the safety of her circle. "If you'll excuse me, Mr. Lester, I should return to my friends."

Jack could have wished it otherwise but he was, once more, under control. Without a blink, he nodded, removing the glass from her fingers and placing it on a nearby table. Then he held out a hand.

Steeling herself against the contact, Sophie put her hand in his. He drew her to her feet, then tucked her hand into his elbow, covering her fingers with his. Hers trembled; with an effort, she stilled them. She glanced up and saw him frown.

Jack studied her face, still pale. "Sophie, my dear—please believe I would never knowingly do anything to cause you pain."

Sophie's heart turned over. Tears pricked, but she would not let them show. She tried to speak, but her throat had seized up. With a smile she knew went awry, she inclined her head and looked away.

He escorted her to her friends, then, very correctly, took his leave of her.

Jack did not immediately quit the house. Something was wrong, and Sophie wouldn't confide in him. The unpalatable fact ate at him, gnawing at his pride, preying on his protective nature, prompting all manner of acts he was far too experienced to countenance. His restless prowling, disguised beneath an air of fashionable boredom, took him by the alcove where Ned Ascombe stood, keeping a glowering watch over his prospective bride.

His gaze on the dancers, Jack propped one broad shoulder against the other side of the alcove. "It won't work, you know."

The laconic comment succeeded in diverting Ned's attention. He turned his head, his scowl still in evidence, then abruptly straightened, his face leaching of expression. "Oh, excuse me, sir."

Jack sent the youngster a reassuring grin. "Boot's on the other foot. It was I who interrupted you." Briefly scanning Ned's face, Jack held out his hand. "Jack Lester. An acquaintance of the Webbs. I believe I saw you at Lady Asfordby's, as well."

As he had expected, the mention of two well-known and well-respected Leicestershire names was enough to ease Ned's reticence.

Ned grasped his hand firmly, then blushed. "I suppose

you saw…" He abruptly shut his mouth and gestured vaguely, his gaze once more on the dancers. "You were with Sophie."

Jack smiled, more to himself than Ned. "As you say, I saw. And I can tell you without fear of contradiction that your present strategy is doomed to failure." He felt rather than saw Ned's curious glance. Straightening, Jack extricated a note-case from an inner pocket and withdrew a card. This he presented to Ned. "If you want to learn how to pull the thing off, how to win the blond head you've set your eye on, then drop by tomorrow. About eleven." Very used to younger brothers, Jack ensured his worldly expression contained not the slightest hint of patronage.

Taking the card, Ned read the inscription, then raised puzzled eyes to Jack's face. "But why? You've never even met me before."

Jack's smile turned wry. "Put it down to fellow-feeling. Believe me, you're not the only one who's feeling rejected tonight."

With a nod, very man-to-man, Jack passed on.

Left by the alcove, Ned stared after him, his gaze abstracted, Jack's card held tight in his fingers.

"WELL, M'DEAR? DID Jack Lester disappoint you?" Propped against the pillows in the bed he most unfashionably shared with his wife, Horatio Webb slanted a questioning glance at his helpmate, sitting sipping her morning cocoa beside him.

A slight frown descended upon Lucilla's fair brow. "I don't expect to be disappointed in Mr. Lester, dear. I really should have organized that waltz myself. However, matters do seem to be progressing along their customary course." She considered, then banished her frown to cast a smiling glance at her spouse. "I dare say I've just forgotten how agonizingly painful it is to watch these things unfold."

Lowering the business papers he had been perusing, Horatio peered at her over the top of his gold-rimmed spectacles. "You haven't been meddling, have you?"

The slightest suspicion of a blush tinged Lucilla's cheeks. "Not to say *meddling*." She dismissed the notion with an airy wave. "But I really couldn't allow Mr. Lester to sweep Sophie into matrimony before the child had even had a taste of success. Not after her last Season was so tragically curtailed."

"Humph!" Horatio shuffled his papers. "You know how I feel about tampering with other people's lives, dear. Even with the *best* of intentions. Who knows? Sophie might actually *prefer* to have her Season curtailed—if it were Jack Lester doing the curtailing."

Head on one side, Lucilla considered the idea, then grimaced. After a moment, she sighed. "Perhaps you're right. When did you say the horses will be here?"

"They're here now. Arrived yesterday." Horatio had gone back to his papers. "I'll take the troops to view them this morning if you like."

Lucilla brightened. "Yes, that *would* be a good idea. But we'll have to give some consideration to escorts." She touched her spouse's hand. "Leave that to me. I'm sure I can find someone suitable."

Horatio grunted. "Wonder if Lester brought that hunter of his up to town?"

Lucilla grinned but said nothing. Finishing her cocoa, she laid her cup and saucer on the bedside table and snuggled down beneath the covers. Smiling, she reached out to pat her husband's hand. "I'm really quite in awe of your far-sightedness, dear. So clever of you to help the Lesters to their fortune. Now there's no impediment at all to concern you, and you may give Jack Lester your blessing with a clear conscience." An expression of catlike satisfaction on her face, Lucilla settled to doze.

Horatio stared down at her, a faintly astonished expression on his face. He opened his mouth, then abruptly shut it. After a long moment of staring at his wife's exquisite features, Horatio calmly picked up his papers and, settling his spectacles firmly on the bridge of his nose, left his wife to her dreams.

CHAPTER EIGHT

AT PRECISELY ELEVEN the next morning, the doorbell of Jack's townhouse in Upper Brook Street jangled a summons. Jack looked up, his brows lifting. "I believe that will be a Mr. Ascombe, Pinkerton. I'll see him here."

Here was the parlour; Jack sat at the head of the table, Pinkerton, his gentleman's gentleman, had just finished clearing the remains of Jack's breakfast and was lovingly glossing the mahogany surface.

"Very good, sir," Pinkerton returned in his usual sepulchral tones.

Jack nodded and returned to his perusal of the latest edition of the *Racing Chronicle*. "Oh—and bring a fresh pot of coffee, will you?"

"Yes, sir." A sober individual who considered it a point of professional etiquette to carry out his duties as inconspicuously as possible, Pinkerton slipped noiselessly from the room. As the sounds of voices penetrated the oak door, Jack folded the *Chronicle* and laid it aside. Easing his chair back from the table, he stretched, trying to relieve the tension that seemed to have sunk into his bones.

The door latch lifted; Pinkerton ushered Ned Ascombe in, then departed in search of more coffee.

"Good morning, sir." Feeling decidedly awkward, not at all sure why he had come, Ned surveyed his host. Jack Lester was clearly not one of those town beaux who considered any time before noon as dawn. He was dressed in a blue coat which made Ned's own loosely-fitting garment look countrified in the extreme.

Jack rose lazily and extended a hand. "Glad to see you, Ascombe—or may I call you Ned?"

Grasping the proffered hand, Ned blinked. "If you wish." Then, realizing that sounded rather less than gracious, he forced a smile. "Most people call me Ned."

Jack returned the smile easily and waved Ned to a chair.

Dragging his eyes from contemplation of his host's superbly fitting buckskin breeches and highly polished Hessians, Ned took the opportunity to hide his corduroy breeches and serviceable boots under the table. What had Clary called him? Provincial? His self-confidence, already shaky, took another lurch downwards.

Jack caught the flicker of defeat in Ned's honest brown eyes. He waited until Pinkerton, who had silently reappeared, set out a second mug and the coffee-pot, then, like a spectre, vanished, before saying, "I understand from Miss Winterton that you would wish Miss Webb to look upon you with, shall we say, a greater degree of appreciation?"

Ned's fingers tightened about the handle of his mug. He blushed but manfully met Jack's gaze. "Sophie's always been a good friend, sir."

"Quite," Jack allowed. "But if I'm to call you Ned, I suspect you had better call me Jack, as, although I'm certainly much your senior, I would not wish to be thought old enough to be your father."

Ned's smile was a little more relaxed. "Jack, then."

"Good. With such formalities out of the way, I'll admit I couldn't help but notice your contretemps with Miss Webb last night."

Ned's face darkened. "Well, you saw how it was," he growled. "She was encouraging an entire company of flatterers and inconsequential rattles."

There was a pause, then Jack asked, "I do hope you didn't tell her so?"

Ned fortified himself with a long sip of coffee and nodded darkly. "Not in those precise words, of course."

"Thank heaven for small mercies." Jack fixed his guest with a severe glance. "It seems to me, my lad, that you're in desperate need of guidance in the matter of how to conduct a campaign in the *ton*."

"A campaign?"

"The sort of campaign one wages to win a lady's heart."

Ned glowered. "Clarissa's heart has always been mine."

"I dare say," Jack replied. "The trick is to get her to recognize that fact. From what I saw last night, if you continue as you are, you're liable to go backwards rather than forwards."

Ned frowned at his mug, then glanced up at Jack. "I'm not really cut out to shine in town. I don't know how to do the pretty by the ladies; I'm more at home in the saddle than in a ballroom."

"Aren't we all?" At Ned's questioning look, Jack elaborated. "The vast majority of gentlemen you'll see at any evening's entertainments would rather be somewhere else."

"But why attend if they don't wish to?"

"Why were you at Mrs. Webb's little affair?"

"Because I wanted to see Clarissa."

"Precisely. The only inducement capable of getting most of us across the threshold of a ballroom is the lure of the ladies. Where else do we get a chance to converse, to establish any connection? If you do not meet a lady first at a ball, it's dashed difficult to approach her anywhere else, at least in town. So," Jack concluded, "if you're set on winning Clarissa Webb, you'll have to accept the fact that you'll be gracing the *ton*'s ballrooms for the Season."

Ned wrinkled his nose. "My father was against my coming up to town—he thought I should just wait for Clarissa to come back. Mr. and Mrs. Webb are very sure she'll not appreciate the racketing about and will want to return to the country."

"I have inestimable faith in the senior Webb's perspicacity. However, don't you think you're extrapolating just a little too far? Taking Clarissa just a little too much for granted?"

Ned flushed again. "That's what worried me. It's why I came to town."

"And your instincts were right." Jack eyed him straitly. "From what little I've seen, I would predict that, whatever her inclinations, Clarissa Webb is sure to be one of the hits of the Season. That means she'll have all the puppies fawning at her feet, eager to paint unlikely pictures of a glowing future should she bestow her hand on them. And, despite the fact she may remain at heart a country miss, one should not lose sight of the fact that there's no shortage of gentlemen who are also inclined to the country. Such men would not baulk at taking a wife who dislikes town life. Most, in fact, would consider her a find."

Ned's brow furrowed. After a moment's cogitation, he looked Jack in the eye. "Are you telling me Clarissa will be sought after by other gentlemen who would wish to retire to the country?"

Jack nodded decisively.

"And if I don't make a…a push to fix her interest, she may accept one of them?"

Again came a definite nod.

Ned looked slightly shaken. After a long silence in which he studied the coffee at the bottom of his mug, and during which Jack sat back, at ease, and waited patiently, Ned raised his head, his jaw set, and regarded Jack with determined honesty. "I thank you for your warning, Jack. You've given me a great deal to think about." Despite his efforts, Ned's features contorted in a grimace which he immediately hid behind his mug. "Dashed if I know what I'm to do about it, though," he mumbled from behind the mug.

"No need to panic." Jack waved a languid hand. "I've loads of experience I'm perfectly willing to place at your disposal. I dare say once you learn the ropes, you'll find the whole business a challenge."

Surprised, Ned looked up from his mug. "Do you mean…" he began, then took the bull by the horns. "Are you suggesting you'd be willing to help me?"

"Not suggesting. I'm *telling* you I'm prepared to stand your mentor in this."

Ned's open face clouded. "But…why?" He flushed vividly. "I mean…"

Jack laughed. "No, no. A perfectly understandable question." He viewed his guest with a quietly assessing eye. Then he smiled. "Let's just say that I can't bear to see one so young so tangled in the briars. And, of course, I, too, have an interest in the Webb household." He made the admission with easy assurance and was rewarded by Ned's instant comprehension.

"Sophie?" His eyes growing round, his gaze openly speculative. Ned considered Jack—and his revelation.

Jack inclined his head.

"Oh."

As Jack had hoped, Ned seemed to accept that his interest in Sophie was sufficient excuse for his interest in him. While he was certainly drawn to Ned's open earnestness, it was Sophie's transparent concern for her cousin that had prompted him to take Ned under his wing. It formed no part of his own campaign to have Sophie in a constant fidget over her cousin, always keeping one eye on the younger girl. It was natural enough that she do so; to one who was himself imbued with a strong sense of sibling responsibility, Sophie's concern for Clarissa demonstrated a highly laudable devotion. Nevertheless, Sophie's cousinly concern could rapidly become a distraction.

And Jack was quite certain he did not wish to share Sophie's attention—not With Clarissa, nor anyone else.

Ned was frowning, clearly still uncertain.

"Consider my offer in the light of one doing his damnedest to ensure his lady is not distracted by unnecessary ructions amongst her family," Jack suggested somewhat drily.

Ned glanced up, struggling to hide a grin. "I suppose that's true enough. Sophie's always been like an elder sister to Clarissa."

Jack inclined his head. "I'm so glad you see my point."

Ned nodded. "If that's the way it is, I have to admit it wouldn't sit well to walk away from a fight. But I do feel totally at sea." He grinned at Jack. "Do you think you can turn me into a dandy?"

Jack grinned back. "Not a chance. What I'm sure we *can* do is to turn you out as a gentleman of the *ton*." Sobering, he fixed Ned with a meaningful glance. "You should never forget, nor attempt to hide, your origins. There is, if you'll only stop to consider, no taint attached to being a husbander of acres. Most of the highest in the *ton* are also the largest landholders in England and I can assure you they're not the least apologetic for the fact. Many spend considerable amounts of time managing their estates. Drawing one's fortune directly from the land is nothing to be ashamed of."

Ned coloured slightly. "Thank you. I don't know how you knew but that's exactly what I felt."

"I know because I've been there before you. I, too, have an estate to manage. That, however, has never stopped me from feeling at home in London."

"Oh." The revelation that Jack, too, had firm links with the country eased Ned's mind of its last doubt. "So, what do I do first?"

"A tailor," Jack declared. "Then a barber. You can't do anything until you look the part. And then we'll see about introducing you to some of the necessary establishments a gentleman of the *ton* must needs frequent—like Manton's and Jackson's Boxing Saloon. After that, we shall plan your campaign in more detail." Jack smiled. "You're going to have to learn that finessing the feminine mind takes the wiles of a fox and the devotion of a hound."

"I'll do whatever I need to," Ned averred. "Just as long as I can make Clarissa stop looking at those trumped-up popinjays as she was last night."

Jack laughed and rose. "Onward, then. No time like the present to make a start."

WHILE NED WAS sipping coffee in Upper Brook Street, Horatio Webb was busy introducing his children and his niece to the mounts he had had brought down from the country.

"These should be just the ticket for jaunts in the Park," he said as he ushered his charges into the stables. "Quite the thing, I hear, to be seen riding in the morning."

"Golly, yes!" returned Jeremy, eyes aglow. "All the crack."

Horatio's eyes twinkled. "Now these two, you two should recognize."

"By Jupiter! They're the ones you bought from Lord Cranbourne, aren't they, sir?" George, together with Jeremy, stared round-eyed at the two glossy-coated chestnut geldings their father had indicated.

Horatio beamed. "I thought they needed a little exercise. Think you can handle them?"

A garbled rush of words assured him that they could.

"We'll cut a dash on these," Jeremy declared.

With both boys absorbed, Horatio smiled down at Amy, clutching his hand. "Now for you, my miss, I've brought down Pebbles. Old Maude wouldn't have appreciated the traffic, you know."

Struck dumb at the thought of advancing beyond Old Maude's plodding gait, Amy stared at the placid grey mare who ambled up to look over the stall door. "Look!" she piped, as the mare reached down to nudge hopefully at her pockets. "She knows me!"

That, of course, took care of Amy. Leaving her to get properly acquainted with the mare, Horatio smiled at his two remaining charges. "Now, my dear," he said, beckoning Clarissa forward. "I fear I couldn't improve on Jenna, so I brought her down for you. I do hope you're not disappointed."

Clarissa smiled delightedly as she reached up to stroke the velvety nose of her beautiful chestnut mare. "How could I possibly be disappointed with you, my pet," she crooned softly as the mare nudged her cheek. "I was afraid you would want to spell her for a bit," she told her father. "I rode her all winter."

"Old Arthur seemed to think she was moping, missing all her rides. You know how soft-hearted he is." Horatio patted Jenna's nose, then turned to Sophie.

"And now for you, my dearest Sophie." Taking her arm, he led her to the next stall, where an elegant roan mare was bobbing her head curiously. "I hope Dulcima here suits you. Not as powerful as the Sheik, of course, but rather more suited to the confines of the Park."

Sophie was staring at the beautiful horse. "But…she's new, isn't she?"

Horatio waved dismissively. "Found her at Tattersall's. She's well broken and used to being ridden in town. Quite a find."

"Well, yes. But I would have been quite happy with one of your other horses, uncle. I do hope you didn't buy her just for me?"

"No, no. Nonsense—of course not." Under Sophie's disbelieving gaze, Horatio looked down and tugged at his waist-coat. "Besides," he said, looking up, a sudden impish twinkle in his eye. "Dare say Mr. Lester will be riding in the Park on the odd occasion. Never do for him to think I don't take all care of you, m'dear."

The comment cut off Sophie's protests. Taken aback, she frowned, opened her mouth, then closed it again.

"Leave you to get acquainted." With a farewell pat for the mare, Horatio strode back to see how his sons were faring.

Sophie looked after him, her eyes narrowing. Then she snorted disgustedly and turned back to the mare. As if in argument, the mare shook her head, then snorted once, ears pricking forward. Sophie grinned. "Aren't you a clever creature?" she crooned.

The mare nodded vigorously.

When, at length, they were ready to leave their equine partners, they strolled together back along the mews and around to the house, Horatio with them.

In reply to Jeremy and George's eager question, Horatio replied, "You should give them a day or two to get over their journey, and for those not used to the noise to become more accustomed, before you take them out."

The boys whooped. "Monday, then!"

"However," Horatio smoothly continued, cutting across their transports. "You cannot, I'm afraid, simply take off with a groom here in town." He glanced first at Sophie, then at Clarissa, walking on either side of him. "Neither your aunt nor I would be happy with that."

"But Toby will be here soon, will he not?" Clarissa ventured.

Horatio nodded. His eldest son, presently at Oxford, was expected to join the family any day. "True. But even so, you must remember that Toby is barely twenty. It would hardly be fair to foist the responsibility for all of you onto his shoulders.

Indeed, although your mother and I have no doubt of his willingness to act as your escort, he is not yet experienced enough to adequately guard against the dangers which might face you here in the capital. This is not Leicestershire, as you know."

"What, then?" Sophie asked, knowing he was right. "Where will we find a suitable escort?"

Horatio smiled his most inscrutable smile. "Your aunt has promised to see to it."

TUESDAY AFTERNOON SAW the Webb ladies taking the air in the Park. The weather continued unseasonably mild; everyone was out to take advantage. Bright walking gowns splashed colour across the lawns. One or two ladies had even felt the need for parasols.

From her perch in the barouche beside her aunt, with Clarissa gaily smiling from the opposite seat, Sophie nodded and waved greetings, determined thus to keep her mind on noting any newcomers, rather than allowing her gaze to wander farther afield, searching for one she would do well to forget.

After completing a leisurely circuit, her aunt directed her coachman to pull up alongside Lady Abercrombie's carriage.

Her ladyship, as sociable as her husband was not, was all smiles. "Lucilla, dear! How positively delightful! Do you intend to remain all Season?"

While Lucilla exchanged gossip with her ladyship, both Sophie and Clarissa did what young ladies were supposed to do on such occasions: they responded to any query directed their way but otherwise allowed their gaze to idly roam the passing scenery, which was to say, the passing crowd.

Engaged in this necessary occupation, Sophie greeted any acquaintances who passed, exchanging commonplaces all but automatically, while her wandering gaze became gradually more intent. When it finally occurred to her what she was doing, she frowned and shook herself.

With a determined air, she looked about for distraction. And discovered Mr. Marston, waiting, sober and serious as a judge, to greet her.

"Oh, good day, sir." Annoyed at her awkwardness—she was surely more experienced than this!—Sophie summoned a smile. "I did not know you had intended to come to London."

Phillip Marston took her hand and bowed. He shook hands with both Clarissa and Lucilla, who, on hearing his voice, had turned, brows flying upward. After exchanging a few words, Lucilla turned back to Lady Abercrombie, leaving Mr. Marston to gravely tell Sophie, "Indeed, Miss Winterton, it was not my intention to join the frivolity." A disdainful glance at two young gentlemen who came up to speak to Clarissa declared his opinion very clearly. "Nevertheless, I felt that, in this case, my presence was necessary."

Sophie was mystified. "Indeed, sir?"

"I flatter myself that I am fully cognizant of the inherent sensibility of your mind, Miss Winterton. I greatly fear that you will find little to entertain a lady of your refined nature here in the capital." Phillip Marston cast a glance at Lucilla, once more deeply engrossed with Lady Abercrombie, and lowered his voice. "As your aunt was determined to bring you to town, I felt that the least I could do, as I assured my dear mama, was to journey here to do what I may to support you through this time."

Utterly dumbfounded, Sophie silently searched for the prescribed reply to that revelation, and discovered that there wasn't one. In fact, as the full implication of Mr. Marston's declaration impinged on her mind, she decided she did not approve—of him or it. Drawing herself up, she fixed him with a distinctly frosty gaze. "I must inform you, sir, that I find the entertainments to which my aunt escorts me quite fascinating."

A condescending smile lifted Mr. Marston's thin lips.

"Your loyalty to your aunt does you credit, my dear, but I feel I must point out that the Season has not yet begun. The entertainments thus far are doubtless mild enough. You will understand my concern once the more…rackety gentlemen are included. Then, I venture to say, you will be only too glad of my escort."

Sophie struggled for words. She dragged in a deep breath, glanced up—and felt a surge of inexpressible relief. Her heart leapt. She promptly tried to dampen her reaction, only to see the corners of Jack Lester's lips lift.

With determined calm, Sophie coolly extended one hand. "Good afternoon, Mr. Lester."

"Miss Winterton." With suave grace, Jack bowed. "I had hoped to discover you here." He ignored Mr. Marston beside him.

Mr. Marston, Sophie noticed, was not ignoring him. He drew himself up, his nostrils pinched as if Mr. Lester's appearance was offensive. Just what he could find amiss with that supremely elegant figure Sophie was at a loss to guess. "Ah…I believe you have met Mr. Marston before, Mr. Lester? He's down from Leicestershire. I was just commenting on what a surprise it was to see him here." Sophie watched as the two men exchanged glances, Marston visibly bristling.

"Marston." With a brief nod, Jack dismissed the fellow from his thoughts and turned to Clarissa as her two admirers withdrew. "Miss Webb." Jack shook her hand, then indicated the figure beside him. "I believe Mr. Ascombe is known to you both?"

Sophie blinked, then smiled delightedly. From the corner of her eye, she saw Clarissa's jaw drop. Ned had been to a tailor—a good one. His coat of Bath superfine now hugged his shoulders, doing far more justice to his lean frame than his previous suiting ever had. And he had had a haircut—his crisp brown locks were now in fashionable disarray. His breeches, his boots—all were new and all contributed to a remarkable transmogrification. Taking it all in with one comprehensive glance, Sophie retained sufficient wit to respond to the subtle prompt in Jack's steady blue gaze. She held out her hand and smiled warmly. "Indeed, yes. It's good to see you, Ned."

Some of Ned's stiffness faded. He slanted Sophie a grin. "You look ravishing, Sophie. Determined to cut a swath through the *ton?*"

Sophie was impressed by the clear confidence in Ned's tone. A quick glance to her right showed that she wasn't alone. Clarissa was staring at Ned, confusion clearly writ in her large blue eyes. "I'm certainly determined to enjoy myself this Season," Sophie responded. "Will you be in town for the duration?"

"I expect so," Ned replied, his gaze fixed on Sophie. "I hadn't realized before just how many distractions there were to be found in the capital."

"Hello, Ned."

At Clarissa's somewhat tentative greeting, Ned turned to her with an easy but in no way especial smile. "Good afternoon, Miss Webb. You're looking quite splendid. Have you been enjoying your stay thus far?"

Sophie bit her lip. The quick glance she sent Jack was a mistake. The devilish light in his blue eyes very nearly overset her control.

Clarissa, clearly bemused by the change in her childhood companion, mumbled a disjointed response, lost as Mr. Marston cut in.

"Afternoon, Ascombe." Phillip Marston eyed Ned's new finery with a critical eye. "Your father, I suspect, would be quite surprised to see you thus decked out."

Used to Phillip Marston's sober declarations, Ned merely grinned and shook his hand.

Sophie smothered a giggle. Jack caught her eye; she looked away, her jaws aching.

Then Lucilla joined the fray. She greeted Jack as an old acquaintance, complimented Ned on his good sense, and, under cover of a rapid-fire monologue on the varied entertainments to be found in the capital, managed to divulge that her charges would dearly like to ride in the Park in the mornings but lacked suitable escorts. "For even when Toby arrives," she declared, "I would not be happy to allow a group of such innocents to brave the Park without someone more experienced to handle the reins, as it were."

Stunned, Sophie directed a look of pointed reproof at her aunt. Lucilla pretended not to notice. Predictably, a deep voice answered.

"Mr. Ascombe and I would be only too happy to be of assistance, Mrs. Webb. Would you be content to release your charges to our care?"

Impotent, Sophie watched as Lucilla bent a look of shining approval on Jack. "Indeed, Mr. Lester. I cannot think of anyone I'd trust more."

Jack very nearly winced but inclined his head in acceptance of her commission. In this instance, her stipulation that he was being entrusted with her charges and therefore, as a gentleman, expected to respect her confidence, was no handicap.

And there was hay yet to be made from the situation. "Perhaps Miss Winterton and Miss Webb would care to stroll the lawns while we discuss the most appropriate time to meet?"

Lucilla's eyes widened slightly.

Sophie was not at all certain of the wisdom of strolling beside Jack Lester, even in the middle of the Park. Maintaining an appropriate distance was imperative; closing the physical distance between them was unlikely to help her cause.

"What a perfectly splendid idea!" Clarissa turned to Lucilla, her eyes bright and eager.

With a sigh and a lifted brow, Lucilla relaxed against the squabs. "By all means—but only for fifteen minutes. I'll await you here."

To Sophie's immense relief, Phillip Marston said nothing, merely frowning into the distance in an abstracted fashion. Then, rather abruptly, he bowed and took his leave of them.

Jack barely noticed. He handed Sophie down from the carriage, his satisfaction implicit in his smile. She was a picture in muslin the colour of old gold, a fairy princess with a touch of rose in her cheeks.

With her hand snugly tucked in his arm, they strolled across the broad expanse of clipped grass. Beside them, Clarissa, on Ned's arm, kept shooting shy glances up at him. Very correctly, the party remained together, clearly within sight of Lucilla in the barouche.

Aware, again, as she paced beside him of that strength that seemed an integral part of Jack Lester, impinging on her senses as if she had no defence, Sophie struggled to remain calmly aloof. Just friends—only friends. To her surprise, her companion proved to have a ready line of patter to meet even this occasion, one she doubted he had had much previous experience of.

"The *ton* seems uncommonly eager to commence this Season," Jack commented, idly scanning the host dotting the lawns. "I don't think I've seen such a turnout this early for years."

"My aunt was commenting on that fact," Sophie returned, keeping her gaze firmly on their surroundings. "I believe that a number of ladies are considering holding coming-out balls next week."

"My own ball will be held on Friday," Clarissa volunteered, suppressed excitement quivering in her tone. "Mama says there's no reason not to get into the swing of things."

"Your mother is indeed very wise, Miss Webb." Jack smiled down at Clarissa's delicately flushed face. A few days of Ned's company had more than sufficed to bolster his instinctive liking into solid support. He was quite determined that, come the end of the Season, Ned would retire from the lists with Clarissa's favour firmly in his possession. "I suspect there are few subjects on which you would not be wise to heed your mother's advice."

"Have you been on an excursion to the Royal Exchange, Miss Webb? I'm told the wild beasts are a fearsome spectacle." Ned's tone was commendably even, devoid of overeagerness.

Hearing Clarissa, still warily suspicious but too unsure of this new Ned to risk any airs, answer with unaffected openness, Sophie was hard put to hide her grin.

Seeing her lips quirk, and deciding he had done enough today in furthering Ned's enterprise, Jack slowed his pace.

Sophie noticed. Her head came up. Looking her escort firmly in the eye, she raised a brow at him. When he merely smiled back, maddeningly, she surrendered to temptation. "Am I right, sir, in supposing you are helping Ned to adjust to town life?"

Jack smiled and leaned closer, lowering his voice. "Ned's a likeable chap. But having come up fresh from the country, he was facing opposition of unfair proportions. I thought it only fair to even the odds a little."

Sophie felt her lips soften. "Indeed?" she replied, her eyes on his. "So your actions are prompted by nothing more than a passing interest in righting an inequity?"

"I'm very keen on righting inequities," Jack informed her, his brows rising arrogantly. Then, abandoning his haughty attitude, he added, his tone deepening, "Not that I don't have reasons of my own to wish Clarissa settled."

"Oh?" Sophie held his gaze, warmly blue. Caution went winging. "And what might those be, sir?"

"Jack." Glancing ahead, Jack asked, "Do you think I'm succeeding?"

Although his glance had taken in Clarissa and Ned immediately ahead of them, his gaze had swung back to her on his question. Sophie, her heart increasing its tempo, was not sure how to reply. With a determined effort, she switched her gaze forward to where Clarissa was still viewing Ned curiously, like some specimen she did not yet understand. "My cousin certainly seems enthralled by Ned in his new guise."

A heartfelt sigh came from beside her. "Perhaps I should take a leaf out of his book? Mayhap Percy could give me some hints."

At his defeated tone, Sophie swung about, her eyes automatically travelling the length of his elegantly accoutred frame before, realizing she had fallen into his trap, her gaze snapped up to meet his. Warm amusement, and a clear invitation to play this game—with him—glowed in the deep blue. Abruptly, Sophie dropped her gaze and murmured, "Time is flying; we should return to my aunt, sir."

A gentle, somewhat wry smile softened Jack's lips. "I dare say you're right, Miss Winterton." So saying, he drew her hand once more through his arm. A few quick strides brought them up with the younger couple.

Ned turned, a glimmer of relief showing briefly in his eyes. But before they could retrace their steps to the barouche, they were hailed from the nearby carriageway.

"Jack!"

They all turned. Sophie recognized Gerald Lester—and his new phaeton. Ned had noticed the phaeton, too—and Gerald had noticed Clarissa. Naturally, they had to pause while introductions were performed and accolades on the phaeton and pair duly exchanged.

"No doubt but that I'll see you at one of the balls," Gerald said, impartially addressing them all. Then he flicked his whip and waved. "Tally-ho!"

"Puppy!" Jack snorted, but he was grinning.

Sophie watched the expensive carriage roll away, then turned towards the barouche.

One more reason why Jack Lester would have to marry well.

She risked a glance up at him; he was scanning the couples between them and the barouche. With Ned and Clarissa in tow, he steered her clear of any interference, making directly for the carriage where Lucilla sat awaiting them. Sophie bit her lip and looked down.

Gerald Lester was clearly a young gentleman unaccustomed to habits of economy. Jack's elegance declared that he, too, was not one to count the cost in presenting himself to the *ton*. The Lesters, at least those she had thus far encountered, knew their place, knew to a nicety how to behave within the circles into which their birth and estates elevated them. Equally obviously, they thought nothing of financing their expensive style of life on tick.

Well, she amended moodily, perhaps not on tick—but there was little doubt that Jack needed a rich wife.

It was not, Sophie reflected dourly, an uncommon occurrence in the *ton*—families inured to living well beyond their means. She could only curse the fate that had made the Lesters one of them.

Then the barouche was before them and it was all she could do to behave normally, agreeing to ride the next morning in the Park, then acknowledging the farewells, smiling as he bowed over her hand, as if there were no black cloud lowering on her horizon, about to deprive her of the warmth of his gaze.

CHAPTER NINE

RESIGNED TO THE INEVITABLE, Sophie was the first of the Webb contingent to appear in the hall the next morning. As she came down the stairs, buttoning her gloves, a wary smile twisted her lips. She should have expected Lucilla to seize the opportunity to throw Ned and Clarissa together, especially now that Ned had captured Clarissa's attention in what was, for her cousin, a wholly novel way. And Jack Lester, of course, was an undeniably capable escort. The children, for some mystical reason, had accorded him favoured status; he had only to speak and they tumbled to obey. Sophie grimaced. Descending the last flight, she tried to ease the knot of nervous tension that was tightening within her. The situation, she told herself, could have been worse. Mr. Marston might have spoken first.

Busy with her thoughts, her gaze abstracted, she did not see the young gentleman who emerged from the library.

"Sophie! Just the person! How are you?"

Before she could answer, Sophie was engulfed in a hug which owed more to enthusiasm than art. "Toby!" she gasped, recognizing her assailant. "Watch my hat, you clunch!"

"That wispy thing ain't a *hat,* Sophie." Toby flicked her riding hat, composed of a pheasant's feather and a scrap of velvet, with one finger. "Wouldn't keep the rain off you for a moment."

"As I should hope you are by now aware, Tobias Webb, having attained the years of wisdom, the importance of a modish hat lies not in its ability to protect one from the elements." Sophie's severity was belied by the affectionate twinkle in her eyes. "How was the trip down?"

"Enjoyable enough." Toby assumed a nonchalant air. "Peters and Carmody and I all came down together."

"I see." Sophie hid her smile. "Have you seen your father and mother yet?"

Toby nodded. "Papa told me you were planning to ride this morning with Ned Ascombe and a Mr. Lester. Thought I might join you."

"By all means," Sophie replied, only too glad of another distraction to counteract Jack Lester. "But they should be here with the horses any moment."

"I've already sent around to the stables for mine, so I shouldn't keep you. I'll just change my coat."

As Sophie stood in the hall watching Toby briskly climb the stairs, pausing at the top to greet Clarissa, about to descend, the clop and clash of many hooves on the cobbles beyond the massive oak door heralded the arrival not only of their mounts, but also of Jeremy, Gerald and Amy, who had been keeping watch from a window upstairs.

After whooping in greeting about their eldest brother, who admonished them with mock severity, the tribe descended to whirl about Sophie, eager to be off on this, their first excursion in the Park.

Thus it was that, admitted by a benignly beaming Minton, Jack, with Ned behind, came upon his golden head knee-deep in commotion. However, the expression of resigned calm on Sophie's face assured him she was not about to succumb to the vapours, despite the din.

"Quiet, you vexatious imps!" His firm greeting immediately transformed said imps into angels.

Sophie struggled to keep her lips straight. Jack's eyes lifted to meet hers and she lost the battle, her lips curving in a generous smile. "Good morning, sir. You see us almost ready."

"Almost?" Taking her hand, Jack lifted an eyebrow, then turned to nod to Clarissa.

"My eldest cousin, Toby, has rejoined the family. He's just gone to change." Nodding to Ned, Sophie wondered if it would be possible to tug her fingers free of the warm clasp which held them trapped. Despite her firm intention to remain aloof, her heart, unreliable organ that it was whenever he was near, was accelerating. "Toby's a keen rider and would not wish to miss our outing."

"Naturally not," Jack agreed, his gaze touching the children's eager faces. "Not when we've such an august and intrepid company as shall make all the *ton* stare."

He smiled as he made the statement, which was greeted with hoots from the younger Webbs. Sophie, however, was suddenly visited by a vision of how their cavalcade would appear to others in the Park. With a sudden sinking feeling, she realized that Lucilla, in her usual cryptic manner, had made no mention of the children.

As the children fell to fitting on their hats and gloves and swishing their skirts, Sophie lowered her voice to say, "Indeed, Mr. Lester, I would understand if you feel my aunt was not sufficiently open with you—she did not mention the children, and I dare say you will not care to be seen with such an entourage in the Park."

Jack turned to regard her in genuine surprise. Then he smiled. "If I were a Tulip of the *ton,* I might be concerned. However, such as I am, I feel sure my standing is sufficient to weather being seen with the Webbs, *en famille.* Besides which, my dear, I like your cousins."

Gazing up into his face, and seeing the gentle amusement therein, Sophie could not doubt his sincerity. It eased her mind and brought a calm smile back to her lips.

Which, to Jack's mind, was a perfectly satisfactory recompense for the trouble he could see looming before him.

Then Toby came bounding down the stairs, his enthusiasm only slightly less than that of his younger siblings. Introduced to Jack, he wrung his hand good-naturedly, nodded to Ned with easy familiarity and suggested they be off.

By Jack's side, Sophie was the last to quit the house. Standing at the top of the steps, she beheld a scene of veritable pandemonium. Luckily, her uncle's grooms had come to hold the horses; used to their master's children, the grooms did not blink as the youngsters rowdily mounted. As Jack drew her protectively closer, Sophie quieted her misgivings with the reflection that, once on horseback, she would not have to deal with her apparently inevitable reactions to his nearness. Riding, when all was said and done, should be safe enough.

It was not until they paused beside Dulcima that Sophie realized that there were hurdles, even when riding in London. Hurdles such as gaining her saddle atop the tall mare.

Jack, of course, saw no obstacle before him. He placed his hands about Sophie's slim waist and easily lifted her up.

Gently deposited in her saddle, Sophie tried to hide her blush, vowing to make a special effort, as of today, to stop reacting that way to his touch. Her heart was thudding madly; the tension within her had twisted tight. She felt the warmth of Jack's blue gaze upon her face but refused to meet it. By the time she had settled her skirts, he had swung up to the saddle of his black and the party was ready to depart.

Determined to appear unaffected by his proximity, she forced herself to look up and smile. She watched as Jack brought his sleek black alongside her mare; with the others ranged neatly before them, they brought up the rear of the procession as it clattered, eager but restrained, down Mount Street, towards the leafy precincts of the Park.

Grateful to feel her cheeks cool once more, Sophie kept

her gaze fixed ahead. Jack's black swung his head towards Dulcima's, then snorted and shook his mane, setting his harness jingling. Dulcima calmly trotted on. The black repeated the manoeuvre, this time nudging Dulcima's shoulder. Sophie frowned. Four paces on, as the black turned to her mare again, Dulcima whinnied and tossed her head.

"Mr. Lester." Sophie felt compelled to support her mare's protest. She turned to Jack, gesturing to the black. "Your horse, sir."

Jack's expression turned rueful. He obligingly tightened his reins, leaning forward to pat the black's glossy neck. "Never mind, old boy. Delicately reared ladies are always the hardest to win over. Pretend they don't even see one. I know just how you feel."

For an instant, Sophie's mind went quite blank. Finding her gaze locked with Jack's, she glared at him. Then, with a toss of her head that came perilously close to mimicking her mare, she looked straight ahead, thereby proving Jack's point.

To her immense relief, the gates of the Park appeared ahead. They entered and proceeded down a ride at a leisurely pace, glorying in the sunshine that continued to defy all predictions. About them, the rich smell of warming earth spiced the air, while birds trilled in the branches arching high overhead.

Glancing at Sophie, Jack inwardly smiled. Prey to an unnerving uncertainty, he had not again called to take her driving. But their stroll in the Park had reassured him, even though she had pulled back the instant he had drawn closer. Feminine nerves—that was the problem. He would just have to bide his time, and give her time to grow accustomed to his interest, to become more at ease with him.

So, holding his restless black to a sedate walk, he ambled beside her, his thoughts filled not with the joys of burgeoning spring, but with resigned acceptance of the tales that would no doubt be told in his clubs that night. He consoled himself with the reflection that, as his pursuit of Sophie would keep him in the ballrooms for most of the Season, he would not be spending much time at his clubs.

And if his pursuit of his bride did not keep him sufficiently busy, there was always his self-imposed task of keeping Ned Ascombe from doing himself an injury.

"I dare say the preparations for your coming-out ball must be exercising your imagination, Miss Webb." Jack cut across Ned to put a stop to what, to his experienced eyes, had been all too much like backsliding.

Caught out, reminded of the role he had been instructed it was in his best interests to play, Ned looked guilty.

"Yes, indeed," Clarissa readily replied. "But Mama had taken care of all the details. The theme is to be classical, although personally I would rather have had the Rites of Spring. But Mama held that that has been quite done to death these last years."

Clarissa glanced at Ned.

"I'm sure Mrs. Webb knows what's best" was his verdict.

Sophie bit her lip.

After a moment's blank astonishment, Clarissa stiffened slightly. When no expression of empathetic understanding joined Ned's bare statement, she pointedly looked ahead.

Jack grinned and drew back, sure Ned would not again lapse into his habitually easy relationship with Clarissa. At least, not today.

"Are we allowed to gallop in the Park, sir?" Toby brought his bay hunter up alongside Jack's black.

At twenty, brown-haired and blue-eyed with the same innate elegance that characterized Lucilla, Toby struck Jack as the sort to be up to all the usual larks, yet wise enough to avoid the grief that often overtook his peers. There was a glimmer of wisdom already detectable in his blue-grey eyes.

No doubt, Jack mused, he had inherited his parents' brains. "You and your younger brothers and sister could conceivably do so. However, neither Miss Webb nor Miss Winterton would be wise to attempt the feat."

Toby wrinkled his nose. "The usual stuffy notions?"

Jack nodded. "As you say."

Lifting a brow at Sophie, and seeing her smile, Toby grinned ruefully. "Sorry, Sophie." Then, turning to his younger siblings, he waved his quirt and challenged, "Last to the oak at the other end of the turf gets to tell Mama what happened today!"

His three juniors responded immediately. All four thundered off.

Exchanging an indulgent smile, Jack and Sophie set their horses into a mild canter in their wake. Ned and Clarissa fell in behind. As they broke from the cover of the long ride and slowed, Sophie noticed their presence was attracting considerable interest. She did her best to appear unaware, until she realized that surprise was the predominant emotion on the faces of the gentlemen they passed.

Turning, she lifted a brow at her companion.

Jack smiled. "I fear I'm not noted for escorting boisterous families on jaunts through the Park."

"Oh." Uncertain, Sophie blinked up at him.

"I don't regret it in the least," Jack supplied, his smile somewhat wry. "But, tell me, my dear Miss Winterton, if you had to make the choice, would it be town or country for you?"

"Country," Sophie immediately replied. "Town is pleasant enough, but only…" she paused, putting her head on one side, "as a short period of contrast." After a moment, she shook herself free of her thoughts and urged Dulcima into a trot. "But what of you, sir? Do you spend much time in the country?"

"*Most* of my time." Jack grinned. "And, although you might not credit it, quite willingly. The estates, of course, need constant attention. When my sister left, she bequeathed me a list as long as my arm of all the improvements required." His brow darkening as a subject that, now, was very close to his heart claimed him, Jack continued, "I'm afraid, before Lenore left, I had not paid as much attention as I should have. She kept us together financially, which was no small feat. Consequently, my brothers and I left the decisions on what projects the family could afford to undertake to her. Although she was not to blame in any way, I should have realized that she did not have an extensive grasp of the estate as a whole, but was entirely familiar with all matters pertaining to the Hall itself. Hence, our ancestral home is in very good repair, but, for my money, I would have given some, at least, of the improvements necessary on the estate a higher priority."

Glancing down at Sophie's face, Jack added, "I fully intend to resuscitate the estate. I know what's needed; now it's simply a matter of getting things done."

A steel vice closed about Sophie's heart. She let her lids veil her eyes. Her features frozen in an expression of rapt attention, she inclined her head.

Encouraged, Jack briefly described those improvements he felt most urgent. "I think it has something to do with being the one to inherit the land," he concluded. "I feel an attachment—a responsibility—now that it's virtually mine. I know Harry feels the same about the stud farm, which will one day be his."

Woodenly Sophie nodded, clutching her reins tightly. From her experience of her father's estates, she knew the cost of Jack's dreams. His words settled, a leaden weight about her heart.

Distraction arrived in a most unexpected form. A brusque hail had them drawing rein; turning, they beheld Mr. Marston astride a showy dun trotting quickly towards them. As he approached, Sophie inwardly admitted that Phillip Marston looked his best on horseback; his best, however, had never been sufficient to raise her pulse. Now, with her expectations conditioned by the likes of Jack Lester, she knew it never would.

"Good day, Mr. Marston." Her expression calmly regal, Sophie held out one hand, refusing to embellish the brief ·greeting with any hypocritical phrases.

"My very dear Miss Winterton." Phillip Marston attempted the difficult feat of bowing over her hand, but was forced to release it quickly as his horse jibbed. Frowning, he restrained the restive animal and, with obvious reluctance, nodded at Jack. "Lester."

Jack returned the nod with a perfectly genuine smile. "Marston."

The dun continued to jib and prance.

Phillip Marston did his best to ignore it—and the fact the dun was no match on any level with the even-tempered black Jack Lester rode. He nodded gravely to Ned and Clarissa, then fixed his pale gaze on Sophie. "I thought I'd take the trouble to find a mount and join you, my dear. I have not, as you know, previously had much experience of town, but I felt sure you would feel more easy in the company of one with whom you share a common background."

Inwardly bridling, Sophie refrained from glancing heavenwards and searched for some acceptable response. She was delivered from her unenviable predicament by the arrival of her younger cousins, whooping gleefully, their faces alight with exuberant joy.

Phillip Marston frowned bleakly. "Really, you young barbarians! Is this the way you behave when out from under your parents' eye?"

Their transports abruptly cut short, their joy fading, Jeremy, George and Amy instinctively looked not to Sophie, but to Jack.

He reassured them with a smile. "Nonsense, Marston," he said, his tone equable but distant. "The Park at this hour is a perfectly acceptable venue for the young to let off steam. Later, perhaps, such behaviour would be frowned upon, but now, with mainly young people and families about, there's nothing the least untoward in such high spirits."

The crestfallen trio were miraculously revived. They shot Jack a grateful glance and fell in beside him, as far as they could get from Mr. Marston. For a moment, Sophie allowed herself to envy them, before regretfully banishing the thought.

Phillip Marston received Jack's wisdom with a stiff little bow. His pinched lips and the slant of his brows left little doubt of his feelings. A charged moment passed in which Sophie bludgeoned her brains for some safe topic—not an easy task with Mr. Marston on one side and Jack Lester on the other—before Marston's particular devil prompted him to say: "I dare say, Lester, not being a *family* man, you don't realize the importance of discipline in handling the young."

Jack controlled his countenance admirably, bending a look of blandly polite enquiry on Marston. As Jack had hoped, Phillip Marston continued, airily declaiming, apparently unaware of Sophie's stunned silence.

"Natural enough, of course. After all, discipline's hardly your style, is it? I mean to say," he hurried on, "that doubtless, having little need for such in your own life, it's hard for you to understand that others live by a different code."

"Indeed?" Jack lifted a brow, his expression remote and slightly bored. "I hadn't, I confess, thought my life so very different from that of the rest of my class."

Phillip Marston laughed condescendingly. "Oh, but it is." He waved airily. "Why, I dare say you'd be stunned to know that some of us spend months on our estates, grappling with such matters as tenants and bailiffs and crop rotation." Oblivious to the flags flying in Sophie's cheeks, Marston continued, "Not all of us can spend our lives in London, frittering away our money at the tables, sipping, unrestrained, from the bowl of life's pleasures."

That was far too much for Sophie. *"Mr. Marston!"* She regarded him with icy indignation. "I'm surprised, sir, that you even know of such things as life's pleasures." The words—so uncharacteristically sniping—shocked her, but she had no intention of recalling them. However, it immediately became clear Mr. Marston stood in no danger of being crushed.

He inclined his head, smiling unctuously. "Quite so, my dear. Such pastimes hold no allure for me. However, I am aware that others find them much more to their taste." He lifted his pale gaze to Jack's face. "No doubt, Lester, you find this squiring of innocents not at all to your liking. Playing nursemaid to a pack of brats is hardly your style, after all." Marston leant forward and spoke across Sophie. "I heard Mrs. Webb trap you into this little jaunt. Dare say you'd rather be anywhere but here. However, as I've nothing better to do with my time, I'll be only too happy to take the responsibility off your hands."

Ned and Clarissa had drawn closer; along with Toby, who had silently rejoined the company, they held their breath and looked, slightly stunned, at Jack. Indeed, every eye in the party was fixed upon him.

They all saw his slow smile.

"On the contrary, Marston," Jack drawled. "I believe you're labouring under a misapprehension. Believe me, there's nothing I would rather be doing than squiring this particular party of innocents. In fact," he went on, his expression growing pensive, "I believe if you consider the matter more closely, you'll see that one such as I, to whom the…ah, pleasures of life are well known, is precisely the most suitable escort."

The relief that swept the party, all except Marston, was palpable.

Jack's smile broadened as he met the other man's gaze. "Indeed, Marston, I wouldn't have missed this morning's jaunt for the world."

Confounded, Phillip Marston glanced at Sophie. Her glacial expression awoke the first inklings of understanding in his brain. His hand tightened on his reins.

The dun, having behaved reasonably for all of ten minutes, reacted predictably, jibbing, then twisting, prancing sideways. Marston struggled to subdue the animal, muttering perfectly audible curses beneath his breath.

Sternly quelling her laughter, Sophie grasped the opportunity. "Mr. Marston, I believe you would be wise to return that horse to the stables forthwith. I confess its antics are making me quite nervous." She managed to imbue her tones with perfectly specious feminine fear.

Which left Phillip Marston with little choice. His expression grim, he nodded curtly. He left, heading straight for the gate.

"Phew!" Toby came up beside Sophie, a grin lighting his face. "I wouldn't want to be the stableman when he returns that horse."

The comment drew laughter all round, banishing any lingering restraint. Restored to their usual high spirits, the youngsters were soon off again. By mutual consent, the party ambled slowly in Mr. Marston's wake.

Summoning the children, coercing them into an orderly retreat, then supervising them through the traffic kept Sophie fully occupied. But when they turned the corner into Mount Street and the youngsters drew ahead, she glanced up at her companion. His features were relaxed; he looked every bit as content as he had claimed. "I feel I must apologize for Mr. Marston's behaviour, sir."

Jack looked down at her. "Nonsense, my dear. It was hardly

something you could control. Besides," he continued, his blue gaze holding hers, "I have yet to see you encouraging him."

"Heaven forbid!" Sophie shuddered, then, seeing the calm satisfaction that infused Jack's expression, wished she'd been rather more circumspect. It was, after all, no business of Jack Lester's whom she encouraged. Taking refuge in the banal, she said, "So the balls are starting at last."

With a slow smile, Jack inclined his head. "Indeed. And your cousin's come-out will be one of the first. Your aunt seems set to steal a march on her peers."

Thinking of Lucilla and her careful scheming, Sophie smiled. "As you say. She's quite determined to make the most of this Season."

Clarissa nudged her horse up beside Jack's. "Indeed," she declared, unusually pert. "Mama is quite set on my come-out being an *unenviable crush*."

Sophie exchanged a wry smile with Jack.

Turning to Clarissa, Jack raised a laconic brow. Obviously, Ned had been faithfully adhering to instructions. "Is that so?" Jack asked. "And what do you know of crushes, Miss Webb?"

Clarissa coloured, then waved a dismissive hand. "Sophie told me all about them."

"Ah." Lips quirking, Jack turned back to Sophie as they halted their mounts before the Webbs' steps.

The junior Webbs had already gone in, leaving the grooms with their hands full. Sophie steeled herself and managed to survive the ordeal of being lifted down to the pavement by Jack Lester with commendable composure.

She looked up—and beheld his slow smile.

"Well, my dear?" Jack lifted a brow. "Was it bearable, riding with me?"

Sophie blushed rosily but was determined to give no ground. Lifting her chin, she looked him in the eye. "Indeed, sir. It was most enjoyable."

Jack chuckled. "Good. Because from what I understand, your cousins wish it to be a frequent event."

With an inclination of her head, Sophie indicated her acquiescence.

Her hand in his, Jack looked down at her, his smile a trifle crooked. "Until your aunt's crush, then, Miss Winterton. Rest assured that, despite the sea of humanity that will no doubt be thrown up between us, I will endeavour to win through to your side." With a rakish grin, he bowed over her hand.

And let her go.

With a very correct nod, Sophie escaped up the steps, refusing to give in to her heart and look back.

At the corner of the street, two horsemen sat their mounts, apparently discussing the weather. In actuality, their interest was a great deal more focused.

"Well, that's a relief! It's the older one Lester's got his eye on—fancy that." Hubert, Lord Maltravers, blinked blearily up at his companion. "A hard night followed by an ungodly early start may have taken its toll on my wits," his lordship mused. "But stap me if I can see why."

Captain Terrence Gurnard's lips lifted in a sneer. "Tarnished his image, that's why. The Webbs are a deal too downy to let their chick fly too close to his snare. But obviously the cousin has enough of the ready to satisfy Lester."

"Odd." His lordship frowned. "Thought she had nothing more than the usual. You know what I mean—expectations but no more. Would've thought Lester needed rather more than that."

"Obviously not. The point, thank Heaven, doesn't concern me. As long as he's *not* got his eye on that juicy little plum, he can have the rest of London for all I care. Come, let's get moving. We've seen all we need."

Side by side, they steered their mounts through the streets in the direction of Hubert's lodgings, the slightly rumpled figure of Lord Maltravers slumped in his saddle, the handsome, broad-shouldered guardsman towering over him.

"Y'know, Gurnard, I've been thinking."

"I thought you didn't do that until after noon."

Hubert snorted. "No. I'm serious. This start of yours—sure there isn't a better way? I mean, you could always try the cent per cents—doesn't hurt to ask."

"In this case, I fear it could hurt." Gurnard winced. "A very great deal."

Realization was slow but it eventually broke on Hubert. "Oh," he said. "You're already on their books?"

"Let's just say that one or two moneylenders could scrape an acquaintance."

"Hmm." Hubert grimaced. "That does rather cut down on your options." As they turned into Piccadilly, he ventured, "No chance this last opponent of yours would consider holding your vowels for latter payment?"

Slowly, Terrence Gurnard turned his head and looked his friend in the eye. "My last opponent was Melcham."

Hubert blanched. "Oh," he said. Then, "Ah." Switching his gaze to the traffic, he nodded. "In that case, I quite see your point. Well, then—when's the wedding?"

CHAPTER TEN

HER AUNT, SOPHIE MUSED, was not to be trusted. At least, not when it came to Jack Lester. Although she had expected to see Mr. Lester at her cousin's come-out ball, Sophie had had no inkling that he would feature among the favoured few who had been invited to dine before the event. Not until he walked into the drawing-room, throwing all the other gentlemen into immediate shade.

From her position by the fireplace, a little removed from her aunt, Sophie watched as Jack bowed over Lucilla's hand. His coat was of midnight blue, the same shade as his eyes at night. His smallclothes were ivory, his cravat a minor work of art. His large sapphire glowed amid the folds, fracturing the light. Beyond the heavy gold signet that adorned his right hand, he wore no other ornament, nothing to distract her senses from the strength of his large frame. After exchanging a few words, Lucilla sent him her way.

Stilling an inner quiver, Sophie greeted him with a calm smile. "Good evening, Mr. Lester."

Jack's answering smile lit his eyes. "Miss Winterton." He bowed gracefully over her hand, then, straightening, looked down at her. "Sophie."

Sophie's serene expression did not waver as she drew her gaze from his; she had had practice enough in the past few days in keeping her emotions in check. Seeing Ned, who had followed his mentor into the room, turn from Lucilla to make his way to Clarissa's side, Sophie glanced up at her companion. "Ned has told me how much you have done for him, even to the extent of putting him up. It's really very kind of you."

Having drunk his fill of Sophie's elegance, Jack reluctantly looked out over the room. Tonight, his golden head appeared warm yet remote, priestess-like in a classically styled ivory sheath, draped from one shoulder to fall in long lines to the floor. Forcing himself to focus on his protégé, Jack shrugged. "It's no great thing. The house is more than large enough, and the proximity increases the time we have to... polish his address."

Sophie arched a sceptical brow. "Is that what you term it?"

Jack smiled. "Polish is all Ned needs."

Sophie slanted him a glance. "And that's the secret of gentlemanly success—polish?"

Jack looked down at her. "Oh no, my dear." His gaze grew more intent. "Such as I, with more sophisticated game in sight, often need recourse to...weapons of a different calibre."

Sophie tilted her chin. "Indeed, sir? But I was thanking you for helping Ned—and must also convey all our thanks for your assistance this morn. How we would have coped had you not removed Jeremy, George and Amy from the house, I simply do not know."

Meeting his eyes, Sophie smiled serenely.

Jack smiled back. "As I've told you before, your cousins are the most engaging urchins; playing nursemaid, as Marston had it, is no great undertaking. I trust all came right in the end?"

With Ned in tow, Jack had arrived on the Webbs' doorstep that morning, as he had for the past two, to find the house in the grip of the usual mayhem coincident with a major ball. Knowing neither Sophie nor Clarissa would be free, he and Ned had nevertheless offered to take the youngsters to the Park—a boon to all as, with the house full of caterers, florists and the like, and the servants rushed off their feet, the youthful trio had been proving a severe trial. They had already caused havoc by pulling the bows on the sheaves of flowers the florists had prepared all undone, then been threatened with incarceration when they had discovered the pleasures of skidding across the newly polished ballroom floor.

"Yes, thank Heaven," Sophie replied, watching further arrivals greet her aunt. "I don't know how Aunt Lucilla manages to keep it all straight in her head. But the storm and tempest did eventually abate, leaving order where before there was none."

Jack's grin was wry. "I'm sure your aunt's order is formidable."

Sophie smiled. "I rather suspect the ball tonight ranks as one of her more spectacular undertakings."

"With both your cousin and yourself to launch, it's hardly surprising that she's pulled out all stops."

Sophie blinked, her smile fading slightly. Then, with determined brightness, she inclined her head. "Indeed. And both Clarissa and I are determined she will not be disappointed."

A subtle reminder that she, too, was expected to find a husband. Just as he would have to find a wife. Sophie was all too well aware that, through shared moments, shared laughter and some indefinable attraction, she and Jack Lester had drawn far closer than was common between gentlemen and ladies who remained merely friends. Nevertheless, that was all they could be, and the time was fast approaching when their disparate destinies would prevail. She was steeling herself to face the prospect.

"Sophia, my dear!" Lady Entwhistle bustled up, her silk skirts shushing. "You look positively radiant, my dear—doesn't she, Henry?"

"Set to take the shine out of the younger misses, what?" Lord Entwhistle winked at Sophie, then shook her hand.

"And Mr. Lester, too—how fortunate." Her ladyship presented her hand and looked on with approval as Jack bowed over it. "A pleasure to see you again, sir. I hear Lady Asford-by's in town; have you run into her yet?"

Jack's eyes briefly touched Sophie's. "I have not yet had that pleasure, ma'am."

"A deuced shame about the hunting, what?" Lord Ent-whistle turned to Jack. "Not that you younger men care—just change venues, far as I can see." His lordship cast a genial eye over the room.

"As you say, sir," Jack replied. "I fear there are few foxes to be found in London, so naturally we're forced to shift our sights."

"What's that? Forced? *Hah!*" His lordship was in fine fet-tle. "Why, I've always heard the tastiest game's to be found in the capital."

Sophie struggled to keep her lips straight.

"Really, Henry!" Her ladyship unfurled her fan with an audible click.

"But it's true," protested Lord Entwhistle, not one whit abashed. "Just ask Lester here. Few would know better than he. What say you, m'boy? Don't the streets of London offer richer rewards than the fields of Leicestershire?"

"Actually," Jack replied, his gaze returning to Sophie, "I'm not sure I would agree with you, sir. I must confess I've re-cently discovered unexpected treasure in Leicestershire, after a year in the *ton*'s ballrooms had yielded nothing but dross."

For an instant, Sophie could have sworn the world had stopped turning; for a moment, she basked in the glow that lit Jack Lester's eyes. Then reality returned, and with it aware-ness—of the conjecture in Lord Entwhistle's eyes, the star-tled look on her ladyship's face, and the role she herself had to play. Smoothly, she turned to Lady Entwhistle. "I do hope Mr. Millthorpe has found his feet in London. Will he be here tonight?"

The surprise faded from her ladyship's eyes. "Yes, indeed. Lucilla was kind enough to invite him for the ball. I'm sure he'll attend. He was very much taken with Clarissa, you know." She glanced across the room to where Clarissa was surrounded by a small coterie of young gentlemen. "Mind you, I expect he'll be in good company. As I told your aunt, fully half the young men in town will be prostrating themselves at Clarissa's feet."

Sophie laughed and steered the conversation towards the social events thus far revealed on the *ton*'s horizon. She was somewhat relieved when Jack chipped in with the news of the balloon ascension planned for May, thus distracting Lord Entwhistle, who declaimed at length on the folly of the idea.

His lordship was still declaiming when Minton entered, transcending the impression conveyed by his severe garb to announce in jovially benevolent vein that dinner was served.

Lord and Lady Entwhistle went together to join the exodus. Jack turned to Sophie. "I believe, dear Sophie, that the pleasure of escorting you in falls…to me."

Sophie smiled up at him and calmly surrendered her hand. "That will be most pleasant, sir."

With her hand on his arm, Jack steered her into the shuffling queue.

Laughing chatter greeted them as they strolled into the dining-room. The surface of the table, polished to a mellow glow, reflected light fractured by crystal and deflected by silver. A subtle excitement filled the air; this was, after all, the first of the large gatherings, and those present were the chosen few who would start the ball of the Season rolling. Horatio, genially rotund, took his place at the table's head; Lucilla graced the opposite end, while Clarissa, sparkling in a gown of fairy-like silvered rose silk, sat in the middle on one side. Ned beside her. Jack led Sophie to her place opposite Clarissa, then took the seat on her right.

As she glanced about, taking note of her neighbours, Sophie took comfort from Jack's presence beside her. Despite his apparently ingrained habits, he always drew back whenever she baulked—smoothly, suavely, ineffably rakish, yet a gentleman to his very bones. She now felt confident in his company, convinced he would never press her unduly nor step over that invisible line.

There was, indeed, a certain excitement to be found in his games, and a certain balm in the warmth of his deep blue gaze.

The toast to Clarissa was duly drunk; her cousin blushed prettily while Ned looked on, a slightly stunned expression on his face.

As she resumed her seat, Sophie glanced at Jack. He was watching her; he raised his glass and quietly said, "To your Season, dear Sophie. And to where it will lead."

Inwardly Sophie shivered, but she smiled and inclined her head graciously.

On her left was Mr. Somercote, a distant Webb cousin, a gentleman of independent means whom her uncle had introduced as hailing from Northamptonshire. While obviously at home in the *ton,* Mr. Somercote was reserved almost to the point of rudeness. Sophie applied herself but could tease no more than the barest commonplaces from him.

The lady on Jack's right was a Mrs. Wolthambrook, an elderly widow, another Webb connection. Sophie wondered at the wisdom of her aunt's placement, but by the end of the first course, her confidence in Lucilla had been restored. The old lady had a wry sense of humour which Jack, in typical vein, recognized and played to. Sophie found herself drawn into a lively discussion, Mrs. Wolthambrook, Jack and herself forming a nexus of conversation which served to disguise the shortcomings of others in the vicinity.

It was almost a surprise to find the dessert course over.

With a rustle of silk skirts, Lucilla rose and issued a charming directive sending them all to the ballroom.

While ascending the stairs on Jack's arm, Sophie noticed the glimmer of a frown in Lady Entwhistle's sharp eyes. It was, Sophie decided, hardly to be wondered at: installing Jack Lester as her partner at dinner had clearly declared her aunt's hand. Lucilla was playing Cupid. It was inconceivable that, after nearly three weeks in the capital, her aunt was not *au fait* concerning Jack Lester's state. But Lucilla was not one to follow the conventions in matters of the heart; she had married Horatio Webb when he was far less well-to-do than at present, apparently without a qualm. Sophie's own mother, too, had married for love. It was, in fact, something of a family trait.

Unfortunately, Sophie thought, casting a fleeting glance at Jack's darkly handsome profile, it was not one she was destined to follow. Hiding her bruised heart behind a serene smile, she crossed the threshold of the ballroom.

Under the soft flare of candlelight cast by three huge chandeliers, the efforts of the florists and decorators looked even better than by day. The tops of the smooth columns supporting the delicately domed ceiling had been garnished with sprays of white and yellow roses, long golden ribbons swirling down around the columns. The minstrels' gallery above the end of the room was similarly festooned with white, yellow and green, trimmed with gold. Tall iron pedestals supporting ironwork cones overflowing with the same flowers filled the corners of the room and stood spaced every few yards along the long mirrored wall, with chaises and chairs set between. The opposite wall contained long windows giving onto the terrace; some were ajar, letting in the evening breeze.

The guests dutifully oohed and aahed, many ladies taking special note of the unusual use of ironwork.

Jack's blue eyes glinted down at her. "As I said, my dear, your aunt's efforts are indeed formidable."

Sophie smiled, but her heart was not in it; it felt as if her evening was ending when, with a graceful bow, Jack surrendered her to her duty on the receiving line.

He had bespoken a waltz, she reminded herself, giving her emotions a mental shake. Conjuring up a bright smile, she dutifully greeted the arrivals, taking due note of those her aunt introduced with a certain subtle emphasis. Lucilla might be encouraging Jack Lester, but it was clear she was equally intent on giving Sophie a range of suitable gentlemen from which to make her choice.

Which was just as well, Sophie decided. Tonight was the start of her Season proper; she should make a real start on her hunt for a husband. There was no sense in putting off the inevitable. And it would no doubt be wise to make it abundantly plain that she was not infected with Lucilla's ideals. She could not marry Jack Lester, for he needed more money than she would bring. Embarking on her search for a husband would clarify their relationship, making it plain to such avid watchers as Lady Entwhistle and Lady Matcham that there was nothing to fear in her friendship with Jack.

Stifling a sigh, Sophie pinned on a smile as her aunt turned to greet the latest in the long line of guests.

"Ah, Mr. Marston," Lucilla purred. "I'm so glad you could come."

Sophie swallowed a most unladylike curse. She waited, trapped in line, as Mr. Marston greeted Clarissa with chilly civility, his glance austerely dismissing the enchanting picture her cousin made.

Then his gaze reached her—and Sophie privately resolved to send a special thank-you to Madame Jorge. Mr. Marston's distant civility turned to frigid disapproval as he took in her bare shoulders and the expanse of ivory skin exposed by the low, slanting neckline of her gown.

Sophie smiled sunnily. "Good evening, sir. I trust you are well."

Mr. Marston bowed. "I…" He drew himself up, his lips pinched. "I will look to have a few words with you later, Miss Winterton."

Sophie tried her best to look delighted at the prospect.

"Lady Colethorpe—my niece, Sophia Winterton."

With a certain relief, Sophie turned to her aunt's next guest and put Mr. Marston very firmly from her mind.

Down in the ballroom, Jack wended his way through the throng, stopping here and there to chat with old acquaintances, constantly hailed as the *ton,* one and all, found their way to the Webbs' ball. Percy, of course, was there. He greeted Jack with something akin to relief.

"Held up with m'father," Percy explained. "He was having one of his turns—convinced he was going to die. All rubbish, of course. Sound as a horse." Smoothing down his new violet silk waistcoat, Percy cast a knowledgeable eye over Jack's elegance, innate, as he well knew—and sighed. "But what's been going on here, then?" he asked, raising his quizzing glass to look about him. "Seems as if every squire and his dog have already come to town."

"That's about the sum of it," Jack confirmed. "I just met Carmody and Harrison. The whole boiling's in residence already, and raring to get started. I suspect that's what's behind the eagerness tonight. Lucilla Webb's gauged it to a nicety."

"Hmm. Mentioned the Webbs to m'father. Very knowing, he is. He had a word for Mrs. Webb."

"Oh?" Jack looked his question.

"Dangerous," Percy offered.

Jack's lips twitched. "That much, I know. To my cost, what's more. Nevertheless, unless I'm greatly mistaken, the lady approves of yours truly. And, dangerous or not, I fear I'm committed to further acquaintance."

Percy blinked owlishly. "So you're serious, then?"

"Having found my golden head, I'm not about to let her go."

"Ah, well." Percy shrugged. "Leave you to it, then. Where'd you say Harrison was?"

After sending Percy on his way, Jack looked over the heads, curled and pomaded, and discovered that Sophie and her family had quit the doorway to mingle with their guests. He located Sophie on the other side of the room, surrounded by a small group of gentlemen. Eminently eligible gentlemen, he realized, as he mentally named each one. Jack felt his possessive instincts stir. Immediately, he clamped a lid on them. He had already claimed a waltz and the right to take Sophie to supper; Lucilla would frown on any attempt to claim more.

With an effort, Jack forced himself to relax his clenched jaw. To ease the strain on his temper, he shifted his gaze to Clarissa, a little way along the wall. Sophie's cousin was glowing, radiating happiness. As well she might, Jack thought, as he viewed her not inconsiderable court. Puppies all, but Clarissa was only seventeen. She was unquestionably beautiful and, to her and her mother's credit, blissfully free of the silly affectations that often marred others of her calibre. Whether she was as talented as her mother, Jack had no notion—he had seen no evidence of it yet.

Seeing Ned holding fast to his place by Clarissa's side despite all attempts to dislodge him, Jack grinned. As long as Ned circulated when the dancing began, there was no harm in his present occupation. His protégé was maintaining a coolly distant expression, which had made Clarissa glance up at him, slightly puzzled, more than once. Ned was learning fast, and putting his new-found knowledge to good use.

Making a mental note to drop a word of warning in Ned's

ear, to the effect that any female descended from Lucilla Webb should be treated with due caution, Jack allowed his mind to return to its preoccupation.

Was Sophie like her aunt, capable of manipulation on a grand scale? Jack shook aside the silly notion. His Sophie was no schemer—he would stake his life on that. To him, she was open, straightforward, all but transparent. As he watched her smile brightly up at the Marquess of Huntly, Jack's satisfied expression faded. Abruptly executing a neat about-face, he strolled deeper into the crowd.

The first waltz was duly announced, and Clarissa, blushing delicately, went down the floor with her father, a surprisingly graceful dancer. At the conclusion of the measure, Horatio beamed down at her. "Well, my dear. You're officially out now. Are you pleased?"

Clarissa smiled brilliantly. "Indeed, yes, Papa," she said, and meant it.

The crowd parted and she looked ahead. To see Ned leading another young lady from the floor. Clarissa's smile faded.

Horatio noticed. "I had better return you to your court, my dear." Blandly, he added, "But do spare a thought for your old father. Don't line up too many suitors for your hand."

Apparently unaware of Clarissa's startled glance, Horatio guided her back to her circle, then, with a blithely paternal pat on her hand, left her to them.

"I say, Miss Webb." Lord Swindon was greatly smitten. "You waltz divinely. You must have been practising incessantly up in Leicestershire."

"May I get you a glass of lemonade, Miss Webb? Thirsty work, dancing." This from Lord Thurstow, a genial red-haired gentleman whose girth explained his conjecture.

But the most frightening comment came from Mr. Marley, a young sprig who considered himself a budding poet. "An ode...I feel an ode burgeoning in my brain. To your incomparable grace, and the effect it has on your poor followers who have to watch you take the floor in another's arms. *Argh!*"

Clarissa eyed the flushed young man in alarm. Gracious, were they all so unutterably silly?

As the evening wore on, she decided that they were. This was not what she had come to London to find. Being mooned over by gentlemen she classed as barely older than Jeremy and George was hardly the stuff of her dreams. Stuck with her court, surrounded on all sides, Clarissa met their sallies with guileless smiles, while inwardly she considered her options.

When Ned reappeared and rescued her, leading her into the set forming for a country dance, the truth dawned. Smiling up at him, Clarissa shyly said, "It's such a relief to dance with someone I know."

Mindful of his instructions, Ned merely raised a brow. "Is it?" Then he smiled, a touch of condescension in his manner. "Don't worry, you'll soon get used to all the attention."

Stunned, Clarissa stared at him.

"Not a bad ball, this," Ned cheerily remarked. "Your mother must be pleased at the turnout. Don't think I've seen so many young ladies all at once before."

It was, perhaps, as well for Ned that the dance separated them at that point. When they came together again, Clarissa, her nose in the air, treated him to a frosty glance. "As you say," she said, "I'm sure I'll learn how to respond suitably to all the compliments the gentlemen seem so intent on pressing on me. I must ask Mama how best to encourage them."

Again the dance averted catastrophe. By the time the music finally died, Ned, chilly and remote, led Clarissa, equally distant and frigid, back to her circle. After perfunctorily bowing over her hand, Ned quit the vicinity, leaving Clarissa to deal with her importunate followers, her cheeks flushed, a dangerous glint in her large eyes.

A little distance away, Sophie had started to compile a

list of potential suitors. The task was not difficult, for they promptly presented themselves before her, all but declaring their interest. The basis for their attraction had her mystified until Lord Annerby confessed, "The young misses are not really my style." When the movements of the quadrille brought them together again, he admitted, "Been hoping a lady like you would hove on my horizon. Not just in the common way, and not likely to giggle in a man's ear, if you take my meaning."

After that, Sophie paid a little more attention to her would-be swains, and discovered that many were, indeed, like his lordship: gentlemen who had been waiting for a lady such as she, not in the first flush of youth but yet young, presentable and altogether acceptable, to appear and walk up the aisle with them. With their reasons explained, she turned her attention to their attributes.

"I understand your estates are in Northamptonshire, Mr. Somercote. I hail from that county myself."

"Do you?" As they glided through the steps of the cotillion, Mr. Somercote made a visible effort to produce his next statement. "Somercote Hall lies just beyond the village of Somercote in the northwesternmost corner of the county."

Sophie nodded and smiled encouragingly, but apparently that was the full extent of Mr. Somercot's loquacity. As they returned through the crowd to where her admirers were waiting, she mentally crossed his name off her list.

The Marquess of Huntly was her next partner. "Tell me, Miss Winterton, do you enjoy the amenities of London?"

"I do indeed, my lord," Sophie replied. The marquess was Lord Percy's elder brother and, despite his bluff appearance and a tendency to stoutness, was unquestionably eligible.

"I've heard that you ride in the Park. Mayhap we'll meet one fine morning."

"Perhaps," Sophie returned, her smile noncommittal.

As they left the floor, Sophie decided the marquess could remain on her list for the present. Perhaps a meeting in the Park, with her younger cousins in tow, would be useful? She was pondering the point when a deep voice cut across her thoughts.

"I believe our waltz is next, Miss Winterton." Jack nodded to the marquess. "Huntly."

"Lester." The marquess returned his nod. "Seen Percy about?"

"He was chatting with Harrison earlier in the evening."

"Suppose I should go and have a word with him. M'brother, you know," the marquess confided to Sophie. "M'father's been at death's door—should see how he is. If you'll excuse me, m'dear?"

Even as she stared at Lord Huntly's retreating back, Sophie's mental pencil was scrubbing out his name. Such callousness was appalling.

Seeing her shocked expression, Jack abruptly shut his lips on the explanation he had been about to make. He did not consider Huntly a rival—but why make a whip for his own back? Appropriating Sophie's hand, he laid it on his sleeve. "Perhaps we could stroll about the room until the waltz commences?"

Sophie blinked, then frowned. "I really should return to my aunt."

His own frown hidden behind an urbane smile, Jack inclined his head and dutifully led her to where her court was waiting.

An unwise move. He was not impressed by the small crowd of eligibles who apparently could find nothing better to do at the first major ball of the Season than congregate about his Sophie. His temper was not improved by having to listen to them vie to heap accolades upon their compliments. For their part, they ignored him, secure in the knowledge that Sophie's expectations were insufficient to permit him to woo her. The thought made Jack smile inwardly. The smile turned to a suppressed growl when he heard Sophie say, "I do indeed enjoy the opera, Lord Annerby."

She then smiled serenely at his lordship.

"I'll be sure to let you know when the season begins, my dear Miss Winterton." Lord Annerby all but gloated.

Jack gritted his teeth. He had avoided the opera for years— a fact that owed nothing to the performances but rather more to those performing. To his immense relief, the strains of the waltz heralded his salvation. "Miss Winterton?"

Surprised, Sophie blinked up at him even as she put her hand in his. His fingers closed tightly about hers. His words had sounded like a command. An inkling of a difficulty she had not previously considered awoke in Sophie's brain.

Without further speech, Jack led Sophie to the door, drawing her into his arms with an arrogance that bespoke his mind far too well. He knew it, but did not care. The relief as she settled into his arms was balm to his lacerated feelings.

As they joined the swirling crowd on the floor, Jack considered closing his eyes. He would wager he could waltz round any ballroom blindfolded, so accustomed was he to the exercise. And with his eyes closed, his senses would be free to concentrate solely on Sophie—on the soft warmth of her, on how well she fitted in his arms, on the subtle caress of her silk-encased thighs against his.

Stifling a sigh, he kept his eyes open.

"Are you enjoying the ball, Mr. Lester?"

Sophie's calm and rather distant comment drew Jack's eyes from contemplation of her curls. He considered her question, simultaneously considering her invitingly full lips. "I'm enjoying this waltz," he replied.

Raising his eyes to hers, Jack watched a frown form in the sky-blue orbs. Puzzled, he continued, "But when are you going to call me Jack? I've been calling you Sophie for weeks."

He had never before seen a lady blush and frown simultaneously.

"I know," Sophie admitted, forcing herself to throw him a disapproving glance. "And you know you should not. It's not at all acceptable."

Jack simply smiled.

Sophie shot him an exasperated glance, then transferred her gaze to the safe space above his shoulder. As always, being in his arms had a distinctly unnerving affect on her. A fluttery, shivery awareness had her in its grip; breathless excitement threatened her wits. His strength reached out and enfolded her, seductively beckoning, enticing her mind to dwell on prospects she could not even dream of without blushing.

She blushed now, and was thankful to hear the closing bars of the waltz.

Jack saw her blush but was far too wise to comment. Instead, he smoothly escorted her into supper, adroitly snaffling a plate of delicacies and managing to install plate, glasses of champagne and Sophie at a small table tucked away near the conservatory.

He had reckoned without her court. They came swarming about, sipping champagne and, to Jack's mind, making thorough nuisances of themselves. He bore it stoically, repeatedly reminding himself that Lucilla would not consider the first major ball of the Season a suitable venue for him to declare his intentions. When the light meal was over, he insisted on escorting Sophie all the way back to her aunt's side.

The look he bent on Lucilla made her hide a grin.

With Sophie and Clarissa both claimed for the next dance, Lucilla turned her large eyes on Jack. "I must say, Mr. Lester, that you're doing a very good job on Ned."

Somewhat stiffly, Jack inclined his head. "I'm glad the transformation meets with your approval, ma'am."

"Indeed. I'm most grateful. *Immensely* grateful."

Seeing Lady Entwhistle fast approaching, clearly intent on having a word in Lucilla's ear, Jack bowed briefly and drifted into the crowd. As he passed the dancers, he heard a silvery laugh. Glancing up, he saw Sophie, smiling brightly up at Lord Ainsley, a handsome and very rich peer.

Muting his growl, Jack swung into an alcove. What numbskull had invented the practice of wooing? Lucilla's comment, which he felt confident in interpreting as open encouragement, was welcome enough. However, the last thing his passions needed right now was further encouragement, particularly when the object of said passions was behaving in a manner designed to enflame them.

Suppressing his curses, he set himself to endure. He could have left, but the night was yet young. Besides, he was not sufficiently sure of Ned to leave his protégé unsupported. At the thought, Jack drew his gaze from Sophie's bright curls and scanned the dancers for Clarissa.

Predictably, Sophie's cousin was smiling up at an elegant youth as she went down the floor in the dance. Jack silently harrumphed, then switched his gaze back to Sophie. Clarissa was clearly absorbed with her partner.

In so thinking, Jack erred.

Although Clarissa smiled and nodded at Mr. Pommeroy's stilted conversation, her attention was far removed from that blameless young gentleman. From the corner of her eye, she could see Ned dancing with Miss Ellis in the next set. The sight filled Clarissa with a sort of quiet fury she had never before experienced. Regardless of its import, it was quite clearly time to refocus Ned's attention on that which had brought him to town.

Her eyes narrowing, Clarissa herself refocused—on Mr.

Pommeroy. She grimaced. Startled, Mr. Pommeroy stumbled and almost fell. Guiltily, for she had not meant to grimace openly, Clarissa applied herself to soothing her partner's ruffled feathers while looking about her for inspiration.

Her court, unfortunately, had little to offer. They were so young; not even in her wildest dreams could she cast them in the role she was rapidly becoming convinced she needed filled. Back amongst them, responding to their quips with but half her mind, Clarissa grimly watched as Ned joined the crowd about two sisters also making their come-out this year. Inwardly sniffing, Clarissa shifted her gaze—and saw Toby coming towards her, a positive Adonis in tow.

"Ah, Clarissa?" Toby came to an uncertain halt before his sister. "Might I make known to you Captain Gurnard? He's with the Guards." Toby was unsure how his sister would react, but the captain had been keen to gain a personal introduction, something Toby could see no harm in.

Clarissa's wide eyes took in every detail of the tall, broad-shouldered figure bowing before her. The captain was clad in scarlet regimentals; his tightly curled hair gleamed like fool's gold in the candlelight. As he straightened, Clarissa caught the hard gleam in his eyes and the cynical tilt of his mouth before unctuous gratification overlaid them.

Clarissa smiled brilliantly and held out her hand. "How do you do, Captain? Have you been with the Guards long?"

Blinking, Toby inwardly shrugged and took himself off.

Dazzled, Captain Gurnard saw nothing beyond Clarissa's guileless china-blue eyes and her delicately curved lips. He could only conclude that Fate had taken pity on him. With a consciously charming smile, he reluctantly released Clarissa's hand. "I've been with my regiment for some years, my dear."

"Some years?" Clarissa's expression was all innocent bewilderment. "But—" She broke off and shyly put one hand to her lips. "Indeed," she whispered, half-confidingly, "I had not thought you so old as all that, Captain."

Gurnard laughed easily. "Indeed, Miss Webb. I greatly fear I must admit to being quite in my dotage compared with such a sweet child as yourself." His expression sobered. "In truth," he added, his voice low, "I fear I cannot compete with these young pups that surround you. The blithe and easy words of youth have long ago left me."

Ignoring the rising hackles of said pups, Clarissa smiled sweetly and leaned towards the captain to say, "Indeed, sir, I find a little of such blithe and easy words is more than a surfeit. Honest words are always more acceptable to the hearer."

The smile on Captain Gurnard's face grew. "Perhaps, my dear, in order to hear such honest words, you would consent to stroll the room with me? Just until the next dance begins?"

Plastering a suitably ingenuous smile on her lips, Clarissa nodded with apparent delight. Rising, she placed her fingertips on the captain's scarlet sleeve.

As he led her into the crowd, Captain Gurnard could not restrain the smugness of his smile. He would have been supremely disconcerted had he known that Clarissa's inner smile outdid his.

Sophie, meanwhile, had run into a problem, an obstacle to her endeavours. Large, lean and somehow oddly menacing, Jack had left his retreat, where he had been propping up the wall, to gravitate to her side, a hungry predator lured, she suspected, by the smiles she bestowed on the gentlemen about her.

Under her subtle encouragement, her potential suitors preened.

Jack looked supremely bored. Having by dint of superior experience won through to her side, he towered over her, his expression rigidly controlled, his eyes a chilly blue.

Sophie felt distinctly irate. He was intimidating her suitors.

She did not *like* her current course, but it was the only one open to her, a fact she felt Jack should acknowledge, rather than get on his high ropes because… Well, the only conclusion she *could* reach was that he was jealous of the attention she was paying the other men.

But it was from among *them* she would have to chose a husband, and she felt increasingly annoyed when Jack continued to make her task more difficult. When Sir Stuart Mablethorpe, a distinguished scholar, met Jack's gaze and promptly forgot whatever lengthy peroration he had been about to utter, Sophie shot her nemesis a frosty glance.

Jack met it with bland imperturbability.

Thoroughly incensed, Sophie was only too ready to smile at Lord Ruthven, a gentleman she suspected had much in common with Jack Lester, in all respects bar one. Lord Ruthven did not need a wealthy bride.

One of Lord Ruthven's dark brows rose fractionally. "Perhaps, Miss Winterton," he said as he straightened from his bow, "you might care to stroll the room?" His gaze flicked to Jack, then returned to Sophie's face.

Ignoring the glint in Ruthven's eyes, Sophie replied, "Indeed, sir. I'm becoming quite fatigued standing here."

Ruthven's lips twitched. "No doubt. Permit me to offer you an escape, my dear." Thus saying, he offered her his arm.

With determined serenity, Sophie placed her hand on his lordship's sleeve, refusing to acknowledge the charged silence beside her. She was too wise to even glance at Jack as, with Ruthven, she left his side.

Which was just as well. Only when he was sure his emotions were once more under control did Jack allow so much as a muscle to move. And by then, Sophie and Ruthven were halfway down the room. His expression stony, Jack considered the possibilities; only the glint in his eyes betrayed his mood. Then, with his usual languid air, he strolled into the crowd, his course set for a collision with his golden head.

By the time she reached the end of the room, Sophie had realized that Ruthven's green eyes saw rather more than most. All the way down the room, he had subtly twitted her on her keeper. She suspected, however, that his lordship's indolent interest was more excited by the prospect of tweaking Jack's nose than by her own inherent attractions. Which was both comforting and a trifle worrying.

Together, she and Lord Ruthven paused beneath the minstrels' gallery and turned to survey the room.

"Ah, there you are, Ruthven." Jack materialized out of the crowd. He smiled easily at his lordship. "I just saw Lady Orkney by the stairs. She was asking after you."

Sophie glanced round in time to see an expression compounded of chagrin and suspicion flit across his lordship's handsome face. "Indeed?" One brow elevated, Ruthven regarded Jack sceptically.

Jack's smile grew. "Just so. Quite insistent on speaking with you. You know how she is."

Lord Ruthven grimaced. "As you say." Turning to Sophie, Ruthven said, "I fear I must ask you to excuse me, Miss Winterton. My aunt can become quite hysterical if denied." Again one of his lordship's brows rose, this time in resignation. "I dare say Lester will be only too happy to escort you about." With a wry smile, he bowed gracefully over her hand and departed.

Sophie eyed his retreating back through narrowed eyes. She had not seriously considered Ruthven as a suitor but she would certainly not consider a man who aggravated a lady's position, then deserted her, leaving her to face the consequences alone.

As Jack's fingers closed about her hand, she glanced up at

his face. His impassive expression didn't fool her for a moment. Then he looked down at her, his eyes hard and very blue.

"Come with me, Miss Winterton." Her hand trapped on his sleeve, Jack headed towards the windows leading onto the terrace.

Sophie dug in her heels. "I have no intention of going anywhere private with you, Mr. Lester."

"Jack." The single syllable left Sophie in no doubt of his mood. "And if you would rather air our differences in public…" he shrugged. "…who am I to deny a lady?"

Looking up into his eyes, and seeing, as she had twice before, the dark brooding presence that lurked behind them, Sophie felt her throat constrict. But her own temper was not far behind his—he was behaving like a dog in a manger. "Very well, *Mr. Lester,*" she replied, holding his gaze. "But not on the terrace." From the corner of her eye, Sophie could see the rippling curtains that sealed off the music room, built out at the end of the ballroom under the minstrels' gallery. Half-concealed as it was by the gallery above and a row of iron-work urns, it was doubtful anyone else had thought to use the room. They could be private there while still remaining in the ballroom. Her lips firming, Sophie nodded to the curtain. "This way."

Jack followed her into the shadows beneath the gallery, then held back the curtain as she slipped through. He followed her. The heavy curtain fell to, deadening the noise from the ballroom. Candelabra shed ample light about the room, casting a mellow glow on the polished surfaces of the pianoforte and harpsichord. It was a comfortable little nook furnished with well-stuffed chaises and two armchairs. Sophie ignored its amenities and strode to the middle of the Aubusson rug in the centre of the floor.

Chin high, she swung to face Jack. "Now, Mr. Lester. Perhaps we may speak plainly."

"Precisely my thinking," Jack replied, strolling forward until he stood directly before her, no more than a foot away.

Mentally cursing, Sophie had to lift her head higher to meet his eyes.

"Perhaps," Jack suggested, "we could start with what, precisely, you think to achieve with all the gentlemen you've been so busily collecting?"

"A most pertinent point," Sophie agreed. She took a moment to marshall her thoughts, then began, her tone calm and quietly determined. "As I believe I told you, my first Season, four years ago, was cut very short."

Jack nodded curtly.

"As you also know, not only my aunt, but all my mother's friends are very keen…" Sophie paused, then amended, "Positively *determined* that I should wed. Indeed—" she met Jack's gaze challengingly "—I can see no other alternative."

A muscle shifted in Jack's jaw. "Quite."

"Thus," Sophie continued, "I must set about…er, gathering suitable suitors." She frowned slightly. Put like that, it sounded decidedly cold.

Jack frowned too. "Why?"

Sophie blinked. "I beg your pardon?"

Jack gritted his teeth and hung on to his temper. "Why do you need a whole *pack* of eligibles? Won't one do?"

Sophie frowned again, but this time at him. "Of course not," she answered, irritated by what could only be deliberate obtuseness. She drew herself up, her own eyes glittering. "I refuse to marry a man who does not have at least *some* of the attributes I consider appropriate."

Jack's frown intensified. "What attributes?"

"Attributes such as having estates in the country and a willingness to spend most of the year there. And being fond of children." Sophie blushed and hurried on, "And who can… can…well, who likes riding and…"

"Who can waltz you off your feet?" Jack's expression relaxed.

Sophie shot him a wary glance and saw the taunting gleam in his eye. She put up her chin. "There is a whole *host* of attributes I consider necessary in the gentleman I would wish to marry."

Jack nodded. "Nevertheless, coming to appreciate the attributes of the gentleman you're going to marry does not, for my money, necessitate gathering a small crowd with which to compare him."

"But *of course* it does!" Sophie glared. "How *do* you imagine I'm going to know that the one I accept is the right one if I do not—" she gestured with one hand "—look over the field?" Her tone was decidedly belligerent.

Jack frowned, recalling Lucilla's words. Did Sophie really need to compare him with others to be sure?

"And how," Sophie demanded, "am I supposed to do *that,* other than by talking and dancing with them?"

Jack's lips compressed into a thin line.

Sophie nodded. "Precisely. And I have to say," she continued, her nose in the air, "that I consider it most unfair of you to get in my way."

A moment's silence followed.

"Sophie," Jack growled, his voice very low, his eyes fixed on Sophie's face. "Believe me when I say that I have no intention *whatever* of letting you loose amongst the *ton*'s bachelors."

Sophie very nearly stamped her foot. Dragging in a portentous breath, she fixed him with a steely glare. "You are behaving *outrageously!* You do understand that I must marry, do you not?"

"Yes. But—"

"And that I must therefore choose between whatever suitors I may have?"

Jack's expression darkened. "Yes. But—"

"Well, then—with all your remarkable experience, perhaps you'd like to tell me *how* I'm to learn enough about each of them to discover which one will make the best husband?"

Jack's eyes narrowed. "It's very easy."

"Indeed?" Sophie's brows flew. "How?"

Jack focused on her lips, lushly full and all but pouting. "You should marry the man who loves you the most."

"I see," Sophie said, her temper still in alt. "And *how,* pray tell, am I supposed to identify him?" Her tone stated very clearly that she expected no sensible answer.

Very slowly, Jack's lips curved. His eyes lifted to Sophie's. "Like this," he said. Bending his head, he touched his lips to hers.

Sophie shivered, then went quite still. Her lids lowered, then shut as a wave of sweet longing swept through her. His lips were warm, smooth and firm against the softness of hers. His fingers found hers and laced through them; her fingers curled about his, clinging as if to a lifeline. She knew she should draw back, but made no move to do so, held, trapped, not by his desire, but her own. The realization made her tremble; his hands left hers to gently frame her face, holding her still as his lips teased and taunted, soothed and sipped.

Another wave of longing swept through her, keener, sweeter, more urgent. Sophie felt her senses start to slide into some blissful vale; she raised her hands and gripped his lapels as she leant into the kiss, offering her lips, seeking his.

Jack shuddered as his passions surged. Ruthlessly he quelled them, refusing to rupture the magic of the moment by allowing them free rein. Sophie's lips were warm and inviting, as sweet as nectar, just as he had imagined they would be. She drew nearer, her breasts brushing his chest. Her lips softened under his, she shivered delicately—and he knew he had been right from the start. She was his.

He felt his passions swell, possessively triumphant; he stood firm against their prompting, even though his arms ached to hold her. Unable to completely resist the beguiling temptation of her lips, he allowed the kiss to deepen by imperceptible degrees, until he had to struggle to shackle the need to taste her passionate sweetness.

Reluctantly he drew back, bringing the kiss to an end, his breathing sounding harsh in his ears. He forced his hands from her face, willing them to his sides.

Slowly Sophie's eyes opened. Her wise, starry gaze searched his face.

Bemused, bewildered, Sophie eased her grip on his lapels and lowered her hands. But she did not step back. She stared up at him and struggled to understand. She was teetering on the brink of some abyss; her senses pushed her on, urging her into his arms. Dimly she wondered what magic it was that could so overset her reason.

She wanted him to kiss her again. She needed to feel his arms close about her—even though she knew it would only further complicate an already difficult situation.

Jack read her desire in her eyes, in the parting of her full lips. He tensed against his instincts, against the building urge to sweep her into his arms.

Sophie saw the dark prowling beast that raged, caged, behind his eyes. And suddenly she understood. She caught her breath, fighting the excitement the welled within her, an unknown, never-before-experienced longing to meet his passion with her own. To fling herself into the dark depths of his gaze.

Jack saw the spark that lit her eyes, the glow that softened her face. The sight shredded his will. His control wavered.

The curtain cutting off the ballroom lifted and the noise of the ball rushed in.

As one, Sophie and Jack turned to see Phillip Marston

holding the curtain back. His expression could only be described as severely disapproving.

"There you are, Miss Winterton. Permit me to escort you back to your aunt."

Sophie did not move. She drew in a breath, then slanted a glance at Jack. He met it, his expression arrogantly distant. Sophie held her breath; she thought she saw one brow lift slightly. Then, to her relief, he offered her his arm.

"You're mistaken, Marston; Miss Winterton needs no other escort than mine."

A delicious little thrill coursed down Sophie's spine; sternly, she suppressed the sensation and placed her hand on Jack's sleeve.

"Miss Winterton was overcome by the heat in the ballroom," Jack glibly explained. "We retired here to allow her to recover." He glanced down at Sophie's slightly flushed cheeks. "If you're feeling up to it, my dear, I'll take you back to your circle."

But not willingly, said his eyes. Sophie ignored the message and graciously inclined her head. "Thank you, sir." At least he wasn't abandoning her to Mr. Marston.

Jack allowed Marston to hold back the curtain as they emerged into the cacophony of the ball, now in full swing.

Sophie held her head high as they slowly wended their way through the crowd. Phillip Marston kept close by her other side.

Jack bided his time until Sophie's little group of would-be suitors, vaguely at a loss having misplaced their focus, loomed large before them. Then he adroitly lifted Sophie's hand from his sleeve and, stepping behind her, interposed himself between her and Phillip Marston. "We have not yet finished our discussion, Sophie."

His words were muted as he raised her hand.

Sophie, her expression once more calm and remote, lifted

her chin. "Indeed, sir, I urge you to believe that we have had all the discussion we are ever likely to have on that particular topic."

Jack's expression remained impassive but his eyes held hers. Very deliberately, he lifted her hand and, turning it, pressed a brief kiss to her palm. "I'll speak with you later."

Sophie snatched her hand back, grateful that his bulk shielded them from almost everyone. She opened her mouth to protest—only to find him bowing gracefully. The next thing she knew, she was surrounded on all sides by gentlemen trying to claim her attention. By the time she had smoothed over her absence, Jack had disappeared.

But he hadn't left.

From an alcove by the steps, shielded by a potted palm, Jack kept a brooding watch over his golden head until the last note had sounded and the last of her would-be suitors had been dismissed.

CHAPTER ELEVEN

WITHIN TWENTY-FOUR HOURS, Jack had come to the conclusion that Fate had decided to live up to her reputation. He had fully intended to pursue his discussion with Sophie, rudely interrupted by Phillip Marston, the very next morning. Fickle Fate gave him no chance.

True, they went riding as usual, a mere ball being insufficient to dampen the Webbs' equestrian spirits. The children, however, prompted, Jack had no doubt, by Sophie, hung about him, bombarding him with questions about the projected balloon ascension. When Percy hove in sight, Jack ruthlessly fobbed the children off on his friend, who, by pure chance, was an amateur enthusiast. But by that time, the gentlemen who had discovered Sophie and Clarissa the night before had caught up with them.

Jack spent the rest of the ride po-faced by Sophie's side.

And there was worse to come.

As Jack had predicted, Clarissa Webb's come-out ball became the de facto beginning of the Season. It had been voted an horrendous crush by all; every hostess with any claim to fame rushed to lay her own entertainments before the *ton*. The days and evenings became an orgy of Venetian breakfasts, alfresco luncheons, afternoon teas and formal dinners, all crowned by a succession of balls, routs, drums and soirées. And beneath the frenzy ran the underlying aim of fostering suitable alliances—an aim with which Jack was, for the first time in his career, deeply involved.

Indeed, as he leaned against the wall in an alcove in Lady Marchmain's ballroom, his gaze, as always, on Sophie, presently gliding through a cotillion, the only thing on Jack's mind was a suitable alliance. He had come to town to use the Season as a backdrop for his wooing of Sophie. By his reckoning, the Season was now more than a week old. Then how much longer did he have to hold off and watch her smile at other men?

"I wonder…need I ask which one she is? Or should I make an educated guess?"

At the drawled words, Jack shifted his gaze to frown at Harry. Observing his brother's interrogative expression, Jack snorted and returned to his occupation. "Second set from the door. In amber silk. Blond."

"Naturally." Harry located Sophie by the simple expedient of following Jack's gaze. His brows slowly rose. "Not bad at all," he mused. "Have I complimented you recently on your taste?"

"Not so I've noticed."

"Ah, well." Harry slanted Jack a rakish smile. "Perhaps I'd better converse with this paragon before I pass judgement."

"If you can shake the dogs that yap at her heels."

Harry shook his head languidly. "Oh, I think I'll manage. What's her name?"

"Sophie Winterton."

With a smile which Jack alone could view with equanimity, Harry sauntered into the crowd. His lips twisting wryly, Jack settled to watch how his brother performed a feat he himself was finding increasingly difficult.

"Thank you, Mr. Somercote. An excellent measure." Sophie smiled and gave Mr. Somercote her hand, hoping he would accept his dismissal. He was, unfortunately, becoming a trifle pointed in his interest.

Mr. Somercote gazed earnestly into her face, retaining her

hand in a heated clasp. He drew a portentous breath. "My dear Miss Winterton…"

"It is Miss Winterton, is it not?"

With abject relief, Sophie turned to the owner of the clipped, somewhat hard tones, beneath which a certain languidness rippled, and beheld a strikingly handsome man, bowing even more elegantly than Jack Lester.

This last was instantly explained.

"Harry Lester, Miss Winterton," the apparition offered, along with a rakish grin. "Jack's brother."

"How do you do, Mr. Lester?" As she calmly gave him her hand, Sophie reflected that in any contest of handsomeness, it would be exceedingly difficult to decide between Jack and Harry Lester, not least because they were so unalike.

The gentleman currently shaking her hand, then appropriating it in a manner she recognized all too well, was fair where Jack was dark, with green eyes where Jack's were blue. He was as tall as Jack, but leaner, and there hung about him an aura of dangerous elegance that was distinctly more sharp-edged than Jack's easy assurance. This Lester possessed an elegance that was almost extreme, an aesthetic's adherence to Brummel's dictates, combined with a well-nigh lethal grace.

Harry's glance flicked to Mr. Somercote, then returned to Sophie's face. "Perhaps you would care for a stroll about the rooms, Miss Winterton?"

The arrogant smile that curved his fatally attractive lips assured Sophie that, despite their physical dissimilarity, the Lesters were certainly brothers beneath the skin. "Indeed, sir. That would be most pleasant." He had already settled her hand on his sleeve. With a gentle nod for the deflated Mr. Somercote, Sophie allowed Harry to lead her along the floor.

"You've come to town with your aunt and cousins, have you not?"

Sophie glanced up to find a pair of green eyes lazily regarding her. "Yes, that's right. The Webbs."

"I'm afraid I've not had the pleasure of making their acquaintance. Perhaps you could introduce me if we meet?"

Sophie quickly discovered that Harry, like his brother, had a ready facility for filling in time in a most agreeable, and surprisingly unexceptionable, manner. As they chatted, threading their way through the crowd, she found herself relaxing, then laughing at a tale of a most hilarious excursion in the Park when he and Jack had first come to town. It was only the arrival of her next partner, Mr. Chartwell, that put an end to their amble.

Jack's brother yielded her up with a flourish and a wicked smile.

Smiling herself as she watched him disappear into the crowd, Sophie wondered at the steely danger so apparent in him. It contrasted oddly with Jack's strength. Not that she had felt the least threatened by Harry Lester—quite the opposite. But she did not think she would like to lose her heart to him.

Her mind had little respite from thoughts of Lesters; Jack claimed her immediately the dance with Mr. Chartwell concluded, barely giving that gentleman time to take his leave. However, having detected an expression of chagrin in Mr. Chartwell's mild grey eyes, Sophie was too grateful for her rescue to remonstrate.

Her gratefulness diminished markedly when it became apparent that Jack's difficulties in accepting their fate had not yet been resolved.

"Sophie, I want to talk to you. Privately." Jack had given up trying to manoeuvre such an interlude subtly. Sophie had proved the most amazingly stubborn female he had ever encountered.

Sophie lifted her chin. "You know that would be most unwise, let alone inappropriate."

Jack swallowed a curse. "Sophie, I swear…" The music for the waltz started up; Jack shackled his temper long enough to sweep Sophie into his arms. Once they were whirling slowly down the room, hemmed in on all sides, he continued, "If I have to put up with much more of this, I'll—"

"You'll do nothing that would force me to cut the connection, I hope?" Sophie kept her eyes wide and her expression serene; they might have been discussing the weather for all anyone could see. But her chest felt tight and her heart had sunk. She held Jack's gaze and prayed he'd draw back.

A savage light lit his eyes. Then, with a muttered curse, he looked away. But the tightening of his arm about her told Sophie the argument was far from over. He was holding her far too tight. Sophie made no demur. She had long ago given up hypocritically protesting his transgressions—such as his insistence of using her first name.

She felt a quiver run through her, felt her body respond to his nearness. That, she supposed, was inevitable. He wanted her—as she wanted him. But it wasn't to be; their world did not operate that way. They would both marry others, and Jack had to accept the fact gracefully. If he did, then perhaps they could remain friends. It was all she could hope for, and she was selfish enough to cling to his friendship. He shared so many of her interests, much more so than any of the gentlemen vying for her hand. Indeed, she was loweringly aware that not one of them measured up to Jack Lester and that whenever they gave signs of wanting to fix their interest, she felt an immediate aversion for their company. Her heart, no longer hers, was proving very difficult to reconquer.

Sensing an easing in the tension surrounding her, Sophie slanted a glance at Jack's face.

He was watching her, waiting. "Sophie…I'll accept that you need time to look about you. But I'm not an inherently patient man." The muscle along his jaw twitched; he stilled it, his eyes never leaving hers. "If you could find some way to hurry up this phase, I'd be eternally grateful."

Sophie blinked, her eyes widening. "I...I'll try."

"Do," Jack replied. "But just remember, Sophie—you're mine. *Nothing,* no amount of pretty phrases, will *ever* change that."

The possessiveness in his expression, intransigent, unwavering, stunned Sophie even more than the essence of his arrogant demand. A slow shudder shook her. "Please, Jack..." She looked away, her whisper dying between them.

Jack shackled the urge to haul her into his arms, to put an end to this wooing here and now. Instead, as the music ceased, he drew her hand through his arm. "Come. I'll escort you back to your aunt."

At least she had called him Jack.

"SOMETHING'S WRONG."

It was two nights after Lady Marchmain's ball. Horatio, already propped amid the pillows, turned to study his wife as she sat at her dressing-table, brushing out her mane of silver-blond hair. "What makes you say that?" he asked, unperturbed by her intense expression.

Lucilla frowned. "Sophie isn't happy."

"Isn't she?" Horatio blinked behind his glasses. "Why not? I would have thought, with a horde of would-be suitors, Jack Lester to the fore, she'd be as happy as a young lady could be."

"Well, she's not—and I think it has something to do with Jack Lester, although I cannot, for the life of me, imagine what it could be. Why, the man's positively eaten by jealousy every time she so much as smiles at another. Anyone with eyes can see it. I really don't know what more Sophie wants. Jack Lester will be the catch of the Season."

"Hmm." Horatio frowned. "You're quite sure it's Jack Lester she wants?"

Lucilla snorted. "Believe me, my dear, there's no man So-phie wants even a tenth as much. Indeed, if I was intent on doing my job by the book, I should have warned her long ago not to be so blatant in her preference."

"Ah, well." Horatio shuffled his ever-present documents and laid them aside as Lucilla stood and came towards the bed. "I dare say it'll work itself out. These things generally do."

Lucilla slipped beneath the covers and snuggled down. She waited until Horatio had blown out the candle before saying, "You don't think I should…well, find out what the problem is?"

"You mean *meddle?*" Horatio's tone made his opinion quite clear even before he said, "No. Let the young make their own mistakes, m'dear. How else do you expect them to learn?"

Lucilla grimaced in the dark. "Doubtless you're right, dear." She reached under the covers and patted Horatio's hand. She waited all of a minute before saying, "Actually, I was thinking of organizing a short respite from town. The circus of the Season can become a mite tedious without a break. And I wouldn't want Sophie or Clarissa to become jaded just yet. What say you to a little house party at Aunt Evangeline's?"

Protected by the dark, Horatio slowly smiled. "Whatever you think best, m'dear."

It wouldn't hurt for the young people to have a little time together—time enough to correct their mistakes.

BUT FATE HAD NOT yet consented to smile again on Jack. And as for Sophie, she was finding it hard to smile at all.

The thought that Jack wanted her to marry as soon as pos-sible was depressing enough. The idea of what he imagined would happen after was even more so. Her dreams were in tatters; Sophie found it increasingly hard to support her se-rene façade. She had made a habit of joining circles with Belle

Chessington, relying on her friend's unquenchably cheery constitution to conceal her flagging spirits. But her glow was entirely superficial. Inside was all deepening gloom.

She had just returned to her circle on the arm of Mr. Chartwell, who was becoming more assiduous with every passing day, when a deep voice set her heart thumping.

"I do hope, Miss Winterton, that you've saved me a dance." Jack smiled into Sophie's eyes as he took her hand and drew her away from her court. "I've been teaching Ned how to tie his cravat, and it took rather longer than either of us expected."

Sophie felt her nerves knot and pull tight. Was this, she wondered, as they strolled down the room, how it was going to be later? Would he simply arrive and appropriate her at will? Tensing, she lifted her chin. "I'm afraid my card is full, Mr. Lester."

Jack frowned slightly. "I had rather supposed it would be. But you have kept a dance for me, haven't you?"

They both nodded to Miss Berry, ensconced on a chaise, then continued onward in silence. Sophie struggled to find words for her purpose.

Somewhat abruptly, their progress halted and her escort drew her to face him.

"Sophie?" Jack's frown was gathering force.

Sophie's eyes met his, cloudy, turbulent, intensely blue. Her heart thudding uncomfortably in her throat, she slid her gaze from his. "As it happens, I have not yet accepted anyone for the second waltz."

"You have now." Smothering the dark, almost violent passion that had threatened to erupt, Jack trapped her hand on his sleeve and continued their stroll.

He pointedly returned Sophie to her aunt, some little way from her cloying court. Surrendering her up for their delectation was presently beyond him. His expression somewhat grim, he bowed over Sophie's hand. "Until the second waltz, Miss Winterton."

With that, he left her, his mood even more savage than when he had arrived.

For Sophie, the second waltz arrived far too soon. She had not yet regained her composure, seriously strained by the events of the past weeks and now close to breaking. Jack's arm about her whirled her effortlessly down the floor; Sophie held herself stiffly, battling the impulse to surrender to his strength.

So absorbed was she with her struggle that the first she knew of their departure from the ballroom was the cool touch of the night air on her face.

"Where...?" Distracted, Sophie glanced about and discovered they were on a terrace. But that, apparently, was not their destination, for Jack, his arm still hard about her waist, urged her on. "Jack!" Sophie tried to dig in her heels.

Jack stopped and looked down at her. "You were obviously finding the waltz a trial. I thought you might need some air."

Sophie relaxed slightly, and found she was moving again. "Where are we going?"

The answer was a garden room, built onto the house beyond the end of the terrace. Walls of windows let the moonlight pour in, silvering everything in sight. A few padded cane chairs and two little tables were scattered about the small room, which was, Sophie realized as she heard the door click behind them, mercifully empty.

Which was just as well, for Jack demanded without preamble, "How much longer, Sophie?"

Sophie swung about and found him advancing on her.

"How much longer are you going to make me suffer?"

Her hand rose as if to ward him off; it came to rest on his chest as he halted directly before her. Feeling the warmth of his body through his coat, Sophie shivered. She looked up into his shadowed face, the planes hard and unyielding, and a small spurt of temper flared inside. How did he think *she* felt, having to give up the man she loved—and having that man urge her to do it? Her chin lifted. "I'm afraid the decision is not that simple. In fact, I find the attentions of my present admirers not at all to my taste."

That admission went a long way towards easing the tension that held Jack in its grip. He could feel it flowing from him, the muscles of his shoulders and back relaxing.

Still considering her suitors, Sophie frowned. "I'm afraid I would not be happy accepting any of my present suitors."

An icy chill stole over Jack's heart. It beat three times before he asked, "None?"

Sophie shook her head. "I don't know what to do. I must accept *someone* by the end of the Season."

The chill was slowly spreading through Jack's veins. He touched his tongue to his lips, then asked, "Why not me?"

Startled, Sophie glanced up at him. "But…" She frowned. "I can't marry you—you know I can't." She could see very little of his expression through the shadows veiling his face. And nothing at all of his eyes.

"Why not?" Sight wouldn't have helped her; Jack's expression was hard, impassive, all emotion suppressed. "We both know I've all the attributes you seek in a husband: a country estate, a wish to reside in the country, a desire for children, to have a family about me. That's what you want, isn't it?"

Sophie stared up at him.

"And, of course," Jack continued, his lips twisting in an uncertain smile, "we have something else between us." Raising a hand, he delicately drew the tip of one finger from the point of Sophie's shoulder, exposed by her wide neckline, across to the base of her throat, then down to where the deep cleft between her breasts was visible above her gown. Sophie shivered and caught her breath.

"A…compatibility," Jack said, "that makes all the rest fade into insignificance." His eyes rose to trap Sophie's stunned gaze. "Isn't it so, Sophie?"

Sophie swallowed. "But I have no fortune. Nothing but expectations."

"That doesn't matter." Jack's gaze sharpened. He drew a deep breath. "Sophie—"

In a sudden breathless rush, Sophie put her fingers over his lips. "No!" she squeaked, and cursed her quavering voice. At last she understood—and knew what she must do. Drawing in a determined breath, consciously steeling herself, she drew back, forcing herself to hold his gaze. "I'm afraid you don't understand, Jack. I've never been wealthy in my life— I came to London determined to marry well." The lie came out so easily. Her eyes falling from his, Sophie searched for more words to shore it up. "I know I didn't say so, but I thought you understood. Nothing…" She paused to make sure her voice would not waver. "Nothing I've seen in London has changed my mind; I require that my preferred suitor has considerable wealth."

The words came out more than creditably. Sophie heard them; her heart thudded painfully in her breast but she held herself erect, head high. Far better he think her lost to all sensibility than that he offer to marry her, mortgaging his future, turning his back on those responsibilities that were so very important to him. He was just like Lucilla—ready to sacrifice all for love. She wouldn't allow it.

"But…" Jack couldn't have felt more stunned had she slapped him. His brain reeled, grappling with the fact that Sophie did not know of his true circumstances. He had assumed Horatio would tell Lucilla, who in turn would have told Sophie. Obviously not. The facts were on his lips. Chill reason froze them there.

He looked down at Sophie's face, calm and serene in the

moonlight, the face of the woman he had thought he understood. But she was intent on marrying for money—so intent she would happily put aside what was between them, turn away from his love, and hers, in exchange for cold hard cash. Fate was playing games with him; his golden head had gold on her mind. Did he really want to win her by revealing his disgusting wealth? How would he feel when she smiled and came to his arms, knowing that it had taken money to get her there?

There was a bitter taste in his mouth. Jack drew a sharp breath and looked up, over Sophie's head. He felt cold. A steel fist had closed about his heart, squeezing unmercifully.

He took a jerky step back. "I regret, Miss Winterton, if my…attentions have been unwelcome. I will not trouble you more. I realize my actions must have complicated your search for…a suitable suitor. You have my apologies." With a curt bow, Jack turned to leave. And hesitated.

His face in profile, Sophie saw his lips twist in the travesty of a smile. Then he turned his head to look down at her. "I can only hope, my dear, that when you find your pot of gold at the end of the rainbow you're not disappointed." With a curt nod, he strode away, opening and shutting the door carefully.

Leaving Sophie in the centre of the empty room.

For a long moment, she remained as she was, proudly erect, then her shoulders slumped. Sophie bowed her head, drawing in an aching breath, squeezing her eyes tight against the pain that blossomed inside.

Ten minutes later, she returned to the ballroom, no trace of misery on her face. Coolly composed, she joined her little circle, brightly responding to Belle Chessington's quips. A quick glance about revealed the fact that Jack's dark head was nowhere to be seen. Sophie crumpled inside. She had done the right thing. She must remember that.

If this was what it took to ensure he prospered and lived the life he should live, so be it.

From an alcove by the card room, almost at the other end of the floor, Jack brooded on Sophie's ready smiles. If he had needed any further proof of the superficiality of her feelings for him, he had just received it. Raising his glass, he downed a mouthful of the golden liquor it contained.

"There you are. Been looking all over." Ned ducked round the palm that blocked the opening of the alcove. His eyes fell on Jack's glass. "What's that?"

"Brandy," Jack growled and took another long sip.

Ned raised his brows. "Didn't see any of that in the refreshment room."

"No." Jack smiled, somewhat grimly, across the room and said no more. Ned didn't need to drink himself into a stupor.

"I danced the last cotillion with Clarissa," Ned said. "Her blasted card was virtually full and that bounder Gurnard's taking her in to supper. Should I hang around here or can we leave?"

His gaze on Sophie, Jack considered the point. "I don't advise leaving until after supper, or it'll be said you only came to dance with Clarissa."

"I *did* only come to dance with Clarissa," Ned groaned. "Can we just cut and run?"

Very slowly, Jack shook his head, his attention still fixed across the room. "I told you, this game's not for the fainthearted." For a long moment, he said no more; Ned waited patiently.

Abruptly, Jack shook himself and straightened from the wall. He looked at Ned, his usual arrogant expression in place. "Go and join some other young lady's circle. But whatever you do, don't be anywhere near Clarissa at suppertime." At Ned's disgusted look, Jack relented. "If you survive that far,

I don't suppose it would hurt to talk to her afterwards—but no more than fifteen minutes."

"Wooing a young lady in the *ton* is the very devil," Ned declared. "Where do all these rules come from?" With a disgusted shake of his head, he took himself off.

With his protégé under control, Jack leaned back into the shadows of the alcove, and kept watch on the woman who, regardless of all else, was still his.

FOUR DAYS LATER, Sophie sat in the carriage and stared gloomily at the dull prospect beyond the window. Lucilla's little excursion, announced this morning, had taken the household by surprise. In retrospect, she should have suspected her aunt was planning something; there had been moments recently when Lucilla had been peculiarly abstracted. This three-day sojourn at Little Bickmanstead, the old manor belonging to Lucilla's ancient Aunt Evangeline, was the result.

Despondent, Sophie sighed softly, her gaze taking in the leaden skies. In perfect accord with her mood, the unseasonably fine spell had come to an abrupt end on the night she had refused to let Jack offer for her. A rainstorm had swept the capital. Ever since, the clouds had threatened, low and menacing, moving Lucilla to veto their rides.

Glumly, Sophie wondered if Jack understood—or if he thought she was avoiding him. The miserable truth was, she did not think she could cope with any meeting just now. Perhaps Fate had sent the rain to her aid?

Certainly Jack himself seemed in no hurry to speak with her again. Perhaps he never would. He had been present at the balls they had attended over the past three nights. She had seen him in the distance, but he had not approached her. Indeed, once, when they had passed close while she had been strolling the floor on one of her would-be suitors' arms, and their gazes had met, he had merely inclined his head in a distant fashion. She had replied in kind, but inside the ache had intensified.

Sophie closed her eyes and searched for peace in the repetitive rocking of the coach. She had done the right thing—she kept telling herself so. Her tears, perforce, had been shed discreetly, far from Lucilla's sharp eyes. She had stifled her grief, refusing to dwell on it; suppressed, it had swelled until it pervaded her, beating leaden in her veins, a cold misery enshrouding her soul. A misery she was determined none would ever see.

Which meant she had to face the possibility that Jack might take up the invitation Lucilla had extended to join them at Little Bickmanstead. The guest list numbered some twenty-seven souls, invited to enjoy a few days of rural peace in the rambling old house close by Epping Forest. But Jack wouldn't come, not now. Sophie sighed, feeling not relief, but an inexpressible sadness at the thought.

The well-sprung travelling carriage rolled over a rut, throwing Clarissa against her shoulder. They disentangled themselves and sat up, both checking on Lucilla, seated opposite, her dresser, Mimms, by her side. Her aunt, Sophie noted, was looking distinctly seedy. A light flush tinted Lucilla's alabaster cheeks and her eyes were overbright.

Touching a lace-edged handkerchief to her nose, Lucilla sniffed delicately. "Incidentally, Clarissa, I had meant to mention it before now—but you really don't want to encourage that guardsman, Captain Gurnard." Lucilla wrinkled her nose. "I'm not at all sure he's quite the thing, despite all appearances to the contrary."

"Fear not, Mama." Clarissa smiled gaily. "I've no intention of succumbing to the captain's wiles. Indeed, I agree with you, there's definitely something 'not quite' about him."

Lucilla shot her daughter a narrow-eyed glance, then, apparently reassured, she blew her nose and settled back against the cushions.

Clarissa continued to smile sunnily. Her plans were proceeding, albeit not as swiftly as she would have liked. Ned was proving remarkably resistant to the idea of imitating her other swains; he showed no signs of wanting to prostrate himself at her feet. However, as she found such behaviour a mite inconvenient, Clarissa was perfectly ready to settle for a declaration of undying love and future happiness. Her current problem lay in how to obtain it.

Hopefully, a few days in quieter, more familiar surroundings, even without the helpful presence of the captain to spur Ned on, would advance her cause.

The carriage checked and turned. Sophie looked out and saw two imposing gateposts just ahead. Then the scrunch of gravel announced they had entered the drive. The house lay ahead, screened by ancient beeches. When they emerged in the forecourt, Sophie saw a long, two-storey building in a hotchpotch of styles sprawling before them. One thing was instantly apparent: housing a party of forty would not stretch the accommodations of Little Bickmanstead. Indeed, losing a party of forty in the rambling old mansion looked a very likely possibility.

Drops of rain began spotting the grey stone slabs of the porch as they hurried inside. A fleeting glance over her shoulder revealed a bank of black clouds racing in from the east. The other members of the family had elected to ride from town, Horatio keeping a watchful eye on his brood. Minton and the other higher servants had followed close behind, the luggage with them. The forecourt became a scene of frenzied activity as they all hurried to dismount and stable the horses and unpack the baggage before the storm hit.

The family gathered in the hall, looking about with interest. The rectangular hall was dark, wood panelling and old tapestries combining to bolster the gloom. An ancient butler had admitted them; an even more ancient housekeeper came forward, a lamp in her hand.

As the woman bobbed a curtsy before her, Lucilla put out a hand to the table in the centre of the room. "Oh, dear."

One glance at her deathly pale face was enough to send them all into a panic.

"My dear?" Horatio hurried to her side.

"Mama?" came from a number of throats.

"Mummy, you look sick," came from Hermione, gazing upwards as she held her mother's hand.

Lucilla closed her eyes. "I'm dreadfully afraid," she began, her words very faint.

"Don't say anything," Horatio advised. "Here, lean on me—we'll have you to bed in a trice."

The old housekeeper, eyes wide, beckoned them up the stairs. "I've readied all the rooms as instructed."

Minton was already sorting through the bags. Sending Clarissa ahead with Mimms and the housekeeper, Sophie came to her aunt's other side. Together, she and Horatio supported a rapidly wilting Lucilla up the stairs and along a dim and drafty corridor to a large chamber. Mimms was in charge there; the bed was turned down, the housekeeper dispatched for a warming pan. A fire was cracking into life in the grate.

They quickly helped Lucilla to bed, laying her back on the soft pillows and tucking the covers about her. Once installed, she regained a little colour. She opened her eyes and regarded them ruefully. And sniffed. "This is terrible. I've organized it all—there are twenty-seven people on their way here. They'll all arrive before dinner. And if the rain persists, they'll need to be entertained for the next two days."

"Don't worry about anything," Horatio said, patting her hand. But even he was frowning as the ordeal before them became clear.

"But you haven't a hostess." Lucilla put her handkerchief to her nose, cutting off what sounded like a tearful wail. She blinked rapidly.

Sophie straightened her shoulders. "I'm sure I can manage, with Uncle Horatio and Great Aunt Evangeline behind me. It's not as if you were not in the house—I can check any details with you. And it's not as if there were no chaperons. You told me yourself you've invited a number of matrons."

Lucilla's woeful expression lightened. Her frown turned pensive. "I suppose…" For a moment, all was silent. Then, "Yes," she finally announced, and nodded. "It just might work. But," she said, raising rueful eyes to Sophie's face, "I'm awfully afraid, my dear, that it will be no simple matter."

Relieved to have averted immediate catastrophe, for if Lucilla broke down, that would certainly follow, Sophie smiled with totally false confidence. "You'll see, we'll contrive."

Those words seemed to have become a catchphrase of her Season, Sophie mused as, an hour later, she sat in the front parlour, off the entrance hall, the guest list in her hand.

After assuring themselves that Lucilla was settled and resigned to her bed, she and Clarissa and Horatio had gone to pay their respects to Aunt Evangeline. It had been years since Sophie had met her ageing relative; the years had not been kind to Aunt Evangeline. She was still ambulatory, but her wits were slowly deserting her. Still, she recognized Horatio, even though she was apparently ineradicably convinced that Clarissa was Lucilla and Sophie her dead mother, Maria. They had given up trying to correct the misapprehension, concentrating instead on explaining their current predicament. Whether or not they had succeeded was moot, but at least Aunt Evangeline had given them a free hand to order things as they wished.

Nevertheless, the prospect of having to keep a weather eye out for an old dear who, so the housekeeper had gently informed them, was full of curiosity and prone to wandering the corridors at all hours draped in shawls that dragged their fringes on the floor, was hardly comforting.

A sound came from outside. Sophie lifted her head, listening intently. The wind was rising, whistling about the eaves. Rain fell steadily, driving in gusts against the windows, masking other sounds. Then came the unmistakable jingle of harness. Sophie rose. The first of her aunt's guests had arrived. Girding her loins, she tugged the bell-pull and went out into the hall.

From the very first, it was bedlam. The Billinghams—Mrs. Billingham and both of her daughters—were the first to arrive. By the time they had descended from their carriage and negotiated the steps, their carriage dresses were soaked to the knees.

"Oh, how dreadful! Mama, I'm *dripping!*" The younger Miss Billingham looked positively shocked.

Mrs. Billingham, if anything even damper than her daughters, was not disposed to give comfort. "Indeed, Lucy, I don't know what you're complaining about. We're all wet—and now here's a to-do with Mrs. Webb ill. I'm not at all sure we shouldn't turn round and return to town."

"Oh no, Mama—you couldn't be so cruel!" The plaintive wail emanated from the elder Miss Billingham.

"Indeed, Mrs. Billingham, there's really no need." Smoothly, Sophie cut in, clinging to her usual calm. "Everything's organized and I'm sure my aunt would not wish you to withdraw purely on account of her indisposition."

Mrs. Billingham humphed. "Well, I suppose with your uncle present and myself and the other ladies, there's really no impropriety."

"I seriously doubt my aunt would ever countenance any," Sophie replied, her smile a trifle strained.

"We'll stay at least until the morning." Mrs. Billingham

cast a darkling glance out of the open door. "Perhaps by then the weather will have eased. I'll make a decision then."

With that declaration, Mrs. Billingham allowed herself to be shown to her chamber.

Hard on the Billinghams' heels came Lord Ainsley. His lordship had unwisely driven out in his curricle, and he was soaked to the skin. He tried hard to smile, but his chattering teeth made it difficult.

Sophie was horrified, visions of guests catching their deaths whirling through her mind. Issuing orders left and right—for hot baths and mustard to ward off chills, for the staff to make sure all the fires were blazing—she turned from the sight of Lord Ainsley's back disappearing up the stairs to behold a bedraggled Lord Annerby on the doorstep.

And so it went, on through the afternoon, while outside a preternatural darkness descended.

Belle Chessington and her equally cheery mother were amongst the last to arrive.

"What a perfectly appalling afternoon," Mrs. Chessington remarked as she came forward with a smile, hand outstretched.

Sophie heaved an inward sigh of relief. The Marquess of Huntly, another who had unwisely opted to drive himself, was dripping all over the hall flags. Her little speech now well rehearsed, Sophie quickly made Lucilla's indisposition known, then smoothed away their exclamations with assurances of their welcome. Horatio had retreated to the main parlour to play host to those gentlemen who had already descended, looking for something to warm themselves while they waited for the dinner gong.

The Chessingtons and the marquess took the news in their stride. They were about to head upstairs when a tremendous sneeze had them all turning to the door.

Mr. Somercote stood on the threshold, a pitiful sight with water running in great rivers from his coattails.

"My dear sir!" Belle Chessington swept back along the hall to drag the poor gentleman in.

His place in the doorway was immediately filled by Miss Ellis and her mother, closely followed by Mr. Marston, Lord Swindon and Lord Thurstow. Of them all, only Mr. Marston, clad in a heavy, old-fashioned travelling cloak, was less than drenched. Sophie left the marquess; she tugged the bell-pull twice, vigorously, then hurried forward to help the others out of their soaked coats.

Mentally reviewing the guest list, she thought most had now arrived.

Mr. Marston moved to intercept her, unwrapping his cloak as he came. He was frowning. "What's this, Miss Winterton? Where is your aunt?"

His question, uttered in a stern and reproving tone, silenced all other conversation. The latest arrivals glanced about, noting Lucilla's absence. Suppressing a curse, Sophie launched into her explanation. Mr. Marston did not, however, allow her to get to her reassurances. He cut across her smooth delivery to announce, "A sad mischance indeed. Well—there's nothing for it—we'll all have to return to town. Can't possibly impose on the family with your aunt so gravely ill. And, of course, there are the proprieties to consider."

For an instant, silence held sway. The others all looked to Sophie.

With an effort, Sophie kept her smile in place. "I assure you, Mr. Marston, that my aunt has nothing more than a cold. She would be most unhappy if such a trifling indisposition were to cause the cancellation of this party. And with my great-aunt, my uncle and Mrs. Chessington and the other matrons all present, I really don't think the proprieties are in any danger of being breached. Now," she went on, smiling around at the others, "if you would like to retire to your chambers and get dry—"

"You'll pardon me, Miss Winterton, but I must insist that you fetch your uncle. I cannot be easy in my mind over this most peculiar suggestion that the party proceed as planned." Supercilious as ever, Phillip Marston drew himself up. "I really must insist that Mr. Webb be consulted at once. It is hardly a minor matter."

An utterly stunned silence ensued.

It was broken by a stupendous thunderclap—then the night outside lit up. The blaze in the forecourt threw the shadow of a man deep into the hall.

As the brilliance beyond the door died, Sophie, along with everyone else, blinked at the newcomer.

"As usual, Marston, you're mistaken," Jack drawled as he strolled forward. "Mrs. Webb's indisposition undoubtedly is, as Miss Winterton has assured us, entirely minor. Our kind hostess will hardly thank you for making an issue of it."

A most peculiar *frisson* frizzled its way along Sophie's nerves. She could not drag her gaze from the tall figure advancing across the floor towards her. The long folds of his many-caped greatcoat were damp, but it was clear he, alone amongst the gentlemen invited, had been wise enough to come in a closed carriage. Beneath the greatcoat, his dark coat and breeches were dry and, as usual, immaculate.

With his usual grace, he bowed over her hand. "Good evening, Miss Winterton. I trust I see you well?"

Sophie's mind froze. She had convinced herself he wouldn't come, that she would never see him again. Instead, here he was, arriving like some god from the darkness outside, sweeping difficulties like Mr. Marston aside. But his expression was impassive; his eyes, as they touched her face, held no particular warmth. Sophie's heart contracted painfully.

Glancing about, Jack bestowed a charming smile on the

other, much damper, guests. "But pray don't let me detain you from giving succour to these poor unfortunates." His smile robbed the term of any offence.

Gently, he squeezed Sophie's hand.

Sophie dragged in a sharp breath. She retrieved her hand and pinned a regal smile to her lips. "If you and Mr. Marston don't mind, I shall see these others to their rooms."

Still smiling, Jack politely inclined his head; Phillip Marston hesitated, frowning, then nodded curtly.

Determinedly calm, Sophie moved forward to deal with the last of her aunt's guests. As she did so, Ned slipped in through the door. He grinned at her. "Shall I shut it? Jack was sure we'd be last."

Sophie smiled and nodded. "Please." As she helped Minton ease Lord Thurstow from his sodden coat, she wondered whether Jack Lester had purposely arrived last for greatest effect—or whether his lateness was a reflection of reluctance.

The heavy door clanged shut on the wild night; to Sophie, it's resounding thud sounded like the knell of an inescapable doom.

CHAPTER TWELVE

SHE BARELY HAD TIME to scramble into an evening gown and brush out her curls before the dinner gong sounded, echoing hollowly through the long corridors. The meal had already been put back twice to accommodate the travellers and their recuperation.

With a last distracted glance at her mirror, Sophie hurried out. The corridor was dark and gloomy, the ubiquitous wood panelling deepening the shadows cast by the candles in the wall sconces. Feet flying over the worn carpet, Sophie turned a corner only to find a cordon, formed by two determined figures, across her path.

Jeremy frowned, threatening sulky. "We can come down to dinner, can't we, Sophie?"

Sophie blinked.

"It's not as if we'd cause any ruckus," George assured her.

"It's *boring* here, Sophie. Having dinner with Amy and the twins—well, it's just not fair." Jeremy's jaw jutted pugnaciously.

"It's not as if we're children." George fixed his blue eyes on her face and dared her to contradict him.

Sophie swallowed a groan. With all the trials of the afternoon, and those yet to come, she had precious little patience left to deal with the boys' prickly pride. But she loved them too well to fob them off. Draping an arm about each, she gave them a quick hug. "Yes, I know, loves—but, you see, we're a bit rushed this evening, and although the party's informal, I don't really think it's quite the same as when we're at Webb Park."

They both turned accusing eyes on her. "I don't see why not," Jeremy stated.

"Ah—but if you don't get an early night, you won't be up in time to go shooting tomorrow."

Sophie jumped. The deep, drawling voice brought goosebumps to her skin. But both boys turned eagerly as Jack strolled out from the shadows.

"Shooting?"

"You mean you'll take us?"

Jack raised a brow. "I don't see why not. I was discussing the outing with your father earlier. If the rain eases, we should have tolerable sport." Jack's blue gaze flicked to Sophie, then returned to the boys' glowing faces. "But you'd have to get an early night—and that, I fear, means dining in the nursery. Of course, if that's beneath you…"

"Oh, no," Jeremy assured him. "Not if we're to go shooting tomorrow."

George tugged his brother's sleeve. "Come on. We'd better let Jack and Sophie get to dinner and go find ours before the twins scoff all the buns."

Restored to good humour, the boys hurried off.

Sophie breathed a sigh of relief, then glanced up at Jack. "Thank you, Mr. Lester."

For a moment, Jack's gaze rested on her face, his expression impassive. Then he inclined his head. "Think nothing of it, my dear. Shall we?"

He gestured towards the stairs. With a nod, Sophie started forward. As they strolled the short distance in silence, she was excruciatingly aware of him, large and strong beside her, her skirts occasionally brushing his boots. He made no move to offer her his arm.

They descended the stairs and turned towards the drawing-room. Minton was hovering in the hall. "Could I have a word with you, miss?"

Sophie's heart sank. "Yes, of course." With a half smile for Jack, she glided across the tiles. "What is it?"

"It's the footmen, miss. That's to say—there aren't any." Looking supremely apologetic, Minton continued, "The old lady apparently didn't see the need and Mrs. Webb didn't imagine we'd need more. Even with old Smithers—that's the old lady's butler—there'll only be two of us and that'll make service very slow. Naughton—Mr. Webb's man—said as he'd help, but still…"

Minton didn't need to spell it out; Sophie wondered what next the evening had in store. Where on earth could she find footmen to wait at table at a minute's notice "I don't suppose the coachman…"

Minton looked his answer. "I'd rather have the maids. But you know how it'll look, miss, having women wait at table."

She did indeed. Sophie's shoulders slumped.

"If I could make a suggestion?"

Sophie turned as Jack strolled forward. He glanced at her, his expression merely polite. "I couldn't help overhearing. I suggest," he said, addressing Minton, "that you ask my man, Pinkerton, to assist. Huntly's man, too, will be well-trained, and Ainsley's and Annerby's. The rest I can't vouch for, but Pinkerton will know."

Minton's worried expression cleared. "Just the ticket, sir. I'll do that." He bobbed to Sophie. "All under control, miss, never fear." And with that, Minton hurried off.

Sophie knew a moment of blessed relief, superceded by the knowledge that more hurdles doubtless awaited her. She glanced up at Jack. "I have to thank you again, Mr. Lester. I would never have thought of such a solution; I only hope it serves." The last was uttered softly, a slight frown playing about her brows.

Not a glimmer of expression showed on Jack's face as, looking down, he studied hers. "Don't worry. Such arrangements are not uncommon—no one will remark on it."

From beneath her lashes, Sophie glanced up. "Thank you," she murmured, a tentative smile touching her lips.

Jack's hand closed about the knob of the drawing-room door. "After you, Miss Winterton."

Sophie entered to find most of the company already assembled. She moved among the guests, seeing that all had everything they needed. Most had recovered from their soaking and regained their spirits. Only Mrs. Billingham and Mrs. Ellis, a delicate lady, had elected to take trays in their rooms. Clarissa was surrounded by her usual little band, Ned included. Her cousin had drawn the other younger ladies into the charmed circle; the sound of shy laughter now ran as a counterpoint to more sober conversations. Her uncle, together with the more mature gentlemen, was deep in discussion of the sport to be found in the vicinity.

Great-Aunt Evangeline provided an unexpected distraction. She had come down to examine the guests who had invaded her home. Blithely calling Sophie "Maria" and Clarissa "Lucilla," she happily chatted with the ladies, her remarkable shawls threatening to trip her at every step.

When Minton announced dinner, the old lady squeezed Sophie's arm. "I'll take mine in my room, dear. Now remember, Maria—you're in charge. Keep an eye on Lucilla, won't you?" With a motherly pat, Great-Aunt Evangeline retired.

Dinner, as it transpired, posed no further problems. As one course was smoothly followed by the next, Sophie gradually relaxed. She had led the way into the dining-room on the Marquess of Huntly's arm. He was now seated on her right with Lord Ainsley on her left. A hum of good-natured conversation hovered over the table; everyone was reasonably well acquainted and, so it seemed, determined to enjoy themselves.

Further down the board, Belle Chessington had taken on the challenge posed by Mr. Somercote; she was bending his ear unmercifully. Sophie smiled and let her gaze travel on, to where Clarissa and Ned, together with Lord Swindon and Mr. Marley, were deep in discussion of some passingly serious subject. Beyond them, Jack Lester was devoting himself primarily to Mrs. Chessington. Sophie had seen him offer that lady his arm in the drawing-room even as she herself had placed her hand on the Marquess's sleeve.

Rousing herself from her thoughts, Sophie conjured a smile and beamed at the marquess. "Do you intend to make one of the shooting party tomorrow, my lord?"

Once the covers were removed, Sophie led the ladies back to the drawing-room. The gentlemen were disposed to linger over their port, yet there was still an hour before the tea trolley was due when they strolled back into the room.

As ladies and gentlemen merged, then fractured into the inevitable smaller groups, Sophie wondered how to keep them amused. She hadn't had time to organize any of the fashionable little games that were so much a part of country-house parties. She was cudgelling her brains for inspiration when Ned stopped by her chair.

"We thought we might try charades, Sophie. Jack mentioned it was all the thing for the younger crowd."

Relieved, Sophie smiled. "By all means; that's an excellent idea."

She watched as Ned and Clarissa rounded up the younger members of the party and cleared an area of the large room. Many of the matrons seemed disposed to look on indulgently. Rising, Sophie glanced about—and found her uncle approaching.

Horatio beamed and took her hand. "You're doing magnificently, my dear." He squeezed her fingers, then released them. "Lester's taken Huntly, Ainsley and Annerby off to try their luck at billiards. I'll just go and have a word with Marston." Horatio glanced about the drawing-room. "The rest I fear I'll have to leave to you—but I'm sure you can manage."

With Mr. Marston off her hands, Sophie was sure of it, too. Belle Chessington seemed reluctant to let Mr. Somercote escape, which left only Mr. Chartwell, Miss Billingham and a few relaxed matrons for her to take under her wing. Sophie smiled. "Indeed, Uncle, it seems we've contrived amazingly well."

"Indeed." Horatio grinned. "Your aunt will be delighted."

To Sophie's relief, the rain cleared overnight. The morning was damp and dismal, but sufficiently clement to allow the shooting party to proceed. By the time the ladies descended to the breakfast parlour, the gentlemen had taken themselves off. Even Mr. Marston had seized the opportunity to stretch his legs.

The ladies were content to stroll the gardens. Sophie went up to check on the twins and Amy. She eventually ran them to earth in the attics; their nurse, who had been with the Webbs for many years, had had the bright idea of turning them loose in such relatively safe surrounds. The trio were engaged in constructing a castle, later to be stormed. Great-Aunt Evangeline was with them. Sophie left them to it and went to look in on her aunt. She found Lucilla sleeping, which of itself spoke volumes. Mimms confirmed that her aunt's indisposition had eased, but she was still very weak.

The gentlemen returned in time for luncheon, an informal meal at which their prowess with their guns was discussed and admired, the ladies smiling good-naturedly at claims of prizes flushed from coverts or taken on the wing.

Listening to the genial chatter, Sophie spared a thought for Lucilla's expertise. Her aunt had selected her guests with a knowing hand; they had melded into a comfortable party despite the presence of such difficult elements as Mr. Marston and Mr. Somercote.

But by the end of the meal, the rain had returned, gusting in from the east in leaden sheets. By unvoiced consensus, the gentlemen retired to the library or billiard room, while the ladies took possession of the morning-room and parlour, to chat in little groups ensconced in the comfortable armchairs or wander in the adjoining conservatory.

With everyone settled, Sophie went to the kitchens to confer with Cook. Belowstairs, she stumbled on an army, the depleted ranks of Aunt Evangeline's aged servitors swelled beyond imagining by the maids, coachmen and valets of the guests, as well as the doyens of the Webb household. But all seemed to be cheery, the bulk of the men gathered about the huge fire in the kitchen. Minton, beaming, assured her all was well.

Climbing back up the stairs, her chores completed, Sophie decided she could justifiably seize a moment for herself. The conservatory had proved a most amazing discovery; it was huge and packed with ferns and flowering creepers, many of kinds Sophie had not before seen. She had had time for no more than a glimpse; now, she pushed open the glass door and slipped into the first avenue, half an hour of peace before her.

As the greenery surrounded her, Sophie closed her eyes and breathed deeply. The humid scent of rich earth and green leaves, of growing things, tinged with the faint perfume of exotic flowers, filled her senses. A smile hovered on her lips.

"There you are, Miss Winterton."

Sophie's eyes flew open; her smile vanished. Swallowing a most unladylike curse, she swung round to see Mr. Marston advancing purposefully upon her. As usual, he was frowning.

"Really, Miss Winterton, I cannot tell you how very displeased I am to find you here."

Sophie blinked; one of her brows rose haughtily. "Indeed, sir?"

"As you should *know,* Miss Winterton." Mr. Marston came to a halt before her, giving Sophie an excellent view of his grim expression. "I do not see how your uncle can reconcile this with his conscience. I knew from the first that continuing with this affair was unwise in the extreme. Unconscionable folly."

Sophie straightened her shoulders and looked him in the eye. "I fear, sir, that I cannot allow you to malign my uncle, who, as everyone knows, takes exceptional care of me. In truth, I cannot follow your reasoning at all."

Mr. Marston appeared to have difficulty restraining himself. "What I mean, Miss Winterton," he finally replied, his tones glacially condemnatory, "is that I am *shocked* to find you—a young lady whom I consider of sound and elevated mind and a naturally genteel manner—here." He paused to gesture about them. "Quite alone, unattended, where any gentleman might come upon you."

Sophie hung on to her patience. "Mr. Marston, may I point out that I am in my great-aunt's house, within easy call not only of servants but many others whom I consider friends? Is it not all the same thing as if I had chosen to walk the pavements of Covent Garden unattended?"

Mr. Marston's grey eyes narrowed; his lips were set in a thin line. "You are mistaken, Miss Winterton. No lady can afford to play fast and loose with her reputation by courting—"

"Really, Marston. No need to bore Miss Winterton to tears by reciting the Young Ladies' Catechism. They all have to learn it by heart before being admitted to Almack's, you know." Jack strolled forward, green leaves brushing his shoulders. His expression was easy and open, but Sophie saw a glint of something harder in his eyes.

The sudden rush of mixed emotions—relief, nervousness

and anticipation among them—on top of her rising temper, left her momentarily giddy. But she turned back to Mr. Marston, lifting her chin challengingly. "Mr. Lester is correct, sir. I assure you I need no lectures on such topics."

She made the comment in an even voice, giving Mr. Marston the opportunity to retreat gracefully. He, however, seemed more intent on glowering at Jack, a futile gesture for, as she shifted her gaze to her rescuer's face, Sophie found he was watching her.

She would have given a great deal, just then, for one of his smiles. Instead, he simply bowed, urbanely elegant, and offered her his arm. "I came to collect you, my dear. The tea trolley has just been brought in."

Sophie tried a small smile of her own and placed her fingers on his sleeve.

Phillip Marston snorted. "Ridiculous! Taking lessons in comportment from a—" He broke off as he met Jack's gaze.

One of Jack's brows slowly rose. "You were saying, Marston?"

The quiet question made Phillip Marston glower even more. "Nothing, nothing. If you'll excuse me, Miss Winterton, I find I am not in the mood for tea." With a curt bow, he turned on his heel and disappeared into the greenery.

Sophie didn't bother to stifle her sigh. "Thank you again, Mr. Lester. I must apologize for Mr. Marston. I fear he's labouring under a misapprehension."

As they strolled towards the parlour, Sophie glanced up at her knight-errant. He was looking down at her, his expression enigmatic.

"No need for apologies, my dear. Indeed, I bear Marston no ill-will. Strange to say, I know just how he feels."

Sophie frowned, but she got no chance to pursue his meaning; the tea trolley and the bulk of her aunt's guests were waiting.

WHEN SOPHIE AWOKE the next morning, and tentatively peeked out from under the covers, she was met by weak sunshine and a pale, blue-washed sky. She relaxed back against her pillows, feeling decidedly more confident than she had the morning before.

The previous evening had passed off smoothly, much in the manner of the first. The only exceptions had been the behaviour of her suitors, who, one and all, had recovered from the dampening effects of their arrival and were once more attempting to pay court to her. That and the behaviour of the elder Miss Billingham, who had all but thrown herself at Jack Lester.

Sophie grimaced, her eyes narrowing. After a moment, she shook herself. And rose to meet the day.

She looked in on Lucilla on her way downstairs. Her aunt was sitting up in bed sipping her morning cocoa. "Indeed, I would love to see how things are progressing, but I still feel quite weak." Lucilla pulled a face. "Maybe this evening?"

"You will remain abed until you are well," declared Horatio, coming through the door with a laden tray.

Leaving her aunt to her husband's fond care, Sophie descended to the breakfast parlour. There, her suitors lay in waiting.

"This kedgeree is quite remarkable, m'dear," offered the marquess. "Quite remarkable."

"Perhaps you would care for some bacon and an egg or two, Miss Winterton?" Mr. Chartwell lifted the lid of a silver platter and glanced at her enquiringly.

Sophie smiled on them all, and managed to install herself between Mr. Somercote, engaged in silent communication with Belle Chessington, who was chattering enough for them both, and Mrs. Chessington, who smiled understandingly.

Further down the board, Jack was apparently absorbed with Mrs. Ellis and her daughter. Beside him, Ned was chatting to Clarissa, Lord Swindon and Mr. Marley openly eavesdropping. Sophie hid a smile at her cousin's rapt expression.

She escaped the breakfast parlour unencumbered, using the pretext of having to check on her younger cousins. Jeremy and Gerald had been tired out by a day in woods and fields; they had happily eaten with Amy and the twins the night before. When she reached the nursery she was greeted by an unnatural silence, which was explained by Nurse when she hunted that worthy down. The children had been taken on a long ride by the grooms; peace, therefore, was very likely assured. Smiling with both relief and satisfaction, Sophie descended—into the arms of her suitors.

The marquess took the lead. "My dear Miss Winterton, may I interest you in a stroll about the gardens? I believe there are some early blooms in the rose garden."

"Or perhaps you would rather stroll about the lake?" Mr. Chartwell directed a quelling look at the marquess.

"There's a very pretty folly just the other side of the birch grove," offered Lord Ainsley. "Nice prospect and all that."

Mr. Marston merely frowned.

Sophie resisted the urge to close her eyes and invoke the gods. Instead, she favoured them all with a calm smile. "Indeed, but why don't we all go together? The gardens, after all, are not that large; doubtless we can see the rose garden, the lake and the folly before lunch."

They mumbled and shot frowning glances at each other but, of course, they had to agree. Satisfied she had done what she could to improve the situation, Sophie resigned herself to an hour or two's insipid conversation. At least she would get some fresh air.

As they wandered the lawns and vistas, they came upon little groups of their companions likewise employed. They nodded and smiled, calling out information on the various sights to be found, then continued with their ambles. In the distance, Sophie saw the unmistakable figure of Jack Lester, escorting Mrs. Ellis and Mrs. Doyle. Neither lady had her daughter with her, but Miss Billingham the elder had attached herself to the group. Viewing the gown of quite hideous puce stripes that that young lady had donned, along with a chip bonnet from under which she cast sly glances up at Jack Lester, Sophie gritted her teeth and looked elsewhere. To her mind, her own walking gown of pale green was far superior to Miss Billingham's attire, and she would never cast sheep's eyes at any man—particularly not Jack Lester.

Swallowing a humph, Sophie airily remarked, "The light is quite hazy, is it not?"

Her court immediately agreed, and spent the next five minutes telling her so.

Nevertheless, the brightness seemed to have gone out of her day. Not even the spectacle of her suitors vying for the right to hand her up the steps could resuscitate her earlier mood. She forced herself to smile and trade quips throughout luncheon but, as soon as the meal was over and it became clear that the guests were quite content, she escaped.

Donning a light cloak, she gathered her embroidery into a small basket and slipped out of the morning-room windows.

IN THE SMALL summer-house at the very end of the birch grove, hidden from the house by the shrubbery, Jack paced back and forth, his expression decidedly grim. He wasn't all that sure what he was doing at Little Bickmanstead. He had taken refuge in the summer-house—refuge from Miss Billingham, who seemed convinced he was just waiting to make her an offer.

Not a likely prospect this side of hell freezing over—but she did not seem capable of assimilating that fact.

It was another woman who haunted him, leaving him with a decision to make. A pressing decision. Sophie's suitors were becoming daily more determined. While it was clear she harboured no real interest in them, she had declared her requirement for funds and they each had plenty to offer. It could only be a matter of time before she accepted one of them.

With a frustrated sigh, Jack halted before one of the open arches of the summer-house and gripped the low sill; unseeing, he gazed out over the wilderness. He still wanted Sophie—regardless.

A movement caught his eye. As he watched, Sophie came into view, picking her way along the meandering path that led to the summer-house.

Slowly, Jack smiled; it seemed for the first time in days, Fate had finally remembered him, and his golden head.

Then he saw the figure moving determinedly in Sophie's wake. Jack cursed. His gaze shifted to the left, to the other path out, but the thought of leaving Sophie to deal with Marston alone occurred, only to be dismissed. Besides, Horatio had had to leave for Southampton on business immediately after lunch; it was, Jack decided, undoubtedly his duty to keep watch over his host's niece.

Glancing about, he noticed a small door in the back wall of the summer-house. Opened, it revealed a small room, dark and dim, in which were stored croquet mallets, balls and hoops. Shifting these aside, Jack found he could stand in the deep shadow thrown by the door and keep the interior of the summer-house in view. Propping one shoulder against a shelf, he settled into the dimness.

On reaching the summer-house, Sophie climbed the stairs, listlessness dogging her steps. With a soft sigh, she placed her basket on the small table in the centre of the floor. She was turning to view the scene from the arch when footsteps clattered up the steps behind her.

"Miss Winterton."

In the instant before she turned to face Phillip Marston,

Sophie permitted herself an expressive grimace. Irritation of no mean order, frustration and pure chagrin all had a place in it. Then she swung about, chilly reserve in her glance. "Mr. Marston."

"I must protest, Miss Winterton. I really cannot condone your habit of slipping away unattended."

"I wasn't aware I was a sheep, nor yet a babe, sir."

Phillip Marston frowned harder. "Of course not. But you're a lady of some attraction and you would do well to bear that in mind. Particularly with the likes of Mr. Lester about."

Her accents frigid, Sophie stated, "We will, if you please, leave my aunt's other guests out of this discussion, sir."

With his usual superior expression, Mr. Marston inclined his head. "Indeed, I'm fully in agreement with you there, my dear. In fact, it was precisely the idea of leaving your aunt's other guests entirely that has prompted me to seek you out."

Sophie felt her spirits, already tending to the dismal, slump even further. She searched for some soothing comment.

Mr. Marston fell to pacing, his hands clasped behind him, his frowning gaze fixed on the floor. "As you know, I have not been at all easy in my mind over this little party. Indeed, I did not approve of your aunt's desire to bring you to town. It was quite unnecessary. You did not need to come to London to contract a suitable alliance."

Sophie cast a pleading glance heavenward. Her mind had seized up; no witty comment occurred to her.

"But I will say no more on what I fear I must term your aunt's lack of wisdom." Phillip Marston pursed his lips. "Instead, I have resolved to ask you to leave your aunt and uncle's protection and return to Leicestershire with me. We can be married there. I believe I know you too well to think you will want a large wedding. Such silly fripperies might be well enough for the *ton* but they are neither here nor there. My mother, of course, fully approves—"

"Mr. Marston!" Sophie had heard quite enough. "Sir, I do not know when I have given you cause to believe I would welcome an offer from you, but if I have, I most sincerely apologize."

Phillip Marston blinked. It took him a moment to work through Sophie's words. Then he frowned and looked more severe than ever.

"A-hem!"

Startled, both Sophie and Marston turned as first the marquess and then Mr. Chartwell climbed the steps to the summer-house. Sophie stared. Then, resisting the urge to shake her head, she drifted to the table, leaving her three most eager suitors ranged on the other side.

"Er, we were just strolling past. Couldn't help overhearing, m'dear," Huntly explained, looking most apologetic. "But felt I had to tell you—no need to marry Marston here. Only too happy to marry you myself."

"Actually," cut in Mr. Chartwell, fixing the marquess with a stern eye, "I was hoping to have a word with you later, Miss Winterton. In private. However, such as it is, I pray you'll consider my suit, too."

Sophie thought she heard a smothered snort, but before she could decide who was responsible, Mr. Marston had claimed the floor.

"Miss Winterton, you will be much happier close to your family in Leicestershire."

"Nonsense!" Huntly exclaimed, turning to confront his rival. "No difficulty in travelling these days. Besides, why should Miss Winterton make do with some small farmhouse when she could preside over a mansion, heh?"

"Chartwell Hall is very large, Miss Winterton. Fifty main rooms. And of course I would have no qualms in giving you a free hand redecorating—there and at my London residence." Mr. Chartwell's attitude was one of ineffable superiority.

"Marston Manor," Phillip Marston declaimed, glaring at Huntly and Chartwell, "is, as Miss Winterton knows, a sizeable establishment. She shall want for nothing. My resources are considerable and my estates stretch for miles, bordering those of her uncle."

"Really?" returned the marquess. "It might interest you to know, sir, that my estates are themselves considerable, and I make bold to suggest that in light of my patrimony, Miss Winterton would do very much better to marry me. Besides, there's the title to consider. Still worth something, what?"

"Very little if rumour is to be believed," Mr. Chartwell cut in. "Indeed, I fear that if we are to settle this on the basis of monetary worth, then my own claims outshine you both."

"Is that so?" the marquess enquired, his attitude verging on the belligerent.

"Indeed." Mr. Chartwell held his ground against the combined glare of his rivals.

"Enough!" Sophie's declaration drew all three to face her. Rigid with barely suppressed fury, she raked them with a glinting, narrow-eyed gaze. "I am *disgusted* with all of you! How *dare* you presume to know my thoughts—my feelings—my requirements—and to comment on them in such a way?"

The question was unanswerable; all three men shuffled uncomfortably. Incensed, Sophie paced slowly before them, her glittering gaze holding them silent. "I have never in my life been so insulted. Do you actually believe I would marry a man who thought *I* was the sort of woman who married for *money?*" With an angry swirl, Sophie swung about, her skirts hissing. "For wealth and establishments?" The scorn in her voice lashed at them. "I would draw your attention to my aunt, who married for love—and found happiness and success. My mother, too, married purely for love. My cousin Clarissa will unquestionably marry for love. *All* the women in my family marry for love—and I am no different!"

Sophie blinked back the tears that suddenly threatened. She was not done with her suitors yet. "I will be perfectly frank with you gentlemen, as you have been so frank with me. I do not love any of you, and I will certainly not marry any of you. There is no earthly use persisting in your pursuit of me, for I will not change my mind. I trust I make myself plain?"

She delivered her last question with a passable imitation of Lucilla at her most haughty. Head high, Sophie looked down her nose and dared them to deny her.

Typically, Phillip Marston made the attempt. As startled as the others, he nevertheless made an effort to draw his habitual superiority about him. "You are naturally overwrought, my dear. It was unforgivable of us to subject you to such a discussion."

"Unforgivable, ungentlemanly and totally unacceptable." Sophie wasn't about to quibble. Mr. Chartwell and the marquess shuffled their feet and darted careful, placating glances at her.

Heartened, Mr. Marston grew more confident. "Be that as it may, I strongly advise you to withdraw your hasty words. You cannot have considered. It is not for such as us to marry for love; that, I believe is more rightly the province of the *hoi polloi*. I cannot think—"

"*Mr.* Marston." Sophie threw an exasperated glance at the heavens. "You have not been listening, sir. I care not what anyone thinks of my predilection for love. It may not be conventional, but it is, I should point out, most fashionable these days. And I find I am greatly addicted to fashion. You may think it unacceptable, but there it is. Now," she continued, determined to give them no further chance to remonstrate, "I fear I have had quite enough of your company for one afternoon, gentlemen. If you wish to convince me that you are, in fact, the gentlemen I have always believed you, you will withdraw and allow me some peace."

"Yes, of course, my dear."

"Pray accept our apologies, Miss Winterton."

Both the marquess and Mr. Chartwell were more than prepared to retreat. Phillip Marston was harder to rout.

"Miss Winterton," he said, his usual frown gathering, "I cannot reconcile it with my conscience to leave you thus unguarded."

"Unguarded?" Sophie barely restrained her temper. "Sir, you are suffering from delusions. There is no danger to me here, in my great-aunt's summer-house." Sophie glanced briefly at Mr. Chartwell and the marquess, then returned her gaze, grimly determined, to her most unwanted suitor. "Furthermore, sir, having expressed a desire for your absence, I will feel perfectly justified in requesting these gentlemen to protect me—from you."

One glance was enough to show Phillip Marston that Mr. Chartwell and the marquess would be only too pleased to take out their frustrations on him. With a glance which showed how deeply against the grain retreat went with him, he bowed curtly. "As you wish, Miss Winterton. But I will speak with you later."

Only the fact that he was leaving allowed Sophie to suppress her scream. She was furious—with all of them. Head high, she stood by the table and watched as they clattered down the steps. They paused, exchanging potent looks of dislike, then separated, each heading towards the house by a different route.

With a satisfied humph, Sophie watched them disappear. Slowly, her uplifting fury drained. The tense muscles in her shoulders relaxed. She drew in a soft breath.

It tangled in her throat as she heard a deep voice say from directly behind her,

"You're wrong, you know."

With a strangled shriek, Sophie whirled round. One hand

at her throat, she groped with the other for the table behind her. Eyes wide, she stared up at Jack's face. "Wh—what do you mean, wrong?" It was an effort to calm her thudding heart enough to get out the words.

"I mean," Jack replied, prowling about the table to cut off her retreat, "that you overlooked one particular danger in assuring Marston of your safety." He met Sophie's stare and smiled. "Me."

Sophie took one long look into his glittering eyes and instinctively moved to keep the table between them. As the truth dawned, she lifted her chin. "How *dare* you eavesdrop on my conversations!"

Jack's predatory smile didn't waver. "As always, your conversation was most instructive, my dear. It did, however, leave me with one burning question."

Sophie eyed him warily. "What?"

"Just what game are you playing, my dear?"

The sudden flare in his eyes startled Sophie anew. "Ah—you're a gentleman, Mr. Lester." It seemed the time to remind him.

"Gentleman *rake,*" Jack replied. "There's a difference."

Sophie was suddenly very sure there was. Eyes wider than ever, she took a step back, then smothered a yelp as, with one hand and a single shove, Jack sent the table shooting over the floor.

Sophie's gaze followed it, until it came to a quivering halt by the wall, her basket still balanced upon it. Then she looked round—and jumped back a step when she found Jack directly in front of her. He advanced; she retreated another step. Two more steps and Sophie found the wall of the summer-house at her back. Jack's arms, palms flat against the wall, one on either side, imprisoned her. She eyed first one arm, then the other. Then, very cautiously, she looked up into his face.

His expression was intent. "Now, Sophie—"

"Ah—Jack." Any discussion was potentially dangerous; she needed time to consider just what he had heard, and what he might now think. Sophie fixed her gaze on his cravat, directly before her face. "I'm really quite overset." That was the literal truth. "I—I'm rather overwrought. As you heard, I just turned away three suitors. Three offers. Not a small thing, after all. I fear my nerves are a trifle strained by the experience."

Jack shifted, leaning closer, raising one hand to catch Sophie's chin. He tipped her face up until her wise gaze met his. "I suggest you steel yourself then, my dear. For you're about to receive a fourth."

Sophie's lips parted on a protest; it remained unuttered. Jack's lips closed over hers, sealing them, teasing the soft contours, then ruthlessly claiming them. Head whirling, Sophie clutched at his lapels. She felt him hesitate, then his head slanted over hers. Sophie shuddered as he boldly claimed her warmth, tasting her, teasing her senses with calculated expertise. Her fingers left his lapels to steal upwards, to clutch at his shoulders. He released her chin; he shifted, straightening, pulling her against him, one large hand gripping her waist. The kiss deepened again; her senses whirling, Sophie wondered how much deeper it could go. Then his hand swept slowly upward to firm about her breast, gently caressing even as he demanded her surrender.

Sophie tried to stiffen, to pull away, to refuse as she knew she should. Instead, she felt herself sink deeper into his arms, deeper into his kiss. Her breast swelled to his touch, her body ached for more.

Jack drew her hard against him, then lifted his head to breathe against her lips, "Will you marry me, Sophie?"

Sophie's heart screamed an assent but she held the words back, hanging on to her wits by her fingernails. Slowly, she opened her eyes, blinking up into the warm blue of his. She licked her lips, then blushed as his gaze followed the action. She tried to speak, but couldn't find her voice. Instead, she shook her head.

Jack's blue eyes narrowed. "No? Why not?" He gave her no chance to answer but kissed her again, just as deeply, just as imperiously.

"You said you would only marry for love," he reminded her when he again consented to lift his head. His eyes rose to hers, satisfaction flaring at her dazed expression. "You're in love with me, Sophie. And I'm in love with you. We both know it."

His head lowered again; Sophie realized she was in desperate straits. Faced with another of his kisses, and their increasingly debilitating effect on her wits, she seized the first word that crossed her mind. "Money," she gasped.

Jack stopped, his lips a mere inch from hers. Slowly, he drew back, enough to look into her eyes. He studied them for a long moment, then slowly shook his head. "Not good enough this time, Sophie. You told them—your three importunate suitors—that you would never marry for money. You said it very plainly. They had money, but not your love. I've got your love—why do I need money?"

His gaze did not leave hers. Sophie could barely think. Again, she shook her head. "I can't marry you, Jack."

"Why not?"

Sophie eyed him warily. "You wouldn't understand if I explained."

"Try me."

Pressing her lips together, Sophie just shook her head. She knew she was right; she also knew he wouldn't agree.

To her dismay, a slow, thoroughly rakish smile lit Jack's face. He sighed. "You'll tell me eventually, Sophie."

His tone was light, quite unconcerned. Sophie blinked and saw him look down. She followed his gaze—and gasped.

"*Jack!* What on earth are you doing?" Sophie batted in-effectually at his hands, busy with the buttons of her gown. Jack laughed and drew her closer, so that she couldn't reach his nimble fingers. Then the gown was open and his long fingers slipped inside. They closed about her breast; Sophie's knees shook.

"Sophie—" For an instant, Jack closed his eyes, his hand firming about her soft flesh. Then he bent his head and caught her lips with his.

For a giddy moment, a tide of delight caught Sophie up and whirled her about. Then Jack drew his lips from hers and the sensation receded, leaving a warm glow in its wake. Desperate, Sophie clung to reality. "What are you doing?" she muttered, her voice barely a whisper.

"Seducing you," came the uncompromising reply.

Sophie's eyes flew open. She felt Jack's lips on her throat, trailing fire over her suddenly heated skin. She shuddered, then glanced wildly about the room—what she could see of it beyond his shoulders. "Here?" Her mind refused to accept the notion. The room was bare of all furniture, no chaise or day-bed, not even an armchair. He had to be teasing.

She felt rather than heard Jack's chuckle. "The table."

The *table?* Sophie's shocked gaze swung to the innocent wooden table, now standing by the wall. Then she looked back at Jack, into his heated gaze. "No," she said, then blushed furiously at the question in her tone.

Jack's gaze grew warmer. "It's easy," he murmured, bending his head to drop wicked little kisses behind her ear. "I'll show you."

"No." This time, Sophie got the intonation right. But her eyes closed and her fingers sank into Jack's shoulders as he continued to caress her.

"But yes, sweet Sophie," Jack whispered in her ear. "Unless you can give me a good reason why not."

Sophie knew there had to be hundreds of reasons—but she could think of only one. The one he wanted to hear. She opened her eyes and found his face. She tried to glare. His fingers shifted beneath her bodice; Sophie sucked in a breath. She didn't have the courage to call his bluff. He probably wasn't bluffing. "All right," she said and felt his fingers still. She leaned against him, seeking his strength as she sought for her words. "I told you I'm a lady of expectations, nothing more," she began.

"And I've told you that doesn't matter."

"But it does." Sophie glanced up, into the warm blue eyes so close to hers. She put all the pleading sincerity she could into her eyes, her voice. "Your dreams are mine: a home, a family, estates to look after. But they'll remain nothing but *dreams* if you don't marry well. You know that."

She saw his face still, his expression sober. Sophie clung to him and willed him to understand.

Her heart was in her eyes, there for Jack to see. He drank in the sight, then closed his eyes against the pain behind. He dropped his forehead to hers and groaned. "Sophie, you have my heartfelt apologies."

Sophie felt like sagging—with relief or was it defeat?

"I should have told you long ago." Jack pressed a soft kiss against her temple, hugging her to him.

Sophie frowned and pushed back to look up at him. "Told me what?"

Jack smiled crookedly. "That I'm horrendously wealthy—disgustingly rich."

Sophie's face crumpled; her eyes filled with tears. "Oh, Jack," she finally got out around the constriction in her throat. "Don't." Abruptly, she buried her face in his shoulder.

It was Jack's turn to frown and try to hold her away. "Don't what?"

"Don't lie," Sophie mumbled against his coat.

Jack stiffened. Thunderstruck, he stared down at the woman in his arms. "Sophie, I'm not lying."

She looked up, her eyes swimming, softly blue, her lips lifting in a heart-rending smile. She raised a hand to his face. "It's no use, Jack. We both know the truth."

"No, we do not." Jack withdrew his hand from her breast and caught her hand, holding it tightly. "Sophie, I swear I'm rich." When she simply smiled, mistily disbelieving, he swore. "Very well. We'll go and ask your aunt."

The look Sophie sent him made Jack grimace. "All right, not Lucilla. Horatio, then. I assume you'll accept your uncle's word on my finances?"

Surprised, Sophie frowned. Horatio, she well knew, was a man of his word. Not even for love would he so much as bend the truth. And Jack was suggesting Horatio would bear out his claims. "But my uncle's just left. We don't know when he'll return."

Jack swore some more, distinctly colourfully. He considered his options, but the only others who knew of his recent windfall were relatives, friends or employees, none of whom Sophie would believe. "Very well." Grimly, he surveyed Sophie's doubting expression. "We'll wait until he returns."

Her mind reeling, Sophie nodded, struggling to see her way forward. She glanced down, and blushed rosily. Tugging her fingers from Jack's clasp, she drew back enough to do up the buttons of her gown. Whatever the truth, she would have to keep Jack at arm's length until Horatio returned—or it wouldn't matter what her uncle said.

"Sophie?" Jack sensed her withdrawal. He had half a mind to draw her back to him, back into his arms where she belonged.

From under her lashes, Sophie glanced up at him almost guiltily. "Ah, yes." She tried to step back but Jack's arm was firm about her waist. "Now, Jack," she protested, as she felt his arm tighten. She braced her hands against his chest. "We've agreed, have we not?" The light in his eyes left her breathless. "We'll wait until my uncle returns."

Jack's blue eyes narrowed. "Sophie…" His gaze met hers, full of breathless anticipation, yet, for all that, quite determined. Jack heaved a disgusted sigh. "Very well," he bit out. "But *only* until your uncle returns—agreed?"

Sophie hesitated, then nodded.

"And you'll marry me three weeks after that."

It was not a question; Sophie only just stopped her nod.

"And furthermore," Jack continued, his blue gaze holding hers, "if I'm to toe the line until your uncle gets back, then so shall you."

"Me?"

"No more flirting with your suitors—other than me."

"I do not flirt." With an offended air, Sophie drew back.

"And no more waltzing with anyone but me."

"That's outrageous!" Sophie disengaged from Jack's arms. "You don't know what you're asking."

"I know only too well," Jack growled, letting her go. "Fair's fair, Sophie. No more going to supper with any gentleman but me—and certainly no driving or going apart with anyone else."

Smoothing down her skirts, Sophie humphed.

Jack caught her chin on his hand and tipped her head up until her eyes met his. "Are we agreed, Sophie?"

Sophie could feel her pulse racing. Her eyes met his, intensely blue, and she felt like she was drowning. His face, all hard angles and planes, was very near, his lips, hard and finely chiselled, but inches away. "Yes," she whispered and breathed again when he released her.

With his customary grace, Jack offered her his arm.

Drawing her dignity about her, Sophie picked up her basket and placed her hand on his sleeve. She allowed him to lead her down the steps and back towards the house, all the way struggling to cope with the sensation of being balanced on a knife-edge. Determined to give the reprobate by her side no inkling of her difficulty, she kept her gaze on the scenery and her head very high.

Jack viewed the sight through narrowed eyes. Then he smiled, slowly, and started to plan.

CHAPTER THIRTEEN

THE PARTY BROKE up the next morning. By then, everyone was aware that something had changed, that Jack stood, in some unspecified way, as Sophie's protector. Despite her disapproval of his tactics, Sophie could not help feeling grateful, especially when he helped shoulder the responsibility for their return to the capital. Even with Lucilla all but fully recovered, with her uncle absent, she had not been looking forward to travelling with all her cousins, Toby the only adult male in sight.

But by mid-morning, when she emerged from the door of her great-aunt's home, all was under control. Her younger cousins were to ride as before, much to their delight. With Jack, Toby and Ned to keep them in line, Sophie had no residual qualms. The carriage stood waiting, Clarissa already aboard. Her arms full of rugs and cushions, Sophie glanced back.

Lucilla came slowly through the hall, leaning heavily on Jack's arm. Although still wan, her aunt showed no signs of faintness. Sophie turned and hurried down the steps to prepare Lucilla's seat in the carriage.

At the top of the steps, Lucilla paused to breathe in the crisp morning air. Blue skies had returned; fluffy white clouds held no lingering menace. With a small, highly satisfied smile, she glanced at Jack beside her. "I'm very glad you did not disappoint me, Mr. Lester."

Recalled from his study of Sophie's curvaceous rear, neatly

outlined as she stood on the carriage step and leaned in, Jack looked down at Lucilla, one brow slowly rising. "That was never my intention, ma'am."

Lucilla's smile broadened. "I'm so glad," she said, patting his arm. "Now, if you'll give me your arm...?"

Jack got his revenge by lifting her easily and carrying her down the steps. As he settled her amid Sophie's cushions and rugs, Lucilla favoured him with a dignified glare. Then her lips twitched and she lay back on the seat, waving him away.

His own lips curving, Jack handed Sophie up, resisting the temptation to bestow a fond pat on her retreating anatomy. And then they were away.

FIVE NIGHTS LATER, under the glare of the chandeliers in the Duchess of Richmond's ballroom, Sophie dimly wondered why she had imagined awaiting her uncle's return in the bosom of the *ton* would be safer than at Little Bickmanstead. Mere hours had sufficed for Jack to make it patently clear that he had meant every word he had uttered in Great-Aunt Evangeline's summer-house. Twenty-four hours had been enough for her to realize that, that being so, the possibility of ever denying him receded even further with every successive day.

Casting a glance up at him as he stood, planted immovably by her side, starkly handsome in severe black and white, Sophie stifled a sudden tremor.

Jack caught her glance. He bent his head to hers. "There's another waltz coming up."

Sophie shot him a warning glance. "I've already danced one waltz with you."

His rakish grin surfaced. "You're allowed two dances with any gentleman."

"But not two waltzes, if I'm wise."

"Don't be wise, my Sophie." His eyes gently teased. "Come dance with me. I promise you no one will remark unduly."

Resistance, of course, was useless. Sophie allowed him to lead her to the floor, knowing any show of reluctance would be pure hypocrisy. She loved being held in his arms; at the moment, waltzing was the only safe way to indulge her senses.

As they circled the floor, she noted the looks of resignation many of her mother's old friends turned upon them. In contrast, Lady Drummond-Burrell, that most haughty of Almack's patronesses, smiled with chilly approval.

"Amazing," Jack said, indicating her ladyship with an inclination of his head. "Nothing pleases them more than the sight of a fallen rake."

Sophie tried to frown but failed. "Nonsense," she said.

"No, it's not. They'll all approve once the news gets out."

Sophie did frown then. Jack had told her how the change in his fortune had come about. "Why hasn't it got out by now? Presuming it's real, of course."

The arm about her tightened, squeezing in warning. "It's real," Jack replied. "But I confess I purposely neglected to mention it to anyone."

"Why?"

"You've met the elder Miss Billingham; just imagine her sort, multiplied by at least a hundred, all with yours truly in their sights."

Sophie giggled. "Surely you weren't afraid?"

"Afraid?" Jack raised an arrogant brow. "Naturally not. I merely have an innate dislike of tripping over debs at every turn."

Sophie laughed, the delicious sound teasing Jack's senses, tightening the tension inside him until it was well-nigh unbearable. He metaphorically gritted his teeth. The wait, he promised himself, would be worth it.

At the end of the dance, he escorted Sophie back to her aunt and took up his position—by her side.

Sophie knew better than to argue. Lord Ruthven stopped by, then Lord Selbourne joined them. With practised ease, Sophie laughed and chatted. While there were many gentlemen who still sought her company, her suitors, not only the three she had already dismissed but all the others who had viewed her with matrimony in mind, rarely hove in sight. Jack's presence, large and dark by her shoulder, was more than enough to make them think twice. Their rides in the Park every morning continued, but with Jack by her side, she found herself blissfully free of encumbrances. It was impossible to misinterpret his interest; as he was so tall, whenever he spoke with her, he bent his head to hers, and she, motivated by her instincts, naturally turned into his strength, reinforcing the image that they were one, wanting only the official announcement. Horatio's absence explained their present hiatus; none doubted the announcement would eventually come, as her mother's old friends' attitudes clearly showed.

She was his, and every passing day made her more aware of that truth. And that much more nervous of her uncle's return. She still doubted Jack's story; she had seen the passion in him and knew his love to be strong enough to motivate the most enormous lie. Regardless of what he said, it was possible. Only Horatio could lay her doubts to rest—and none knew when he would return.

With an inward sigh, Sophie mentally girded her loins. She glanced across at Clarissa, holding court on the other side of her aunt's chaise. Her cousin looked radiant, charming her many youthful swains yet, as Sophie had noticed, careful to give none any particular encouragement. Beside her, Ned occupied a position that had much in common with Jack's. Sophie's lips twitched; she returned her gaze to Lord Selbourne. There was a light in Ned's eyes that she did not think Clarissa had yet noticed.

Ned, in fact, was almost as impatient as Jack. But both his

and Clarissa's parents had agreed that no formal offer should be considered until after Clarissa's Season. Which meant he had a far longer wait ahead of him; and, to his mind, far less assurance of gaining the prize at the end.

Which left him feeling distinctly uneasy. His silver princess still smiled on her court; he had even heard her laugh with that bounder Gurnard.

"This wooing business seems to drag on forever," he later grumbled to Jack as they both kept watch over their ladies, presently gracing the floor in other men's arms.

Jack shot him a sympathetic glance. "As you say." After a moment, he continued, "Has Clarissa let slip any information as to when they might retire to Leicestershire?"

"No," Ned replied. He cast a puzzled glance at Jack. "But I thought they were staying until the end of the Season. That's more than a month away, isn't it?"

Jack nodded. "Just a thought." As Sophie whirled past in Ruthven's arms, Jack's easy expression hardened. "As you say, this business of wooing is an ordeal to be endured."

While Jack, Ned and the ladies of his family were thus engaged, Toby had embarked on amusement of a different kind. At that moment, he was strolling along the pavement of Pall Mall, along the stretch which housed the most notorious gaming hells in town, in company with Captain Terrence Gurnard.

The captain stopped outside a plain brown door. "This is the place. A snug little hell—very exclusive."

Toby smiled amiably and waited while the captain knocked. After a low-voiced conversation with the guardian of the portal, conducted through a grille in the door, they were admitted and shown into a sizeable room, dimly lit except for the shaded lamps which shed their glow onto the tables. There were perhaps twenty gentlemen present; few raised their heads as Toby followed Gurnard across the room.

With his usual air of interested enquiry, Toby glanced about him, taking in the expressions of grim determination with which many of the gentlemen applied themselves to their cards and dice. There was a large table devoted to Hazard, another to Faro. Smaller tables attested to the hell's reputation for variety; there were even two older gentlemen engaged in a hand of Piquet.

This was the third night Toby had spent with Gurnard, and the third hell they had visited. He was, as usual, following one of his father's maxims, that which declared that experience was the best teacher. After tonight, Toby felt, he would have learned all he needed of gaming hells. His real interest tonight lay in the play. Gurnard had allowed him to win for the past two nights; Toby had begun to suspect the captain's motives.

Initially, Gurnard had brushed against him with apparently no particular intent; they had subsequently struck up an acquaintance. It was after their sojourn at Little Bickmanstead that the captain had sought him out and, being apparently at a loose end, had offered to show him the sights. Toby had accepted the offer readily; he had not previously spent much time in the capital.

Now, however, he wondered whether the captain had taken him for a flat.

By the end of the evening, which Toby promptly declared once his losses had, almost mysteriously, overtaken his current allowance, he was quite sure the captain had done just that. Comforting himself with the reflection that, as his father was wont to say, there was no harm in making mistakes just as long as one didn't make the same mistake twice, he frowned slightly as he looked across at Gurnard. "I'm afraid I won't be able to meet that last vowel until the pater returns to town—but he should be back any day."

He hadn't expected to outrun his ready funds. However, as his father had settled a considerable sum on him two years before, and managed it for him under his direction the better to teach him the ways of finance, Toby had no real qualms about asking Horatio for an advance. "I'll speak to him as soon as he returns."

Gurnard sat back, his face flushed with success and the wine he had steadily consumed. "Oh, you don't want to do that." He held up his hand in a fencer's gesture. "Never let it be said that I caused father and son to fall out over the simple matter of a few crowns."

Toby could have set him straight—he fully expected his father to have a good laugh over his adventure—but some sixth sense made him hold back. "Oh?" he said guilelessly. There were rather more than "a few crowns" involved.

Gurnard frowned, his face a mask of concentration. "Perhaps there's some way you can repay the debt without having to apply to your pater?"

"Such as?" Toby asked, a chill stealing down his back.

Gurnard looked ingenuous. He frowned into space. Then his face cleared. "Well, I know I'd count it a blessing to have a few minutes alone with your sister."

He leant across the table and, with just the slightest hesitation, conspiratorially lowered his voice. "Your sister mentioned that your party are planning to attend the gala at Vauxhall. Perhaps, in repayment of your debt, you could arrange for me to meet with her in the Temple of Diana—just while the fireworks are on. I'll return her to you when the show's over, and no one will be any the wiser."

Not only a flat—a foolish flat. Toby hid his reaction behind a vacant expression. The poor light concealed the steely glint in his eyes. "But how will I get Clarissa to agree?"

"Just tell her you're taking her to meet her most ardent admirer. Don't tell her my name—I want to surprise her. Women like the romantic touch." Gurnard smiled and waved a languid hand. "Dare say you haven't noticed, but your sister and I are deeply in love. You needn't fear I'll take advantage. But with all the attention that's focused on her we've found it hard to find the time to talk, to get to know each other as we'd like."

Concluding that the captain was the sort of gentleman he should hand over to higher authorities, Toby slowly nodded. "All right," he agreed, his tone bland. He shrugged. "If you'll be happy with that instead of the money...?"

"Definitely," Gurnard replied, his eyes suddenly gleaming. "Ten minutes alone with your sister will be ample recompense."

"TOBY, IS ANYTHING wrong?"

Bringing up the rear as his exuberant siblings tumbled back into the house after their morning ride, Toby jumped and cast a startled glance at Sophie. Seeing the conjecture in her cousin's open face, she nodded.

"I thought so." With a glance at the horde disappearing up the stairs, Clarissa trailing absent-mindedly behind, she linked her arm with Toby's. "Come into your father's study and tell me all."

"It's nothing really dreadful," Toby hurried to assure her as they crossed the threshold of his father's sanctum.

"Then there's probably no reason for you to be so worried about it," Sophie returned. Sinking into one of the armchairs by the hearth, she fixed Toby with a commanding if affectionate eye. "Open your budget, my dear, for I really can't let this go on. Doubtless I'm imagining all sorts of unlikely horrors; I'm sure you can set my mind at rest."

Toby grimaced at her, too used to Lucilla to take offence. He fell to pacing before the hearth, his hands clasped behind his back. "It's that bounder Gurnard."

"Bounder?" Sophie looked her surprise. "I know Ned's been calling him that for ages, but I thought that was just Ned."

"So did I—but now I know better. Dashed if Ned wasn't right."

Sophie looked pensive, then cast a glance up at Toby. "I've just remembered. Your mother said she didn't trust the man, and Clarissa agreed."

"Did she?" Toby brightened. "Well, that makes it easier, then."

"Makes what easier?" Sophie stared at Toby, consternation in her eyes. "Tobias Webb, just what is going on?"

"No need to get into a flap. At least, not yet."

When Toby said no more but continued to pace the hearthrug, Sophie straightened her shoulders. "Toby, if you don't tell me what this is all about immediately, I'll feel honour bound to speak to your mother."

Toby halted, his expression horrified. "Saints preserve us all," he said. And proceeded to tell Sophie the story.

"That's *iniquitous!*" Sophie was incensed. "The man's worse than a mere bounder."

"Undoubtedly. He's a dangerous bounder. That's why I want to wait until Papa gets back to lay this before him. I think it would be best for all concerned if Gurnard is stopped once and for all."

"Unquestionably," Sophie agreed. After a moment, she added, "I don't think it would serve any purpose to tell Clarissa. She doesn't like the man as it is; I can't see her doing anything rash."

Toby nodded.

"And I really don't think telling your mama would be a good idea."

"Definitely not." Toby shuddered at the thought.

"I suppose," Sophie suggested, "we could seek professional assistance."

"The Runners? And risk a brouhaha like they made over

Lady Ashbourne's emeralds?" Toby shook his head. "That's not a decision I'd like to make."

"Quite," Sophie agreed. "Still, at least we know Gurnard's unlikely to make a move before the gala."

"Precisely." Toby's blue gaze rested consideringly on Sophie. "All we really need do is hold the fort until then."

AN HOUR LATER, Jack sat in his chair in his parlour in Upper Brook Street, the table before him spread for an early luncheon, and attacked the slices of sirloin on his plate with an air of disgruntled gloom. "Permit me to warn you, brother mine, that this wooing business is definitely plaguesome."

Harry, who had looked in on his way down to the country, raised an amused brow. "You've only just discovered that?"

"I cannot recall having wooed a lady—nor any other kind of female—before." Jack scowled at a dish of roast potatoes, then viciously skewered one.

"I take it all is not proceeding smoothly?"

For a full minute, Jack wrestled with a conscience that decreed that all matters between a lady and a gentleman were sacrosant, then yielded to temptation. "The damned woman's being noble," he growled. "She's convinced herself that I really need to marry an heiress and is determined not to ruin my life by allowing me to marry her."

Harry choked on his ale. Jack rose to come around the table and thump his back but Harry waved him away. "Well," he said, still breathless, "that was the impression you wanted to give, remember."

"That was then, this is now," Jack answered with unshakeable logic. "Besides, I don't care what the *ton* thinks. My only concern is what goes on in one particular golden head."

"So tell her."

"I've already told her I'm as rich as Croesus, but the witless woman doesn't believe me."

"Doesn't believe you?" Harry stated. "But why would you lie about something like that?"

Jack's expression was disgusted. "Well might you ask. As far as I can make out, she thinks I'm the sort of romantic who would marry a 'lady of expectations'—her words—and then valiantly conceal the fact we were living on tick."

Harry grinned. He reached for the ale jug. "And if things had been different? If we hadn't been favoured by fortune and you'd met her—what then? Would you have politely nodded and moved on, looking for an heiress, or would you do as she suspects and conceal the reckoning?"

Jack shot him a malevolent glance. "The subject doesn't arise, thank God."

When Harry's grin broadened into a smile, Jack scowled. "Instead of considering hypothetical situations, why don't you turn that fertile brain of yours to some purpose and think of a way to convince her of our wealth?"

"Try a little harder," Harry offered. "Be your persuasive best."

Jack grimaced. "Can't be done that way; believe me, I've tried." He had, too—twice. But each time he resurrected the subject, Sophie turned huge eyes full of silent reproach upon him. Combined with a brittlely fragile air, such defences were more than enough to defeat him.

"I need someone to vouch for me, someone she'll believe. Which means I have to wait until her uncle returns to town. He's off looking over the Indies Corporation's next venture at Southampton. The damnable situation is that no one has any idea of when he'll be back."

Viewing his brother's exasperated expression, evoked, so it seemed, by the prospect of having to wait a few days to make a certain lady his, Harry raised a laconic brow. Everything he had heard thus far suggested that Jack was poised to take the final momentous step into parson's mousetrap and, amazing though it seemed, he would have a smile on his face when he did so. Love, as Harry well knew, was a force powerful enough to twist men's minds in the most unexpected ways. He just hoped it wasn't contagious.

The sound of the knocker on the door being plied with determined force disrupted their peace.

Jack looked up.

Voices sounded in the hall, then the door opened and Toby entered. He glanced at Jack, then, noticing Harry, nodded politely. As the door shut behind him, Toby turned to Jack. "I apologize for the intrusion, but something's come up and I'd like your opinion on the matter. But if you're busy I can come back later."

"No matter." Harry made to rise. "I can leave if you'd rather speak privately."

Jack raised a brow at Toby. "Can you speak before Harry?"

Toby hesitated for only an instant. Jack had spent all the Season at Sophie's feet, concentrating on nothing beyond Sophie and her court. Harry Lester, on the other hand, was by reputation as much of a hellion as Jack had been and had not shared his brother's affliction. Toby's gaze swung to Harry. "The matter concerns a Captain Gurnard."

Harry's eyes narrowed. "Captain Terrence Gurnard?" The words sounded peculiarly flat and distinctly lethal. When Toby nodded, Harry settled back into his seat. "What, exactly, is that bounder up to?"

Jack waved Toby to a seat. "Have you eaten?" When Toby shook his head, his eyes going to the half-filled platters still on the table, Jack rang for Pinkerton. "You can eat while you fill us in. I take it the problem's not urgent?"

"Not that urgent, no."

While he fortified himself, Toby recounted his outings with Gurnard and the ultimate offer to discount his losses against an arranged clandestine meeting with Clarissa.

"So you won for the first two nights but lost heavily on the third?"

Toby nodded at Harry. "He was setting me up, wasn't he?"

"It certainly sounds like it."

Jack glanced at his brother. "I've not heard much of Gurnard—what's the story?"

"That, I suspect, is a matter that's exercising the minds of quite a few of the man's creditors." Harry took a long sip of his ale. "There are disquieting rumours doing the rounds about the dear captain. Word has it he's virtually rolled up. Fell in with Duggan and crew. A bad lot," Harry added in an aside to Toby. "But the last I heard, he'd been unwise enough to sit down with Melcham."

"Melcham?" Jack tapped a fingernail against his ale mug. "So Gurnard's very likely up to his eyebrows in debt."

Harry nodded. "Very possibly over his head. And if Melcham holds his vowels, as seems very likely, his future doesn't look promising."

"Who's Melcham?" Toby asked.

"Melcham," Jack said, "is quite a character. His father was a gamester—ran through the family fortune, quite a considerable one as it happened, then died, leaving his son nothing but debts. The present earl, however, is cut from a different cloth than that used to fashion his sire. He set out to regain his fortune by winning it back from those who had won it from his father. Them and their kind, which is to say the sharps who prey on the susceptible. And he wins. Virtually always."

"The sharps can't resist the challenge," Harry added. "They line up to be fleeced, knowing Melcham's now worth a not-so-small fortune. The catch is that he's also won a lot of powerful friends—and paying one's debts is mandatory."

"In other words," Jack summed up, straightening in his chair, "Gurnard is in a lot of trouble. And once the news gets out, he'll no longer be the sort of escort wise mamas view with equanimity."

"But not yet," Harry said. "The news hasn't hit the clubs. That was privileged information, courtesy of some friends in the Guards."

Jack nodded. "All right. So Gurnard has decided that the most sensible way to get himself out of the hole he has nearly buried himself in is to marry an heiress—a very wealthy heiress."

"Clarissa?" asked Toby.

"So it appears." Jack's expression was as grim as Harry's. "And time is not on his side. He'll have to secure his heiress before his pressing concerns become public knowledge." Jack turned to Toby. "Exactly how did he want this meeting arranged?"

Toby had started to repeat the directions Gurnard had been at pains to impress upon him when the door opened and Ned walked in. Toby broke off in midsentence. Ned's amiable smile faded as he took in Toby's expression and Harry's grim face. He looked at Jack.

Jack smiled, a predatory glint in his eye. "What did Jackson say today?"

Drawing a chair up to the table, Ned dropped into it. "I have to work on my right hook. The left jab's coming along well enough." Ever since Jack had introduced him to Gentleman Jackson's Boxing Saloon, Ned had been taking lessons, having uncovered a real aptitude for the sport. His eyes slid around the table once more.

"Excellent." Jack's gaze was distant, as if viewing some invisible vista. Then he abruptly refocused on Ned. "Strangely, I believe we may have found a use for your newly discovered talents."

"Oh?" Jack's smile was making Ned uneasy.

The smile grew broader. "You want to consolidate your position in Clarissa's affections, don't you?"

"Yes," Ned admitted, somewhat cautiously.

"Well, I'm pleased to announce that a situation has arisen which calls for a knight-errant to rescue a fair damsel from the unwanted attentions of a dastardly knave. And as the fair damsel is Clarissa, I suspect you had better polish up your armour."

"What!"

It took another ten minutes to explain all to Ned's satisfaction and by then Jack had been sidetracked. "You told all this to Sophie?" he asked, fixing Toby with a disbelieving stare.

Toby looked guilty. "I couldn't avoid it—she threatened to speak to Mama."

Jack looked disgusted. "Meddlesome female," he growled, and he didn't mean Lucilla.

"I pointed out that we needn't worry until the gala. If Papa returns before that, there'll be no reason for Sophie to worry at all."

Jack nodded. "Well, don't tell her anything more. We can take care of it—and the fewer complications the better."

Toby nodded, entirely in agreement.

"But how, exactly, are we to take care of it?" Ned's expression was grimly determined.

Succinctly, assisted by helpful suggestions from his inventive brother, Jack laid their campaign before them.

By the time he'd finished, even Ned was smiling.

"ARGH!" JACK STRETCHED his arms above his head, then relaxed into his chair. "At last I think I see the light."

Harry grinned. "Think Ned can pull it off?"

The brothers were once more alone, Ned and Toby having taken themselves off with some vague intention of keeping a watchful eye on Clarissa during her afternoon's promenade in the Park.

"Think?" Jack replied. "I know it! This performance should land Clarissa firmly in his arms, relieving Sophie of further anxiety on the point and myself of the charge of overseeing that youthful romance once and for all."

"Has it been such a burden?" Harry drained his tankard.

"Not a burden, precisely. But it hurts to watch one of us succumb so young."

Harry chuckled. "Well, at least neither of us fell young, and I don't think you need worry about Gerald."

"Thank God. At least I have the excuse of being the head of the family—it's expected, after all."

"Rationalize it any way you want, brother mine; I know the truth."

Jack's blue eyes met Harry's green ones across the width of the table. Their gazes locked, then Jack sighed. "Well, at least with Ned safely settled, I'll be able to give my full attention to a certain golden head. And with Horatio Webb's help, I'll conquer her stubbornness."

"Let me be the first to wish you happy."

Jack glanced at Harry and realized his brother was serious. He smiled. "Why thank you, brother mine."

"And I'll give you a warning, too."

"Oh?"

"The news is out."

Jack grimaced. "Are you sure?"

"Put it this way." Harry set his tankard down. "I was at Lady Bromford's affair last night, and lo and behold, Lady Argyle made a play for me. Not a blush in sight, what's more. She had her daughter in tow, a chit just out of the schoolroom." Harry wrinkled his nose. "Her ladyship was as clinging as Medusa. Totally unaccountable, *unless* she'd heard rather more than a whisper of our affairs."

"And if she's heard, others will, too." Jack grimaced even more.

"Which means it won't be long before we're the toast of the tea parties. If I were you, I'd secure your golden head with all speed. An announcement in the *Gazette* should just be enough to buy your escape. As for myself, I've decided to run for cover."

Jack grinned. "I did wonder over your sudden penchant for the lush green fields."

"In the circumstances, Newmarket looks considerably safer than London." Harry's grin was crooked as he rose. "Given the danger, I feel confident I'll find enough in the country to keep me amused for the rest of the Season."

Jack shook his head. "You won't be able to run forever, you know."

Harry raised an arrogant brow. "Love," he declared, "is not about to catch me." With a last, long look, he turned to the door. His hand on the knob, he paused to look back, his grin distinctly wry. "Good luck. Just don't get so distracted by the excitement at the gala that you forget to keep your back covered. Until your golden head says yes, you're no safer than I."

Jack had raised his hand in farewell; now he groaned. "God help me! Just when I thought I was home and hosed."

HARRY'S DIRE PREDICTION was confirmed that evening at Lady Summerville's ball. Jack bowed gracefully over her ladyship's hand, disturbingly aware of the relish in her gimlet gaze. Luckily her duties prohibited her from pursuing him immediately, but her promise to look him up later left little doubt that his news was out. Fully alert, Jack artfully avoided two ostriched-plumed matrons, as imposing as battleships, waiting to ambush him just yards from the ballroom steps. He was congratulating himself on his escape when he walked straight into Lady Middleton's clutches.

"My dear Mr. Lester! I declare, Middleton and I have not seen much of you this year."

Biting back the retort that, if he had had his eyes about him, her ladyship would have seen even less of him, Jack bowed resignedly. On straightening, he was subjected to the scrutiny of her ladyship's protuberant eyes, grotesquely magnified by lorgnettes deployed like gunsights. "Indeed, ma'am, I fear I have been greatly occupied thus far this Season."

"Well! I hope you're not going to be too *occupied* to attend my niece's coming-out ball. She's a sweet thing and will make some gentleman an unexceptionable wife. Your Aunt Harriet was particularly fond of her, y'know." This last was accompanied by a pointed glance. Jack looked politely impressed. Her ladyship nodded, apparently satisfied. "Middleton and I will expect you."

With a snap, she shut her lorgnettes and used them to tap him on the sleeve.

Choosing to interpret this as a dismissal, Jack bowed and slid into the crowd. It was, indeed, as Harry had foreseen; despite his efforts to make his intentions crystal clear, he was not yet safe. Doubtless, nothing less than the announcement of his betrothal would convince the matchmaking mamas that he had passed beyond their reach. Yet another good reason to add to the increasingly impressive tally indicating that the speedy curtailment of Miss Sophia Winterton's Season was a highly desirable goal.

Looking about him, he spotted his quarry, elegant as ever in a gown of pale green figured silk, her curls glowing warmly in the candlelight. His height was both advantage and disadvantage, allowing him to scan the crowds but making him far too conspicuous a target. By dint of some rapid tacking by way of evasive action, he gained Sophie's side without further difficulty.

As always, his appearance coincided with a thinning of

the ranks about her. Sophie no longer noticed. She gave him her hand and a warmly welcoming smile. "Good evening, Mr. Lester."

"Actually," Jack said, straightening and scanning their surroundings, "it probably isn't."

"I beg your pardon?" Sophie stared at him.

"As an evening, I've probably faced better," Jack replied, tucking her hand into his arm. "Ruthven, Hollingsworth— I'm sure you'll excuse us." With a nod for those two gentlemen, Jack led Sophie into the crowd.

Hearing Lord Ruthven chuckle, Sophie glanced back to see his lordship explaining something to a puzzled Mr. Hollingsworth. "What is it?" she asked, looking up at Jack.

"I've been pegged up for target practice."

"Whatever do you…" Sophie's words trailed away as she noticed the simpering glances thrown Jack's way—mostly by debutantes who, two days ago, would certainly not have dared. She shot a suspicious glance at Jack. "You've put the story of your fortune about?"

Under his breath, Jack growled. "No, Sophie. I have not *put* the news about. It *got* out—doubtless from the other investors involved in the Indies Corporation." He cast an exasperated glance down at her. His temper was not improved by the wary frown he saw in her eyes. "Devil take it, woman!" he growled. "No rake in his right mind, having declared his intention to wed, would then call the dragons down on his head by *inventing* a fortune."

Sophie swallowed her giggle. "I hadn't thought of it in quite that way."

"Well, do," Jack advised. "It's the truth—and you're not going to escape it. And speaking of escape, I do hope you realize that, until your uncle returns and our betrothal can be announced, I expect you to assist my cause."

"In what way?" Sophie asked.

"By lending me your protection."

Sophie laughed, but the smile was soon wiped from her face. A succession of cloying encounters set her teeth on edge; some of the warm hints directed at Jack left her positively nauseous. Somehow, he managed to keep a polite expression on his face and, by dint of his quick wits and ever-ready tongue, extricated himself from the ladies' clutches. She admired his address, and was more than ready to acquiesce to his unvoiced plea. She remained fixed by his side, anchored by his hand on his sleeve, and defied all attempts to remove her. That she managed to do so while restraining her comments to the realms of the acceptable was, she felt, no reflection on the provocation provided. Indeed, on more than one occasion she found herself blushing for her sex. Miss Billingham proved the last straw.

"My mama was quite bowled over to hear of your windfall, sir," she declared, batting her sparse lashes and simpering. "In light of our time spent together at Mrs. Webb's house party, she has charged me to ask you to call. Indeed," she went on, dropping her coy smile long enough to shoot a venomous glance at Sophie, "Mama is very keen to speak to you immediately." Greatly daring, Miss Billingham placed her hands about Jack's arm and smiled acidly at Sophie. "If you'll excuse us, Miss Winterton?"

Sophie stiffened, then smiled sweetly back. "I greatly fear, Miss Billingham," she said, before Jack would speak, "that I cannot release Mr. Lester. There's a waltz starting up." With calculated charm, Sophie smiled dazzlingly up at Jack. "Our waltz, I believe, Jack."

Jack's slow smile was triumphant. "Our waltz, dear Sophie."

They left Miss Billingham, open-mouthed, staring after them.

Sophie was seething as they took to the floor. "How *dare*

she? How can they? They're all quite shameless. I thought it was only rakes who were so."

Jack chuckled and drew her closer. "Hush, my sweet Sophie." When she glared in reply, her full breasts swelling with indignation, he brushed a most reprehensible kiss across her curls. "It doesn't matter. You're mine—and I'm yours. When your uncle returns, we can tell the world."

Sophie took comfort in the warmth of his gaze, and in the delight she saw behind it. Did he really find it so surprising that she would fly to his aid?

Whatever the case, she thought, as she felt the waltz, and him, weave their accustomed magic, Horatio had better return soon. In such difficult circumstances, there was no telling what scandalous declaration she might feel obliged to make.

CHAPTER FOURTEEN

GALA NIGHT AT VAUXHALL was a treat few among the *ton* cared to miss. With their party, swollen by the presence of Jeremy and Gerald, who had been included by special dispensation, Sophie strolled beside Jack down the Grand Walk. She saw many familiar faces, all bright with expectation of the night's revelries. None were as bright as hers.

She glanced up at Jack and smiled, feeling her brittle tension tighten. Horatio was due back tonight; her uncle had sent word that despite the business that had delayed him, he would return this evening to join them at the Gardens. Jack smiled back, his hand warm over hers where it rested on his sleeve. He said nothing, but the expression in his eyes left her in no doubt of his thoughts.

Determined at least to appear calm, Sophie gave her attention to their surroundings, duly exclaiming at the brightly lit colonnade, which had been added since her last visit. Jeremy and George, and, to a lesser extent, Toby, Ned and Clarissa, looked about with avid interest, speculating on the age of the elms lining the gravelled promenade and eyeing the dense shrubbery separating the walks.

"I think the booth your uncle has rented is this way."

Jack steered her to the right of the section of promenade known as the Grove. Toby followed with Lucilla on his arm, Ned and Clarissa behind with the two boys bringing up the rear. In the centre of the Grove, a small orchestra was setting up. Arranged about the perimeter were a large number of wooden booths, many already filled with patrons come to enjoy the night's entertainments.

Their booth proved to have an excellent view of the orchestra.

"Ah, yes." Lucilla settled herself on a chair by the wide front window. "A most satisfactory location. From here, one can see almost everything."

Sophie noticed her aunt's gaze was not on the musicians. Indeed, it seemed as if all of fashionable London were a part of the passing scene. Gentlemen and ladies of all degrees strolled upon the paths; many stopped to exchange pleasantries with her aunt before moving on. Then there were the bucks and their ladybirds, the bright lights of the *demi-monde*. Sophie found herself fascinated by one particular redhead— or rather her gown, a wispy concoction of silk and feathers that barely concealed her charms. Until she noticed the interest the lady evinced in return, and realized it was not for her. A frown threatening, Sophie glanced at her companion—the focus of the red-head's attention—only to find he was watching her. A slow smile lifted his lips; one dark brow rose.

Sophie blushed vividly, and pointedly transferred her gaze to the orchestra. As if sensing her need, they promptly laid bow to string, filling the night with their magic. Soon, a bevy of couples was whirling in the light of the Chinese lanterns, suspended high overhead.

Jack rose. "Come," he said, holding out his hand, a smile and an invitation in his eyes. "No one counts the dances at Vauxhall."

For an instant, Sophie met his gaze. Then, with a calm decisiveness that surprised even her, she lifted her chin and put her hand in his. "How accommodating."

Her uncle had better arrive soon; she couldn't bear to wait much longer.

Luckily, Jack proved most efficient at distracting her, until her mind was filled with nothing beyond thoughts of him, of his teasing smile and the beckoning warmth behind his blue eyes. He danced with her twice, then relinquished her to Ned, who in turn passed her to Toby before Jack once more drew her into his arms.

Sophie laughed. "I find myself quite breathless, sir."

Jack smiled down at her, a slow crooked smile. "Jack," he said.

Sophie looked into his eyes; her breath vanished altogether. "Jack," she whispered, letting her lashes fall.

Jack's arm tightened about her; he swept her into the waltz.

Supper was provided in the booth, laid out on a narrow trestle table at the rear, along with a jug of lemonade and another of the famous Vauxhall punch. When they lifted the linen cloths from the dishes, they found delicate cucumber sandwiches, a selection of pastries and a large platter of the fabled wafer-thin ham.

"Exactly as I recall," Lucilla declared, holding up one near-transparent slice. She looked at Sophie. "When your mother and I were debs, we were always famished after a night at Vauxhall." Nibbling the ham, she added, "I told Cook to lay out a cold collation for when we get back."

Jack, Ned and Toby looked relieved.

Somewhere in the gardens, a gong clanged. The music had stopped some minutes before and the heavy note vibrated through the twilight.

"Time to view the Grand Spectacle!"

Jeremy's shout was echoed from all around. There was a surge of bodies as people left their booths to join the throng flocking to where a looming mountain, now brilliantly lit, rose craggily from amidst the otherwise unremarkable landscape. Fifteen minutes were spent in oohing and aahing at the various elements, some mechanical, others purely decorative, artfully placed within the alpine scene. Then the lights were doused. Chattering and exclaiming, the patrons returned to the walks, the booths and the dancing.

The last of their company to return to their booth, Sophie and Jack strolled through the twilight, her hand on his arm. She could feel the tension that gripped him, lending steel to the muscles beneath her fingertips.

"Sophie?"

Wreathed in shadows, Sophie looked up.

Jack stared at the pale oval of her face, the wide eyes and slightly parted lips. For a moment, he was still, then, concealed by the shadows, he bent his head and swiftly kissed her.

Sophie's lips met his, her heart leaping at the brief caress. Her hands fluttered; her arms ached to hold him.

Jack caught her hands. "Not yet, sweetheart." His smile was decidedly crooked. "Just pray your uncle's carriage doesn't break an axle."

Sophie sighed feelingly and allowed him to resettle her hand on his sleeve.

Covering her hand with his, Jack gently squeezed her fingers. "We'd better get back to the booth." As they strolled out of the shadows, he added, "The fireworks come later."

Puzzled, Sophie looked up. "I hadn't imagined fireworks to be one of your abiding interests."

Jack glanced down at her, then his slow, rake's smile curved his lips. "There are many kinds of fireworks, my dear."

For an instant, Sophie glimpsed the dark, powerful passions behind his blue eyes. A distinctly delicious sensation slithered down her spine. But further discovery was denied her; they were caught up in the dancers and dragged into the heart of the revels once more.

The orchestra was now accompanied by a vocalist, a tenor whose pure notes drifted high over the booths to disappear into the increasing darkness. Stars speckled the sky as night slowly enfolded the scene. The Chinese lanterns came into their own, shedding their rosy glow over dancers and musicians alike. Laughter and the mellow murmur of conversation, softer now, muted by the effects of good food and fine wines, rippled through the shadows.

Throughout the evening, again and again, Sophie's eyes met Jack's. A magical web held them bound; neither was aware of those about them. And what passed between them was magical, too, carried in the weight of shared glances and the lingering touch of lovers' hands.

Their surroundings were part of the magic. At the conclusion of the musical interlude, the tenor embarked on a solo performance. Breathless, conversing softly, the dancers headed back to their booths. As she strolled on Jack's arm, Sophie noticed Belle Chessington on the arm of Mr. Somercote—surely a most unlikely Vauxhall patron. Belle waved and smiled hugely, her eyes sparkling. Mr. Somercote, too, smiled broadly, clearly both pleased and proud.

"Well, well," Jack murmured. "You'll have to tell your aunt she's achieved a minor miracle. Somercote's silence has been tripping the matchmakers up for years. It looks as if he's finally found his tongue."

Sophie laughed. "Indeed, you have to admit he won't need many words, not with Belle on his arm."

Jack smiled, then looked ahead.

And tensed. Sophie felt it, and followed his gaze to see the rotund figure of her uncle clearly visible in their booth.

"Just in time." Jack quickened his pace.

As they entered the booth, Lucilla beckoned to Sophie. "Mrs. Chessington just stopped by. Wonder of wonders!"

From the corner of her eye, Sophie saw Jack greet Horatio. They exchanged a few words, Jack very serious, then both turned and left the booth.

Subsiding onto the chair beside her aunt, Sophie forced herself to concentrate enough to follow Lucilla's discourse. It proved a supremely difficult task. Her hands clasping and unclasping in her lap, she was acutely conscious of every little sound, every movement in the booth.

She jumped when the gong rang again.

"The fireworks!"

Once more, the patrons poured from the booths and from the shadowy walks, heading for a small arena surrounded by lawns. Smiling indulgently, Lucilla allowed Jeremy and George to tug her to her feet. Sophie rose uncertainly, glancing about. Ned offered Clarissa his arm; together with Toby they joined the exodus. Jack was nowhere to be seen.

"There you are, m'dear." Horatio materialized outside the booth. "Come along now or you'll miss the fun."

Sophie stared at him, her heart sinking all the way to her slippers. Hadn't Jack asked? Why wasn't he here? Did that mean..? Forcing her shaking limbs to function, she picked up her half-cape. Swinging it about her shoulders, she left the booth.

Horatio offered her his arm. They started to stroll slowly in the wake of the others, now far ahead. But instead of joining his family, Horatio stopped in the shadows, well to the rear of the crowd.

"Now, my dear Sophie, I understand you have had some reservations about Jack's financial situation."

Slowly, Sophie turned to face her uncle, her heart thudding in her throat. She held herself proudly, a silent prayer on her lips.

Apparently oblivious, Horatio rattled on. "It really was quite remiss of him, I agree. He should have told you much earlier. But you'll have to excuse him—not but what, with his experience, you might have expected a little more than the usual impulsive rush. But men in love, you know, tend to forget such minor matters as money." Smiling genially, he patted Sophie's hand.

Sophie drew in a slow, deep breath. "Uncle, are you telling me that Jack is truly wealthy? That he doesn't need to marry a rich bride?"

Horatio's grey eyes twinkled. "Let's just say that for him, expectations alone will be a more than sufficient dower."

A golden rocket burst in a flurry of brilliant stars, gilding Sophie's face. Her eyes shone, reflecting the glory.

"Oh, Uncle!" Sophie flung her arms about Horatio's neck.

Horatio chuckled and reciprocated her, then gently turned her. "Come, let's join the festivities."

Sophie was only too ready to do so. She peered into the darkness, eagerly searching the crowd every time another rocket lit up the scene. They found Lucilla and the boys in the front ranks. The boys pounced on Horatio, bombarding him with questions.

Then a large wheel lit up the night, hissing and spitting as the force of the rockets tied to its spokes whirled it round. In the midst of the crowd, Sophie stood very still, her face slowly draining of expression. The steadier illumination confirmed beyond doubt that Jack, Ned and Toby were not present. Neither was Clarissa.

The memory of Gurnard's plan rushed into Sophie's mind, thrusting all other considerations aside. This was the time Toby was to have taken Clarissa to meet the dastardly captain. Yet Ned had been with them—he wouldn't let any harm come to Clarissa. But where were they? If Jack, Ned and Toby had gone to warn off the captain, where was Clarissa?

Sophie blinked in the glare of a set of coloured flares; elation, guilt and sheer frustration poured through her in a dizzying wave.

Horatio would know. She looked to where her uncle stood, Lucilla beside him, George's hand in his. Jeremy was throwing questions at his father in a never-ending stream. There was no possibility of speaking to Horatio without alerting Lucilla and, potentially worse, the boys.

Everything was probably all right; Jack would surely have the matter in hand.

But maybe Jack was elsewhere, ignorant of Gurnard's threat? Perhaps Toby and Ned had decided to handle it on their own? And Clarissa had followed?

Sophie turned and quietly made her way back through the crowd.

The majority of the patrons were viewing the fireworks, leaving the walks sparsely populated. Here and there, a couple or a small group still wandered, having seen the fireworks too many times. But the crush of revellers that had filled the walks earlier had given way to empty shadows.

Just beyond the booths, Sophie slowed. The Dark Walk, with the Temple of Diana, lay furthest afield, the narrowest and most heavily shaded of the Gardens' promenades. And the most secluded.

Grimacing, Sophie halted. It would be the height of folly to risk the length of the Dark Walk at night, alone. But if she went back up the Grand Wall, wide and well lit, she could take a side path across to the Dark Walk, emerging just a little above the Temple. It was longer, but she was far more certain to reach her goal by that route.

Clutching her cape about her, she turned and hurried up the Grand Walk.

At the Temple of Diana, deep in the shadows of the Dark Walk, Jack waited with Toby, concealed in thick bushes by the temple's side. A small structure in the Ionic style, the temple was little more than a decorative gazebo. The surrounding bushes had grown close over the years, filling the side arches until the space within resembled a room with green walls.

Jack peered through the shadows. Toby had delivered Clarissa to the temple at the appointed time. Ned had earlier hidden himself on the other side of the main archway, awaiting his moment of glory. Gurnard, however, was late.

The scrunch of heavy footsteps on gravel brought Jack's head up. Out on the path, the figure of a man came into view, heading purposefully towards the temple. He made no attempt to conceal his approach; a guardsman's red cape was thrown over one shoulder.

"Here he comes," hissed Toby.

They waited, frozen in the shadows, as Gurnard climbed the short flight of steps and disappeared into the temple.

"So far so good," Jack whispered.

Inside the temple, however, all was not going as either they, or Captain Gurnard, had planned.

Clarissa, delivered by a strangely serious Toby to the dim temple with a promise that her most ardent suitor—Ned, of course—would shortly join her, had entered the shadowy hall with high hopes. It was clear that Sophie would shortly receive the offer she desired; Clarissa, having expended considerable effort in encouraging Ned, expected that he would, tonight, at least take a more definite step in his wooing of her. With any luck, he might kiss her. Why else had he asked her here?

As the minutes ticked by, she had fallen to pacing, hands clasped behind her, her brow furrowed as she wondered how fast she could urge things along. A marriage in September, assuming Sophie did not opt for a long betrothal, seemed a distinct possibility.

She had reached this point in her cogitations when firm footsteps approached and ascended to the temple.

Starry-eyed, Clarissa turned.

And beheld the unmistakable outline of Captain Gurnard.

"What are you doing here?" she demanded, not the least bit pleased at the prospect of having her tryst with Ned interrupted or—even worse—postponed.

Terrance Gurnard blinked. "Why, I'm here to meet you, my dear."

"I'm afraid, sir, that my time this evening is spoken for." If nothing else, Clarissa was Lucilla's daughter. She delivered the captain's dismissal with an affronted dignity that would have done justice to royalty.

For a moment, Gurnard was bewildered. Where was the youthful, wide-eyed innocent he had arranged to meet? Then he shook himself. The hoity young miss was just playing hard to get. "Nonsense, my dear," he purred, advancing on Clarissa. "We all know you're besotted with me. But fear not, for I'm equally besotted with you."

Even in the dimness, Gurnard could not misinterpret the icy rigidity that laid hold of Clarissa's slim frame. She drew herself up and, somehow, succeeded in looking down her nose at him. "My dear Captain, I believe you have lost your wits." The cool incisiveness in her tone bit deep. "If you will but consider, the notion that I, with suitors such as Mr. Ascombe, could consider you, who have nought but your uniform to commend you, is highly insulting, sir!"

Rocked by the strident vehemence in her tone, Gurnard blinked. Then he sneered. "You were ready enough to encourage me to dangle after you—do you deny it?" Abruptly, he closed the gap between them. He did not have all night to accomplish what he must.

"That was because you were being useful." Clarissa, her own considerable temper in orbit, continued with undisguised relish, "Useful in ensuring that *Mr. Ascombe's* attention did not wander."

"Useful, was I?" Gurnard ground out. "In that case, my dear, you'll have to pay the piper." Roughly, he grasped her arms, intending to pull her to him.

Used to wrestling with her brothers, Clarissa anticipated the move enough to wrench one arm free. "Let me *go,* sir!"

Her furious shriek jolted Ned from the dazed stupor into which he had fallen. He shot up the steps, only just remembering their plan in time to change his automatic. "Unhand her, you fiend!" to a relatively normal, if slightly strangled, "Clarissa?"

He saw her immediately, one arm held by Gurnard. With an heroic effort, assisted by the calming effects of the cold rage that poured through him, Ned strolled lazily forward. "There you are, m'dear. I apologize for my tardiness, but I was held up." Commandingly, he held out his hand to Clarissa, his gaze, coldly challenging, fixed on Gurnard's face.

In order to take her hand, Clarissa chose to use the arm Gurnard was holding. She did so without in any way acknowledging Gurnard's grasp, much less his presence.

The action snapped Gurnard's patience. He had no time to play games, nor to brook interference of any sort. He waited until, as Clarissa's fingers slipped into Ned's palm, Ned glanced at her. Then he attacked.

And was immediately sent to grass—or marble, as was the case—by a punishing left jab.

In the bushes to the side, Jack allowed the battle-ready

tension that had instantly gripped him to fade. "He said his left jab was coming along."

Inside the temple, Ned frowned, attempting to shield Clarissa from the sight of the captain stretched out on the marble floor. "I'm sorry, Clary. Not the sort of thing one should do in front of a lady, I know. You aren't feeling faint or anything, are you?"

"Good heavens, no!" Clarissa, eyes alight, both hands clutching one of Ned's forearms, peered around him at the captain's prone form. Satisfied that the captain was, at last temporarily, beyond further punishment, she turned her glowing eyes on Ned. "That was *marvellous,* Ned! How *thrillingly* heroic. You rescued me!"

And with that, Clarissa promptly hurled herself into her knight errant's arms.

The watchers in the bushes heard Ned mutter something that sounded like a weak disclaimer but his heart was clearly not in it. Then came silence.

Jack sighed and relaxed, looking up into the night sky, considering, with a certain rakish satisfaction, the prospect of the immediate future. Beside him, Toby shifted restlessly.

Then they heard Ned's voice, and Clarissa's replying; the pair turned, still hand in hand, Clarissa's head against Ned's shoulder, and made slowly for the steps.

"We'll follow," Jack said. "They may be almost betrothed but they're not betrothed yet."

They followed Clarissa and Ned at a distance; it was questionable whether either was aware of their presence.

When they reached the booth, it was to find Horatio beaming benevolently, and Ned standing, proud but a trifle hesitant, as Clarissa poured the details of her rescue into her mother's ear. Jeremy's and George's eyes were wide as they drank it all in. Seeing Jack, Lucilla smiled and asked, "Where's Sophie?"

Ned and Clarissa looked blank.

Toby blinked.

Jack froze—and looked at Horatio.

Suddenly serious, Horatio frowned. "I spoke with her, then we joined Lucilla and the boys. At the end of the fireworks display, Sophie had disappeared. I thought she was with you."

"She must have gone to the temple," Toby said, genuinely horrified.

"Gurnard's still there," Ned pointed out.

"I'll find her." Jack kept his expression impassive, despite the emotions roiling within. He exchanged a look with Horatio, who nodded. Striding to the door, Jack spared a glance for Lucilla. "Don't worry," he said. The smile that accompanied the words held a certain grim resolution.

Somewhat subdued, the rest of the party settled to listen to the last of the music.

"You know," Lucilla murmured as Horatio took the seat beside her, "I'm really not sure we've done the right thing."

"How so?"

"Well, I'm quite sure Sophie can handle Captain Gurnard. But can she handle Jack Lester?"

Horatio smiled and patted her hand. "I'm sure she'll contrive."

ON GAINING THE Dark Walk, Sophie paused to catch her breath. Peering through the shadows, she could just make out the distant glimmer of the temple's white pillars, set back in a small grove. The path leading to the water-gate lay nearby; somewhere beyond the temple lay one of the less-used street gates.

Dragging in a deep breath, Sophie quit the shadows. There was no one about. Her soft slippers made little sound on the gravel as she neared the temple steps. Standing at the bottom, she peered in but could see nothing but shadows. Surely Clarissa could not be inside?

For a full minute, she vacillated, then, holding her cape close about her, Sophie mounted the steps. If there was no one inside, it couldn't hurt to look.

The shadows within enveloped her. Sophie glanced about, then stifled a shriek as a dark shape loomed beside her.

"Well, well, well. Come to look for your cousin, I take it?"

As the shape resolved itself into Captain Gurnard, Sophie gave an almost imperceptible gasp. Straightening, she nodded. "But as she isn't here—"

"You'll do just as well."

The captain wrapped one hand about Sophie's arm.

Instinctively, she tried to pull away. "Unhand me, sir! What on earth do you believe can come of this?"

"Money, my dear Miss Winterton. Lots of money."

Sophie remembered his scheme. "You appear to have overlooked something, Captain. I am not an heiress."

"No," Gurnard acknowledged. "You're something even better. You're the woman Lester's got his eye on."

"What's that supposed to mean?" Sophie carefully tested the captain's hold.

"It means," Gurnard sneered, convincing her his grip was unbreakable by shaking her, "that Lester will pay and pay handsomely to have you returned to him. And he'll pay even more to ensure you're...unharmed, shall we say?"

Sophie recoiled as Gurnard thrust his face close to hers. "It seems Lester's windfall is to be *my* gain." With an abrupt laugh, he turned and dragged her towards the door. "Come on."

Dredging up every ounce of her courage, Sophie went rigid and pulled back. Her full weight served only to slow the captain, but it was enough to make him turn with a snarl.

Sophie lifted her chin, refusing to be cowed. "There is, as I said, something you appear to have overlooked, Captain. I am *not* going to marry Mr. Lester."

"Gammon," said Gurnard, and tugged her on.

"But I'm *not!*" Sophie placed her free hand over her heart. "I swear on my mother's grave that Mr. Lester has not asked for my hand."

"It's not my fault if he's backward." They had almost reached the top of the steps.

Sophie lost her temper. "You imbecile! I'm trying to make it plain to you that I am *not going to marry Jack Lester!*"

Gurnard stopped and turned to her, fury in every line of his large frame. "You," he began, pointing a finger at her.

"Should learn to accept Fate graciously."

There was a split second of silence, then Gurnard turned.

Only to meet a left jab that had a great deal more power behind it than the one he'd met earlier.

The result was the same. The captain's head hit the marble with a resounding thump.

Sophie glared down at him, prostrate at her feet. "Of all the unmitigated scoundrels," she began.

Jack shook his head and sighed. "Are you and your cousin so lost to all sensibility that you can't even swoon at the sight of violence?"

Sophie blinked at him, then humphed. "If you must know, I'm feeling quite violent myself. Did you know he intended to—"

"I heard." Jack reached for her and drew her to him. "But you don't need to worry about him any more."

Sophie readily went into his arms. "But shouldn't we—"

"It's already taken care of." Jack looked down at Gurnard, then prodded him with the toe of his boot. His victim groaned. "I sincerely hope you're listening, Gurnard, for I'm only going to say this once. I've had a word with an acquaintance of mine, the Earl of Melcham. He was most upset to hear of the method you'd selected to raise the wind. He doesn't approve—not at all. And I'm sure you know what happens to those of whom Melcham disapproves."

There was a stunned silence, then Gurnard groaned again.

Grimly satisfied, Jack turned Sophie towards the steps. "And now, my dear, I think it's time we left." Tucking her hand in his arm, he led her down onto the gravelled walk.

Sophie went readily, her mind seething with questions. "What happened to Clarissa? Did she go to the temple?"

Jack glanced down at her. "She did."

Sophie glared at him. "What happened?"

Jack smiled and told her, adding that Horatio had approved their scheme. "If Clarissa had simply not shown up, Gurnard would have assumed she'd been prevented from doing so, not that she wouldn't go to meet him. He'd have tried again to get her alone, and perhaps we wouldn't have learned of his intentions in time to foil him. It was best to make the situation as clear as possible."

"But what if he turns to some other young lady?"

"He won't have time. As of tomorrow, courtesy of Melcham, to whom Gurnard is deeply in debt, the captain will have entirely too much on his mind to think of persuading any other young lady to his rescue."

Sophie pondered his revelations, her feet following his lead. "So Ned floored the captain?"

"He seems to have floored Clarissa as well." Jack's lips curved in fond reminiscence. He slanted a glance at Sophie. "We all thought the opportunity too good to miss to advance Ned's standing with your cousin."

For an instant, Sophie stared into his smugly satisfied face. Then she burst out laughing. "Oh, dear. Was that supposed to be Ned's great scene—so that Clarissa would think him her hero and respond suitably?"

Frowning, Jack nodded.

"Oh, poor Ned." Sophie could not stop smiling. She glanced confidently up at Jack. "Just for your information, Clarissa settled on Ned some weeks ago, not all that long after we'd come up to town. She's been trying to nudge him along for the past two weeks at least. I'm not at all surprised to hear she flung herself into his arms. After all, what better opportunity she could hope for?"

Jack looked down at her through narrowed eyes. "Remind me," he said, "to tell Ned just what he's getting into, marrying a Webb female."

Sophie pressed her lips tightly together. When she was sure her voice was under control, she said, "I'm related to the Webbs; does that make me a 'Webb female', too?"

Jack's glance was supercilious. "I haven't yet decided."

It was then, when he stood back to usher her through the watergate, that Sophie realized that they had been walking in the wrong direction. A leafy lane stretched before them. Not far ahead, the lane ended by the banks of the Thames. Sophie halted. "Ah…Jack…?"

Jack looked down at her and held out his hand. "Your uncle's returned. He spoke to you, didn't he?"

"Yes." Eyes wide, Sophie studied his face. "He told me there's no reason we can't marry."

"Precisely." Jack smiled, closing his hand about the fingers she had automatically surrendered. He drew her closer and tucked her hand into the crook of his arm. "Which is to say that by common consent, general agreement and the blessing of Fate, my wait is, at long last, over."

"But shouldn't we..?" Sophie glanced back at the dark shrubbery of the Gardens, slowly receding in their wake.

Jack cast her a reproving glance. "Really, my dear. You don't seriously imagine that *I*, such as I am, could consider Vauxhall a suitable venue for a proposal, do you?"

There seemed no sensible answer to that.

But Sophie had no time to ponder the implications. They had reached the water's edge. She glanced about, somewhat surprised at the bustling scene. A stone wharf lined the river and extended out in a jetty where a small flotilla of pleasure craft bobbed gently at their moorings.

"If habits linger, he'll be at the end."

A most peculiar sensation started to creep along Sophie's nerves. She clung to Jack's arm as they wended their way between Garden patrons haggling with the boatmen, and others embarking for a slow ride home. The craft were of a variety of sizes, some holding no more than a couple, while others could comfortably carry a small party. Still others had canopies erected over their bows under which lovers could pursue their acquaintance in privacy, screened by drapes which let down about the sides.

It was towards one of these last that Jack led her.

"Rollinson?"

Sophie suddenly felt quite light-headed.

The beefy boatman in charge of the largest and most opulent craft turned from desultory conversation with his crew to peer up at Jack. "There you be, Mr. Lester!" He grinned, displaying a row of decidedly haphazard teeth, and tipped his felt hat to Sophie. "Got your message. We're here and ready, sir."

"Very good," Jack replied.

Sophie found it hard to follow the rest of their conversation, at least half of which was conducted in boatman's cant. She glanced about, trying to interest herself in the scene, rather than dwell on what their presence here probably meant. If she thought of that, she might feel obliged to protest.

As it was, she was not to escape making some part of the decision on her fate. Their itinerary agreed upon, Jack leapt down to the wooden planking of the boat's hull, which floated a good yard below the jetty.

He then turned to study Sophie, one brow rising. "Well, my dear?" With a graceful gesture, he indicated the boat and the curtain cutting off the bow. His slow, slightly crooked smile twisted his lips. "Will you trust yourself to me tonight?"

For an instant, Sophie stared down at him, oblivious of those about them, of the sly yet careful glances cast her by the boatmen. All she could see was Jack, waiting for her, a very definite glint in his eyes. For an instant, she closed her own. What he was suggesting was perfectly scandalous. Drawing in a deep breath, she opened her eyes and, with a soft smile, stepped to the edge of the jetty.

The familiar feel of Jack's hands about her waist was reassuring, soothing the peculiar jitteriness that, all of a sudden, had afflicted her. He set her down beside him, one arm slipping about her to steady her as he helped her across the rowing benches. Parting the heavy damask curtain that screened the bow, he ushered her through.

Sophie entered a private and very luxurious world of moonlight glinting on water. The curtain fell closed behind them, sealing them in. With a slight lurch, the boat got under way. Jack's arm came to urge her to a seat as the boat nosed out onto the river. Once clear of the craft by the jetty, the boat pulled smoothly, powerfully, upstream.

As her eyes adjusted to the deep shadows beneath the canopy, Sophie, fascinated, gazed about. She was seated amid a pile of huge silk cushions spread over a satin-draped platform, heavily padded, that was constructed to fit snugly across the bow. The platform all but filled the area behind the curtain, leaving barely enough room for a wine cooler, which, she noticed, contained a bottle, already open and chilling, and a small fixed buffet holding glasses and small dishes of unidentifiable delicacies. Jack turned from examining the buffet's offerings to look down at her.

"I think we'll leave the caviar for second course."

Sophie's eyes widened. She didn't need to ask what he fancied for the first. His eyes, even in the shadows, gleamed as they rested on her. Clearing her throat, suddenly dry, she asked, a trifle unsteadily, "You planned this?"

His smile was smugly triumphant. "To the last detail," Jack averred, coming to lounge on the cushions beside her. "It's customary, you know."

"Is it?" Sophie stared at him.

"Mmm-hmm." Jack leaned back, gazing upward to where the canopy overhead was drawn partially back, revealing the black velvet of the sky sprinkled with jewelled stars. "Seductions are never so satisfying as when they're well-planned."

Sophie bit her lip and eyed him warily.

His gaze on her face, Jack laughed and, reaching up, drew her down to lie among the cushions beside him. Sophie hesitated, then yielded to his gentle strength. Propped on one elbow, Jack smiled down into her wide eyes. Then he bent his head and kissed her, long and lingeringly, before whispering against her lips, "I'm not teasing, Sophie."

A thrill of desire raced through Sophie, all the way down to her toes. She opened her lips on a feeble protest—and Jack kissed her again. And kept kissing her until she had no breath left to speak.

"No, Sophie." Jack dropped soft kisses on her eyelids as his fingers deftly unbuttoned her gown. "I've had more than enough of wooing you, my love. You're mine, and I'm yours. And nothing else matters." His voice deepened at the last as he looked down at her breast, the firm ivory flesh filling his palm.

Sophie arched lightly as his thumb circled the rosy peak. Unable to speak, barely able to breathe, she watched him from beneath heavy lids as he caressed her. Then he lowered his head and she stopped breathing altogether, her fingers sinking into his shoulders as his tongue lightly teased, knowingly tantalized.

"Besides," Jack murmured against her soft skin. "We've only one thing left to discuss."

"Discuss?" The word came out weakly on a slow exhalation, the best Sophie could manage, her mind struggling against the drugging haze of his caresses.

"Hmm. We have to discuss what I'll accept as suitable recompense for my torture."

"Torture?" Sophie knew about torture. She was being tortured now, his hands touching her so skilfully she was gripped by an urgent longing. "What torture?"

"The torture of having to woo you, sweet Sophie."

Sophie stirred, consumed by the sweetest ache. "Was it torture?"

"Torture and worse," Jack vowed, his voice deep and raspy.

Sophie sighed. "What do you consider suitable recompense?" She just managed to get the words out before he stole her breath again with a caress so artful she thought she could faint. She didn't, but the sensations didn't stop, darting through her like lightning, spreading like warm fire beneath her skin.

Aeons filled with pleasure seemed to have passed before she heard his soft murmur.

"I know what I want as my reward for wooing you. Will you give it me?"

"Yes." Her voice was a soft whisper on the breeze.

Jack raised his head, a smile twisting his lips. "I haven't yet told you what I want."

Sophie returned his smile with one of her own. "It had better be me—for that's all I have to give you."

For the first time in his rakish career, Jack was lost for words. He looked down into her eyes, passion-filled and mysterious. "Sophie." His voice was hoarse, dark with his turbulent passions. "You're all I'll ever want."

"Then take me," Sophie murmured, wondering, very distantly, how she dared. She reached up and drew his lips to hers before her sane self could resurface and disturb the glorious moment.

Thereafter, her sanity or otherwise was not in question; desire caught her and held her until she glowed with its flame. Jack fed her fires, never letting her cool, until she ached for him to join her. When he did, it was as if the sun shone brightly out of the night-dark sky. Sophie surrendered to joy and delight and rapturous, delirious pleasure. For one timeless moment, she felt that she had flown so high she could touch the stars gleaming in the firmament. Then she softly drifted back to earth, safe, forever, in Jack's strong arms.

The gentle rocking of the boat, and Jack's heavy weight, drew her slowly back to reality.

Surprisingly, Sophie found her mind oddly clear, as if the sensations that had held her body in thrall had proved so overpowering that her wits had disengaged and retreated to a safe distance. She could feel the cool caress of the river breeze on her naked skin and her lover's touch as, propped now beside her, he gently stroked her hair from her face. She opened her eyes and looked up. He was a dark shadow as he hung over her, solid and comforting in the moonlight. Sophie listened for the shush of the water under the hull—and made a discovery. "We're not moving."

Jack's smile gleamed in the moonlight. "We're moored. Off a private park. The men left us nearly an hour ago." He reached up to spread out her curling hair, released from its moorings. "They'll come back later and take us home. My carriage will be waiting at the steps."

Sophie blinked. "You really did think of everything."

His smile grew broader. "I always aim to please." He shifted slightly, drawing her more comfortably into his arms and tucking a silk shawl tenderly about her. "And now that I've pleased you, how soon can we be wed?"

Still slightly dazed, Sophie stared up at him, marshalling her wandering wits.

"Not that I'm trying to rush you, my love, but there are any number of reasons why an early, if not immediate, wedding would suit us best."

As he turned her hand over to press a kiss into her palm, and the touch of his lips stirred the embers that were only now dying within her, Sophie abruptly nodded. "I see your point." She stopped to clear her throat, amazed she could think at all. "My father's due back for a quick visit next month—can we wait until then?"

Jack raised his head to look down at her. "It might be hard." He smiled, his usual crooked smile. "But I suspect we can wait until then."

Sophie sighed, deeply content. She put up a hand to brush back the dark locks from his forehead. "You'll have to marry me; you've thoroughly compromised me. We've been away for far too long."

"I always intended to marry you. From the moment I first saw you in Lady Asfordby's ballroom."

Sophie studied his face in the moonlight. "Did you really?"

"From the moment I saw you dancing with that upstart Marston," Jack admitted. "I was smitten then and there."

"Oh, Jack!"

After the necessary exchange of affection brought on by that revelation, Sophie was the first to return to reality. "Dear Heaven," she exclaimed weakly. "We've been gone for hours."

Jack caught the hint of concern dawning in her voice. "Don't worry. Horatio knows you're with me."

Fascinated, Sophie stared at him. "Did you tell my aunt, too?"

"Good God." Jack shuddered. "What a horrible thought. If I had, I'd lay odds she'd have given me instructions. I don't think my pride could have stood it." Jack dropped a soft kiss on one delectable rosy peak. "Your aunt, my love, is just plain dangerous."

Privately, Sophie agreed but was far too distracted to find words to say so. Sometime later, her mind drifting in dazed consideration of the future he had spread before her, the home, the family—everything she had ever wanted—with him by her side, she returned to his point. "Speaking of marriage, sir, you have not yet asked me to marry you."

"I have—you quibbled and refused."

Sophie smiled into the night. "But you're supposed to ask me again, now that my uncle has given me permission to receive your addresses."

Jack sighed lustily, then shifted to move over her, one elbow planted on either side, his expression arrogantly commanding. His eyes, deep dark pools within which passion still smouldered, transfixed her.

"Very well, Miss Winterton. For the *very last time*—will you marry me? I realize, of course, that you are only a lady of expectations and not an heiress. However, as it transpires, I neither need nor want a wealthy bride. You, my beautiful, desirable Sophie—" Jack bent his head to do homage to her lips "—will do just wonderfully. You, my love, fulfil all *my* expectations." Another kiss stole her breath. "Every last one."

A soft smile curving her lips, her gaze misty with happiness, Sophie reached up to slide her arms about his neck. Her acceptance was delivered, not in words but in those actions which, to her mind, and Jack's spoke best.

As the Webb carriage rocked into motion, leaving the shadows of Vauxhall behind, Lucilla sank back against the squabs. On the opposite seat, Jeremy and George yawned and closed their eyes, their faces wreathed in seraphic smiles. Behind, in the smaller carriage, Toby, Ned and Clarissa were doubtless still exclaiming over their exciting evening. Lucilla, however, was not impressed.

She had just been informed that Jack would be returning Sophie to Mount Street by a different route.

It was several long moments before she trusted herself to speak.

"And you told *me* not to meddle." With an audible humph, she cast a disgusted glance at her spouse.

Horatio was too wise to answer. He smiled serenely, glancing upriver as the carriage rattled over the bridge.

* * * * *

THE SECRETS
OF A COURTESAN

Nicola Cornick

Dear Reader,

Welcome to the Regency world of Fortune's Folly, a town set in the wild Yorkshire Dales where scandal, danger and romance are but a step away!

Eve Nightingale has run away from London and created a new life for herself in the little Yorkshire market town, but when her former lover, the handsome and charismatic Alasdair, Duke of Welburn, arrives in Fortune's Folly, all her secrets are in danger of exposure. Can Eve and Alasdair rekindle the love that once united them or will they be driven apart forever?

It's a very great pleasure to see *The Secrets of a Courtesan* in print for the very first time. This prequel to my Brides of Fortune series has previously only been available in ebook format and I have had so many requests from readers wanting a print copy. Here it is, especially for you!

Very best wishes,

Nicola

For my sister-in-law, Julie.

PROLOGUE

April 1809
Letter from Lord Hawkesbury,
Home Secretary, to Alasdair Rowarth, Duke of Welburn

Rowarth,
I write to you in absolute confidence, requesting your assistance on a matter of national security. Mutual acquaintances tell me that you are an utterly sound fellow. I am sure this is the case because I knew your cousin at Eton. So, Rowarth, here is the situation. For some time now this department has been investigating the criminal activities of one Warren Sampson, a mill owner who has acquired land around the villages of Peacock's Oak and Fortune's Folly in the North Riding of Yorkshire. Sampson is suspected of encouraging civil unrest and sedition and it is *imperative* that we put and end to his influence. *Imperative,* I tell you. The man is a blackguard, an utter scoundrel. And now we may have found a way but it is a matter of considerable delicacy. It involves a certain Mrs. Eve Nightingale or, as you may remember her, Eva Night…

Pray, call on me at your earliest convenience so that I may acquaint you with your task.
Yours in haste,
Hawkesbury

CHAPTER ONE

Fortune's Folly, Yorkshire—May 1809

EVE NIGHTINGALE had never believed that her past would catch up with her. She had run too far and hidden herself too well to be found. And then she saw Alasdair Rowarth, Duke of Welburn, in Fortune's Folly Market Square one morning in spring and knew that everything that she had striven for was in danger.

Eve had been shopping, browsing amongst the market stalls, taking her time to chat to the sellers and enjoying the sunshine. The winter had been long and bitter with so much snow that for a time the village, so high in the Yorkshire dales and fells, had been cut off from the outside world. Now that spring had finally arrived it had brought an influx of visitors, for Fortune's Folly was a spa of some note, not as famous as the local town of Harrogate, but with health-giving mineral waters that were said to be far less disgusting to drink. And on this May morning the square was full of townsfolk and visitors taking the air, gossiping and strolling, perusing the goods in the shop windows, the ladies' parasols a forest of bright colors against the sun, the gentlemen elegant in jackets of blue and green superfine. There was a sense of brightness and hope in the air after such a long and gloomy winter.

Eve had just placed a quart of milk and a piece of creamy Wensleydale cheese in her marketing basket when she felt a strange prickle that raised the hairs on the back of her neck. It was the unmistakable sensation that she was being watched. She turned slowly and met the dark gaze of a gentleman who was standing on the opposite corner of the street.

It was his absolute stillness that attracted her attention first when everyone around him was moving. That, and the fact that he was looking directly at her with a gaze so focused and intent that she could not escape the force of their connection. His head was uncovered and in the spring sunshine his hair gleamed with the colors of fallen leaves, bronze and auburn and dark gold. His eyes looked watchful, conker brown beneath straight, dark brows. He was very tall with a hard, handsome face as unyielding as the local stone. It was given even more character by high, slanting cheekbones and a cleft chin that looked the essence of stubbornness.

Rowarth.

For a moment Eve was utterly unable to accept the evidence of her own eyes. Five years had passed; five very long, difficult, painful years, since she had seen the Duke of Welburn. When she had run from him, run from London, she had thought never to see him again. Yet here he was. He had found her. She, who had never wanted to be found.

For a moment it felt as though her heart had actually stopped before it slammed through her body again and began to race. He held her eyes with a fierce intensity that captured and trapped her. For a moment Eve felt stunned, imprisoned by his gaze. He had already started to move toward her and in that moment of blind panic and fear, all she knew was that she could not face him. Not now, not yet, perhaps never. Her feelings for him were still too raw even after five years. She had to run again.

But it was too late. Her shaking fingers slipped on the handle of the basket and it fell from her grasp, spilling the ham and cheese across the cobbles and sending the milk cascading into the gutter. An enterprising crow swooped down and snatched the ham away. Eve made a grab for the basket, her hands trembling as she tried to gather everything together again.

"Allow me."

Suddenly Rowarth was beside her, his hand on her elbow as he helped her to her feet, his touch searing her through the material of her sleeve. He picked up the slightly squashed cheese and handed it politely to her. Their fingers touched. Eve felt heat ripple through her awakening feelings she had thought long dead. Rowarth was summoning the dairyman and the butcher with authoritative gestures now to replace the items she had lost. Money changed hands. Eve heard the clink of coin and the men's mumbled thanks. She felt hot and dizzy, the sun beating down on her bonnet and dazzling her eyes. She tried to steady her breathing. There was not the remotest chance of escaping a confrontation with Rowarth now. He still held her, lightly but with a touch that made her entire body thrum with awareness.

"Eve."

She looked up and met his eyes and again felt the shock like a physical blow.

"Rowarth." She was proud that her voice was so steady. "What an unexpected…surprise."

His lips curved into a smile that was sinfully wicked but not remotely reassuring. "Is there any other sort?" he murmured.

"There are nice surprises," Eve said.

"And then there is meeting me again." His smile deepened. "Which I imagine falls into a different category given the alacrity with which you ran away from me."

Pain twisted in Eve, bitter and sharp, not even slightly blunted with the passing of time. Yes, she had run from him. She had had no other choice in the world. And now, five years later, the mere sight of him could still affect her so profoundly that she felt faint and light-headed, her emotions stretched as taut as a wire.

But Rowarth's measured tones had nothing but coldness in them for her now. Whatever feelings she still had for him, so deeply held that she had never quite been able to banish them, were not shared. Mistresses came and went, after all. He had been everything to her and there had never been anyone else for her since, but she could hardly expect it to be the same for him.

The crowds had melted away, leaving them alone. People were still staring, though from a discreet distance. *Women* were staring. But then, Eve thought, women had always stared at Alasdair Rowarth. Women had always wanted him. He was handsome, he was rich and he was a duke. What more could one ask for?

"You must let me escort you home," Rowarth said. He was steering her across the market square and down Fortune Alley, one of the twisty little lanes that led away from the main thoroughfare. Already they had left the bustle of the main streets far behind.

"There is absolutely no need, I thank you," Eve said. "I am sure that you have more pressing business." It was impossible, she thought, that Rowarth had come to Fortune's Folly to seek her out. A part of her longed for it to be true; when she had first seen him she had hoped for one heart-soaring moment that he had come looking for her because he still cared for her. Yet even in that moment she had known deep down that it was a foolish thought. The cynic in her, little Eve Nightingale, who had grown up on the streets of London and struggled to survive, knew enough of life to see that as the fairy tale it was. Besides, if by some miracle Rowarth *had* sought her out, that could only bring more lies and more heartbreak. There was no going back.

No, this could be no more than a coincidence. Fate was

laughing at her, bringing Rowarth to this little town, miles from anywhere, where she had thought herself safe. In a moment he would excuse himself and be gone from her life a second time and she would have to try and forget him all over again.

"There was a time when you found my company a great deal more attractive." Rowarth was making no secret of his amusement at her blatant attempt to dismiss him. "Though of course," his tone chilled, "your affections lasted only as long as it took you to find someone you preferred." He looked around at the dingy back streets with their rubbish in the gutters and the smell of rotting vegetables in the air. "What happened, Eve?" he said softly. "I hardly expected to find you here. Did your new lover leave you without a feather to fly?"

"That is none of your business, Rowarth." Eve tried to speak lightly, dismissively, but the words stuck in her throat. In the note she had left him she had told him she had found another protector. It had been the only way she could think of to make him hate her—to make certain that he would not follow her and demand the truth. It had been the only way to set him free.

Rowarth squared his shoulders. "You mistake." His voice, smooth and deep, cut across her thoughts. "It is my business. In fact I have no business here other than to see you, Eve."

For a moment Eve's foolish heart soared again at the thought he might, against the odds, care for her still. But there was something in his voice that warned her; in his tone and in the cool, appraising look that he gave her. And frighteningly he had read her thoughts and seen how vulnerable she was to him, for he smiled again with grim pleasure.

"Have no fear that I am about to importune you with impassioned declarations of love," he said drily. "Nothing was further from my thoughts. This is business only."

Eve felt a little sick at the contempt she could hear in his voice. "What possible business could you have with me after all this time?" she questioned, still striving to keep her voice light. "We have no more to say to one another."

"We'll talk of that in private."

"No, we shall not." Suddenly furious, she freed herself from his grip and spun around to face him. "We shall not do that just because you dictate it, Rowarth. You always were arrogant."

Once they had laughed together about his innate confidence and the way in which people deferred to him because of his position. Eve remembered with a pang what it had been like when she had been his mistress, beside Rowarth on those occasions when they had visited the opera or the theater or a ball. There was a dizzy glamour that had been attached to his title and his status, a glittering, raffish fascination that had beguiled her. When they had lain together, tangled in her sheets in the rapturous aftermath of making love, she had teased him about his importance and his arrogance and the way that people fell over themselves to please him, and he had laughed and kissed her and they had made love again through the hot summer nights. She had loved the fact that behind the closed doors of her boudoir Rowarth was hers, and hers alone, that she was the only one who truly knew him.

Perhaps it had been an illusion, but for a brief time it had made her happy. She had thought that they had both been happy. From the start there had been an instant attraction between them, blazing into vivid life the very first night they had met at the Cyprian's Ball. She, the newest of new courtesans, had been feted and courted as the gentlemen waited to see upon whom she would bestow her favor—and her innocence. Her price was high. And then Rowarth had arrived, cutting through the throng, and everyone else had faded away, pale imitations of men in comparison with his natural authority and overwhelming charm. She had been his from that first moment and miraculously, it seemed, he had been hers. She was not merely his mistress; they had shared everything. It had been so wonderful that for a short while even she, raised on the London streets, the illegitimate child of a seamstress and a sailor, abandoned as a baby and forced to fight for everything she had ever had in her life, had started to believe in happy endings. She had thought that there was more to their relationship than mere lust. She had felt that they had had an instant affinity.

Eve swallowed what felt like an enormous lump in her throat. Those days and nights had been full of color and excitement and joy, so far removed from her existence now that they had been another world, a fading memory but one that was so laced with pain that it could never quite die.

"And you were always the only one who dared oppose me." There was an odd note in Rowarth's voice now. For a moment it sounded almost like regret. "But in this, Eve, you cannot."

"Watch me." She was so cross now that she was prepared to argue with him in the street. She started to hurry away; he followed, effortlessly matching her step, not even remotely out of breath.

"With pleasure, as always." He sounded as imperturbable as ever. "But it will make no odds."

"You are as persistent as a stray dog."

"A charming analogy. You always liked animals, as I recall."

They had almost reached the pawnbroker's shop that Eve now ran. It seemed that Rowarth knew exactly where she lived and what she now did to earn that living. A shiver of apprehension racked Eve as she wondered what else he knew and what he might do with that knowledge. His reappearance in her life was not only shocking, it was dangerous as well. She had lived like a nun since coming to Yorkshire. She had buried her past as Rowarth's mistress and that was the way she was determined it would stay. Small towns were notorious for gossip and she was determined that *nothing* was going to ruin her reputation or her livelihood.

"We are at an impasse," she said coldly, on the doorstep. "I shall not invite you in."

"Then I will take you somewhere else where we may talk," Rowarth said, "and I doubt you will appreciate my methods in conveying you there. Your choice."

Eve looked at him. Would he really carry her kicking and screaming through the streets of Fortune's Folly? Very probably he would, and without disturbing the cut of his jacket in the process. He looked unyielding, implacable. And despite her anger she really did not want a scene in the street.

"Very well," she said, even more frostily. "Since you force my hand."

She pushed open the door of her shop and stepped from the bright sunlight into the cool, dusty shade feeling a strange sense of relief at least to be on her own property. She placed her marketing basket on the counter with a little sigh. In the windows the sale items gleamed in the sun; jewelry sending a shower of sparkling rainbow colors across the display, bone china pawned by the wife of a brewer who was so fond of his own ale that he had spent too much time drinking and too little working, bed linen from a cottager out on the road to Skipton, all manner of goods brought in by people desperate to raise a bit of ready cash. There was also a very fine brace of pistols that Eve suspected belonged to a man who had turned his hand, unsuccessfully, to highway robbery, and a dinner service that a local banker had brought in when his bank had gone bust and he had wanted to avoid his possessions being confiscated by his creditors. All the goods told their own stories, Eve thought, of people struggling in what was a hard economic climate.

Joan, Eve's assistant, came scurrying out of the back room,

wiping her hands on her apron as she heard the ring of the doorbell. She was an older woman, a former servant at Fortune's Hall, the local manor house and home to the squire, Sir Montague Fortune. She was the only person in whom Eve had confided her past and Eve valued her friendship highly.

"I did not realize you were back, madam—" Joan broke off as she saw Rowarth, and her sharp brown gaze swept over him, summing him up in one comprehensive glance. Her sandy eyebrows rose infinitesimally.

"This gentleman and I," Eve said carefully, "have business to discuss. Could you take over here please, Joan?"

"Business, is it?" Joan said tartly. "I thought you had finished with that sort of business, madam."

Eve smiled. She was accustomed to Joan's sharp tongue and knew it hid a protective heart. Joan had been turned off for refusing Sir Montague Fortune's advances and she had some hair-raising tales to tell of the goings-on at Fortune's Hall. She also had no very good opinion of men.

"Don't fret," Eve said. "I am done with it."

Ignoring Joan's snort of disbelief she ushered her visitor behind the counter and through the doorway into the room at the back. The pawnbroker's shop occupied two downstairs rooms in the stone-built terrace. Eve used one as the shop front and the other, a much larger room, as a combined office and a store for all the goods people brought in to pawn. Upstairs there was a tiny bedchamber and some even tinier living quarters. She and Joan clung to their financial independence by their fingertips. The premises were hardly sumptuous but the shop did at least provide an independent living and it had been a lifesaving opportunity for Eve when she had run from London—and from Rowarth—leaving everything behind, broken by a miscarriage, reeling from the news that she would never bear another child. She had left behind the beautiful little town house that Rowarth had given her in

Birdcage Walk, where he had spent all his nights and most of his days with her, the clothes and the jewels, and had climbed on the first stagecoach from the Blue Boar Inn in High Holborn. She had told the driver she would go as far as her money could take her and had ended up in Fortune's Folly, working as an assistant until she had accumulated sufficient savings to buy the shop, working her fingers to the bone, working, always working, as she tried to forget...

She pushed the memories away. Rowarth was standing in her office and looking around him with a lively interest. He looked elegant and polished, the epitome of wealth and privilege, utterly out of place in these shabby surroundings. Never had the differences between them felt so stark.

"So," she said, a little ungraciously, "I can give you two minutes, Rowarth, no more. Whatever your business is with me, I do not want to discuss it."

His gaze came back to rest on her, dark, brooding, and she repressed a little shiver.

"You will give me as long as I require," he said. He straightened. "My business with you is this. I am here on behalf of the Home Secretary. You are under suspicion of criminal activity. If you do not help us we will ruin you. We will expose your true identity and we will take from you *everything* that you possess." He smiled at her. "Now," he said gently, "will you talk to me?"

CHAPTER TWO

S̲ʜᴇ ʟᴏᴏᴋᴇᴅ ᴛʜᴇ same as she had done five years before. Alasdair Rowarth looked at his former mistress and amended his view slightly; she looked almost exactly the same except that there were shadows haunting those glorious lavender blue eyes now, suggesting a sadness that went soul deep. He did not feel any pity to see them; she had left him, walked out on him for another man, so whatever sorrow she had brought on herself was surely richly deserved.

The bitterness and resentment twisted within him and he ruthlessly subdued it. She was nothing to him now. He was here to prove it. But he remembered that it was Eve's clear and candid gaze that had first enslaved him from the moment he had stepped into the ballroom at Albermarle Street, persuaded against his better judgment by his friend Miles Vickery to attend the Cyprian's Ball. He had been bored and restless that evening, he remembered, searching as he always was for something elusive, something he could not even name, grasping after that mysterious entity that would fulfill him and provide a desperately needed balance to the lonely duty that was his life. Rowarth had come into his dukedom young; so many people depended upon him, it seemed that his days were never any more than a round of obligation and responsibility. He had searched for someone to share that weight of duty with him, looked for a wife at Almacks and in the long round of the London Season, and had been bored rigid by the witless pattern-card debutantes he had met.

And then he had attended the Cyprian's Ball and there she had been, Eva Night, bright, dazzling, so very alive, and in some way strangely untouchable even as she was effectively selling her virginity to the highest bidder. He had been entranced. He was rich enough—so he had bought her. And yet from the first he had thought that there was more to the transaction than that. It had not been solely his money for her body. She had given him life and light and warmth, wrapping him around with her generosity of spirit, her very presence lightening the load of the responsibilities he carried. In return he had shared everything with her. Not simply his money but his concerns and his cares, his deepest, darkest fears and his hopes for the future. Even though he was a mature man of one and thirty he had fallen for her like a love-struck youth. He had wanted to marry her. It had been perfect. Or so he had thought until she had left him, run away, denting his pride, making him an utter laughingstock—the foolish duke who had wanted to marry his venal mistress—and breaking a heart that until he had met her he had cynically believed could never be touched.

He had been a fool. That much was clear. The thing that angered him most was that he had loved her and believed his feelings were returned when in fact she had merely been using him for money and advancement. He had been wealthy enough but nowhere near as rich as some of the peers who sought Eve's favor now that she was the toast of the *demi-monde*. It had been madness to think that he could hold her if another man offered more. When he had been a mere ten years old he had seen his mother do precisely the same thing, betray his father, running off abroad to be with her wealthy lover. There had been the most appalling *crim con* divorce case that had dragged through the House of Lords and made his father look like a naive, impotent fool. And Rowarth, who savagely told himself that he should have known better, had almost made the same mistake as his luckless father. He knew he should be grateful that he had not committed the ultimate folly of marrying Eve as he had wanted to.

After Eve's defection he had gone abroad for several years—he had business concerns in India that had occupied him most successfully until the pleas of his estate managers had brought him back to England to face those responsibilities he had neglected. He had believed that he had put aside thoughts of Eva Night until he had come back to London and found himself searching for her face in a crowd or listening for news of her. He had learned that no one had heard of her since she had run away from him. It had been the *on dit* at the time but Eve was now long gone, her star extinguished, the brief time when they had been the glittering couple of the *demimonde* all but forgotten. Rowarth had tried to forget it, too, but every so often the memory of Eve would stab him like a wound that had not completely healed.

Then Lord Hawkesbury's letter had arrived out of the blue, asking for his help. Yes, he would go to Yorkshire and confront his beautiful, treacherous former mistress. Yes, he would ascertain if she were a member of a dangerous criminal fraternity, as Hawkesbury's intelligence suggested. And in doing so he would prove once and for all that he was free of the hold she had once exerted over him.

Criminal she might be. Beautifully, wantonly seductive she most certainly was. Eve's face still had the vivid animation that Rowarth remembered: her creamy complexion was still dusted with amber freckles, her hair was still a fiery red, and the quick, expressive movements of her body were as ridiculously, dangerously appealing to him as ever. Not even her fearsomely respectable worsted gown and dark blue spencer could hide the lush curves of a figure he had known intimately and already ached to explore again in exquisite detail, unable to subdue the desires of his body even while he deplored her and the hold she still had over him.

He had not expected to want her.

He had thought those feelings dead and gone. They should have been—they should have been annihilated, destroyed by her betrayal. He was furious that they were not. Yet he was forced to acknowledge that when he had first seen Eve in the Market Square he had felt all the old emotions of desire and lust and longing as strong as they had ever been and searing in their intensity. He had been told himself then that the memories, the hold she had had over his senses, would never be permitted to cloud his judgment. That resolution had lasted all of five seconds. He had seen her and he had wanted her with a hunger all the more acute for the years of denial.

But his business with Eve was precisely that—business. He was here on Hawkesbury's behalf to ascertain her connection to Warren Sampson and to use her, coldly, ruthlessly, to get to Sampson so that the man could finally be arrested. That was his goal, no more, no less.

"I strongly suggest," he said, "that you do as I ask."

For a moment Eve stared at him, those glorious lavender eyes wide and blank and he wondered if she had even heard him. Then an expression of fury came across her face.

"You bastard!" she said, picking up a very fine silver hairbrush from the desk in front of her and throwing it at his head. "How dare you come here and threaten to take away from me everything that I have worked so hard for?"

Rowarth caught the hairbrush absentmindedly in one hand before it made contact. He had always been good at cricket. Eve was looking absolutely furious, her piquant face flushed and her breathing quick and light. But it was more than anger he could see in her face. It was desperation. There was so much passion and rage in her voice that for a moment the principal emotion he felt was admiration that she was as strong as a tigress in defending the things that mattered to her. Memory stirred again; when she had been his mistress he had given her money and had been puzzled when she appeared to have spent it all on nothing. When pressed it had turned out that she had given it all away to feed and clothe urchins living on the streets. Rowarth had protested at her generosity and Eve had turned on him, saying that he was spoiled and privileged and could not understand—all true, of course, for how could an Eton-and Oxford-educated duke ever understand what it was like to struggle to survive? Most dukes would not even care. They had argued passionately and then made love even more passionately and she had lain in his arms and at last confided the truth in him.

"I did not know my parents," she had said, her head against his shoulder, "and I was cold and hungry and afraid more times than I care to remember." There had been a faraway look in her eyes, as though she were seeing far beyond the walls of her bedchamber. "If I can spare even one child from suffering as I did then that has to be for the good."

Rowarth had felt humbled, made to look beyond the comfort that had shielded him since his youth to another more painful existence. He knew that Eve had chosen to become a courtesan only because she had seen it as a way out of such stark poverty.

"I was pretty," she had once said lightly, "so I used it to escape." But he knew those words hid a wealth of bitterness.

"It is only the rich who can afford moral scruples," she had once flashed at him when he had commented on the hanging of a youth for the theft of a loaf of bread and he knew that she had felt the same way about the choice she had made in selling herself.

Or he had thought he had known her until she had betrayed him.

But that was in the past and nothing to the purpose now.

He put the silver hairbrush on the desk. He suspected it was part of a quantity of stolen goods that Hawkesbury had said Warren Sampson was almost certainly laundering via Eve's pawnbroking business. Which brought him back to the matter in hand.

"You are working with Warren Sampson to pass on stolen goods," he said. "He runs a housebreaking gang that robs property across the county and then his accomplices bring the items here and you sell them, making him a double profit."

She stared at him contemptuously. "That is utter rubbish." She turned away from him with an angry swish of skirts and took a couple of paces away across the room. She could not get any farther away from him because the office was so small and he could sense the anger in her, still simmering like a pot coming back to the boil.

"I barely know the man," she snapped. "And what I do know I dislike intensely. It is both insulting and plain wrong to suggest some criminal conspiracy between us."

Hawkesbury had suggested that Eve might be Warren Sampson's mistress, a cozy arrangement if they were in bed and business together. And Rowarth was not simply going to accept her word that it was not so. Just the thought of her tumbling between the sheets with Sampson made him hot with rage and thwarted desire. Madness, when he had sworn he did not care and did not want to want her.

"Shall we sit," he suggested evenly, "and discuss this calmly?"

She gave him another look of searing disdain. "If we must. If it will hasten your departure."

He bit back a reluctant smile. Never had a woman seemed so anxious to be rid of him. But then, Eve had always been different.

"I shall want to see your accounts in due course," he said. "I need to trace every one of your transactions."

"How tedious for you," Eve murmured.

"I suppose that they are in order?"

"Of course not." Eve glanced at the tottering plies of paper on the desk and the floor. "You may have taught me to read and to compute mathematical sums, Rowarth, but you could not make me like it."

The memory touched him on the raw. It was true that she had been illiterate before he had taught her. There was a bitter taste in his mouth as he thought of the sweetness of those lessons and the gifts he had brought her, the books she had painstakingly learned to read, the columns of figures she had haltingly added up while he had joked that at least that way she would know how *much* money she was giving away to the poor. He slammed the door on such memories. Evidently she had moved on and was able to calculate Sampson's wealth very accurately and certainly well enough to profit by it.

"It was not the only thing that I taught you," he said harshly. "You may have been a courtesan but you were not a tutored one."

Color lit her cheeks at his reference to the fact that she had been a virgin when he had taken her to his bed.

"I do not recall you having any complaints," she snapped.

He had not. It had been blissful. He recalled the sweetness of Eve's lissome body stretched beneath his hands and the pure physical compatibility that they had achieved. And then he thought of her running from him.

"Such debate gets us nowhere," he said harshly. "Now, tell me the truth about Warren Sampson this time." He met her eyes directly. "Was he the man you left me for? Are you his mistress?"

"I do not believe that you have been hearing me," Eve said wearily. She felt sick to her soul that Rowarth, who had once loved her, should now hold her in nothing but contempt. "For the last time, Rowarth," she said, "I barely know Warren Sampson. I am neither his mistress nor his business partner, nor," she added with emphasis, "his associate in any way."

Disquiet stirred in her. It was true that for the past couple of months she had been aware of some very valuable goods passing through the pawnshop. The silver hairbrush was one such item and there had also been some silver plates and a couple of gold snuffboxes. A rather dissolute young man whom Eve had recognized as Tom Fortune, younger brother to the squire, had brought the pieces in. The workmanship on them had been superb and Eve had given him a good price for them. She had asked no questions at the time for she was well aware that people were very sensitive about bringing in property to pawn for money and one of the reasons her clientele liked her was because she was so discreet and kept their secrets. And yet she had not been comfortable about the transaction. A sixth sense had told her that something was wrong even as she had tried to persuade herself that

Tom Fortune was probably only selling off the family silver to pay his gambling debts.

Her disquiet turned to foreboding. Could Hawkesbury be correct, not in his suspicions of her, but in the fact that Warren Sampson might be using her shop to launder stolen goods? Sampson was a deeply unpleasant man, grotesquely, ridiculously wealthy with a fortune that had been made in the mills of Leeds and Bradford. On more than one occasion Eve had caught him looking at her with speculation and lust in his eyes and she had shuddered to imagine that he might know her secrets, her background, her past. What Warren Sampson might do with such knowledge was terrifying. But he had said nothing and had always treated her with outward respect, and Eve had told herself that she was imagining things. Nevertheless, he always made her skin crawl.

Rumor, which swirled around Fortune's Folly like the current of the River Tune, said that Sampson had added to his money through various criminal activities but nothing had ever been proven. Now it seemed that Hawkesbury was set on finding that proof and that Rowarth would use her in any way possible to bring Sampson down.

Eve shuddered. She knew that if Rowarth had Hawkesbury's authority he could enforce whatever he wished and if Hawkesbury believed her guilty of criminal activity then she had no hope. Suddenly she felt so tired, so vulnerable to this man and to the insidious appeal that he still had for her and so miserable that he had nothing but disdain for her now. It appalled and distressed her that he had accepted Lord Hawkesbury's commission to bring her down.

But such regrets would not save her. With a sigh, she gestured Rowarth to a seat on one of the rather rickety wooden chairs at the side of her desk. Accounts and correspondence spilled from the table onto the floor. She gave vent to her feelings by giving the papers a violent shove so that the ones still on the desk cascaded onto the floor.

Realizing that Rowarth was waiting, with impeccable manners, for her to sit first, she pushed some books aside and took a chair. He immediately sat down opposite her. His presence seemed to fill the space between them, powerful, authoritative. The room suddenly seemed too small, cramped and close, and it was nothing to do with the piles of goods that were stored in there. It was simply that Alasdair Rowarth had always been the most overwhelming man that Eve had ever met and she felt angry that he could still affect her in such a profound way.

To cover her nervousness she tilted up her chin and subjected him to a stern appraisal.

"You cannot have any evidence at all to back up these ridiculous accusations," she said. "They are absolutely untrue."

Rowarth inclined his head. His hair, glossy and thick, shone in a ray of sunlight that penetrated the dusty window. He looked self-assured, Eve thought, with all the confidence that privilege and position could bring. It only served to make her feel all the more vulnerable.

"The Home Secretary's agents have had your shop under observation for several months," he said. "They know that you are fencing stolen goods." He picked up the silver hairbrush again and looked thoughtfully at it. "I am sure you are aware there have been a number of robberies locally."

"No," Eve said. Her immediate instinct was to protect herself and Joan and all she had worked to build up. But she could see as soon as the words left her mouth that Rowarth did not believe her. His gaze rested on her face with the perceptive intensity that she remembered. She blushed and saw the corner of his mouth lift in a smile, as though she had just confirmed her guilt. She could have kicked herself.

"If stolen goods *are* being passed through this shop it is entirely without my knowledge," she temporized.

Rowarth held her gaze, his own implacable. Eve shivered to see the coldness there where once there had been nothing but heat and sweetness for her.

"That does not make you innocent," Rowarth said.

"It makes me a victim of Sampson's criminality," Eve said sharply, "not an accomplice."

Rowarth raised his brows in blatant disbelief but he did not challenge her immediately. Instead he picked up a monograph of some very naughty erotic drawings that Eve had failed to notice was lying on the desk. As he flicked through the pictures Eve started to feel unconscionably heated, her mind conjuring up visions of the past, of her body locked with Rowarth's in the most intimate and sensual of embraces, his mouth hot against the bare skin of her inner thigh, her cries of need as his tongue flicked her tender core, the bliss as he took her, pushing her to the extremes of pleasure…

She tried to steady her breathing. Her pulse was fluttering like a trapped butterfly. Her skin tingled and she felt lightheaded. She fanned herself surreptitiously, watching as Rowarth assessed the saucy sketches, brows slightly raised, a faint smile still on his lips. Her fingers were itching to snatch the book away from him and put an end to her embarrassment. And then he looked up and the turbulent desire in his eyes flared strong and elemental, and Eve felt the need knot in her stomach and almost gasped aloud.

"What an interesting variety of items you must take in here," Rowarth said, a rough undertone to his voice. He shifted, clearing his throat. "These, I would guess, are the property of Mr. Tom Fortune. I hear he has an extensive library of such books."

"I never divulge details about my clients," Eve snapped. She pulled herself back from the brink of sensual awareness. If Rowarth could exercise such control against the ghosts of the past then so could she.

Rowarth's gaze had moved on to a rather fine ruby bracelet that was nestling in a cut glass bowl.

"That is pretty."

"It's made of paste," Eve said quickly and untruthfully. The bracelet was not in fact a fake, but Eve was desperately hoping that the Dowager Duchess of Cole, who had brought it in, would find the funds to buy it back. She had seen the look of despair on Laura Cole's face when she had pawned her jewelry and had guessed that it was of great sentimental value. She had given the Dowager Duchess a very generous sum for she knew that Laura Cole and her little daughter were poverty-stricken.

Rowarth permitted the rubies to slide through his fingers before looking up at her. "You seem reluctant to sell."

"I was not aware that you were buying," Eve said. "I thought you were here to threaten me instead."

"Touché." He smiled at her suddenly. It was devastating. "You fight damned hard, Eve."

"I always did."

"I know."

For one short, achingly fragile moment their eyes met and held and Eve's heart tumbled to see the tenderness in his, and then it was gone, swept aside by a coldness so bitter that she felt shrivelled and frozen. Rowarth broke the contact, stretching in his chair, muscles rippling beneath the blue superfine of his coat. "Hawkesbury's intelligence is that you are extremely liberal in the sums you offer to clients, sometimes giving far more than an item is worth," he said. His voice had chilled, too. "Apparently if you know a client is attached to a particular item you will keep it safe for them to reclaim when they can afford it, rather than sell it. If you know some of your clients are pawning their last stick of furniture in order to buy gin to drink themselves into a stupor, you will try to persuade them off the bottle."

"And your point?" Eve asked tartly. "I thought that you were the prosecution not the defense."

"My point," Rowarth said with an edge to his voice, "is that such generosity would make you vulnerable to blackmail. You do not have the skill to make your business profitable by legitimate means and so it seems you have resorted to illegitimate ones in order to keep afloat. Perhaps Sampson was able to blackmail you into his bed and his business because of your poverty?"

"That is entirely false," Eve said, stung by the harshness of his judgment. "I bought the shop, but I could not buy the business acumen to go with it. I have tried my best and yes, you are correct, I struggle because I tend to be too kind to my clients. Nevertheless, I would never resort to criminal means for my livelihood."

She could feel Rowarth's gaze search her face, shrewd, perceptive and as tangible as a physical touch.

"I know you are determined to believe the worst of me," she said bitterly, "but you should at least get your accusations straight. Either you suspect me of being Sampson's mistress— in which case I would hardly be flailing around in poverty watching my business fail but rather enjoying his vast wealth in comfort and privilege—or you think me a blackmail victim. Neither is correct." She snapped a pencil fiercely between her fingers. "You can take your base suspicions and put them in your ducal—" she broke off, in danger of reverting to the street slang of her childhood "—pipe and smoke it," she resumed. "You can prove *nothing,* for there is nothing *to* prove and so you may tell Lord Hawkesbury."

There was another silence and then Rowarth shifted, stretched. "What you have told me may well be true, Eve, but at the very least, you have committed a crime and that *is* proven. You have stolen goods sitting in your shop." He gestured toward the hairbrush. "This piece here, and the candlesticks I saw in the window will, I suspect, match an inventory of goods taken from Broughton Castle two weeks ago. You could be hanged for that alone."

Eve's heart started to thud. She wondered for how long and how often Warren Sampson had been using her shop to launder his stolen goods. His associates had brought the items to her and she, in her ignorance, had paid for them, giving money for items taken by theft. She had been so naive and now her entire life teetered on the edge of extinction. Once again Rowarth's gaze appraised her and Eve had the strangest sensation that he was probing her soul. Would he really condemn her to death? She could not, *would not* believe it. Yes, he had changed—he had a harder edge than the man she had once known—but surely that would be beyond him.

"Then have me arrested," she challenged him. Their gazes clashed, blue eyes and dark. "Send me to the executioner if you can."

There was a long and painful silence and then Rowarth shook his head slowly. "I have another purpose in mind for you," he said, and again his tone was so cold that Eve shivered to hear it. "There is a particular piece of jewelry, a necklace of sapphires, that was taken in the same burglary as the silver. If we can prove it is still in Sampson's possession then we will have him."

"I fail to see how that concerns me," Eve said.

Rowarth looked at her. "I will tell you," he said. "There is a party at Sampson's house at Juniper Hill tonight. You will attend with me. You will seek Sampson out and hint that you know he is using your shop to sell his stolen goods. You will suggest that the two of you go into business formally together in order to make more profit. That should appeal to him. You will ask if he has other items he could pass on to you, jewelry perhaps…" His gaze swept over and seemed to linger on the line of her mouth. "And you will sweeten the offer…"

"With the additional promise of myself?" Eve wrapped her arms about her to ward off the chill that was invading her very bones. "You are blackmailing me to make me prostitute myself to him just so that you can catch him?"

She saw a flicker of expression in Rowarth's eyes that she could not read, and then it was gone.

"That is putting it a little harshly," he said, "but yes, you have it precisely."

Eve felt sick that he could not have made it clearer that she was nothing to him now other than a means to an end. "I would rather that you sent me to jail," she said bitterly.

"I doubt that," Rowarth said.

"I will not do it," Eve said defiantly.

"You will." Rowarth was implacable. "You have no choice."

Eve knew she did not. She was trapped. And she knew Rowarth did not trust her. This was a trial; he was testing her as well as using her, for if it appeared from Warren Sampson's reaction to her that the two of them were already in league, Rowarth would denounce her without a thought. The bitterness turned to ashes in her mouth. Once they had been so much to one another. Now there was nothing left. She supposed that she should not feel so harsh a disillusionment, for she was the one who had betrayed him originally, after all. She had deliberately pushed him away, believing she had no choice, knowing they could have no future. Even so, his ruthlessness shocked her.

She got up and moved toward the door. "I would like you to go now," she said.

Rowarth stood up, too. Suddenly he was very close to her, so close that she could hear his breathing and smell the scent of his skin and see the stubble that darkened his chin and jaw. The light grip of his hand on her elbow sensitized her entire body. Heat scorched her like a flame, making her shake. She felt stunned, trapped and a little dizzy.

"I am sure that you understand," Rowarth said, in a measured tone, "what Warren Sampson's parties entail?"

Eve's mind reeled. She had indeed heard rumors of the scandalous parties at Juniper Hill but she had forgotten about them in the turmoil and shock of seeing Rowarth again and in the horror of his accusations. With a sick lurch of the heart she realized that this would be no respectable dinner or ball. Not only would she be making Warren Sampson an indecent proposal in order to trap him, by her attendance she would be proclaiming to the whole of Fortune's Folly just what sort of woman she was. She closed her eyes for a moment, then opened them and looked up into Rowarth's face.

"If you make me do this you will ruin me as surely as if you tell the world of my past history," she said. She hated the pleading note in her voice but could not avoid it. "Rowarth…" She looked at him but his expression was as unyielding as granite. "If word gets about the town that I am the sort of woman to attend such entertainments," she said desperately, "then you might as well brand me a courtesan in public."

She knew even as she spoke that her words were falling on deaf ears and she felt desolate.

"We shall have to display a certain amount of…pleasure… in each other's company since we shall be attending together," Rowarth said, quite as though she had not spoken. "I trust that you will once again fulfill the role of my mistress with all the experience at your disposal."

Pain twisted in Eve that he could dismiss their past loving as something so tawdry. She could feel him watching her, seeing too much with those dark eyes. Her feelings felt exposed, naked. Could he tell how vulnerable she felt, still so aware of him as a man despite all that had happened to divide them?

She took a deep breath, knowing that the die was cast and there was no escape for her.

"I never was a very good actress but I suppose I can pretend to an affection for you for a short time," she said.

Rowarth laughed.

"Pretense, is it? Why, I could swear that you are not indifferent to me, sweetheart."

He kissed her with no warning and no chance of refusal. Eve's hands closed into tight fists against the smooth material of his jacket, only to open and slide over his chest as she was instantly seduced by the memory of what had once been between them. Hot, sweet, wicked and wanton… He did not plunder but teased, the subtle pressure of his lips tempting hers to open. His tongue caressed hers and her knees weakened and the pleasure curled down to her toes and spread through her whole body as though she was melting.

His arms locked tighter than steel about her and she leaned into him, opening to his kiss, her body quivering like an instrument that recognized a familiar touch. He tasted the same and yet the experience was so different; it shook her, making her shiver, and he held her closer still even as he took her mouth with the same thorough possession that he had once taken her body. Her mind was full of memories and deep, dark desire. She could feel the need in him, held under tight restraint, and suddenly she wanted to push beyond that control and make him feel with the same powerless intensity that she was feeling.

But then Rowarth released her abruptly, stepping back. His eyes were almost black with lust, desire distilled.

"Pretense," he said again. "If that was counterfeit, then you are a damned fine actress after all, Eve."

And then he was gone, leaving her staring blankly at the panels of the door as he slammed it behind him.

CHAPTER THREE

ROWARTH WATCHED EVE as the carriage rolled up the drive toward Warren Sampson's mansion at Juniper Hill. It had been easy enough to procure an invitation to one of Sampson's notorious parties. The man was an inveterate social climber and when he heard that the Duke of Welburn, no less, was interested in attending he had been expansive in his welcome. Whether or not Sampson would be equally easy to trap into revealing his crimes was a moot point, but in that Rowarth did at least have the support of two of the Home Secretary's finest men, his old friend Miles, Lord Vickery and Nathaniel, Lord Waterhouse. Both would be attending that evening and both were part of Lord Hawkesbury's mysterious and elite group of counterspies, the Guardians, who worked to keep the country safe.

Rowarth could tell that Eve was nervous as the coach traveled up the long drive. She was sitting forward, her gloved hands clasped tightly together, her eyes anxiously scanning the road ahead as though she were dreading the moment they actually arrived and was hoping that fate would intervene in that short time and save her the ordeal. Rowarth felt a treacherous pang of tenderness to see her anxiety. He knew that he should not care a rush for her feelings after the way that she had deserted him but his emotions, it appeared, were not susceptible to rational argument. He had come to Yorkshire determined to fulfill his commission, certain he would feel nothing for Eve and that he could lay the ghosts of the past.

Yet almost as soon as he had seen her, his feelings had started to change. It had been unconscionably difficult to force her to fulfill Hawkesbury's demands with the callousness the situation required. Instead he had felt protective of her, which was the last thing he had either expected or wanted. When he agreed to work for Hawkesbury he had fully anticipated leading Eve into the lion's den and watching as she was thrown to her fate. Yet now, seeing her fear and the courageous way in which she confronted danger, he had been forced to reappraise the situation. Seeing Eve again, speaking to her, witnessing her bravery and her resilience and her determination under threat had reminded him of what a fine person he had once believed her to be, before betrayal had so disillusioned him. His instinct was stubbornly telling him that Eve simply could not be complicit with Warren Sampson, that she must be a victim of the man's criminality rather than a partner in it. Which meant that his urge was to protect her rather than use her, to defend her instead of sacrificing her. And yet he felt so angry at this impulse to shield her. Eve Nightingale deserved nothing from him. She had ruthlessly cut her ties with him years before. Now it was his turn to use her equally ruthlessly.

The torches that lit the driveway to the house shone through the carriage windows and illuminated Eve's translucent complexion, highlighting the scattering of freckles across her nose and dusting her cheeks with a golden glow. Her lips were painted a deep red and looked luscious and impossibly tempting. In accordance with Rowarth's instructions, she had chosen a fashionable red evening gown that was cut almost indecently low across her breasts. It clung lovingly to her curves and rustled as she moved, emphasizing the swing of her hips. As soon as he had seen her that night Rowarth had found himself possessed by an impatient and overwhelming masculine desire to peel the gown from her body and make love to her on the carriage seat. He wanted to rediscover where else she had those freckles. He wanted to relearn the taste of her, to inhale the scent of her skin and to let himself drown in the warm, silky sweetness of her body as she closed around him tight and hot. Lust, painfully sharp and predatory, twisted within him again as he thought about it. He was in an advanced state of sexual frustration, desperate to take his former mistress with a hunger that had dissipated not one whit. Yet she had spurned him, left him flat. He despised himself for his lack of self-control.

"Where did you go when you left London?" He spoke abruptly.

He had not meant to ask. After he had seen her at the shop he had resolved not to rake up anything of the past, simply to do his job tonight and then go back to London and never see her again. But now old emotions were aroused and old memories stirred and there were some things that he had to know.

He thought for a moment that Eve was not going to reply. The light from the torches skipped across her face in bars of flame and shadow.

"I came here," she said slowly, after a moment. "I have been here for five years. Did Lord Hawkesbury's intelligence not provide you with that information?"

It had. It had been something that had puzzled Rowarth, a doubt nibbling at the corner of his mind. Why choose Fortune's Folly? And if she had run off with another lover, as she had told him in her farewell note, where was he? Who was he? Rowarth had assumed it must be Warren Sampson but now he was not so sure. None of Hawkesbury's informants had mentioned that Eve had a new protector. Either she and her lover had been extraordinarily discreet or the man had not existed at all.

"You told me in your parting note that you had found a

new protector," he said slowly, watching her, "but my information is that no such person ever existed."

He saw her stiffen, a quick, instinctive gesture she could not hide, before she turned her face away and feigned indifference. But it was too late and he was too quick, too perceptive.

"Eve?" he said. "Did you run off with a lover?"

She was stubbornly silent but he already knew the answer. Even after five years apart he knew her so well he did not need words.

"You did not," he said. Urgency beat within him. "There was no new lover, was there, Eve?"

He saw her lips set in a tight line as she capitulated. "No, there was not." Her words fell starkly into the darkness of the carriage. The torchlight flickered over her face and for a split second he saw utter honesty reflected in her eyes.

No new lover. Rowarth's mind reeled. She had not left him for another man. She had not been another man's mistress. Stupefaction, relief, *pleasure* flooded him at her words. He grabbed her hands, his heart lifting with absurd hope.

"Then why…" He had to clear his throat. "Why did you tell me that you had run away with someone else?"

Again it seemed forever before she answered as the carriage drew closer and closer to the door of Juniper Hill.

"I lied because I wanted to be sure that you would never seek me out." She spoke the words so quietly that he had to lean closer to hear them and when he did they were like a blow to the heart. "I did not wish to be your mistress anymore, Rowarth. I had to leave you."

I had to leave you…

Rowarth's hopes crashed before they were barely born. He dropped her hands as he felt a dull pain spread though his chest. Eve had not wanted to be with him. She had felt so strongly that she wanted to make sure that they never saw one another again. The affinity they had apparently shared, physical and emotional, had been nothing to her. She had quenched the restlessness in his soul, she had anchored him and fulfilled the empty need within him and yet she had felt nothing. She had wanted to be free.

"I see." He spoke slowly as he absorbed the blow. "I had no idea that you were so unhappy as my mistress. You should have told me. I would have paid you off. There was no need to run away."

Eve did not reply. She turned away and the light and shadows skipped across her face, hiding all expression.

Rowarth knew that he should be humiliated. He should not want to pursue this further. And yet… And yet once again his instinct prompted him that there was something here that did not make sense, something he strove to understand.

"I tried to find you," he said.

He had never intended to admit it. She had made him a laughingstock in the *ton,* the rich, handsome duke who could not hold on to his mistress and was in danger of making as much of a fool of himself over a woman as his father had done before him. He had looked everywhere for her in such a fever that he could not tell anger, fear and desperation apart; he had inquired everywhere but found no trace of her so that in the end he had been forced to accept that she did not want to be found, that maybe she had gone abroad, that he would never see her again.

"I am sorry." Again her words dropped softly into the silence. She sounded indifferent, as though she were apologizing for stepping on his foot. Her apparent coldness, her *pity,* when his feelings for her were still so strong, was intolerable. His anger broke through five years of restraint. He grabbed her upper arms. The cerise wrap slipped from her shoulders to puddle on the carriage floor.

"Did it really mean so little to you, Eve?" he said fiercely.

"After all we had shared could you really walk away from me so easily?"

The fury inside him was volcanic in its power. He wanted to shake her. He wanted to kiss her, to ravish her, to make her his once more and claim her with all the passion and anger within him. He pulled her close and she closed her eyes, her lashes spiky sharp against the pale curve of her cheek, as though she were warding off the fury in him, trying to defend herself. Her expression was stark in its misery and Rowarth felt in that instant, with a sudden, terrifying conviction that whatever she claimed, she had not left him by choice. Something terrible had happened to her, something she had felt unable to tell him, something that still pierced her soul. All the evidence supported it. Her false claim that she had left him for another man, the fact that she had left behind all her money and jewelry when she could have taken it and lived in luxury, the fact that she had hidden herself away in this little backwater... Whatever she had told him she had not run because she had been unhappy as his mistress. There had to be something else...

All the rage left him then, banished by the misery he could see in her face and feel in every line of her body. He picked up the wrap and placed it gently about her shoulders, wanting to draw her close, shaken by the instinct he felt to comfort her. But again she drew away from him, lonely but indomitable in her strength.

"Do not pursue this, Rowarth," she said. He could see her hands shaking as she wrapped the shawl about herself. "It was a long time ago."

Frustration and determination gripped him in equal measure. Pride and anger prompted him to let the matter drop and yet he found he could not.

"I don't believe you," he said brutally. "I don't believe

that you left me through choice, Eve. You must tell me what happened."

For a brief moment she looked him directly in the eyes. "Nothing happened," she said. Her voice was cool and light again, devoid of emotion. It was as though the unhappiness he was sure he had seen in her only a moment before had never existed.

"You mistake," she said. "I appreciate that it must be difficult for you to accept, but I am afraid that I discovered that the role of your mistress was not one that suited me. So I left. That is all."

Rowarth swore. "So you preferred to go back to an existence where you struggled to hold body and soul together as you had done once before?" he challenged. "You ask too much if you expect me to believe that, sweetheart."

"I never wanted you for your money and status." There was a thread of anger in her voice now. At last he had provoked her out of her self-control. She had always had a temper. "Oh, it was nice to be *rich*—" she invested the word with scorn "—but it was never really my money, was it?" She sighed. "I wanted respect," she said. "*Self-respect* I had earned. I did not have that as a courtesan, using my body to buy survival."

Again Rowarth thought she was dealing in half-truths. He knew how fiercely she hated the depths to which poverty and desperation made men sink and that she had deplored the necessity of selling her body in order to save her life. But he had also thought that between them there had surely been mutual respect and trust.

"You had my respect," he said. "I wanted to *marry* you."

Again she was silent for a moment, biting her lip. "I did not wish to be a duchess."

"No," Rowarth said. "Apparently you wished to be a pawnbroker."

Again she showed a flash of temper. "Is it inconceivable that I might want an honest trade?"

"Rather than be a duchess?" Rowarth drawled. "Frankly, my dear, it is. And besides, pawnbroking is not generally considered to be an honest profession."

She looked furious. "Enough," she said. She turned her shoulder to him. "I am afraid that you will simply have to accept that I left you because I did not wish to be with you. There is no point in discussing the matter further."

The carriage had drawn up in front of the steps of Sampson's mansion and a liveried footman opened the door. Rowarth descended and held out a hand to help Eve down. Her face was serene again, concealing any emotion she might feel inside, but he felt her fingers tremble a little in his.

You will simply have to accept that I left you because I did not wish to be with you...

The words echoed in Rowarth's head as he guided her into the entrance hall. So be it. Eve had made her feelings clear. His instinct that there was more to her betrayal than met the eye was clearly wrong and he would be a fool to pursue it further. She had wanted to be free of him. There was no more to be said.

The hallway at Juniper Hill was a riot of bad taste. Eve's fascinated gaze was drawn upward to the ceiling where naked painted cherubs romped amidst fluffy blue clouds. In the alcoves were statues of hugely endowed Greek gods and artfully draped goddesses, whose state of undress was only equalled by the scandalous *deshabillée* of Warren Sampson's female guests. Those invited tonight were not the respectable citizens of Fortune's Folly but those of the local gentry who hunted hard, especially when it came to women, plus some actresses from the theaters of York and Harrogate, a smattering of Sampson's business associates and those of their wives bold enough to attend.

Servants were circulating with trays of champagne. In the center of the hall was a gigantic ice sculpture of a naked, rampant god Poseidon, his icy erection almost as enormous as the trident in his hand. It rather spelled out the point of the entertainment, Eve thought. And in the middle of all this splendid ostentation was Warren Sampson himself, preening in peacock blue, expansive and vulgar and most frightfully proud, as far as Eve could see, of displaying his money in such an opulent style. He was surrounded by a positive plethora of hangers-on, including the squire's brother Tom Fortune, who smiled very suggestively as Eve approached. As she and Rowarth stepped forward Eve registered the sudden excitement that ran through the ranks of Sampson's guests. The men raised their quizzing glasses and looked Eve up and down from the diamond clasp in her red curls to the tips of her red satin slippers, lingering on the bodice of her gown where her abundant charms were so amply displayed. The women cast glances of lascivious greed at Rowarth who was looking exceptionally elegant in his austere black-and-white evening dress.

A frisson of nerves ran through Eve as Sampson's gaze fell on them and he came forward to greet them, his eyes lighting with self-congratulation to have caught so eminent a guest as the Duke of Welburn.

"My dear fellow…" He stretched out a hand to Rowarth, his voice unctuous. "I am *charmed* that you have been able to join us tonight."

Not by a flicker of expression did Rowarth give away any emotion other than an apparent delight to be there. The perfect courtesy bred in an English gentleman evidently made him able to carry off such a meeting, Eve thought. In contrast, her skin was crawling simply at being in close proximity with Warren Sampson. There was something unwholesome about the man and when he turned his gaze on her she felt a sense of revulsion she was afraid might be almost too strong to conceal.

"Mrs....Nightingale, is it not?" Sampson was working hard to cover his astonishment at seeing her, but could not quite hide his feelings. Eve could not be sure whether his surprise arose from the unexpected appearance of his unwitting stooge or simply from shock at seeing a lady he had previously thought irreproachably respectable flaunting herself in such a shocking gown. His eyes lit with a predatory gleam as his gaze lingered on the swell of her breasts. Eve felt Rowarth stiffen almost imperceptibly beside her but when she flicked a glance up at his face his expression was quite smooth. His hand was in the small of her back, pushing her forward a little so that she could not avoid Sampson's appreciative appraisal. She felt a bitter taste in her mouth, as though Rowarth was whoring her out, which of course, he was. And she had only herself to blame. When he had started to question her on the past in the intimate darkness of the carriage she had lied to him because it was the only way to keep her secrets and to keep the horrible memories of her miscarriage and loss locked away in the dark where it belonged. But she knew that she could not now complain if Rowarth despised her. She had deliberately pushed him away. Even so, a sliver of misery like a lump of ice wedged itself in her heart.

"Mr. Sampson." She forced a smile. "It is such a pleasure to attend one of your parties. Your hospitality is legendary."

Sampson laughed, showing his teeth. "My dear Mrs. Nightingale, had I known of your interest I would have invited you sooner." He took her hand, his touch suggestive, and pressed his lips wetly to her fingers. Eve suppressed a shudder. Sampson's predatory gaze went from her to Rowarth.

"Nor did I realize," he murmured, his breath hot in her ear, "that you were a particular friend of his grace."

"Oh, Rowarth and I are very old acquaintances," Eve said,

with an arch look up at Rowarth who smiled back straight into her eyes. "But should we ever fall out I will let you know, Mr. Sampson."

Sampson laughed. "I live for that day," he said.

Eve smiled. She had never been much of an actress, she was all too well aware that she had too fiery and opinionated a disposition to hide her true feelings well, but since Rowarth wished her to offer herself—since she had to do so to save herself from Hawkesbury's so-called justice—she would ful-fill her role with all the fervor she could.

And hate herself for it later, no doubt. But she could not allow herself to think about that now.

Sampson was still holding her hand and she let it rest there, tightening her fingers with the slightest of pressure.

"I was hoping," she murmured, "that I might have a few moments with you in private later, Mr. Sampson. There is a matter I would very much like to discuss with you—a busi-ness matter to our mutual benefit."

Sampson's eyes almost popped out of his head with a com-bination of lust and excitement, curiosity and, Eve was inter-ested to note, wariness.

"You intrigue me, Mrs. Nightingale," he said. "I will rejoin you as soon as I can arrange it." He kissed her hand again, running his lips over her knuckles in an odiously familiar manner that made Eve want to wipe her hand on her gown.

"Your servant, madam," Sampson said, moving off to greet some of his other guests and giving her one very long, back-ward look.

Rowarth took Eve's hand in a grip so tight she almost flinched.

"He seems to like you," Rowarth said, his voice hard and low.

"Of course he does," Eve said sharply. "There is plenty of me on display to like." She glared at him. "You would also have observed that he was surprised to see me. He was not expecting me to be here tonight. I told you that I barely know him."

Rowarth's gaze narrowed on her. "I accept that," he said slowly.

"Oh, you do, do you?" Eve snapped. "Not that it makes any difference to you. Well, stay close to me, Rowarth, while I trap him for you. You want me to whore myself tonight," she added, seeing him recoil and glad that her bitter words had touched him, "so I will do. I was your harlot so will do whatever you wish."

She was unprepared for Rowarth's response. He caught her arm and pulled her behind the cover of an enormous statue of Apollo. His expression was tight and furious and made her quake inside. "Never refer to yourself like that again, Eve," he said. "Never! Do you hear me?"

Eve was utterly shaken. For a long moment their gazes held, tense and stormy, and then Rowarth swore under his breath and his arms went about her and his mouth came down on hers with absolute mastery, forcing her lips apart, his tongue tangling with hers and plundering her without restraint. Eve was lost from the first moment, her emotions adrift, the sensuality flaring between them in a scalding tide. She forgot where they were, almost forgot everything, in the maelstrom of sensation and desire that swept her away.

"Getting into the swing of things rather well, Rowarth."

An amused male voice had them falling apart, panting, and Eve looked up to see a tall man with brown hair and the wickedest hazel eyes she had ever seen smiling at her and making her an elegant bow.

"A pleasure to meet you again, Mrs. Nightingale," he said, "though I do apologize for interrupting you at such an impossibly awkward moment. You may remember that we met a few times in London. Miles Vickery, entirely at your service." He gave Eve a look of comprehensive admiration that brought a blush to her cheeks. "I wish that Hawkesbury had chosen me for this assignment rather than bringing Rowarth in specially," he drawled, "but then I suppose he does have the prior claim."

Rowarth did not seem amused. "Vickery—" he began, with so much possessive threat in his voice that Miles backed off, raising his hands in a gesture of surrender.

"All right, Rowarth. I understand." He grinned. "Don't forget that I am your oldest friend. There is no need to call me out. I'm here only if you need help tonight. As is Nat Waterhouse." He pointed out a tall, dark man who was across the other side of the hall drinking champagne and flirting with a blond woman with improbably girlish ringlets, whose breasts were tumbling out of the bodice of her clinging blue gown. As they watched, Waterhouse raised one of the blond's ringlets to his lips and she simpered up at him in return.

"Contrary to all appearances," Miles Vickery said drily, "Waterhouse *is* working tonight."

He bowed again and sauntered off, leaving Eve very aware of Rowarth's presence at her side. She had felt the tension simmering in him from the moment they had first greeted Warren Sampson. She turned to see him glaring at her.

"No one will believe that we were *ever* lovers if you look at me like that, Rowarth," she said. "There is no need to behave with such ill-tempered possessiveness."

"Is there not?" Something primitive flared in Rowarth's eyes before he banked it down. "That is what you do to me, Eve. There is business unfinished between us."

"There is nothing between us—" Eve started to say, even as he caught her close again with a demand she was powerless to resist and which made a mockery of her denials.

"You still respond to me," he murmured, his lips brushing the corner of her mouth. "Admit it, Eve."

"And what is that to the purpose?" Eve was really angry with him now both for demonstrating the power he still had over her and arrogantly asserting that it meant anything at all. "I admit that there is some sort of inconvenient attraction still between us," she said, "but it is no more than that." She tapped her fan sharply in the palm of her hand. "You should take a good, long look at yourself, Rowarth, duke or no. You come here and insult me with your false accusations and coerce me into behaving like a harlot in red silk and no underwear and then you behave like a dog in a manger."

They stared at one another, locked in furious confrontation, until recalled to their surroundings by a discreet cough.

"Excuse me, madam." A liveried servant had approached and was standing a little distance away, clearing his throat. Eve tore her gaze away from Rowarth. "Mr. Sampson's compliments and would you care to join him in the library?"

"Thank you," Eve said, casting Rowarth one final glance before she followed him. "I should be delighted."

CHAPTER FOUR

"I DON'T LIKE it," Rowarth said to Miles Vickery. The two of them were stationed on a stone balcony directly above the open terrace windows that led from the library into the gardens. It gave them a perfect means of eavesdropping on the conversation inside the room without being so obvious as to be lurking suspiciously on the terrace. But Rowarth could also see the disadvantages. If Sampson closed the terrace doors then they would hear nothing and more importantly, if Eve needed help it would take them a long time to reach her. Nat Waterhouse, who was downstairs making sure that no one sprung them, was nearer, but he could not know what was happening inside the library.

At the moment Eve was alone and Rowarth was already feeling as strung out as a wire. His tension had ratcheted higher and higher since the confrontation with Eve in the carriage. He had despised the way in which Sampson had looked her over, his hands itching to plant the man a facer. He had almost done the same to Miles, who was a childhood friend. And Eve's words to him in the hall had cut directly through all the bitterness and anger within him and had gone straight to his heart.

You come here and insult me with your false accusations and coerce me into behaving like a harlot...

Rowarth gritted his teeth. He was not proud of himself. There had been a time when he had been a better man than this. Eve had made him so. Now he wondered what would be worse—being obliged to listen to Eve seducing Warren Sampson, for the man was such an exhibitionist and the party so uninhibited that Sampson probably would not trouble to close the windows—or being unable to help her if Sampson turned threatening. Both thoughts were unendurable and it was he who had placed her in this situation, using her as bait, driven by his anger and need for revenge....

"Of course you don't like it," Miles Vickery said, breaking into his thoughts. "The woman you used to love is down there in danger of either seduction or violence or worse." Miles shook his head. "To be honest, old chap, I think you are touched in the attic to have gone so far with this scheme. When Hawkesbury first mooted the idea you should have told him to go hang. I could not believe that you did not."

"Yes," Rowarth said, belatedly recognizing the truth of Miles's assertions. "I should have done."

"I know you were bitter after Eve left you," Miles continued. "I know you were afraid to show weakness like your father, but really, old chap..." He shook his head. "The two cases were very different, were they not? And Eve had been ill, which I am sure must have made matters more difficult—" He broke off, seeing Rowarth's expression. "I know, I know. None of my business."

Rowarth stared at him, wondering if he had misheard. The wind from the gardens came faintly to him, carrying the scent of pine and jasmine with it. It also breathed suspicions into his mind, faint but powerful, no longer possible to dismiss.

"I beg your pardon?" he said.

"None of my business—" Miles began.

"No," Rowarth interrupted. "The other bit."

"Eve had been ill," Miles repeated, as though Rowarth

was a rather slow schoolboy having trouble with his lessons. "I know it was not something that you ever mentioned, but I saw the doctor leaving—"

Rowarth grabbed him by the lapels of his jacket. "What? When?"

"Steady on, old chap," Miles wheezed. "I thought you were supposed to be cool under pressure?"

Rowarth released him. "When?" he repeated, very softly now.

Miles smoothed his jacket down. "Must we do this now, old fellow?" he beseeched. "Try to keep your mind on the job in hand. Sampson will be arriving at any moment."

"Forget that," Rowarth said. "This is more important. You were saying?"

Miles sighed. "I knew it was a mistake for Hawkesbury to recruit an amateur." He caught sight of Rowarth's expression. "Oh, very well. If you must know, I called on you at Welburn House a few days before Eve left you. There was an urgent matter I needed to discuss with you... Well, it is of no consequence now. I did not realize that you were out of town—the servants made no mention of it—so naturally when you were not at Welburn I assumed you were with Eve." He sighed. "I was about to knock on the door of the house in Birdcage Walk when it opened and Dr. Culpepper came out."

"The *doctor?*" Rowarth felt suddenly cold, the fear creeping down his spine.

"Yes, the doctor," Miles said. "Must you repeat everything that I say?"

"Go on," Rowarth said.

"As the maid was showing him out I heard him instruct her to look after her mistress," Miles said. "So I assumed Eve was ill. That's all."

Rowarth took a deep breath. "Why did you never tell me this before?" he demanded.

"I'd forgotten about it until tonight," Miles said simply.

The sharp click of the library door opening and closing again snapped them back to attention. There was the sound of voices.

"That is Tom Fortune," Miles said, listening intently, "not Warren Sampson." He spun around as Rowarth let out an oath and, opening the balcony doors, ran back inside the house.

"I say, old fellow, you can't intervene now," Miles protested. "You'll ruin everything!"

"No, I won't," Rowarth said harshly. "I'll be doing what I should have done long ago, devil take it." He was already slamming out of the room, his footsteps echoing across the floor as he headed toward the stairs.

"As I said, I knew it was a mistake to recruit an amateur," Miles said, but he was smiling as he followed Rowarth out.

Eve had found the library in near darkness, lit only by a single stand of candles that cast long shadows up the wall. It was also empty and for a moment Eve was relieved, for Warren Sampson's absence at least gave her a moment to collect herself. She drew a deep breath, leaning against the long central table, which bore a breathtakingly tasteless vase of lolling lilies. Misery and regret beat through her body as she thought of the bitter words she had exchanged with Rowarth.

It was so pointless, so foolish, to want to go back, to wish to change the past. She had run from Rowarth in the first place because she had had no choice and nothing had changed. Five years ago she had turned her back on all that they had had because he had wanted to wed her and she had known that it was utterly impossible.

When first Rowarth had proposed marriage to her she had

been astounded but he would entertain no opposition nor accept any refusal from her. He had rejected all her objections that she was unsuitable, that she had been born out of wedlock, that she had no education, that she had been his mistress and so it was utterly unacceptable for her to be his wife and even more inappropriate for her to be a duchess. He had swept it all aside, confident and happy, buoyed up by his love for her. He was a duke—he could do as he wished. And for a while Eve had been swept along, too, believing that they could be happy.

But then she had found out that she was pregnant and had lost the baby almost in the same instant. She had been ill, dreadfully ill, and Dr. Culpepper had told her that she would never bear another child. The news had been the bitterest blow that she had ever had to accept in her life. Even now she could not think about it without the pain expanding in her chest and stealing her breath and making her want to weep. She had thought herself hardened to every misfortune that life could throw at her. She had dealt with more than her share. But this grief was a different matter. It was a black, aching emptiness, a jagged pain that caught her at unexpected moments like a thief in the dark. It sapped her soul until she was so tired and worn that sometimes she had not known how she had carried on.

Rowarth had been away on business, visiting his estates in Kent, and by the time he had returned to London Eve had packed up and gone, knowing that she could never be his wife now, that it was all at an end, that fairy tales did not happen to the likes of little Eve Nightingale. Even if a duke *was* unconventional enough to marry his mistress he needed a son to carry on the title and inherit the estates that he had cared for so dutifully all these years. But she would never, ever be able to give Rowarth children and it had broken her heart and it would break his, too, if he ever knew...

Eve straightened, rubbing the tears from her cheeks with impatient fingers.

Fool to cry. She had always known that everything that had once been precious and sweet and true between them was long gone. She had always known there could be no going back for them.

"My apologies for keeping you waiting, Mrs. Nightingale."

Eve had been so wrapped up in her grief that she had not heard the door open but now she saw not Warren Sampson, as she might have expected, but Tom Fortune bearing down upon her, a glass of wine in one hand, a wolfish smile on his lips. She straightened quickly, masking her distress.

"I am sorry," she said, with an attempt at a smile. "I thought that Mr. Sampson was joining me."

Fortune smiled again. "He will be here presently." He came so close to her that she could smell the stale sweat on his body and the wine on his breath. Eve's nerves tightened. There was something feral about Tom Fortune, something dangerous. She had met men like him before and knew precisely what they wanted. She looked around for something with which to arm herself but the fire irons were out of reach, as were the heavy china figurines on the mantel. She wondered where Rowarth and his colleagues had stationed themselves in order to witness her springing the trap on Sampson. She hoped they were close enough to intervene. But of course they would not do so. Her heart plummeted as she thought about it. Since Rowarth was happy enough for her to seduce Warren Sampson in the interests of eliciting a confession, no doubt he expected her to seduce Tom Fortune as well if the situation required it.

"Now then, Mrs. Nightingale," Fortune was saying, "I believe that you had a business proposition you wished to discuss?"

Eve gave him a cool look. "For Mr. Sampson's ears only," she said politely.

Fortune laughed. He ran one finger down Eve's bare arm and she tried not to flinch away. "You can tell me," he murmured. "Mr. Sampson trusts me to handle his business affairs."

"Does he indeed?" Eve said, raising her brows. "Was it Mr. Sampson's business that brought you to my shop?"

Tom Fortune's eyes narrowed and he gave her a very sharp look. "No indeed," he said. "That was a personal financial embarrassment, I fear."

"Selling off your brother's silver to pay your debts?" Eve said. "A pity. I had thought…hoped…that there might be more business potential in the situation than that."

Tom was very still, watching her like a snake watching a mouse. "What exactly are you suggesting, Mrs. Nightingale?"

"As I said," Eve said, turning away and feigning boredom, "that is for discussion with Mr. Sampson only."

Tom laughed. "Then if you will not talk to me," he murmured, "I suggest that we pass the time until Mr. Sampson's arrival in more pleasurable ways." He lingered suggestively over the words. "You must know, Mrs. Nightingale, that in your case Mr. Sampson would deem it a positive delight to mix business with pleasure."

"And you expect a share in that…pleasure, too, I suppose," Eve said, trying to edge away from him. Tom Fortune followed her until they were in danger, Eve thought a little hysterically, of chasing one another around the table.

"I always try the goods out myself first," Tom agreed. He

moved quickly, grabbing her arm and pressing a damp kiss on the curve of her neck. Suddenly his hands seemed to be everywhere, down the neck of her gown, grasping for her skirts. It was intolerable and suddenly Eve knew she would rather be dead than succumb to him, Rowarth and Hawkesbury be damned. She tried to free a hand to strike him, but Fortune was strong and determined. She managed to reach for the huge phallic vase in the center of the table and brought it down on his head. Fortune swore. Water cascaded everywhere. Lilies flew in all directions. And in the same moment the door of the library was flung open and Rowarth, all urbane elegance gone, charged across the room, grabbed Tom Fortune by the neck cloth, dragged him away from Eve and struck him so hard and so scientifically that the man seemed to arc across the library before landing in the fireplace with a crash.

"Damned scoundrel," he growled.

Miles Vickery, who had followed Rowarth into the room, went across to check on Fortune. "Out cold," he said. "You always did have a dangerous left hook, Rowarth."

"Rowarth," Eve said, her hands pressed to her cheeks, torn between laughter and tears, "I do believe you have completely sabotaged your own commission."

"To hell with my commission." Rowarth scooped her up in his arms and strode to the door. His expression was set and hard. "To hell with Sampson. To hell with Hawkesbury. I should have told him to go hang from the start. You and I are going home, Eve. We have matters to discuss."

Outside in the hall it seemed that all hell had broken loose as well. The ice sculpture of Poseidon, partially melted and drooping now, had been toppled onto the floor and was spreading water all around. A very pretty young girl of about eighteen in a peacock-blue mask was struggling in the arms of one of Warren Sampson's guests, who, inebriated and lecherous, was trying to kiss her.

"Don't you know who I am?" the maiden shrieked, pushing him hard. "Unhand me at once, you dolt!"

The man reeled backward and in the same moment Nat Waterhouse erupted across the hall, caught him by the cravat and hit him across the room in much the same way that Rowarth had despatched Tom Fortune. Waterhouse turned on the girl.

"Lizzie," he said, in tones that made a chill trickle down Eve's spine, "what the *devil* are you doing here?"

Despite the mask, Eve had recognized the girl now as Lady Elizabeth Scarlet, half sister of Sir Montague Fortune and of Tom, the very man who had just tried to seduce her in the library. It was evident from Lady Elizabeth's very expensive but demure debutante's raiment and the look of the startled virgin on her face that she could not quite hide, that for all her bravado she was in completely the wrong place.

"I heard there was a party," Lady Elizabeth proclaimed, "and I wanted to see for myself." She sounded ever so slightly drunk.

Her gaze swung around the hall, taking in the seminude women, the couples in various states of debauchery and the overendowed ice sculpture, and Eve saw her gulp. She had heard that Lady Elizabeth was wild but the poor girl had, Eve was sure, overstepped the mark this time.

"I'm taking you home," Nat Waterhouse said to her, still sounding furious.

Across the hallway a couple of drunken young bucks had decided that if there was going to be a mill then they would join in. Half-dressed women ran shrieking for cover as they ploughed enthusiastically into the fight. Before long the servants had joined in and the entire room was a heaving mass of men planting random punches. Miles Vickery was doubled up with laughter.

"A marvelous end to Mr. Sampson's entertainment and to our endeavor," he said cheerfully. "Rowarth—would you like to be the one to explain this to Lord Hawkesbury?"

CHAPTER FIVE

"WE NEED TO talk," Rowarth said. He and Eve were alone in the carriage, having delivered Lady Elizabeth Scarlet secretly and safely back to Fortune Hall and received her incoherent and tearful thanks. Waterhouse and Vickery had bidden them good night and retired to their lodgings at the Morris Clown Inn, mocking Rowarth for the fact that he was so rich that he was staying at the Granby Hotel while their miserable pittance of an income from the Home Secretary condemned them to less salubrious surroundings.

"I don't want to go to the Granby," Eve said. "I have had a sufficiently disreputable evening as it is without creeping into a gentleman's hotel room. That would finish my reputation for good."

Rowarth took her hand. "Then where shall we go?" he asked. His gaze compelled her and a curl of apprehension tightened in her stomach. She knew that there could be no avoiding a final confrontation now. She had felt it from the moment Rowarth had scooped her up into his arms in Sampson's library.

"There is no one at the shop," she said reluctantly. "Joan has rooms at her sister's house in the village."

She saw the flare of satisfaction in Rowarth's eyes and something else, heated and intense. "Just to talk, Rowarth," she reminded him, though her pulse fluttered.

"Absolutely," Rowarth said smoothly.

The tiny room above the shop seemed even tinier with Rowarth in it, his presence dominating the space. Eve stirred the embers of the fire to a bright burning glow and lit a candle that she could ill afford. The soft light gave the room an illusory warmth but she felt cold and on edge inside.

"Would you care for a brandy?" she asked. Her cupboard was scarcely creaking under the weight of wine or spirits but she felt that even if Rowarth refused, she needed a drink for Dutch courage.

He laughed. "You still have a taste for brandy?"

The memories flooded back into Eve's mind. When they had been together Rowarth had teased her once about the unladylike pleasure she took in drinking brandy and she had explained that she liked it because it was expensive, a gentleman's drink, unlike the rough gin that was sold on the streets. Rowarth had gone out and bought her a case of the best brandy the very next day and she had told him that it was not his gift that mattered the most to her, although it touched her, it was his generosity in wanting to make her happy.

"I do not need a drink," Rowarth said.

"I do," Eve said feelingly. She poured for herself, then found that she could not touch the spirit anyway.

"Eve…" Rowarth came to sit next to her on the sofa. "I am sorry," he said. "What I made you do tonight was unconscionable."

"You did not make me do anything in the end," Eve said. "I had already decided that you and Lord Hawkesbury could go to hell in a handcart before I touched Warren Sampson. And I was well able to deal with Mr. Fortune."

"He looked very fetching wearing those lilies," Rowarth said, smiling. The smile faded. "But you know what I mean. I was utterly in the wrong to coerce you so. It was unforgivable."

The breath caught in Eve's throat. She looked at him. He was watching the embers of the fire and his gaze was somber.

"I regret it more than I can tell you," he said. "There are no excuses, but I want to explain. I want you to understand." Then, as she inclined her head he continued: "To my eternal shame, I was so angry with you, Eve, angry and bitter. I should have told Hawkesbury what to do with his commission but when I heard that he had found you all I could think of was to see you again so that I could prove to myself that you no longer had any power over me." He looked up, took her hand, his grip painfully tight. "I think that I feared becoming like my father," he said softly. "His divorce case was so scandalous and sordid. It broke him. I was only ten years old but I saw the change in him. And then he died when I was barely eighteen and I knew my mother's betrayal had killed him in the end." He intertwined his fingers with hers, looking down at their linked hands. "I was furious that I had almost made the same mistake myself."

He shifted, his fingers tightening painfully on hers. "Hawkesbury was able to use me because of that fear and resentment," he said, "and in return I used you."

"I understand," Eve said. Her voice was thick with tears for the boy who had seen his father broken and betrayed and for the young man who had had to step into his shoes at so young an age and take on all a grown man's responsibilities. "It does not matter, Rowarth," she said. "We have both made mistakes. It is all done now."

Rowarth was still holding her hand, his thumb stroking in distracting circles over her palm. "No, it is not," he said, and Eve shivered because she knew what was coming. "Tell me what happened to you, Eve. Why did you run? I do not believe what you told me before. I know that you loved me, so why did you leave me?"

The grief and the misery wrenched at Eve's heart. She looked up and met his eyes and saw nothing but compassion there, all anger spent.

"I cannot tell you," she said. "Oh, Rowarth, don't ask me. Please don't ask me."

His hand came up to cup her chin, forcing her to meet his eyes. "You're afraid," he said softly. His fingers touched her cheek with aching tenderness, cradling her. "Eve, I have to tell you that Miles Vickery told me something tonight that I never knew. He saw you on the day you left. He had come to call on me and he saw Dr. Culpepper leaving, too."

Eve went very still. Icy shivers chased over her skin. Rowarth's words had conjured all the fear and misery of those last days. She struggled to keep the horrible memories locked in the box where they belonged. She sat silent, her heart breaking.

"Eve…" Rowarth was gentle but relentless and she knew he would not give up now, not until he had the truth. She felt trapped. Could she relinquish half the secret, explain a little while keeping those worst, darkest and most devastating of memories safely locked away? She was terrified; she could never tell the worst of it. Even now it would destroy her.

"Were you ill?" Rowarth asked. "Eve, please—"

Eve gave a little hiccup between laughter and tears. "I was not ill. I was pregnant."

There was a moment's silence while Rowarth thought about this. "Did you leave because you thought I would not want our child?" His voice was rough. "Surely you knew me better than that? You knew I wished to marry you—" He broke off as Eve shook her head violently.

"It was not that," she said. "I lost the baby, Rowarth. I had a miscarriage. I lost our child and I could not bear it."

To her enormous relief he did not press her any further but gathered her close, brushing the hair away from her face as she cried now, unable to help herself. He murmured endearments to her, his arms as strong as steel bands about her.

"My darling…that you should have had to suffer that and I was not there for you…"

The warmth of his touch, the bliss of being in his arms after so many barren years, was too much for Eve. Suddenly she desperately wanted to deny the past, forget it and lose herself in this moment. She knew that she and Rowarth could not go back, that too much had happened to force them apart, but she wanted to hold on to this night forever. In the warm intimacy of this tiny room with the door closed against the world and the future, she could fool herself for a little while that she could recapture what they had had.

"I don't want to talk about the past," she said, pressing her fingers to her lips. "I want to spend this one night with you, Rowarth, and forget about all else."

Rowarth went very still at her words. He held himself under absolute control, aching to touch her, hold her and kiss her to within an inch of her life. His body had sprung into almost instant hardness at the images her words conjured. To lie with Eve again, to rediscover the pleasure they could give one another, to hear her soft cries and take her with all the lust and tenderness and regret that was in his soul… But that was not enough. It would never be enough.

"Just the one night?" he asked.

"Yes." The firelight shimmered on some expression in her eyes that he could not understand. "We both know that there cannot be anything else for us, Rowarth."

He would take issue with that, Rowarth thought. Not long ago he might have thought that one night with Eve would be sufficient to sate his need for her and lay to rest the ghosts of the past. Now he knew that it could never be enough. His future would be a desert if Eve were not a part of it. The idea of her walking away from him again in a day, two days, and never seeing her again was intolerable.

His. The possessive desire almost floored him. She had

always been his, from the first moment he had seen her, and she would be his again. They had lost each other a little along the way but soon, very soon, they could wash away the loneliness and grief he had seen in her, and the bitterness and revenge that had been in him. And then he would never let her go again.

Eve moved closer to him, which brought her into his arms, and raised her face to his so that he could kiss her. He was within an inch of forgetting everything except his need for her. With a groan he lowered his mouth to hers and she opened her lips to him and he tasted her, hot, sweet, as seductive as she had always been except that his desire for her was so much more potent now. His tongue grazed hers and she gave a little whimper of pleasure. He scooped her up in his arms, still kissing her, his only thought now to take her to bed and claim her once and for all as his own.

Eve stood on the rug before the fire in her bedroom, shivering. She was terrified. She had gone this far, recklessly, on emotion alone, and now a part of her was excited, wanting to luxuriate in the wonderful, wicked pleasure of rediscovering Rowarth's touch, but she was also nervous, as gauche as a debutante.

He had carried her through to the bedroom and placed her gently on her feet but now he did not touch her. The anticipation and the anxiety thrummed through Eve like a wire. She had thought he wanted her with a hunger that matched her own.

"If you have changed your mind then let us forget the whole matter." It was her pride talking because she could not bear for him to reject her now, after all that they had been through.

He moved then, so fast that she was taken by surprise, catching her hand and drawing her close.

"I have not changed my mind." His voice was amused

but with a rough edge to it now and the excitement flickered through her blood like sheet lightning to hear it. "I wanted you from the first moment I saw you again and I knew this would happen."

"How arrogant of you." How she loved that confidence in him.

Rowarth put a hand under her chin. His eyes scanned her face, eyes so warm, so tender. Eve shivered again, this time with longing as well as fear. She had always known deep down that she still loved Rowarth and tonight she did not want to think about the future. She wanted to banish the darkness, at least for a little while.

He brushed his thumb over her bottom lip and Eve felt her body quiver in response.

"You're nervous." His voice was low. "I swear I will not hurt you."

"I am not afraid of you," she corrected him. At least there would be no physical consequences for her; there could not be when she could no longer bear a child. "It's been a very long time for me," she said.

Five years…

Tenderness warmed his eyes. "Then we shall do this very slowly and stop whenever you wish."

"I don't think I am likely to want that," she murmured.

He was smiling and suddenly, fiercely, she wanted to kiss that smiling mouth, to taste him and lose herself in him.

"May I kiss you?" he murmured.

So sweet to be asked when most men would simply take.

"Please do…" Her voice was husky. His mouth took hers deeply, fiercely, his tongue tangling with hers in intimate dance. Her skin came alive beneath his hands, recognizing him in the most elemental way, tingling with the need to be close with no barriers between them. She freed herself from his ardent grip only so that she could undress him, eager now,

her fingers slipping a little in her haste. She unfastened his
stock and then the neck of his shirt, and stood on tiptoe to
press a kiss on the hot skin at the base of his throat. A groan
rumbled in his chest. She could feel the pulse there beating
against her lips with the same rhythm as his heart. His hand
went to unbutton his coat and waistcoat. Eve was fascinated
to see that he was shaking. He shrugged himself out of the
garments and tossed them aside. They hit the bed and slithered to the floor.

He caught her about the waist to press another kiss on
her lips. Heat spiraled through Eve, twisting and tightening.
Sweet desire flooded her down to the tips of her toes.

"Let me finish…" She pressed her palm against his chest
and felt the warmth of his body through the material of his
shirt "…or I will never get you out of these clothes."

He made a sound like a growl. "Be quick then."

Eve laughed. "I used to think that you were a patient man."

Again she reached up to kiss him, full of feminine power
and a bubbling happiness that took her by surprise. It was so
long since she had felt like this. Joy and discovery, excitement
and nervousness all mingled within her and made her feel
honey-soft inside. She freed his shirt from the waistband of
his pantaloons and burrowed underneath, fanning her hands
out against his stomach. His muscles rippled against her fingers. He caught his breath and ripped the shirt over his head.
Eve stared as the firelight turned his body golden and bronze,
smooth, hard and sculpted. Beautiful. Time had not altered
the physical perfection she remembered so well.

Her throat dried. She reached out to him but he was too
quick for her, picking her up to lay her on the thick rug before the fire. His hands traveled over her, easing the gown
from her, unlacing her stays with quick, practiced movements,
taking her chemise from her so that she was naked but for
her stockings. Eve was quiescent and still, her breath com-

ing rapidly, her eyes fixed on his face where she saw intent concentration and desire distilled.

"Ah…" His eyes went almost black with lust as he exposed her body to his gaze. He sat back on his heels, a flush of arousal along his cheekbones. He had, she noticed, an enormous erection that his pantaloons could barely contain.

"Turn over."

He rolled her onto her stomach. Her breasts, so full and sensitive now, brushed against the soft caress of the rug and she groaned. He leaned over her to press kisses up her spine and over the line of her shoulders. Her nipples hardened, her entire body alive and prickling with arousal. He licked a path down her spine again, his hot, wicked tongue spiraling over her skin, and Eve moaned. When his hands swept up her thighs she allowed her legs to fall open and felt the coolness of the air against her flesh.

"Leave the stockings," she managed to say, as she felt his fingers on her garter, and she heard him laugh. The rough edge to the tone made her heart beat in double time. His caresses rose higher, stealing over her in a seductive circling motion that made the heat pool deep within her, until he reached the softest skin of her inner thighs. His fingers grazed her cleft and she cried out, the sensation blazing through her even as her body grasped for more. His hand was on her hip and he rolled her over so that she was staring up, dazzled by sensual need, into the hard, hot glitter of his eyes.

"I want to see you…" His words were low and harsh. "You always were so very beautiful… I want to touch every part of you…"

Eve *felt* very beautiful, worshipped and adored for the first time in five long years. There was reverence in the way Rowarth touched her, as though she was exquisitely precious, and awe in the way that he looked at her.

At last he moved to unfasten his pantaloons and his erection sprang free of the constraint, thick and hard. He lay beside Eve on the rug and started to kiss her all over again, his hands holding her still as he ravished her mouth deeply, his fingers tangling in her hair. He dropped his head to her breasts and skimmed his tongue over the sensitive underside and up to the nipple, licking and sucking, wrenching a gasp from her lips that was half moan, half plea. She wanted nothing more than to feel him inside her now and she reached for him, but he held off, making her wait.

"Patience…" There was amusement in his voice. "I want you to really want me…"

Oh, she did. She thought she would die of the wanting.

He trailed kisses across the curve of her stomach and she felt her muscles jump and clench. She arched, raising her hips, begging now.

"Darling Eve…" His voice was a dark whisper. "You have always been mine." He moved between her thighs and hung there poised for what felt like the longest moment of her life. The emotion strung out between them, fierce and tight and impossibly tense, and then he slid into her, claiming her, so smooth and deep that she cried out.

Her body shifted to accommodate him as he thrust with strong, slow strokes. Already the pleasure was building within her, shimmering and tantalizing just out of reach. She wanted more. She wanted to explode.

"Faster, if you please…" She dug her fingers into his buttocks to pull him even tighter inside and felt his body jerk in response.

"So polite…" His breathing was ragged. He obliged her by plunging deeper and harder, driving her higher and higher as she smoothed her hands down his back to encourage him on and bit his shoulder in an agony of need and ecstasy. She had lost all coherent thought, everything drowning in pure pleasure and the absolute necessity of fulfillment. And then her body clenched and she came with a blissful, dazzling intensity. Fireworks exploded in her head, flooding her mind with light. Her body clasped his in helpless spasm, and she held him and heard him call her name as he, too, fell into the deepest languor and pleasure. Past, present and future collided in the most perfect reunion.

In the aftermath she felt him draw her close, tucking her into the curve of his arm as though she was the most precious thing on earth, her head on his shoulder and the beat of his heart against hers, and it felt like coming home.

Eve woke to see the light flooding the room and to feel a quick, uncomplicated joy. Rowarth was lying beside her, his arm about her waist in casual possession, his legs tangled with hers. She could smell his skin, at once familiar and exciting. Her body quickened again and she shifted, feeling the ache inside that was the aftermath of bliss and the promise of pleasure to come. It had been so perfect. She had never imagined it would be like that again.

The happiness fled. The loss she had staved off the previous night came flooding back, filling the emptiness within her soul with its bitter harvest. She had gone into this knowing that she loved him but that she could never keep him. Not Rowarth, with his responsibilities and his obligations, not least amongst which was his need to produce an heir for his dukedom with some suitable, blue-blooded, fertile aristocrat. She had borrowed him for one last night, loving him too much to deny either of them. And now she would have to give him up because that was the only thing to do.

"Sweetheart…" He was stirring. He stroked a palm over the soft skin of her stomach. He sounded happy. Another crack appeared in her heart.

He rolled over, looked at her, and at the expression in his eyes she felt sudden acute apprehension. Her heart was thumping. She knew he was going to ask her to be his mistress again and she was so sorely tempted to agree. To have Alasdair Rowarth in her life again, even if it was only for a little while… Would she sacrifice the independence she had achieved here and all she had worked for in order to be with him? And could she watch him wed another woman and produce an heir when she had thought once that she would be his wife and she knew that she loved him more than anyone else ever could?

"I once asked you to be my wife, Eve," Rowarth said. "Now I am asking you again. Will you marry me?"

"Oh, no!" Eve could not quite bite back the words in time. This really was a disaster. She had not imagined, not dreamed, that this could happen. And of course it was utterly impossible, for all the same reasons that it had been before.

Rowarth was looking quizzical and a little chagrined at her outburst.

"I did not think the idea would be so abhorrent to you," he said.

"I thought you were going to ask me to be your mistress again," Eve said helplessly.

Rowarth did not look pleased. In fact he looked most forbidding. "That position is not on offer."

Oh, dear. She knew she had offended him. No, she had hurt him. She could see it in his eyes. She loved him so much that it made her want to cry, she who had once thought herself as hard as diamonds. "I… I cannot." Her heart was breaking piece by little piece. She wanted to explain why, but it hurt so much to open up those final dark secrets that she did not think she could force out the words. Besides, she *could not bear* to see his face when he knew the truth and to hear him retract his proposal. Like her, he knew that a man, a duke, needed an heir to his dukedom. He cared for Welburn so much, had done so since his youth with both a sense of responsibility and a deep love. It would be imperative for him to pass on that love and that duty to the next generation.

"My life is here now, Rowarth," she said. "Flattered as I am by your proposal, I believe that it would be a mistake to try to re-create what we had."

He had gone very still. There was a hard, determined light in his eyes. "Last night you told me that you loved me."

Had she? She had no recollection of it at all, but during their impassioned lovemaking it would have been fatally easy to pour out all the feelings she had harbored for him during those five long, lonely years.

"Did I say that?" She forced lightness into her tone, making the entire experience sound no more than a pleasant tumble rather than something that had touched her soul. "A figure of speech, my dear. I certainly *enjoyed* it—"

He looked as though he was going to argue. He looked as though he did not believe her. Her defenses felt perilously weak. One word from him and she might falter. She moved to put a stop to it before it had started.

"I believe a gentleman can accept a refusal with good grace?"

Now he looked really angry. "If you wish to put it like that…" He bit the words out. "You tie my hands, madam. I will say no more."

He leaped from the bed, magnificently unconcerned about his nudity, and gathered up his clothes, throwing them on haphazardly with swift, angry movements before wrenching open the door. Then he looked back.

"Farewell, Eve," he said.

She heard his furious steps on the stairs, heard also Joan's startled squeak as they met in the shop doorway and heard the door slam behind him. She lay still and forced herself not to watch him walk away from her because she knew that if she did she would change her mind and run after him and that was the one thing she could not permit herself to do.

It had been the most damnably miserable day. No matter that the sun poured down from a cloudless sky and the pavements of Fortune's Folly bustled with people shopping, taking the waters or walking on Fortune Row. Eve was unhappy and Joan shook her head over her and brought her endless cups of tea for solace.

"I told you so," Joan said. "No good ever comes from tangling with handsome gentlemen."

"I am not tangled," Eve snapped. "He has gone."

Business was improving. A young lady had called by that morning. Miss Alice Lister had brought in a footstool to sell with an enormous, vulgar coat of arms on it.

"I'm afraid my mother embroidered it," she said sadly. "She will sew our family crest on anything that doesn't move away fast enough. Please, could you get rid it for me? I truly cannot bear to look at it."

Eve had chatted with her and had smiled and sorted out the stock that had come in over the past few days and the time had dragged, the hands of the clock edging around so slowly into a future that now seemed colorless and gray. She had sent Rowarth away again because it was the only thing that she could do, for his sake and her own. Now all she had to do was forget him for a second time; no easy matter when she ached for him with every particle of her being.

At three-thirty the doorbell clanged again. Eve had been dealing with the accounts—hateful job—while Joan was in the village. She came out into the shop in time to hear the key turn in the lock and the shutters rattle closed.

"What on earth—"

Rowarth.

Impossible.

He was standing just inside the door. He had the key in

his hand. Shaking, Eve moved several of the counter items at random. "I thought you had gone," she said foolishly, since he was standing right before her.

"I've come to claim something I lost." He sounded confident, authoritative, the humor lurking just below the surface. Eve's heart leaped and she tried to quell its insistent beat.

"This is a pawnbroker's shop," she said, "not a lost property office."

Rowarth smiled. Her stomach dipped. "I appreciate that. And there is another difficulty, too, I fear. I cannot pay you. What I want is beyond price. You have to give it to me freely."

"That isn't the way that I do business."

"It is now. I want your love. Your hand in marriage."

"My *love?*" Her voice sounded squeaky as a rusty gate. "*Marriage?* Rowarth, I told you this morning—"

"You told me that your words of love meant nothing. I think that you lied. I think you sent me away because you are afraid to take the risk."

Eve stared at him, unwilling, unable to lie again. That morning it had been painful enough. "I cannot be held to anything I said in the throes of passion. It was so blissful I probably would have said *anything…*"

Rowarth smiled again, devastating, wicked. She felt lightheaded, dizzy with love for him. "Eve…" He shook his head. "Take the risk. I love you—you make me happy, a better man. I hope I make you happy, too. So we will wed."

The blunt male logic of it made it sound so simple.

Eve's throat closed with tears. How to dissuade him now? He had come several steps closer. There was a smile in his eyes and a confidence about him that said he knew now how this would end. She could not hurt him again, could not lie.

"We cannot marry," she said defiantly. "I was your mistress. I am unsuitable. Everyone will talk scandal."

He looked unmoved. "I have had a great deal more women

than you have had men, my dear." He shrugged. "Does the past matter, if we love each other?"

Actually she found it did. She was consumed with jealousy for all those women. She wanted to rip them to shreds.

"If you believe that my past does not matter, you are mistaken," she said. "No one will receive me."

He looked regretful. "Some will because of the title. But I know that it is a great deal to ask of you. Do you love me enough to do it?" Then, as she hesitated, knowing she was only making excuses anyway, he added, "Eve, you know that I am no callow youth with unrealistic ideals. I'm old and cynical yet despite that I know that once I have found love—the real thing—I cannot afford to let it go if I am ever to be happy again."

Eve picked up a cuckoo clock, concentrating fiercely on it. "I cannot. I am illegitimate, and ill-educated—"

He took the clock from her, placed it carefully on the desk and then took her hands, his gaze suddenly intent. "You may recall that we have had this conversation before. I do not care about your parentage or your education. You are loving and generous and warm and the most special woman in the world and I knew it from the moment we first met."

She could not look at him. She tried to free herself and was held fast.

"Rowarth," she said again, and she could hear the unsteady note in her voice and cursed herself for it. "How many dukes do you know who married their mistresses?"

He was actually counting. She could see it. "Three," he said, at last. "Dunston, Glenroth and Shefford. The Duchess of Shefford called herself an actress but we all knew—"

"Rowarth!"

"I beg your pardon." He sounded genuinely apologetic. "But you are scared, Eve. You are making excuses."

She was. It was true. She so desperately wanted to accept

him and to lay to rest the very last secret between them, yet she knew that if she did she ran the biggest risk of all, that of losing him for good.

"Eve, look at me," Rowarth said. "Tell me what truly troubles you."

It was pointless to resist. He was determined and his gentleness undermined every last defense she had.

She let go of her last secret. "I told you that I lost our baby five years ago." She looked up into his eyes. "What I did not tell you, Rowarth, was that Dr. Culpepper explained that I would never bear more children." She took a deep, painful breath. "I had not even known I wanted a child but then to be told I could never again bear one…it almost destroyed me." She covered her face briefly then let her hands fall. She needed to end this. When he had gone she could break down. "But the point is that we cannot wed, Rowarth. We could not then and we cannot now, for I would never be able to give you an heir. That was why I ran away."

There, it was out. The painful truth that she had nursed to herself all these years was finally exposed in the light. She had never talked of it with anyone. It was too difficult. The wound had never healed, for the hurt had run too deep. It had scarred over, her defenses imperfect, aching when something reminded her, or when, like now, the barrenness of her future was spread before her in all its sterile detail.

Rowarth's expression had changed. She had known it would. She could not hit him with such a shocking truth and expect everything to be the same. He would withdraw from her now, free himself and beat a hasty retreat. He would do it charmingly, of course, with expressions of deep regret and commiseration even as he headed for the door, but he would leave her nevertheless.

"Eve, I am so very sorry."

He sounded sincere. Eve was sure he was. She stifled a

strong desire to throw herself into his arms and beg him to make everything right, because of course he could not. No one could. She drew herself up.

"Thank you." Inexplicably he was still holding her hands and she realized that he had made no move to go. He was watching her, the deepest compassion in his face. She swallowed the enormous lump in her throat.

Why did he not go? She did not want his sympathy. It would be unendurable.

"Thank you," she said again, very quickly. "But you must see…" She wished she did not have to spell it out. "It would be quite impossible for us—for you. You need an heir for Welburn. I know you love the place very deeply and would want to pass it on to your son. So…"

So why do you not simply go, put an end to this, walk away?

He dropped her hands at last and straightened up. Her body sagged with relief as well as misery.

"I am afraid that I do not." He sounded terribly polite. Eve felt confused.

"Do not what?"

Unbelievably, there was still a spark of humor in his eyes. Her battered heart lifted to see it before plunging back down again. How could she feel even remotely happy when she was banishing forever the love of her life?

"I am afraid that I do not see why this makes it impossible for us to be together."

She stared at him, utterly unable to comprehend what she was hearing.

"But, Rowarth—"

"My darling Eve." Now, his arms went about her. Now the comfort and the peace she craved was so close but she did not quite dare to reach out to grasp it. He pressed his lips to her hair and spoke softly. "I am sorry for all you have suffered,

Eve. I am even more sorry that I was not beside you when you needed me. I cannot imagine what you have been through or what it feels like for you, though I would do anything in my power to take away those memories. Alas, I cannot. But I can promise to devote myself to your future and your happiness always, if only you will let me."

"But, Rowarth—" Her throat was clogged with tears. She never normally cried and now she was turning into a watering pot. It was infuriating. "The dukedom! Pray, do not be so foolish—"

"My darling Eve," he said again, his lips moving to brush her ear, making her shiver, "my current heir is my nephew, and he loves Welburn almost as much as I did at his age. I am sure he has been secretly praying that I will never wed so that he can inherit. And I should be glad if he did."

"Oh!" Eve felt taken aback, almost shocked. "But surely a man wants a son?"

Rowarth was strong enough not to deny it.

"It would have been very special," he acknowledged, "to have had a son—or a daughter—with you." For a moment they stood locked together in contemplation of a different future, one that could not be. Then Rowarth's arms tightened about her.

"But I want you, Eve, more than anything else in the entire world. You are the one who completes me. You are all I need."

Eve felt his compassion and his tenderness and his love touch her soul, taking away the darkness, and she turned her face up to his.

"I have never loved anyone but you," she whispered. "I cannot believe this is true. It makes me feel quite giddy."

She saw a smile curve his sensuous mouth. "My sweet, I have always said that you are a very inexperienced courtesan. To love only one man in your entire life…"

She touched his cheek lightly, lovingly. "And you love me, too."

"So much that it consumes me," Rowarth said. "I love you even more than I did five years ago. I had no idea it could be like this."

"So we may learn about love together." Her heart unfurled, light banishing the darkness, healing her. A tear escaped from the corner of her eye and Rowarth caught it with one finger and traced the line of her cheek.

"You have worked very hard for all that you have achieved here," he said, as the cuckoo clock chimed loudly from the desk.

"That's true. I have." Eve looked around at the shabby shop and felt a rush of affection for it.

"You once said that you preferred being a pawnbroker to being a duchess."

"Perhaps I shall have to reconsider."

"I thought," Rowarth said, "that you might wish to keep the shop anyway. Perhaps Joan could run it for you?"

"I think that she would like that very much." Eve pressed her fingers to his lips. "How generous you are to risk offering me a means of escape should I find I really do prefer being a pawnbroker to being a duchess."

"You will not want to escape." His arms about her told her that he would never let her go now he had found her again. The happiness swelled within Eve and this time she dared to trust it. "You are arrogant," she whispered.

He laughed. "So you keep telling me." His voice changed. "Accept me, Eve. Come away with me."

Her heart was so light and full of joy she thought she might burst. "I thought that you had a job to do," she teased. "You have not yet caught Warren Sampson."

"The other Guardians can do that," Rowarth said. "Hawkesbury will not rest until he has Sampson behind bars."

"And what will you be doing meanwhile?" Eve asked, standing on tiptoe to kiss him.

"I shall be on my wedding trip with you," Rowarth said. He bent his head and his lips met hers. "We can go wherever you wish, my love. Wherever you are is my heart's home and it always will be."

* * * * *

HOW TO WOO A SPINSTER

Kasey Michaels

CHAPTER ONE

LADY EMMALINE DAUGHTRY sat in the gardens of Ashurst Hall on one of the first bright days of spring, completely and entirely alone.

It was her twenty-eighth birthday.

On her lap was the letter that had arrived in the morning post from her nieces, Lydia and Nicole. In order to keep to one sheet, thus saving on the postage, Lydia had written her rather formal, excruciatingly correct wishes in her finest copperplate. Nicole, being Nicole, had scribbled her good wishes upside-down between Lydia's lines, her usual exuberance evident in both her atrocious spelling and her latest affectation of marking all her *i*'s with small hearts.

The twins were back with their mother, the thrice-widowed Helen Daughtry, at their small estate of Willowbrook, as Helen was once again between husbands and had remembered that she had daughters to fuss over in her own fashion.

That would change in a few weeks, when Helen went tripping off to London for the Season, and Lydia and Nicole were once again shuttled back to Ashurst Hall "to bear their dearest spinster aunt their Comfort and Presence, as you must be So Devastatingly Lonely isolated in the back of beyond." Or so Helen's last letter, all but pinned to the twins' luggage, had stated so cruelly. But all under the guise of being caring and compassionate.

Lady Emmaline knew her late brother's widow could be a

kind person, in her own way. She simply wasn't a kind person *frequently*.

In that way, Helen had fit very well with the Daughtry family, who seemed to belong to another age, the more rough and tumble—and most definitely profane—age of two decades past. Marital fidelity was a joke to them, kindness considered a weakness and selfishness a near art form. Or else today's Society had simply learned to hide their failings and vices better...

Her morals had, however, been the only way her sister-in-law resembled the Daughtrys. Helen always said she'd married the wrong brother when she'd wed the second son, but even that marriage had been quite above her social station. Yet, ever resourceful, she'd made do with a husband who had tired of her within a few months, and built her own life, her own circle of London friends.

When Emmaline's brother Geoffrey had died, Helen had tricked herself out in crushingly expensive widow's weeds, impatiently waited out a full month of mourning and then deposited her son, Rafael, and the twins on the doorstep of Ashurst Hall and returned to London and those friends. Over the years, the children had spent more time at Ashurst Hall than on their own estate, until Rafe had left to serve with Wellington.

Emmaline had been as thrilled by these additions to the family as her only surviving brother had been appalled—which may have been one of the reasons Emmaline had been so delighted. After all, it wasn't as if there was any love lost between Charlton and herself.

Charlton and Geoffrey were so very much older than Emmaline, and males to her female, so it was not surprising that the three had never been especially close. And Emmaline could have accepted that. But Emmaline's mother had departed this earth the same day her only daughter was born, and for that, Charlton and Geoffrey would never forgive her. Even their father, the Duke of Ashurst, had been no more than occasionally aware of his daughter's existence. Not that he'd much cared for his sons, either. Emmaline always thought his children would have garnered more affection from their sire if they could run on four legs, go up on point when they spotted the fox and then lay at his feet at the banquet whilst he celebrated his latest glorious kill.

And then Geoffrey had died, and their father had looked around and noticed that, by Jupiter, he was in danger of being outnumbered by petticoats. Charlton's wife was enough to have twittering about Ashurst Hall, complaining that he came to dinner in his hunting clothes, or tossing fierce looks at him when he belched or scratched satisfyingly whenever the spirit moved him. It was time to marry off the one he could get rid of, by Jupiter!

So Emmaline had been hauled off to London upon the occasion of her eighteenth birthday, where she was put under the supposedly watchful eye of Helen Daughtry. Which is the same as to say Emmaline was left to her own devices while Helen flirted outrageously with any man who happened to look at Emmaline in a matrimonial way.

Not that Emmaline hadn't had her chances during the Seasons she'd suffered through under Helen's haphazard chaperonage. There had been at least a few gentlemen who hadn't taken one look at Helen's décolletage and deserted Emmaline as if she'd just told them she had contracted the plague. There had been Sir William Masterson, a widower with six children under the age of ten. He'd made no bones that he was looking for a woman to ride herd on his…well, on his herd. Lord Phillipson had loved her; Emmaline had been very aware of that fact from the way he had all but drooled on her shoe tops, but as his breath would fell an ox at ten paces, she'd felt she had to decline his proposal.

There had been no third Season, as her father had died, and Emmaline had insisted on a full year of mourning (Helen had actually laughed when she'd heard that, which was, in fact, as she headed out the door on her way to London less than two hours after the duke had been put to bed for his eternal rest in the family mausoleum).

Charlton, now the thirteenth duke, had given Emmaline one more chance the following Season, sending her off with a warning that an only passably pretty woman of three and twenty shouldn't be so damned choosy and she'd better find some fool who'd come up to scratch because he was done paying through the nose for gowns and gloves and other fripperies.

The Season hadn't gone well. Emmaline sometimes wondered if she had deliberately sabotaged herself and her matrimonial hopes simply to spite the new duke.

On the event of her twenty-fourth birthday, Charlton's gift to her had been a half dozen white, embroidered spinster caps and the information that, while he and his sons George and Harold (their mama having succumbed to a putrid cold three years previously) would be going to London for the Season, she was to remain at home.

Emmaline hadn't protested. Indeed, at the time, she had been rather relieved. After all, in her many Seasons in London she had met, danced and spoken with nearly every eligible bachelor not risking his life on the Peninsula, and none of them had excited her in the least. She could find little attraction in men who cared more for the cut of their evening jacket than they did the notion that Bonaparte might somehow best Wellington and they'd all be speaking French. How on earth was she supposed to take any of these men seriously when none of them had been any better than her brother and nephews, some of them actually worse?

But now the war was at last over and Bonaparte was on his

way to a deserved exile, and the world could welcome home all its fine, brave soldiers…who to a man would surely be on the lookout for ladies much younger than Lady Emmaline.

No, she was destined to remain forever on this estate, sitting in this same garden, season after season, year after year, birthday after birthday, waiting for her perfect lover who would never arrive. How she had tired of watching Charlton eat with his fingers at the dinner table, hearing George and Harold brag about their latest bouts of drinking and gambling, wretches that they were, not to mention listening in some fear to her brother threaten to send her off to their great-aunt in Scotland because he was weary of looking at her.

Yes, having Rafael and Lydia and Nicole so often in residence these past years had been Emmaline's main comfort, and she missed them sorely.

She did not miss Charlton or his sons, who had left her alone without a kind word about her birthday, most probably because they'd forgotten the date. No, they'd gone off five days ago to play with George's newest toy, a yacht he had won at the gaming tables. As if any of them knew the first thing about steering a boat, or whatever it was one did with a boat.

Would it be terrible of her to hope that all three of them spent most of their voyage hanging over the side, sick as dogs and casting up their suppers into the Channel?

Emmaline sighed, folding up the letter from her nieces as she tried to shake off her depressing thoughts. She wished her good friend Charlotte Seavers, who lived in Rose Cottage with her parents, right next door to Ashurst Hall, could share her birthday with her, but her mother was still not quite well. But, no, Emmaline wouldn't think about that particular sadness tonight, either.

Cook had promised her a special treat for supper, and she really should go change out of her simple sprigged muslin gown and into something more festive. She didn't wish to disappoint the servants, who she knew had been busily polishing silver especially for what would be a solitary meal in the cavernous dining room, followed by a quiet evening of reading and an early bedtime.

Perhaps she should reconsider those caps Charlton had given her along with the warning that she was only living under his roof because of his kind and generous nature. She considered this idea for a full three seconds before declaring to the flowers and the trees: "The devil I will. With or without my family, I'm going to celebrate my birthday. *By Jupiter.*"

And then, after surprising herself with her outburst, Emmaline quickly bit her lips between her teeth as she heard the sound of firm, purposeful footsteps approaching along the brick path. How wonderful. Now she was talking to herself, a very spinsterlike thing to do, and someone may have heard her.

She turned her head at the sound of her name. "Yes. Here I am," she said, knowing she did not recognize the male voice that had called to her.

The gentleman who appeared momentarily was a complete stranger to her, for she surely would have remembered such a tall, darkly handsome man as this if she had ever seen him.

"Lady Emmaline?"

"Yes…um, yes, I am she," Emmaline said, feeling rather shaken by the sight of the man's coal-black hair and blazingly blue eyes. As her own eyes were a very ordinary brown and her hair so typically English blond, she had always had an attraction to dark hair and blue eyes. Indeed, she had secretly envied young Nicole her ebony curls and nearly violet eyes, knowing that when she and the differently beautiful Lydia came of age and headed to Mayfair, their suitors would probably have to be beaten away with stout sticks.

"Please pardon the intrusion, ma'am. Your butler told me I would find you here."

Belatedly, Emmaline held out her hand to the man, her hopefully subtle inspection unnoticed by him. She recognized his uniform as belonging to the Royal Navy. *And on my birthday, too—what a lovely present.*

She mentally slapped herself for her frivolous thoughts, probably old-maid thoughts, or those more often entertained by someone like Helen. Then again, Emmaline reminded herself, she was not exactly a debutante, was she? "Captain?"

"Alastair. Captain John Alastair, ma'am," he said after only a slight hesitation, taking her hand in his and bowing over it before releasing her and rising to his full height once more. "I've brought news. If we might step inside, ma'am? And do you have other family in residence at the moment?"

Goodness, what a glorious uniform, right down to the bicorne hat he had tucked up under his arm. Now *this* was a man worth meeting. *Stop that!* she warned her inner self, who was certainly not behaving as a spinster should. But, my, he was so handsome...

"No, I'm quite alone," Emmaline answered after a moment, feeling slightly dazed. When he'd taken her hand she'd felt a tingle of awareness skip up her arm, and knew she was disappointed that he had not kissed her hand. Which was ridiculous. It wasn't as if someone had sent her the man as a birthday present, for goodness' sake. Still, the image of him being presented to her, all tied up with a lovely satin bow, persisted in her traitorous brain. If this was what reaching the lofty age of eight and twenty got her, what would she be doing at thirty? Chasing men down the streets of the village? Shame on her!

His frown told her she had given him an answer he could not like. "Then perhaps your maid? A companion?"

Reluctantly, Emmaline brought her mind back to attention. "Captain Alastair, I don't understand. I'm certainly past the age of needing a chaperone. Or have you come to the front door of Ashurst Hall and introduced yourself to my brother's butler all with the intention of either robbing us or killing us, or both? If so, you may want to reconsider housebreaking as a way to make your way in the world now that the hostilities are a thing of the past."

Had she really said all of that? Why, she was babbling, that's what she was doing. But he looked so serious. So handsome and so serious. It seemed necessary to keep speaking, even babbling, so that he didn't say what he had obviously come here to say. Something he would say that, it would seem, required that she have some other female conveniently on hand for the moment when she would either erupt in hysterics or faint dead away.

A sudden fear invaded her. "Has this to do with Rafe? My nephew, Captain Rafael Daughtry? He is with Wellington. But no, that can't be it. For one, the hostilities are over. And you are a navy captain, and Rafe is with the—I'm sorry. I should stop asking questions and ask you to accompany me inside, shouldn't I, as that is what it would seem you wish me to do?"

"That was another question," Captain Alastair pointed out, not unkindly. "If I may?" He held out his arm to her, and she took it, suddenly believing she might need some sort of support.

Neither spoke as they made their way along the brick path to one of the many sets of French doors leading into the large formal saloon. The captain held open the door for her, and Emmaline stepped inside to see that not only was the silver tea service already set up on the table between the two couches near the center of the room, but that both Grayson and the housekeeper, Mrs. Piggle, were standing just outside the room, pretending not to be watching for her.

She shot them a look they both seemed to understand, and the double doors were closed. Not that Emmaline didn't feel certain that both servants had stepped no more than an inch away from the doors. Knowing Mrs. Piggle, the woman was probably already down on her knees, one eye to the keyhole.

"This is about my brother, isn't it?" Emmaline asked as she sat down and waited for the captain to take up his seat on the facing couch. "What have he and his sons done? Did they somehow ram and sink one of His Majesty's boats? Has the Navy put them under arrest?"

"No, ma'am," the captain said, reaching for the teapot. "May I?"

"Oh! I should have offered. I'm so sorry…yes, please do. Would you rather some wine?"

He looked across the table at her, those blue eyes unreadable. "I'm pouring the tea for you, ma'am. You might consider it a restorative, unless you'd rather a glass of wine. I'm afraid I'm the reluctant bearer of very sad news."

"Yes, I believe I've rather sensed that, Captain Alastair. Please forgive me for attempting to delay delivery of this very sad news. I'm trying to keep my wits about me. Unfortunately, I believe I'm sadly failing at the effort. I'm imagining all sorts of things, none of them very palatable."

"Then please allow me to say this as quickly as I can, and I apologize now for being so abbreviated. Lady Emmaline, it is my sad duty to inform you that your brother and his sons were lost at sea last evening off Shoreham-by-Sea. My own ship arrived on the scene just as the yacht was disappearing beneath the waves with all save one soul still onboard. I'm… I'm profoundly sorry we could not save them."

Emmaline sat very still. She may have breathed, but she couldn't be sure. Her mind objected in the most ridiculous way: *But it's my birthday. Isn't it just like them to do this to me on my birthday?*

She twisted her hands in her lap, and then pinched herself, just to be sure she was awake, and not in the middle of a nightmare that incongruously somehow included a man best described as the perfect lover of her more pleasant dreams.

"Lady Emmaline? May I please summon someone now?"

She shook her head, unable to speak. She waited for the tears, but they didn't come. In all, she felt rather numb. What had been the last words Charlton had said to her five days ago before climbing into his traveling coach behind George and Harold? Oh yes, she remembered. *Make me a happy man, sister mine. Run off with one of the grooms before we get back!*

Her nephews had laughed hard and long at their father's joke. She could still hear them laughing as the coach moved off down the drive.

Emmaline snapped herself back to the moment at hand.

"Was...um, was there a storm?" She didn't know why she asked this. But she felt it was something at least halfway sensible to say, something to break the oppressive silence.

"No, ma'am. Not anything I'd call a storm, at least. As I understand the thing from speaking with the survivor, a Mr. Hugh Hobart, the captain was intoxicated and belowdecks at the time, and one of your nephews was at the helm. Waves are powerful things, ma'am, even on a day that could only be called choppy from the wind along the Channel. Ride with the waves and you fly across the water. Hit one of them wrong, and even a sturdy ship can crack like an egg."

He looked at her, wincing. "I'm sorry. That was stupidly clumsy of me. I shouldn't say that the tragedy could be laid at your nephew's door."

"The yacht was a recent...acquisition. I can't imagine what either George or Harold could have been thinking, to attempt to take the wheel like that. But that's what this Mr. Hobart told you?"

The captain nodded. "The man was rather overset and unintelligible. But, yes, he said his friend Harold was at the helm. That is—was—one of your nephews, correct?"

Emmaline nodded, still waiting to cry. She should be crying, shouldn't she? Clearly Captain Alastair believed she should be weeping, in need of comfort. She was an unnatural sister, that's what she was, and an unnatural aunt.

Because all she could feel, of the little she seemed capable of feeling, was relief...

CHAPTER TWO

JOHN ALASTAIR WAS certain he'd felt more uncomfortable in his lifetime, but at the moment he could not recall anything that measured remotely close to the impotence he felt as he sat across from the bravely stoic Lady Emmaline Daughtry.

He wasn't certain what he'd been expecting from the woman once he'd delivered his terrible news. Tears, protestations that he was wrong, slightly buckling knees or even an outright swoon necessitating burnt feathers being passed beneath her nose to revive her.

He was in considerable awe of the woman, even as he was grateful that he wouldn't have to deal with a hysterical female, as he did not believe playing the role of sympathetic comforter was one of his stronger suits.

Although the thought of having Lady Emmaline in his arms as he comforted her probably appealed to him more than it should.

The late duke's valet, whom John had run to ground at a tavern in Shoreham-by-Sea, had rather grudgingly informed him that Lady Emmaline was the late duke's closest relative, and then gone back to drinking himself under the table, bemoaning the loss of his master. John had asked that the man accompany him to Ashurst Hall, but the valet had demurred, pointing out that there was nothing for him there anymore so he'd stay where he was for the nonce before returning to Ashurst Hall, thank you very much, and then maybe take himself to London to find a new position. When the valet began loudly complaining that he'd have to find that new employment without aid of a written recommendation, considering that the duke was currently fish food, John left the useless man where he was, and good riddance.

He left feeling certain that whatever belongings of the duke and his sons had remained in their rooms at the tavern would soon be sold in order to line the servant's pockets, but it wasn't as if he could command the fellow to show him the way to Ashurst Hall. Instead, he'd commandeered the duke's crested traveling coach and set out to be the Bearer of Sad News.

News Lady Emmaline Daughtry seemed to be taking exceedingly well. What sort of men were the late duke and his sons? The valet had cried…the sister had not?

John studied her as she spooned sugar into her tea and then added cream, her hands steady, her movements graceful. She was a mature woman, little of the girl about her. Her blond hair was styled very simply, swept up and back, away from her face, which showed her smooth chin line and remarkable cheekbones to his admiring eyes. Her brown eyes were rather long, their shape definitely bordering on the exotic, although she did not use them to their best advantage.

Not that he'd expected her to flirt with him. For the love of heaven, what was he thinking? This was probably what happened when a man hadn't stepped foot onshore, let alone been in the company of a beautiful woman, in more than half a year.

"Lady Emmaline?"

"Yes, Captain?" Still slightly bent toward the tea tray, she looked up at him from beneath her curiously dark eyelashes. *Now* she was using her eyes as they were meant to be used. Except he doubted she realized that, even as he was certain she couldn't know how his traitorous body had reacted to the look of vulnerability he saw in those soft brown depths.

"I apologize again for being the one to bring you such disturbing news, and feel I have intruded on your sorrow long enough. I took advantage of having your coachman drive me here in the duke's coach, so I would be most appreciative of the loan of a horse so that I might be installed at an inn before nightfall. I'll see that the horse is returned tomorrow."

"You...you're leaving?"

It seemed a strange question. But he couldn't ignore the sudden apprehension in her voice. What was wrong with him? She'd told him she was alone here. Alone, and most probably completely at sea as to what she should next do.

As if to help decide the question of his departure, there was a loud boom of thunder just as the skies seemed to open in a downpour that would have had him soaked to the skin in moments were he to step outside.

Lady Emmaline turned to look out through the panes of the French doors, and then returned her gaze to him. "You were very kind to have come here today, Captain. Please, allow me to offer you the hospitality of Ashurst Hall for the night. Unless it is imperative that you return to your boat?"

"Ship," he corrected with a slight smile. "A frigate, to be exact. But not mine. I was merely traveling with the *Fervant*, as my duties have concluded. I was on my way home via the port of Hove, in fact, when we came upon...when we came upon the wreckage."

She ignored his mention of her brother's yacht. "Have you been away from your home and family for a long time, Captain?"

"My home, yes, my lady. Four years or a little more, when last I thought about it. As for my family, my three sisters are wed and gone. My parents are also gone—to their eternal rewards. Not to belabor the thing, but as I have spent a solitary bachelor existence at sea for so very long, I will be returning to a home as empty as this one must feel to you at the moment."

"Then I wouldn't be delaying you overmuch if I were to shamelessly beg you to remain here until I...until I can think what next to do. I should be doing *something,* shouldn't I? Should I be asking you to take me to Shoreham-by-Sea?"

John shook his head. "There's nothing for you to do there, no, my lady. The *Fervant* circled the area for hours, and only Mr. Hobart was located. He'd somehow been lucky enough to free the small boat the yacht had been dragging with it before it, too, was pulled beneath the surface."

"How fortunate for Mr. Hobart. Will there be an inquiry, do you suppose?"

John didn't have an answer to that question. "I suppose that will be up to the authorities in charge of such things. But Captain Clark has already written his recounting of what we found, what we did. I'm fairly certain the ruling will be death by accident, not misadventure."

"Yes, I would agree with that. Not misadventure, but adventure. Is that what men call heading out to sea with a drunken captain, and with less knowledge of how to pilot a boat—ship—than a strutting barnyard rooster?" She entwined her fingers together as she looked at John in some surprise. "Why, yes, that's it. *That's* what I'm feeling. I wasn't certain. But now I know. I'm angry, Captain Alastair. My brother and my nephews are dead, leaving me to do Lord only knows what, and I'm very, very *angry* with the three of them. Is that wickedly unnatural of me, Captain?"

John lifted his shoulders in a small shrug. "I suppose that, in some ways, you could believe that they've behaved rather inconsiderately toward you. Dying, that is."

They looked at each other for a long moment, and then John felt the corners of his mouth attempting to embarrass him with a smile.

But rather than be appalled by his inappropriate levity, Lady Emmaline's brown eyes began to twinkle, and a smile played about her lips, as well, before she stood, so that he, too, hastened to his feet.

"I need to have Grayson summon all the servants and inform them of the duke's demise. Oh, dear. The duke's demise. That sounds rather like a farce at Covent Garden, doesn't it? Do you know something, Captain Alastair? I think I may be about to become slightly hysterical, after all."

"I sincerely hope not," John told her frankly. "I've no experience with hysterical women, and I was hoping to be of some use to you as long as it would appear I am to be your guest for the evening." He was liking this woman more with each passing moment. Her courage, her strength—her honesty. And those lovely soft brown eyes...

"Very well, then, I won't be hysterical. Not even slightly, I promise. But you'll come with me, won't you? You'll speak to Grayson for me?"

"Would you rather I hunted him down and brought him in here?"

"I suppose. But you won't have to look far, I'm sure. Just open the door. Oh, and be careful Mrs. Piggle doesn't topple in on your feet."

Lady Emmaline's strange warning had John thinking that the woman still wasn't very far from a complete breakdown, but when he opened the doors that led into the foyer, it was to see a rather red-cheeked, pudgy woman of an indeterminate age attempting to regain her feet just on the other side of the door.

"You could at least have offered your arm in helping me up, Mr. Grayson," she complained to the butler, who was now eyeing John as if he was some bit of vermin he'd unintentionally let into the house.

"Let me assume that you've heard the news," John said before turning to close the doors behind him, blocking Lady

Emmaline's view. She'd mentioned a farce, and he sought to spare her the one now taking place in this foyer.

"How can we know they're dead? We've only your word for it. And who are you?" Grayson asked, accused, the moment those doors were shut.

John nearly told him, but then mentally bit his tongue. A duke of the realm and his two heirs didn't all perish together without repercussions that would reverberate for weeks, if not months. There was enough turmoil at Ashurst Hall at the moment, without him making some grand announcement. Besides, Lady Emmaline might not be as ready to appeal to him for help if she knew who he really was. As things stood now, she could accept his assistance and retain the illusion that she was in charge. John believed she needed to feel in charge, competent.

"I am who I said I was when I arrived here, Grayson. Captain John Alastair, late of His Majesty's Royal Navy. I'm also the man who would consider your words an insult to his honor if not for the grief that has just settled over this household."

Grayson's chin lowered slightly, the older man seeming to understand that he had spoken out of turn to a gentleman who didn't take insolence lightly.

"I'll have one of the grooms ride to the village to summon the vicar. Lady Emmaline will wish for spiritual guidance."

"Hummph," Mrs. Piggle snorted, and then quickly covered her mouth as she turned her less than laudatory reaction into a cough. "Suppose someone'll want the chapel taken out of Holland covers. Ain't been a Daughtry in there since the last duke was carried in feetfirst. I'll set the maids to it first thing tomorrow."

"We all worship the Almighty in our own ways, Mrs. Piggle." Grayson quelled the woman's insolence with a stare that would have made any sergeant-major proud. "Lady E. attends services in the village, you understand. His Grace and his sons…preferred to worship our Lord in their own way."

"You don't need to explain. I will tell you that I'll be staying here tonight at Lady Emmaline's request," John said, not wishing for any more confidences from the servants at the moment. "See to it that a chamber is made ready for me. My bags are still in the coach, I imagine. I'd like to bathe and change into a fresh uniform before the dinner bell is rung."

"Oh, laws, Lady E.'s birthday! Mr. Grayson, we forgot. Lady E.'s birthday celebration. And Cook has prepared all of her favorites, and now we're all at sixes and sevens, what with the duke and those horrid boys drowning and all. Ah, what a misery this day is. Poor little dab. What a misery…"

John cocked a look at the butler. "It's Lady Emmaline's birthday?"

"Just as Mrs. Piggle said, yes. She's had more than her share of birthdays under this roof, that's what His Grace would always say. He may have forgotten this one, I'm afraid."

"They'd all still be alive if he'd remembered this one. Excepting he probably would have gone sailing at any rate." Mrs. Piggle took a step away from the butler as Grayson frowned. "I'm only speaking the truth, you know. I can't remember the last birthday any of them paid a bit of mind to. Poor little dab."

John took a step toward the butler. He was beginning to feel rather proprietary toward Lady Emmaline Daughtry. "But we're not going to forget it, Grayson, are we? Whatever has been planned shall go forward. So, what is planned?"

Mrs. Piggle answered. "Just her favorite meal, sir, and a simple confection she also favors. And all to be served in the main dining saloon, with the table shining with all the silver and candles and such. The staff is quite fond of Lady E."

"Thank you, Mrs. Piggle. It all sounds lovely and thoughtful. I would ask that another place be laid, as I will be joining Lady Emmaline at table. There's time enough for the vicar tomorrow, Grayson. For tonight, we will discuss the duke's death only if her ladyship wishes it. Agreed?"

Grayson nodded. "Agreed, sir. And I will inform the staff. Her ladyship should not have to worry her head about a thing, not if we can be of assistance." He frowned, hesitated and then added, "The new duke will be here soon enough, if he's not dead, too."

"And who might this new, perhaps deceased duke be, Grayson?" John asked, anxious to get back to Lady Emmaline, who probably shouldn't be left alone with her grief for too long.

Grayson sighed. "The most unlikely person, that's who. The late duke's brother's son. One Rafael Daughtry, and a captain serving under Wellington. I cannot imagine anyone less suited for the title."

"And don't be forgetting the mother," Mrs. Piggle said, rolling her rather bulging eyes. "There's one would make a stone statue blush, what with her outlandish ways. We're to be taking orders from the likes of her?"

"Shush, Mrs. Piggle. That will be quite enough." Grayson turned to John once more. "Forgive us, sir, the both of us. We've had quite the shock. We've known the late duke ever so long, and the boys since before they were born. And then, of course, Lady Emmaline holds all our hearts. It's…it's a trying time. But we will overcome it, sir."

"Then you're all finished with being shocked now, aren't you, and from this moment on you will all do whatever is in your power to assist Lady Emmaline during this trying time—without further comment. Am I correct? Very good." What a poorly run household this was, John thought. He'd never met the Duke of Ashurst or his sons, but he felt fairly certain he had nothing to regret in not making their acquaintances.

At last, the butler seemed to pull himself together. "Yes,

Captain. I'll see to having your bags taken up to the west wing and a bath called for. I'll have one of the footman escort you directly. Dinner is at six."

"Thank you, Grayson. But before you do that, please summon Lady Emmaline's maid to her and explain that I will rejoin her in an hour."

"Yes, of course. And again, Captain, our apologies. We will strive to draw ourselves together and carry on." The butler put his hand to the small of the housekeeper's broad back. "Come along, Mrs. Piggle. I know you can't wait to be the one who tells everyone the terrible news."

John looked at the closed doors to the main saloon, part of him wishing to rejoin his hostess, while another part of him longed to be out of his uniform and sunk in hot soapy water to his chin. Bathing aboard ship was always a spotty thing, and he was sorely in need of not only soap and water but clean linen and even a razor.

He should have stopped at an inn along the way from Shoreham-by-Sea and made himself more presentable, but he'd believed time was of the essence, that news of the duke's demise—as Lady Emmaline had termed it—must be brought to his estate as quickly as possible.

Still, it wouldn't hurt to just step back inside the room for a moment, to assure himself that the woman was still as bravely stoic as she'd been since first hearing of her now vastly altered family situation.

Giving in to his curiosity, if that was the proper term for it, he opened the door only slightly and peered toward the couches set in the middle of the large room.

Lady Emmaline was no longer seated on one of the couches.

John stepped fully inside, casting his gaze around the room, only to discover that it was empty of all but its furnishings.

Where could she have gone? A quick glance toward the French doors told him that the rain was still coming down hard, so she wouldn't have gone back outside into the gardens.

Then he noticed another door in the far right-hand corner of the room, and he approached it quietly, to see that it was slightly ajar.

"Lady Emmaline?"

"Yes. One moment."

He stepped back from the doorway and she joined him in a few moments, as promised, a new look of determination on her beautiful face.

"How do I best get a message to Paris?" she asked him without preamble. "Or at least to France. I think Rafe's in France."

"Rafe. Your nephew?"

Lady Emmaline nodded. "Yes, my nephew. He has to come home, doesn't he? Ashurst Hall cannot be without its master."

"You should not be alone here, no. I would suggest a personal courier, ma'am. Perhaps a former soldier? A Bow Street Runner? It's an orderly turmoil now that Bonaparte has retreated to Paris, but it is still turmoil, and will be until the man officially abdicates."

She looked up at him, her eyes fearful. "Is Rafe in any danger?"

"Hopefully not. But as I said, Bonaparte is still in Paris, and one can never consider the man as being entirely toothless."

"Oh, dear," she said as she turned and stepped back into the room she'd just left. She crossed to a small table, the top of which was more than completely covered by what looked to be an open Bible. "I want Rafe to be safe. There's no question of that. But there is more than just Rafe's safety that is at stake now."

John walked over to the table and looked down at the writing on the inside of the back cover of the Bible. "The next in line after your nephew is a real rotter?" he asked, hoping to make her smile.

"Hardly. The next in line after Rafe is *nobody*. I was certain that is the case, but felt it necessary to check my conclusion by looking at our family tree in the Bible. And there is nobody. The titles, these lands, this estate and others, they would all revert to the Crown. That can't happen, it simply cannot. Someone must be sent to find him, immediately, and bring him back here." She laid both her hands on his forearm and looked up into his face. "Please, Captain Alastair. Help me."

"I will. I promise." He didn't know how he would help, but if she'd asked him to move a mountain he would have agreed to that chore, as well. How could he deny this woman anything when she looked at him with those soulful brown eyes?

CHAPTER THREE

EMMALINE SURREPTITIOUSLY TURNED her head toward her left shoulder and sniffed. Maryanne, her maid, had sworn to her that the black gown did not smell of camphor after being packed away in the attics these past half dozen years or more, since her father's death, but Emmaline was still not convinced.

What she was convinced of, however, was that the gown, never a favorite, was woefully out of fashion. According to her sister-in-law, Helen, it had been out of fashion the moment it had been stitched up by the seamstress in the village, as anyone with any sense knew there was no hope of cleverness to be found in Mrs. Watley's hamlike fingers. To Emmaline, that had meant that Mrs. Watley had flatly refused to lower Helen's bodice another two inches for fear that the deceased would take one look at those exposed bosoms and sit up straight in his coffin.

The last time Emmaline had worn this gown (the one with the depressingly *ordinary* neckline) had been during her year of mourning for her father. That grief, although not overwhelming by any means, had been genuine, as it was difficult to fault the twelfth duke for being the man he had been: rough, gruff and fairly oblivious. Summoning up authentic grief for her brother and his sons was still proving problematic, however, and she'd once again felt a fraud as she'd come down to dinner in this gown.

Emmaline paced the main saloon, unable to settle herself,

wondering where she'd summoned the courage—no, the audacity!—to enlist a complete stranger's assistance in dealing with the repercussions of her brother's death. But there was something about Captain John Alastair that instilled confidence in him and his ability to, if not make things right for her, at least shepherd her through the next difficult days.

She closed her eyes and thought about him, and the way he'd looked as he'd approached her out in the gardens. His tall, handsome form so splendid in his impressive uniform, his bicorne hat neatly tucked beneath his arm, the slight shadow of an evening beard on his lean cheeks. He'd looked weary, and more than a little nervous, most probably because he was certain he would momentarily be presented with a wildly hysterical, weeping woman.

Emmaline walked along behind one of the couches, lightly running her fingertips over its curved back, and then stopped to look up at the portrait of her father that still hung in its place of honor above the fireplace. Yes, she'd wept when the twelfth duke had died. Why couldn't she seem to weep for the thirteenth duke and his two sons?

There had to be something unnatural about a woman who would see their deaths as a problem to be solved rather than the tragedy that it was. There had to be something perverse about a woman whose primary occupation since hearing of those three deaths had been to worry for her own future… when she wasn't peering into every mirror she could find to assure herself she and this horrid gown wouldn't frighten Captain Alastair when next he saw her.

"Emmaline?"

Emmaline turned in time to see Charlotte Seavers racing into the room, tossing her shawl in the general direction of Grayson, who was now wearing a black armband and a suitably stern expression.

"I just heard the news," Charlotte said, approaching Emmaline and taking her hands. "Is it true? Harold's dead?"

Charlotte, who lived on a small estate that bordered Ashurst Hall, was not only Emmaline's dearest friend. She had also recently been betrothed to her younger nephew, a fate Emmaline had considered worse than death for that beloved friend. Indeed, for the past month, since Charlotte had become betrothed to Harold and she had learned the circumstances behind that engagement, Emmaline had lost any remaining love she'd harbored for her brother and nephews.

"All three of them, yes. It's over, Charlotte. You're free."

"Oh, but I…that is, I shouldn't…" Charlotte shook her head and sighed. "Surely I'm going to hell, Emmaline. I want to dance a jig!"

"Oh, thank God," Emmaline said, pulling Charlotte down on the couch beside her. "You're the only one who understands how I feel, and I don't have to pretend with you. We can travel to hell together."

"Perhaps not. Lord knows George and Harold and your brother are already there. Perhaps we'll go somewhere else. Would you like to see Paris, Emmaline?"

"I know you're joking, but perhaps we could. It is imperative that Rafe be informed of his changed station as quickly as possible. Would you like to see Rafe, Charlotte?"

The younger woman colored, her eyelids fluttering shut for a moment. "No. I…I wouldn't know what to say to him. It has been six years. We're no longer children, are we?"

"He will be coming back here as the new duke," Emmaline reminded her friend. "You won't be able to avoid him. And if you were to tell him the truth, he'd certainly understand. Or I could explain everything to him for you."

Charlotte shook her head. "No, don't do that, please. He can't know. I couldn't possibly look him in the eye once he knew, not knowing what I'd see. Please, Emmaline, let's not speak of this anymore. Just take this," she said, pulling off the heavy betrothal ring and putting it in her friend's hand. "There, that's better. It was as if I had a small millstone circling my finger. From now on, we shall pretend it was never there, and Rafe never needs to know. Are we agreed?"

"Agreed, although I doubt such a secret will stand for long, not once Rafe has returned." Emmaline examined the fine Ashurst ruby set inside a cluster of diamonds. "This ring has been in our family for untold generations. How often do you think such a pretty thing was employed to hide an ugly truth?"

They sat silently for a few minutes, each lost in their own thoughts, before Charlotte asked what she might be able to do for Emmaline in the coming days.

"I really can't be sure. There are no…that is, there is nothing to be laid to rest in the family mausoleum. I suppose, for the sake of propriety, there must be a service of some kind at some point. The few relatives we have left need to be notified. Nicole and Lydia. Oh, dear. You know whom else that means, don't you?"

"Helen," they said at the same time, and then Emmaline smiled.

"I could say I sent a letter off to London and it became lost in the post?"

Charlotte nodded, not quite suppressing a smile of her own. "The post has been notoriously erratic recently, hasn't it? Why, by the time your letter arrived in Grosvenor Square, it could be whole *days* after the service, and with the Season already begun. No one could expect Helen to leave Mayfair in the midst of the Season."

"Least of all Helen," Emmaline pointed out, her smile widening, until the two of them dissolved into guilty laughter, which is how Captain Alastair discovered them a few moments later as he entered the main saloon.

"I'm sorry. Am I interrupting?"

Emmaline wiped at her moist eyes and looked up at the captain, who appeared bathed and shaved and positively resplendent in his brushed and pressed uniform. "Oh, no, no. Miss Seavers and I were…we were just reminiscing about a family memory. Captain, may I introduce you to my dear friend and neighbor, Miss Charlotte Seavers. Charlotte, Captain John Alastair, who was kind enough to personally inform me of…of the tragedy."

She quickly explained the man's continued presence to Charlotte, and his generous offer to help her wade through the necessities that must be dealt with in the coming days.

"Captain, I cannot thank you enough for your kindness to my friend," Charlotte said, holding out her hand. He bowed over it elegantly, Emmaline thought. And then Charlotte got to her feet after only one quick, interested look at Emmaline, saying she was needed at home and must leave. "My mother is not quite well," she explained to the man. "I only stole a moment to sneak here once the rain stopped, to see how you were, Emmy."

"You can't stay for supper?" Emmaline inwardly winced, wondering if her lack of disappointment was evident in her voice.

"No, I'm sorry, I can't. Oh, but I forgot!" Charlotte reached into her pocket and pulled out a small package wrapped in ivory paper and tied with a small red bow. "Happy birthday, Emmy. It's only a silly bookmark, and I'm afraid my embroidery isn't what it should be. But please know I give it with love," she said, and then kissed her friend's cheek. "Captain," she said, dropping into a quick curtsy, "it was a pleasure to meet you, and I thank you for being so considerate as to offer your support to Lady Emmaline during this trying time. I'm sure I'll see you again, at the memorial service?"

The captain looked to Emmaline, who realized she was

suddenly holding her breath, and then back to Charlotte. "Why, yes, Miss Seavers, I shall look forward to that."

Emmaline watched the captain as he watched Charlotte depart the room, and then she quickly looked away as he turned back to her, so that he shouldn't know that she'd been staring. But who could resist staring, when the man's presence seemed to fill the room with light, charging the very air with an excitement she could not name, yet knew she had never before experienced.

"May I add my congratulations to Miss Seavers's sentiments, ma'am, and wish you as pleasant a birthday as possible under the circumstances," he said, inclining his head toward her.

She didn't know where the words came from, what part of her normally reticent self had allowed such a thought to enter her head yet alone escape her lips, but suddenly Emmaline heard herself saying, "Captain, I would consider my natal day to be more of a blessing and less of a reminder of my continuing gallop into old age if you could please resist addressing me as *ma'am* again."

His low chuckle sent hot color flooding into her cheeks. "A thousand apologies, Lady Emmaline. Are you feeling quite decrepit? Surely you're not anything so ancient as *ma'am* would suggest. At six and thirty, I believe I have some years on you."

"Good Lord, yes," Emmaline shot back, suddenly willing to give as good as she got. "You're positively tottering on the brink of the grave." Then she realized what she'd just said. "Oh, dear. No matter what anyone says, we seem to keep circling back to Charlton and the boys, don't we? I still imagine they'll all come storming back in here at any moment to put the lie to what I know is true."

Did she sound as if that was a prospect much to be wished, or the thing she would dread most in the world? Really, she had to take control of her tongue, and quickly, or the captain would wonder if he'd blundered into a madhouse.

"May I?" Alastair asked, indicating with a small gesture that he'd like to join her on the couch.

"Oh, yes, please do," she said, tucking her horrid black skirts more closely around her just as if he'd planned to plop himself down right next to her when the couch could easily accommodate a half dozen people. "And would you care for some wine?"

"Thank you, no," he said as he sat, and then bent down to pick up something that had fallen to the floor. "Yours?" he asked, holding up the ruby ring.

Denying the dratted thing would open up questions about Charlotte, and as the story could only reflect badly on her brother and Harold, she quickly claimed the ruby as her own. "Thank you, Captain," she said, reaching for it. "It was my mother's, and always much too large for me."

And then the dratted ring made a liar out of her by stopping at her second knuckle as she attempted to slip it on her finger. She resisted the urge to fling it across the room.

"Ma'am—Lady Emmaline…?"

"Just Emmaline, please," she said, sighing. "And I shall call you John, since we're just the two of us here. And then, John, I should tell you that I just quite blatantly lied to you, shouldn't I?"

"About the ring. Yes. But you don't have to explain."

She relaxed. "Good, because I really don't want to." She slipped the ring into her pocket and picked up the small wrapped present. "Shall we open this instead? I love presents, and Charlotte is always so inventive with hers, even if she insists she has no talents. Just this past Christmas she gave me a small, smooth rock she'd painted to look like a toad."

Actually, Charlotte had given the toad a face that greatly

resembled that of her nephew George, but the captain didn't have to know that.

The captain put his hand on her wrist. "Lady...Emmaline," he said, so that she forgot all about Charlotte's present. "I should leave."

"Leave?" Emmaline squeezed her eyes shut for a moment, hating that she had seemed to *squeak* out the word. "But...but why? I know the rain has stopped, but it's coming on to dark soon, and we'll be called in to dinner at any moment, and—"

"I didn't mean tonight," he said, cutting her off, thankfully, before she could say something so silly as to mention how much she really wanted him to stay. "I would go only as far as the nearest inn, if you still wish my assistance for a few days, until we can summon your brother's solicitor, set up a search for your nephew and anything else I might do for you."

"You're saying without saying it that we are unchaperoned here."

"No, I'm saying without saying it that *you* are unchaperoned here. I would suggest that Miss Seavers come bear you company, but as she is quite young, and there's the problem of her mother being unwell..."

"John, there are twenty-seven servants in this house, at least three of whom, I have every certainty, are spying on us even now. I hardly call that being unchaperoned."

"No. However, Society would. You've just been dealt a serious shock, Emmaline, but one of us must think clearly."

She nearly let her shoulders sag as she realized what he was saying. "You feel *responsible* for me. Because it was you who brought me the news about Charlton and the boys. And I did nothing to dissuade you of that impression, absolve you of your gentlemanly impulse to protect a clearly helpless woman."

His slow smile sent her stomach to doing a small flip inside her. "That sounds so very noble, doesn't it? Actually, I came here to deliver my news and then depart as quickly as possible. Until I saw you out there in the gardens and thought you the most exotically beautiful woman I'd ever seen. You've had the most immediate and remarkable impact on me, Emmaline. I am in no hurry to leave."

"Oh."

"Yes—oh. And, hopeful idiot that I surely am, I don't think you have taken me in disgust. Now do you understand? The proprieties must be adhered to, no matter the circumstances. I won't go far, unless you've now decided that I should, but I cannot remain here, the two of us beneath the same roof."

"There are sixteen bedchambers under this roof," Emmaline said, as if that meant anything to Society, that same Society that had condoned Charlton's behavior, George's and Harold's behavior, but would condemn her, a confirmed spinster, for the most minor infraction of their silly rules. "There's no need for you to be put to the expense of staying at the inn."

His smile in response to that statement had her looking at him strangely, and she quickly attempted to explain what she'd said.

"Not that I'm intimating at all that you might be…that you cannot afford, um, that is—oh, stop that! I'm not saying anything in the least amusing."

He took her trembling hands in his and raised the right one to his lips, turned it over, and pressed a bone-melting kiss against her palm. Just for an instant, the tip of his tongue lightly stroked her sensitive skin. And then, holding her hands against his chest, he looked at her with those soul-destroying eyes. "Now, Emmaline? Now do you see why I need to take myself off to an inn tomorrow morning?"

"Yes…I rather suppose I do."

CHAPTER FOUR

JOHN DIDN'T KNOW if Grayson's entrance into the main saloon to announce that dinner was being served had been fortunate, or if it had been the worst timing in the history of Affectionate Old Family Retainers. Probably the former, as John hadn't known what in bloody blazes he was going to do next, once he was looking so deeply into Emmaline's glorious eyes.

He had wanted to kiss her. No, he had needed to kiss her. He *would* kiss her before this night was over. As a man who had spent many years at war, he knew that opportunities were just that, and often fleeting. For too many years of his life, he'd put his own wishes aside in the name of the Better Good. Now it was time for him to think about what John Alastair wanted.

And he wanted Lady Emmaline Daughtry.

Curiously, knowing this, he was finding it best suited to his purpose to keep his true identity hidden just a little while longer. He wanted Emmaline to see him as Captain John Alastair, accept him that way...perhaps discover feelings for him that way; the simple man, the man she could be concerned about if he had to pay for his lodgings at the local inn.

He also wanted to know more about the late duke and his two sons, but would she find it as easy to confide in him if she realized his true rank? Emmaline had been shocked by the news of their deaths—anyone would have been shocked at the suddenness of it—but John felt certain he'd also seen a measure of relief in her eyes.

Having experienced much the same feelings when he'd opened the letter from Warrington Hall, informing him of his father's departure from this earthly coil by way of collapsing after a hard ride on one of the local tavern wenches, John wondered what sort of man the late duke had been. What sort of brother he'd been to Emmaline. Obviously not a beloved one.

John sensed that applying to Grayson for enlightenment would get him nowhere, but he had higher hopes of Mrs. Piggle, and planned to speak to the woman in the morning. In the meantime, he would not press Emmaline for details, not knowing how painful it might be for her to share them with him.

This decision left him free to concentrate on Emmaline herself, which was what he'd much prefer to do in any case.

He entered the cavernous dining room with Emmaline on his arm, only to see that their places had been set at opposite ends of a table that could easily serve as a bowling green. Once he'd assisted her to his chair and Grayson had withdrawn his disapproving face, John picked up his gold charger plate, utensils, serviette and wineglass and carried them all down the length of the table, placing them to Emmaline's right.

"This way we won't have to shout at each other," he said as he sat down. "And I might add that I cannot think of more pleasant company than you in this, my first meal in months in which I won't have to worry about my wineglass sliding off the table as the ship cuts through the waves."

"Grayson will not be pleased," Emmaline told him as a young girl entered, two bowls of soup balanced on a tray. "He's quite the stickler for propriety."

"Among other things, yes, I can see that propriety would be one of his sticking points. Does that worry you?"

Emmaline cocked her head slightly to one side, as if considering the question. "No. No, I don't think it does. Thank you, Mary. It smells delicious."

"Yer fav'rit, milady. Cook remembered. All yer fav'rits tonight. All whats yer likes best, right here."

"Yes, I believe you're right," Emmaline said, sneaking a quick look at John from beneath her lashes, a delightful flush coloring her cheeks.

The soup was country thick and flavorful, or so John remembered it later, even though the rest of the courses were eaten without him tasting them. He was much too well-occupied answering Emmaline's intelligently probing questions about his service in the Royal Navy, much too enthralled by the way the candlelight danced in her golden hair, the grace with which she patted her lips with the snow-white serviette... the way she listened to him as if he was reciting words he'd brought down from some mountain on stone tablets.

He did remember the dessert course, because it seemed that Emmaline's favorite sweet consisted of a simple dish of strawberries and heavy cream. Whenever some of the cream clung to her upper lip, and she surreptitiously employed the tip of her tongue to swipe it away, John began to wonder if taking himself off to the inn the next morning could be seen as in the way of cruel and unusual punishment for a man who definitely had another destination in mind.

At last the meal was over, and John suggested they take a stroll in the gardens now that the rain had disappeared and a setting sun still lent enough light for a pleasant inspection of the grounds.

Good Lord, he sounded so stiff, didn't he?

"Emmaline—I want to be alone with you," he whispered in her ear as he pulled out her chair for her. "And to hell with the posies."

She looked up at him, her smile tremulous, and laid her hand on his as she got to her feet. "The herb garden is well away from the house at the bottom of the gardens. And fenced," she said quietly. "With rather tall shrubbery."

"I've always liked herbs," he said as, together, they departed the dining room through the French doors conveniently placed there so that gentlemen could end their meals by stepping outside to blow a cloud, spit or relieve themselves over the railing of the stone terrace. John's father used to hold contests as to who could aim best and shoot farthest, much to his son's embarrassment. He pushed the memory from his mind.

"Rosemary is one my favorites," Emmaline told him as they descended the flagstone steps into the gardens.

"Mine, as well. Along with parsley and sage and…"

"Thyme," she finished for him. "I've always thought *Scarborough Fair* a most confusing poem. If you wish someone to be your true love, why would you then make impossible demands on that person in order to become that true love?"

John bent and broke off a perfect pink rose, stripped it of its thorns and then bowed as he handed it to her. "'Love imposes impossible tasks,'" he quoted from memory, "'though not more than any heart asks.'"

"Oh? And do you think that sounds as asinine as I do, John? Why should a heart that cares make demands?" Emmaline asked as she held the rose beneath her nose and sniffed. "Ah, nothing complicated about a rose, is there? It is pretty, it smells heavenly, and if you aren't careful in the way you handle it, it pricks your finger. Still, you can see the thorns, so it isn't as if you weren't warned, correct?"

They threaded their way along the curving brick path. "Am I being warned, Emmaline?"

She stopped, turned to look up into his face. "Someone probably is, but I'm not sure which one of us that person might be. John…I think you should know that I'm not a very…nice person."

"Is that so?" He cocked one eyebrow as he offered her his

arm once more and they continued down the pathway. "Do you abuse kittens? Snore in church? No, wait, I have it—you pull faces behind Grayson's back."

"Well, sometimes—that last bit about Grayson. But I'm attempting to be serious here, John. I'm…I'm an unnatural sister, an unnatural aunt. I've been trying all day long to work up even a single tear over Charlton and the boys, and I simply can't manage it."

"You didn't love them?"

"No, no, of course I *loved* them. One doesn't have much choice in that, seeing as we're related. The question is, did I *like* them? And I didn't."

John kept moving toward the tall thick shrubbery that he was sure concealed the herb garden. "They weren't likeable?"

"I suppose that would depend on whom you applied to for their opinion. Their friends seemed to like them well enough."

"And did you like their friends?"

They stopped at a slatted wooden gate and John opened it. "No, I didn't. Why would you ask that?"

He ceremoniously bowed her through the entrance to the herb garden, where they were immediately cast in the shade of the towering evergreens. "I don't know. It simply occurred to me that, if you didn't care for the people who cared for them, then perhaps the only reason you cared for your brother and nephews at all was because of an accident of birth. We can't choose our relatives, Emmaline. Only our friends."

"You're only trying to make me feel less guilty."

"I know," he said, leading her to a curved stone bench at the center of the small garden. "Am I succeeding?"

She sat down, gracefully arranging her skirts around her, and looked at him. "Why, yes, I believe you are. Charlton and his sons are dead, and I'm sorry they didn't lead better lives while they had the chance. I think I could weep for that."

He joined her on the bench. "Now?"

Emmaline was slowly twirling the rose stem between her fingers, and looked up at him in some confusion. "Pardon me? Now what?"

"I was asking if you were going to weep now," he explained, biting back a smile.

"Oh. Oh, no, I don't think so. But at the service it will be better if I don't disappoint Vicar Wooten. So then I shall think about what might have been." She sighed. "What might have been is always so sad, isn't it? What we could have done, what we should have done. What we missed because we didn't dare to—"

John brought his mouth down on hers, cutting off any chance that either of them would ever look back at this moment and think, *If only.*

He pulled back slightly, smiling into her eyes. "I'm sorry, I couldn't seem to resist. In fact, I still can't..."

This time when he kissed her he also slid his arms around her, pulling her closer against his chest. She responded by sliding her arms around his back, signaling without words that she didn't dislike what he was doing to her.

What she was doing to him.

A kiss. A simple kiss. And yet his world was tilting on its axis. He prodded at her with his tongue, and she responded by opening her mouth to him, and the flame she had lit inside him the first time he'd seen her threatened to consume him.

He kissed her hair, her perfect shell-like ear, her throat. He heard her quick intake of breath as he moved his hands forward, to her rib cage...and then slowly slid them upward, to cup her firm breasts.

"John..." she breathed, but not in protest, as she still held him tightly, her head tipped back as he dared to press his lips against her bare flesh above the neckline of her gown.

Her mourning gown.

Christ!

He took her hands in his and raised her to her feet, not letting go of her as he looked deeply into her eyes. "I'm sorry. I had no right..."

"You were not lacking an invitation, Captain Alastair," Emmaline told him quietly, shifting her gaze to the ground at her feet. "Shall we just put this down to an aging spinster feeling reckless, even desperate, on the event of her twenty-eighth birthday?"

"I don't think so, no. Not unless we explain my behavior with the notion that I've been too long at sea, and haven't seen a woman in months and months, so that any woman will do. You're not that old, Emmaline, and I'm not that young."

She smiled weakly and pulled one hand free, turning so that they could retrace their steps to the house. "You've quite the way with words, or else I'm eager to be convinced."

She shivered then, only slightly, as the setting sun had slipped behind a blanket of thick clouds, and John slipped his arm around her shoulders, pulling her closer beside him as they walked along the path.

"I had an idea as I dressed for dinner," he told her as they approached the doors to the main saloon. "I've remembered the name of the brother of Josiah Coates, my steward aboard ship. Phineas. Yes, I'm positive that's it. Phineas Coates. He's with the Bow Street Runners, but Josiah told me the man is unhappy with his position, so that he's actively seeking employment as a valet. Josiah and his other brothers are all gentleman's gentlemen, in one form or another, you understand."

"Not really, not yet," Emmaline admitted as they stepped inside the main saloon, to see that Grayson had already ordered the evening tea tray, a not-quite subtle hint that he believed her ladyship should soon be saying her good-night to the captain. "But you'll explain?"

John availed himself of the well-stocked drinks table, pouring a glass of wine while Emmaline prepared a cup of tea for herself. He returned to the main seating area, but did not sit down.

"Josiah left for his home at the same time I was coming here, to Ashurst Hall. I know his direction, and I'm sure he'll be there by the time a letter from me reaches London." He didn't add that Josiah had only gone to the city to visit his widowed mother before heading to Warrington Hall, as that was information best kept to himself for the moment.

"Ah, you're thinking this Phineas Coates might be the man who can find Rafe for me."

"Yes, that's exactly what I'm thinking. You could go through the War Office, but the extremely busy people there might not consider the mission as important as you'd like."

"And, since Mr. Coates is a Bow Street Runner, he should have no problem in *running* down Rafe if we tell him what we know, that my nephew is in Paris. He could even, considering the man's desire to leave the Runners, offer his services as the new duke's valet, and stay with him, accompany Rafe home to Ashurst Hall. All very neat and tidy."

"Only if you're agreeable. I don't know Phineas, but I can vouch for Josiah."

"Very well, then, that's what we shall do. I'll write to Rafe tonight, and you can include the letter along with your instructions? And, yes, I'd feel much more comfortable if this Mr. Phineas Coates stayed at Rafe's side until he's home safe. I might even suggest they stop in London for a few days, to do something about Rafe's wardrobe. The boy has been in uniforms for half a dozen years. Now he has to dress himself as befits a duke. Oh, dear, I wonder if he's going to like that. He left here a boy, but he's a man now. I wonder if he's going to like any part of this, to be truthful. He had no ambitions in this direction, and no training, when it comes to that."

"Three hearts away from the title, two of them young and I'll assume vital, I can see why your nephew might not have considered that such a day might arrive. The title, this estate and, I'm sure, several others? He's inherited considerable responsibility. Is he up to it, do you think?"

Emmaline nodded. "Rafe is a good, sound person, boy or man, I'm sure. He may be somewhat discommoded to see how his sisters have blossomed in his absence, and I don't envy him having to ride herd on his mother once she decides she is now the dowager duchess—but, no, I have no serious qualms for the title now that it is in Rafe's hands."

She put down her cup. "John...about what happened in the gardens..."

He shook his head slowly. "No, let's not talk about that now. You've had a long and extremely trying day, one way or another, and I certainly wasn't any great help to you."

"I feel as if I've just been told to take myself off to bed," she said to him, smiling. "All right. And I'll have that letter for you in the morning. Oh, and I suppose there are others I'll need to write. To some distant aunts...perhaps the newspapers?"

"Tomorrow, Emmaline. There is nothing you can do anymore tonight that can't wait until tomorrow."

"Do I look that exhausted?"

"No, Emmaline. You look that vulnerable. And I'm not as strong as I thought myself. Not since I kissed you, at any rate."

He watched as hot color invaded her cheeks once again. "Oh. Well, then, all right. It has been a long day."

"Until tomorrow, which is already much too far away," he told her, not daring to kiss her hand because he knew neither of them would be able to stop with such a simple, formal gesture.

He watched her walk, chin held high, toward the foyer, and then drank the rest of his wine, resisting the temptation to then fling the glass into the fireplace.

What in bloody hell had he done out there in the gardens?

The woman had just had a terrible shock. Had he really believed that seducing her was the answer to all her problems?

And lying to her? How was that helping her?

His deception had begun easily enough, but there had been ample opportunity for him to correct her when she addressed him as captain.

She'd been impressed to hear he was a captain in the Royal Navy, that he had, like her nephew, gone to war to defend his country. And all of that was true enough.

She'd also felt comfortable with him, possibly because he was, to her mind, a relatively simple man. She'd felt free with him. Free to tell him the truth, bare her troubled soul to him. Free to lean on him in her time of need.

Free to let him kiss her.

She was Lady Emmaline Daughtry, daughter of a duke, sister of a duke, aunt to a duke. There would be no real social consequences for her if she kissed a captain in the Royal Navy. Kissed him…or more.

John poured himself a second glass of wine, preparing to settle himself in for at least another few hours of thinking, and most probably drinking. He had to tell her. He couldn't put off telling her.

How would he tell her?

"Your Grace?"

John's head turned toward the door before he could stop himself, and he watched as Grayson entered the main saloon, to bow in front of him.

"Excuse me, Grayson? That's Captain, not Your Grace."

"No, Your Grace, it's not. I took it upon myself to personally unpack your bag. There were letters inside. I left them tied as they were, but could not avoid reading what few lines I saw. You are His Grace, Captain Jonathan Alastair, Duke of Warrington. I've taken the liberty of removing your belongings to the large bedchamber just to the left at the top of the landing, Your Grace."

"Lady Emmaline?"

"Doesn't know, no, Your Grace. May I ask why?"

"I was just sitting here asking myself the same question, Grayson. She seemed...she seemed pleased that I served in the Navy."

Grayson nodded, transformed from the stiff and stern butler to the sort of old family retainer who had come to look upon his employers as well-loved children. "Her ladyship is very admiring of those who chose to defend this country from that rascal Bonaparte, yes, Your Grace." The butler bowed, turned to leave, and then turned back to look at John, his expression stern once more. "She is also, begging Your Grace's pardon, quite fond of honesty and truthfulness."

"Yes, thank you, Grayson. Lady Emmaline is, indeed, a very truthful, forthright person. She deserves nothing less in return."

Grayson bowed again. "As you say, Your Grace."

CHAPTER FIVE

...SUCH SAD AND shocking news. I imagine you reading this wherever you are, and marveling at how quickly lives can change. In truth, I have been thinking much the same thing ever since Captain Alastair walked into the gardens of Ashurst Hall this afternoon.

Emmaline lifted her pen and stared at her words. Why had she written them? She should tear up this letter, as well, and put it with the other discarded efforts she had begun and then abandoned. But it would make no difference if she began again; no matter how she tried to concentrate on the matter at hand, John Alastair kept creeping back into her thoughts, and onto the page of the letter to her nephew.

She dipped the pen once more and continued:

You are, of course, needed home as soon as you are able, but I understand the demands of your service, and wish to assure you that we are all quite safe here, and capable of holding things together until you find it possible to return. I ask only that you write to us as often as you can, and that you allow Mr. Coates to be of any and all assistance to you.

Rafe, you will make an exemplary Duke of Ashurst. You hold my deepest confidence and blessings.

Yrs. In Greatest Affection,
Emmaline

Before she could change her mind, Emmaline sanded the page, folded it and then used the Ashurst seal to press the warmed wax onto the folded page. There, it was done. She'd arrange for funds to be given to Mr. Coates, who would carry them with him to Paris, so that Rafe would not feel penny-pinched as he made arrangements for his transport back to England.

She kept the letter separate from the small stack that would go out with the morning post, informing a few distant aunts of Charlton's death, and then reluctantly added the letter to Helen, Rafe's mother, to them. She could not in good conscience delay sending that particular letter, especially since the London newspapers were bound to make a huge announcement in the next few days.

After all, it wasn't every day that a duke and both his heirs drowned in the Channel thanks to their own utter stupidity.

"Stop it," Emmaline muttered under her breath as she rose from the small writing desk in her bedchamber and turned to contemplate the mantel clock. She was surprised to see that it had only gone past midnight. She'd hoped for more, perhaps that it was already after three, or even four.

How long before she would see John again at the breakfast table? Knowing she would not sleep, could not sleep, she believed the hours between now and then could be more easily measured in months.

In any event, it was no longer her birthday, although she could still consider it such until the sun rose in the morning. The next time she marked her birthday, it would also mark the day she'd learned that her brother and nephews had died. How odd. Which was worse, she wondered: to grow older every year, or to be reminded how many years it had been since those deaths?

"If they were going to die, anyway, they could have been just a *little* bit more considerate," Emmaline told her reflection in the dressing table mirror as she pinched at her cheeks to bring color into them and then checked the neckline of her ridiculously virginal white night rail and dressing gown.

And then, before her better self, her saner self, could talk her out of it, Emmaline headed for the door to the hallway, intent on spending her twenty-ninth birthday thinking back over a much nicer memory of her twenty-eighth.

She headed for the west wing, hoping her courage wouldn't desert her, but halted before she got to the center staircase, having seen light peeking out from beneath the double doors to the bedchamber reserved for their highest-ranking guests. The prince regent himself had stayed in the chamber twice, this last time breaking a fine antique chair just by sitting his bulk in it.

Why would Grayson put John in this chamber? It wasn't like the butler to stray from the strict rules of social protocol that made up such things. Captain Alastair should have been put in the west wing, and probably at the end of the corridor at that, right next to the servant stairs.

Perhaps Grayson had taken a liking to John. Although Grayson rarely took a liking to anyone.

And what did it matter where Grayson had put John, or why? She told herself that all she was doing now was standing in a drafty hallway, possibly to be seen by any servant who might be up and about for some reason. Either she was going to do something for herself or she was going to die old and dry and with a regret that had her sighing into her teacup while her relatives murmured behind her back: "Poor old Emmy, unlucky in love, you know."

She raised her hand, hesitated as she took one last, deep steadying breath, and then closed her fist and rapped her knuckles on one of the doors.

Emmaline winced as the sound of that knock seemed to fill the quiet night like cannon shot woke the world to mark a dawn battle.

"You wanted something, Emmaline?"

She nearly jumped out of her skin, whirling about to see John standing almost directly behind her.

"Why aren't you in bed?" she asked, saying the first thing that came into her head.

"I should perhaps ask you the same thing," he responded, his magnificent eyes slipping lazily up and down her dressing-gown-clad body.

Her toes curled in her slippers.

"I didn't hear you come down the hallway."

"Or up the stairs, either, I'd imagine," he said, smiling. "Perhaps, next time, I should have one of the footmen lead the way, blowing on a trumpet."

"Now you're making sport of me."

"No," he said, his tone serious as he stepped closer to her. "I'd never do that. For one thing, I'm too grateful to see you. It has been hours and hours."

"Yes, it has," Emmaline told him, daring to look straight into his eyes. "And it's just as you said, John. Tomorrow is much too far away…"

He put his hands around her upper arms and then leaned in ever so slowly, touching his mouth to hers with a gentleness that brought her closer to tears than she had felt all day.

At first she thought she was floating, but quickly realized John had picked her up, lifting her high against his chest, even as he went on kissing her. She sensed his knees bending slightly as he tried to manage the brass latch. She was about to tell him that romance was lovely but perhaps they were both a few years too old for such gallantry when the door opened and he walked her inside, kicking it closed behind him.

By now she had her face buried against the side of his neck. "That was quite…impressive," she whispered, keeping her eyes shut as he carried her across the large chamber and toward the bed that had housed kings, queens and rotund princes.

"Thank you. I thought so, too," John told her as he laid her on the already turned-down bed. Bless Grayson, he was nothing if not efficient.

Standing next to the bed, John stripped off his uniform jacket before joining her on the lush satin sheets, pulling her once more into his arms. His mouth mere inches from hers, he said, "I've wanted this for so long."

Emmaline thought that a lovely thing to say. "We barely know each other."

"No. We've known each other forever, my dearest one, always known the other of us was out there somewhere in the world, waiting. We only just happened to meet today."

They made love slowly, because it was her first time, because they had the rest of their lives, because to rush something this beautiful, this perfect, would be tantamount to a crime.

He kissed away her silent tears when the lovemaking threatened to undo her; the unexpected intensity of her arousal, the tenderness of his every intimate touch, swelling her heart and wordlessly telling her she was cherished, she was beautiful to him, she was desirable.

But there was more. She hadn't expected what she'd felt so far, what he'd caused her to feel, and her surprise manifested itself in a rather startled gasp as he found the very heart of her most intimate place and touched it, teased and stroked it, doing amazing things to her suddenly eager body.

She lifted her hips to him, wanting to know more, wanting to learn her feelings even as he was learning her body. A new tension invaded her every muscle, urging her forward, telling him without words that, yes, yes…there. And again, there. Do that…please do that. Don't stop doing that…right there…*please*…

And when he mounted her, when her body relieved her of the responsibility to think and just reacted to his, when he settled himself deep inside her, Emmaline knew that every word he'd said to her was true. She'd been waiting for him all of her life.

Their bodies had become one, their hearts and minds, as well. He whispered sweet words in her ear, urging her to move with him, feel with him, fly with him.

Emmaline had already waved goodbye to all of her misgivings and inhibitions of eight and twenty long years. She lifted her hips to him, met his every thrust as she held on tight, pulling him deeper, deeper inside her. She felt her most secret parts bud, unfurl, bursting into the full flower of her womanhood.

And then more. Just when she felt she had nothing more to give, to take, to feel, her body began to throb around him, sending stunning sensations through her, glories both wonderful and frightening.

"John!"

And he knew, somehow he knew. His hold tightened on her and he thrust one more time as he held her close, his mouth on hers, taking in her frantic breaths, her wondrous sighs.

She felt his body clench. Clench, and then release. Again

and again and again, until he seemed to collapse bonelessly against her, his warm breath audible next to her ear.

"I will never...leave your side. Never. At last I'm alive..." he whispered, and her tears fell once more as he kissed her hair, her eyelids, even the tip of her nose, before settling once more against her mouth. "Neither of us will ever be alone again."

EMMALINE ALLOWED herself to be convinced another black gown she'd always loathed would be extremely fine for the morning, especially since she would have to meet with the vicar at some point, and headed down the stairs to see if John was already at breakfast in the morning room.

He'd proposed to her an hour before dawn, promising her his love and all of his worldly goods. He'd gone down on his knees; he'd held both her hands in his as he looked so deeply into her eyes. Had she said yes before he'd kissed her, before they'd fallen onto the bed once more?

And did it matter? He had to know her answer was yes.

She would still have a personal maid when she was John's wife, as well as a cook and housekeeper, if not a butler. Her dowry was such as to make them both comfortable, and to support any children that might come of their union.

Children. Emmaline stopped on the bottom stair and smiled into the middle distance. She'd never thought she would have children, and now she wanted a houseful. And she and John would never neglect them, never treat them as if they were a nuisance.

No. They'd live in a lovely thatched cottage, possibly near the sea—John loved the sea—and they would spend their lives quietly, happily. Watching their children grow, together. The two of them growing old, together.

After all, being the daughter of a duke had gained her

nothing. She had no qualms about exchanging that role for that of wife and mother.

There was a knock on the door and one of the footmen hastened to open it, stepping back quickly as Helen Daughtry swept (Helen swept better than most anyone else in the world) into the foyer.

"Emmaline!" she called out, already drawing off her black gloves and untying the smallest wisp of a black bonnet that must have cost the earth. And if the bonnet had cost the earth, the black cashmere shawl tipped with ermine and the black mourning gown covered in lace and edged with pearls had cost the remainder of the universe. "I came as soon as I heard. Oh, the horror!" And then her eyelids narrowed. "Has my son been notified? He's the duke now, you know."

"Yes, Helen, I know," Emmaline said, descending the last few stairs and allowing herself to be lightly embraced by her sister-in-law's scent as the woman pursed her lips and kissed the air about an inch from Emmaline's ear. "And you are now the dowager duchess."

Helen Daughtry's eyes widened in horror. "Dowager? Oh, no. Oh, no, no. I think not! We'll have to do something about that. But for now," she said, taking Emmaline's hand and leading her down the hallway, "I'm famished. Ah, Grayson, there you are."

"Your Grace," the butler said, his bow stiff, as if it was restricted by a rusty hinge rather than a spine. "I'll have someone see to your luggage, and that your usual chamber is prepared."

"Oh, no, don't do that. I'm staying only a few miles away with Lord Edmunds—dearest Ferdie—marvelous house party. You weren't invited, Emmaline? Shame on them! Just because you said your last prayers years ago doesn't mean you couldn't be included, at least for the tamer entertainments. At any rate, I heard the news, and knew I must have someone drive me over here for a few hours," Helen said with a wave of her hand.

"How fortunate you managed to pack that gown," Emmaline said without inflection.

"Yes, isn't it, darling? I had to borrow the bonnet, but I wear black quite often in the evening, as it shows off my hair so well. Strange that we're both blonde, and yet black…well, perhaps a little visit to the paint pots, hmm? At any rate, I'm only here to make certain my son is being installed as he should be…and to lend you my support of course, my dearest Emmaline. So alone in the world now. How difficult it must be to be a spinster. Being a widow is *much* more fun! Why, only Rafe's charity will keep a roof over your head now, won't it? But not to worry—I'm sure he'll find someplace to put you."

Grayson and Emmaline exchanged looks as Helen wandered off ahead of them. "As my late brother said, Grayson, the woman has a tongue that runs on wheels, but only rarely engages with her brain box. She means well."

"As you say, my lady. His…that is, your guest awaits you in the morning room."

Emmaline hastened down the hallway, realizing that putting Helen within fifty yards of any young, handsome man was akin to setting a plate of sugar cookies within easy reach of a precocious child.

She stopped to take a settling breath, and then turned the corner and entered the morning room, just in time to see John bowing over Helen's hand.

Her sister-in-law turned to her with a wink and a smile. "Well, now, aren't you the naughty one? While the cat's away the mice will dance, hmm? Or did Charlton know about this… houseguest of yours?"

"Captain Alastair was there on the scene, just after the yacht sank, Helen. It is he who brought me the sad news."

"And then decided to stay for the funerals? How accommodating of you, Captain. I may have to attend the services myself, after all," Helen said, once more turning her back on Emmaline. "Alastair? John *Alastair*. Now why is that name so familiar to me, hmm?"

John shot a quick look past Helen, to where Emmaline stood. "John is a fairly common name, Your Grace."

"Common as dirt, yes. But Alastair? No, I think I…oh, wait! I think I remember now. Not John Alastair. *Jonathan* Alastair. You're William's son. The sailor. How he loathed that you'd put the line in jeopardy, haring about on the high seas and all of that nonsense. Poor William, although Dame Rumor has it that he died quite happily." Helen sank into a graceful curtsy. "It is so delightful, again, to meet you, Your Grace."

Emmaline found that she couldn't breathe.

And Helen, who always noticed such things, noticed. "Emmaline, dearest? Are you quite all right? How could you have forgotten to tell me that the Duke of Warrington is your houseguest? Your Grace, you simply *must* return to River's Edge with me, as there is nothing quite so dull and dreary as a house of mourning. So sorry you won't be able to join us, Emmaline. What with your brother so newly dead and all."

"Emmaline, I—Emmaline, wait!"

But Emmaline was gone, turning about so quickly she nearly tripped over the hem of her gown before running out of the room.

He caught up with her in the large foyer, before she could

mount the stairs and lock herself in her bedchamber, where she would remain for the next hundred years, if possible.

"Grayson," he said, his eyes on Emmaline, his hand holding tight to her arm, "if you'd be so kind as to keep Her Grace occupied elsewhere."

"But…but how should I do that, sir?"

"I don't care if you tie her to a chair. And it wouldn't depress me if you included a gag. The woman is a feather-witted menace. Go, and everyone else—leave."

"John, you cannot just go ordering the servants to—and let go of my arm."

"I was going to tell you, Emmaline, I swear I was. This morning. I don't know why I didn't tell you immediately… but it all just seemed…easier if you thought me a more…a more simple man."

"I thought we'd live in a cottage. And…and raise our children. I thought…I thought I would be your helpmeet, your companion."

"And how does my being a duke change any of that? Granted, Warrington Hall is not a cottage, but as for the rest of it? Being duke and duchess does not preclude us from being loving parents. From loving each other, staying true to each other. We won't ever have to go to London at all, if you don't want to go. Is that it? Have you taken a firm dislike to London, to Society?"

She shook off his hand. "I'm not a recluse, John. Charlton refused to take me, that's all. I adore London, at least most of it."

"Oh, good," he said, relaxing slightly. "Because I really think we need to go there from time to time. That is, if you can love a duke even half as much as you could love a simple sea captain?"

Emmaline looked down at the floor. "I'm being silly, aren't I? I saw us as being so simple, our lives so uncomplicated. Being Charlton's sister was…very complicated." She turned her gaze on the man she loved. "How did you know I felt that way?"

"I don't know. I felt that if I told you who I am, about the damned title, then you'd not relax your guard around me, tell me the sorts of things you told me yesterday. About your family, about your life."

"Well, I wouldn't have, you're correct about that. I don't think I would have worried about how you'd pay for your room at the inn, either."

"Darling, do you remember when I said we can't choose who we love, but we can choose who we like?"

"Yes," she said, allowing him to take her hands in his.

"I knew I loved you the moment I first saw you. That was the easy part. But then I knew I *liked* you when you showed such concern for my welfare, when you were more worried for me than concerned with the suddenly altered circumstances of your life. Now, am I forgiven?"

"I don't know," she said coyly—imagine, a twenty-eight-year-old almost-virgin, being coy! "I really believe I may have had my heart set on a thatched cottage near the sea."

He slipped his arms more fully around her and brought his mouth down to nearly meet hers. "We'll work on that…"

EPILOGUE

THERE WERE TWO musty old aunts in the second pew, a quiet and reserved-looking Charlotte Seavers and her father in the third, and only Emmaline and John sitting in the first pew as the vicar looked uncomfortable in the small chapel hung in black crepe but glaringly absent of coffins.

Helen Daughtry had not only sent her regrets, but had forbidden her twin daughters from attending the service. "Much too depressing for the young dears," she'd insisted, which was, Emmaline knew, another way of saying, "If they're there, then I have to be there, and I don't want to be there."

Last night, while the two of them were in bed together after the rest of the household was asleep, John had proposed a wine toast to Helen's absence. If it were possible to love him even more, she did, because he was so impervious to Helen's beauty and wiles.

The quickness of the memorial ceremony and the absence of the trio who would provide raucous entertainment for them had kept Charlton's friends firmly in London. As for George and Harold, they were the sort who had acquaintances, men to whom they either owed money or were owed money. Not friends.

It was a sad statement about three wasted lives, lives that could have been so rich as well as privileged.

Now Rafael Daughtry was the Duke of Ashurst, even if he was probably still unaware of his new title. His mother would drive Grayson and the other servants to distraction when she was in residence, and Nicole and Lydia would make them happy again, as all the staff adored the twins.

But Emmaline, who had thought she'd never leave Ashurst Hall, would be departing in the next few weeks to become the Duchess of Warrington. It was obscene, unheard of, for a woman in mourning to wed so hastily, but when she and John had realized that neither cared what Society thought, Emmaline had set her maid to bringing down trunks from the attic so that they could begin packing up her belongings.

"We mourn our brothers, Charlton, George, Harold," Vicar Wooten droned on—he'd been droning on for nearly an hour and even he seemed fatigued. "Dust to dust, ashes to ashes… um, well, not perhaps in this particular case, begging your pardon."

One of the aunts stifled a giggle and, for some reason she would never understand, that caused Emmaline to shed her very first tears for her brother and nephews.

Not in this case. No, nothing was quite like *this case.* The deaths had been senseless, unnecessary and much too soon.

She dabbed at her moist eyes with the corner of her hand-kerchief, knowing her tears now were for what might have been, for the past that could never be changed.

And then John slipped his hand into hers, squeezed it, and she turned to look at this man she loved. Every question she'd ever had, any answer she'd ever sought. They were all there, in his eyes. She smiled through her tears as she saw her future.

* * * * *

Look for Kasey Michaels' sparkling new novel,
WHAT AN EARL WANTS,
coming soon from Harlequin HQN!

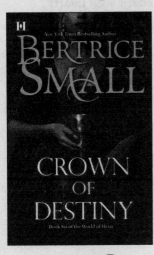

REQUEST YOUR FREE BOOKS!

2 FREE NOVELS
FROM THE ROMANCE COLLECTION
PLUS 2 FREE GIFTS!

YES! Please send me 2 FREE novels from the Romance Collection and my 2 FREE gifts (gifts are worth about $10). After receiving them, if I don't wish to receive any more books, I can return the shipping statement marked "cancel." If I don't cancel, I will receive 4 brand-new novels every month and be billed just $5.99 per book in the U.S. or $6.49 per book in Canada. That's a saving of at least 25% off the cover price. It's quite a bargain! Shipping and handling is just 50¢ per book in the U.S. and 75¢ per book in Canada.* I understand that accepting the 2 free books and gifts places me under no obligation to buy anything. I can always return a shipment and cancel at any time. Even if I never buy another book, the two free books and gifts are mine to keep forever.

194/394 MDN FELQ

Name	(PLEASE PRINT)	
Address		Apt. #
City	State/Prov.	Zip/Postal Code

Signature (if under 18, a parent or guardian must sign)

Mail to the **Reader Service:**
IN U.S.A.: P.O. Box 1867, Buffalo, NY 14240-1867
IN CANADA: P.O. Box 609, Fort Erie, Ontario L2A 5X3

Not valid for current subscribers to the Romance Collection
or the Romance/Suspense Collection.

Want to try two free books from another line?
Call 1-800-873-8635 or visit www.ReaderService.com.

* Terms and prices subject to change without notice. Prices do not include applicable taxes. Sales tax applicable in N.Y. Canadian residents will be charged applicable taxes. Offer not valid in Quebec. This offer is limited to one order per household. All orders subject to credit approval. Credit or debit balances in a customer's account(s) may be offset by any other outstanding balance owed by or to the customer. Please allow 4 to 6 weeks for delivery. Offer available while quantities last.

Your Privacy—The Reader Service is committed to protecting your privacy. Our Privacy Policy is available online at www.ReaderService.com or upon request from the Reader Service.

We make a portion of our mailing list available to reputable third parties that offer products we believe may interest you. If you prefer that we not exchange your name with third parties, or if you wish to clarify or modify your communication preferences, please visit us at www.ReaderService.com/consumerschoice or write to us at Reader Service Preference Service, P.O. Box 9062, Buffalo, NY 14269. Include your complete name and address.

ROM11